MURDER in
DRURY LANE

Vanessa Riley is the author of:

The Lady Worthing Mystery series

Murder in Westminster

Murder in Drury Lane

The Rogues and Remarkable Women Romances

A Duke, the Lady, and a Baby

An Earl, the Girl, and a Toddler

A Duke, the Spy, an Artist, and a Lie

Historical Fiction

Island Queen

Sister Mother Warrior

Queen of Exiles

VANESSA RILEY

MURDER in DRURY LANE

KENSINGTON
PUBLISHING CORP.

www.kensingtonbooks.com

KENSINGTON BOOKS are published by

Kensington Publishing Corp.
119 West 40th Street
New York, NY 10018

All Kensington titles, imprints, and distributed lines are available at special quantity discounts for bulk purchases for sales promotion, premiums, fund-raising, educational, or institutional use.

Special book excerpts or customized printings can also be created to fit specific needs. For details, write or phone the office of the Kensington Special Sales Manager: Attn. Special Sales Department. Kensington Publishing Corp., 119 West 40th Street, New York, NY 10018. Phone: 1-800-221-2647.

The K with book logo Reg. U.S. Pat. & TM Off.

Library of Congress Card Catalogue Number: 2023941470

ISBN: 978-1-4967-3867-7
First Kensington Hardcover Edition: November 2023

ISBN: 978-1-4967-3873-8 (ebook)

10 9 8 7 6 5 4 3 2 1

Printed in the United States of America

For my mother, the mystery and night soap opera TV watcher—*Murder She Wrote, Dynasty,* and *Dallas.*

Thank you for instilling a love of drama and literature.

Cast of Characters

Character List	Alternate Names and Titles
Abigail Carrington Monroe	Lady Worthing
	Baroness
	Abbie
Stapleton Henderson	Commander Henderson
	Physician, Abbie's neighbor
Neil Vaughn	Godfather, Abbie's godfather
	Mr. Vaughn
	Uncle Vaughn (Florentina's uncle)
Florentina Sewell	Flo
	Abbie's cousin
Mrs. Smith	Abbie's housekeeper
Miss Bellows	Abbie's personal maid
Mr. Rodgers	Abbie's butler
James Monroe	Lord Worthing
	Baron
	Abbie's husband
Mr. Rawlins	Abbie's driver
John Carrington	Abbie's father
Wilson Shaw	Abbie's solicitor
Dinah Carrington	Abbie's half sister
The Sewells	Florentina's parents
	Abbie's aunt (by blood), Abbie's uncle (by marriage)
	Vaughn's brother and sister-in-law
Mr. Sheridan	Richard Brinsley Butler Sheridan
	Drury Lane Theatre Owner
	MP Sheridan

Alexander Hildebrand	Famed actor
Martin Simpkins	Duke of Culver
	Formerly the Viscount Culver
Joanna Mathews Danielson	Mrs. Danielson
	Miss Mathews
	Stapleton's friend
	Ward of the Mathews
Anthony Danielson	Budding playwright
	Partner of Watson,
	Joanna's husband
Lucas Watson	Watson
Barbara Banyan	Actress
Lord Ellenborough	Ellenborough
Lord Sidmouth	Sidmouth
	Siddy
Lord Lauderdale	Lauderdale
Baron Grenville	Prime Minister,
	William Grenville, 1st Baron
	Grenville
William Wilberforce	Wilberforce
Mary Edwards	Mrs. Edwards
	Human computer

MURDER in DRURY LANE

Prologue

The right woman can make the worst scoundrel change his ways. Anthony Danielson focuses on the line he's just penned. His handwriting, the fancy cursive, makes him smile. His love is enamored with the flourishes of his *S*s and *C*s in every letter he sends.

His lips curl more as giddy glee fills his chest. Then he flips through his stacks of foolscap, the many piles neatly arranged on his makeshift desk at Drury Lane. This play will set the world on fire. Clutching the sides of his silken waistcoat, he savors a deep breath. The musty air circulating and the old props and canvas backdrops of performances from years past crowd him. The junk, as he calls it, offers nooks to hide his treasures. To Anthony, it's a sweet fragrance. Finishing this play will be the new beginning of the rest of his life.

The sound of a woman's laughter touches his scandalous heart, like sweet music stroking a maestro's ear. The notes of this song remind him of his old world, where farces and cheating consumed his days.

Now he spends them perfecting this play and writing to his beloved.

The words coming from outside the room grow louder. The sailors working the curtains must have pulled them fully open. Even though this room sits far from the stage, the lines of dialogue resound.

"She's a woman, I hope?"

The crowd's chortles pound the walls. It's sort of a welcome sign for the opening of *A Bold Stroke for a Wife*.

Another line creates more ripples of laughter. The clapping and hooting reach from the lower level of the theater, the cheapest seats or the bowels as some call it. His father said that was all Anthony, his third son, would be good for. Things cheap or in the bowels of an animal.

Laughing to himself, Anthony envisions his revenge—a successful play performed in his own theater, or co-owned one.

This being a better man, earning an honest living, doesn't seem so bad. With the love of his world cheering him on, he's unstoppable.

Well, mostly unstoppable. The greater the number of days in which he outdistances himself from his unsavory past, the better. Before he'd fallen head over heels in amour, his tawdry schemes had grown as elaborate. The fruit of the last, a set of IOUs, sits in the pocket of his waistcoat. These markers are his insurance for many things. Above all, the sizable amount would guarantee his play would be performed. How could the debtor say no? In the end, the value of these IOUs will ensure his love is kept in the manner to which she's accustomed—wealthy and decadent.

As a niggling feeling creeps up his spine, a small part of his reformed soul wants to rip up the markers and release the debt obligations of the fellow he might've cheated at cards. No. Anthony can't take the chance.

Turning over a new leaf, navigating the straight and narrow, and earning an honorable income have proven to be more difficult than Anthony had first thought. It definitely takes longer to amass money this way. For him, grift has always been easier.

The door bangs shut. The stench of the Thames drifts inside, thick, sour, and fishy.

"No one's supposed to be in the old-scene store until intermission," he says with his back to the closed door. "The rigging is what you seek. Take the corridor behind the stage. You'll see the ropes hanging. The men will show you how to work the curtains."

A knife flies past Anthony's jaw.

It stabs into a stack of crates with a bone-cracking thud.

Heart racing, the gambler inside his skin takes command. Casually, with his fingers twirling about the knife's handle, Anthony takes his time and gets a good hold, then yanks the blade free.

The gold knife belongs to one person. Anthony spins around fast and spies his old partner, his former best friend. "Watson, I told you you're not welcome here. Mr. Sheridan doesn't want you here."

The lean man stomps forward. "The old fool doesn't run me. And I do his bidding pretty often, deliverin' love tokens to whatever bird he's courting. It's you who don't want me here. You think you run this place. Too good for your old pal Lucas Watson."

"Hey, you can be here, but not as a thief or as someone who's going to cause problems."

Watson points at Anthony. "See. I told you, you don't want me here." Then he storms around the room, navigating the tight shelves, the big pieces of painted wall coverings. Gawking, he points at Anthony. "What happened to your nose?"

A gift from the family of his greatest love. They don't want

Anthony near their girl. They don't want him breathing at all. "Nothing but my own clumsiness. Thanks for the concern."

Starting on the neat piles on the desk, Watson flicks the edges of the papers. He taps the expensive bottle of ink that sits close to the stacks. "Forgery work? Is that what Sheridan has you doing?"

Anthony carefully moves the crystal bottle. "No. I said those days are behind me, but I do love India ink."

"Who do you work for? I know you're cozy with the theater owner, but there has to be a bigger score. Are you waiting for a payout from your share of the benefit night? Once all the actors, especially the old legend, take a cut, there won't be much for you."

"I'll manage. I have a reason to do better."

These words leave Anthony's lips easily, but his old friend is right. The way one makes money in the theater isn't from wages but from a night of ticket sales. Depending merely upon receipts from patrons and theatergoers is risky. Maybe once Anthony is more established, benefit nights won't make his pledge to be good feel so isolating.

"Did you leave the streets for a dusty room? One filled with old garbage?" Watson whips a spear from a military production off a top shelf. The blade shimmers in the sconce light. The tip seems sharp. A man could be skewered by it.

"Watson, put it down. I don't need you getting ideas."

"I thought about killin' you when I first met you. No need to do it now. Maybe in a few days, when I learn how you kept me from gaining a mere pence from selling this stuff." He drops the weapon. "What, your old friend is not worth pennies to ya?"

"Watson, no. This all gets reused. Now go."

"Can't have anyone from your old life visiting you at Drury Lane. Do I remind you too much of those good days?"

"A show is going on, Watson. I can't risk you getting me in trouble."

"Oh? I hadn't noticed." The man shrugs, then lifts an awful grin. The one Anthony has seen many times, right before they perfected a swindle.

"Come on, Watson. I've changed. Sheridan can't know my past."

"I risked a lot for you, a spoiled rich man's son who left his snide family for the rookery. In Seven Dials, if it wasn't for me teaching you to survive, you'd been killed your first night on the streets."

Anthony puts the knife on the desk, then slides it to the fellow who'd shown him how to live again, outside the law — through pickpocketing, larceny, forgeries, fixed card games, and good old-fashioned blackmail. "I'm grateful, Watson, but those days are done."

"'Cause of a woman. They always mess things up."

"Someday, Watson. You'll meet someone who'll make you see the world differently. I hope you have the courage to change."

The man scoops up his knife and shoves it into his dark greatcoat. "Well, your changing doesn't get you out of owing me money. I want it." He starts looking at shelves and poking at relics, releasing dust into the air. "Sure I can't sell anything?"

Anthony rounds the desk. "Hey. Hey. Stop. Some of these items are old, but all are fakes. They can be easily broken."

Watson grabs the sharp spear again. He twirls it in the air and then presses the tip against Anthony's chest. "This don't look fake. It's sharp enough to run you through."

Trying hard to keep his eyes from widening and thus exposing his fear — fear of the things he knows Lucas Watson is capable of, fear of the acts he's bragged about committing — Anthony grabs the metal spear's point. "This is iron but was made this year. It won't fetch more than a few pounds."

Tossing the spear aside, Anthony forces a confident smile—one he'd used to compromise the weak, to seduce the mighty, and to open new avenues of financial coercion. He motions Watson to his desk. "Come on, friend. Relax."

When the man follows, Anthony releases a slow breath. "I'm trying to be different. I need to be better. This is my chance."

"I see ya chitchatting with the actress." Watson picks up one of the neat stacks of paper and waves the pages as if he'd tear them to pieces. "She talks to me. Will she change me, too?"

Anthony grabs the papers, gently places them in their correct position, and continues to pretend the man at his back doesn't have the wherewithal to kill him. "You have to know when it's time to change. And my love needs to depend on me. I can't bring her more worries."

Except for the rumblings from the stage, no one says another word.

Then Watson laughs. "You let a whore twist you up, give up our riches—"

Anthony lunges for Watson and grabs him by the neck. With his hands about his friend's throat, he stops short of killing Watson. He lets him breathe and then shoves the fool to the floor. "No one twists me into anything. Yes. I'm in love. I'm willing to be an honest man for her. Besides, our time at petty schemes has run out. These papers are my chance to have it all."

Coughing, Watson sits up and clasps his knees. "You were always a strange bird. A man who once ate from silver spoons wanted to be a common thief. But I shoulda guessed you wouldn't last. Nothing common about you."

After extending his hand, Anthony helps Watson stand. "Look, I'll get you what I owe. I'm grateful for everything. I need time."

The light in Watson's blue eyes glows. "You're on to a bigger gambit. I want in."

The door opens. The lead actress for tonight's show, the beautiful Barbara Banyan, stands at the threshold. Her resplendent costume shimmers, owing to the shiny glass baubles about the waist. They're fake diamonds, but oh, how they make her glitter.

Anthony turns to Watson. "Sir, the cabling is upstairs. I'm glad the manager keeps hiring honest sailors."

Watson nods. "Yes, but this isn't over."

"Of course not. It's intermission, or the lovely actress wouldn't be here. Now please go. And I won't say anything about you getting lost rummaging through the old-scene store."

His old friend offers a mumbled curse and leaves. He passes Barbara and seems to barely notice her trim waist and ample bosom. She's the goddess of Drury Lane.

Her eyes curiously follow Watson.

Then she enters. Her cheeks bear a red cosmetic, but she doesn't need such artifice. When the actress steps fully into the sconce's light, Anthony sees her crystal blue eyes forming tears.

"What is it, Miss Banyan?"

"I've seen him here before. He causes me worries."

If Watson is cornered, he'll expose their horrible past, especially since he thinks he's been left behind.

Anthony glances again at fretful sweet Barbara and decides it's best to allay her fears. "Old Mr. Sheridan has rough-and-tumble sailors around. That's not unusual."

"Such strange happenings. Everyone seems frightened Drury Lane will close. What will someone like me do if it happens?"

Anthony leans closer, further examines her tense countenance. The slight press of her lips, her dour eyes have all the tells of someone in trouble. "What's happened, Barbara? I can tell it's more than typical theater woes."

Sniffling, she blinks a hundred times. "More flowers came."

"The unbidden admirer struck again? I'll find the bastard."

Barbara moves into his arms. Her embrace, her fingers latching about his neck, feels soft and smooth, but Anthony remembers himself and retreats. "Barbara, we . . . we're friendly. I think the world of you. And as a friend, I want to protect you."

Her head tilts, and her blond wig releases a few luscious raven locks. "I know, but you're the only man I can trust. And I long to hear more of this play and your ideas for the theater."

"You helped with this. You're my inspiration."

"Mr. Danielson, you'll still write plays for me?"

He stretches and puts a palm to her cheek. "Yes. You'll be the reigning star at Drury Lane. Bigger parts than the farce you're doing now. My plays will make you known throughout London."

"A legend?"

Her voice sounds sweet, but Anthony understands her desire to be the best. "Of course."

"I thought I'd be known with tonight's play. I'm the main character. Mrs. Lovely is the center of attention. But everyone's waiting for the great Hildebrand's return. I'm nothing."

"Losing anyone's attention is something you never need to fear." After returning to his desk, Anthony carefully stacks his pages. "This play you inspired will help you do it."

She walks over to where he's standing. "Oh, Mr. Danielson . . . Anthony."

"You're one of my muses. My Drury Lane muse. This profession is my calling. Funny. My father always tried to dissuade me. He didn't think it dignified to write for the theater. I know I'm not suited for the church."

"Third sons." She lifts his chin. "I know it makes you sad. Difficulties with a parent can hurt, but hey, don't think about him. Tell me more of your plans, particularly what you'll do when you control Drury Lane."

His brow rises. He's confided so much to this dear woman. To have met her at a different point in his life . . . would've meant disaster, another person on the list of ones he's used and discarded. This friendship is pure.

Anthony again sits on the stool beside his desk and rocks a little. "Drury Lane is everything. It's the key to everyone's future."

She folds her arms about her, as if a chill has swept into this warm, stuffy room. "Will Mr. Sheridan agree to let you control the theater? From the stage, it looks like we have a nice audience. The last-minute announcement in the paper about Alexander Hildebrand's return has brought a few more into the theater. If attendance keeps growing, his money problems won't linger."

Sheridan's debt to Anthony must be paid by week's end, or he will forfeit his collateral, half of Drury Lane. The setbacks, the small audiences, which Anthony may or may not have had a hand in bringing about, have made the normal receipts too low to provide full payment by Friday. "Sheridan's a man of his word. He'll give me what's due."

"He is as bad as my demanding admirer. Can a leech, a cheat be honorable?"

That's the question tormenting Anthony about his own redemption. But Richard Brinsley Butler Sheridan, the playwright, politician, and poor gambler who owes a hefty sum, needs to be a man of honor and pay Anthony.

"Barbara, I'm quite confident. Intermission will be done soon. Get ready to return. I'll make sure the mysterious flower giver doesn't bother you again."

She nods, offers one of those regretful glances that make her crystal eyes look wet and pensive, then leaves.

Anthony waits for the confident thud of the door, which never comes.

Instead, he hears clapping rising from a darkened corner of the old-scene store. The noise sounds as if it originates underneath a stack of sculptures and discarded pieces of wrought-iron fencing.

Dropping low, Anthony claims the discarded spear. He lifts it, bandies it around, and sneers. "Come out. Come out now, or I'll find you and run you through."

In the dim light of his tallow candle, he searches for the thief or thieves. Fools believing the jewels on the costumes are true have struck Drury Lane before. "You chose the wrong night and the wrong man. You've been warned."

A long cough is the answer. "Give me a moment."

Alexander Hildebrand, formerly one of the greatest actors on the stage, now a drunken buzzard, rises from the shadows. His face is unshaven; his gray hair, wild and parted. "Do not run me through, good sir. I'm not the enemy, but an admirer."

The smell of brandy becomes stronger the more he mumbles.

"How are you to do your lines tonight, stinking like the floor of a tavern?"

Hildebrand stumbles but catches himself on the edge of a shelf. "I'll manage. I always do."

"You can't. You're intoxicated."

He wobbles a little, then reclaims his balance. "What does it matter to you? I know you want the play to languish and dry up the box office."

"The brandy has eaten holes in your brainbox. I want Drury Lane to thrive."

Hildebrand pounds the desk. "I've heard what you truly want. You're not exactly the kindly apprentice to old Sheridan. You're a backstabbing schemer."

Fingers gripping tighter about the spear, Anthony weighs his options. Could this talkative fool ruin his plans?

"Now, don't get fussy. Save it for your lady love."

Anthony tosses the spear to the desk. "Old man, go home. I'll get your understudy to do your part."

A few chuckles flee the actor, and he shifts his stance, drawing out his flask. "Decided I'm no harm. Feel secure in what I know and don't?"

"Didn't you tell me security was the chief enemy of mortals?" Anthony slicks back his hair, then tugs at his waistcoat, which wrinkled when he swung the spear. "I'm mortal. I cannot be secure."

"Shakespeare told you, Danielson." Hildebrand steps closer to the desk. After he fingers the sharp point of the spear, the fool draws back a bloody thumb. Suckling the digit with his lips, he says, "I'm merely the vessel to bring his words to life. I'll not tell a soul. I don't even want in on your scheme, unless you feel generous to my heirs."

"Sir, you shouldn't be here in this condition. You're not in tonight's show. Sheridan will replace you."

"Funny, he said that about you. But then he hinted at a business venture between the two of you. It all makes sense."

"Mr. Sheridan can't hold his tongue or his liquor."

The actor laughs then and raises his gaze to the sconce, as if it's a houselight for the stage. "How much did you take my foolish friend for? A thousand? Ten thousand?"

Trying not to blink and give himself or his dealings away, Anthony glares at him. With a hand clutching the buttons of his pin-striped waistcoat, the second thing he's purchased after a wedding band, he shakes his head. "You need to go."

"The part I don't get is Miss Barbara Banyan. Is she in on this or just another mark? She needs money, too. Women fare badly in the theater. They don't get asked back when they grow old."

Anthony looks away to compose a response and immediately regrets the tell—a gambler's signal of something wrong.

Hildebrand laughs louder, almost matching the noise of patrons in the theater. "Why does everyone want the tart? Must be her gorgeous bust. If I were a more youthful fool, I'd pop Barbara's fanny—"

With fists raised, Anthony storms over to Hildebrand. "Don't use such coarse talk to defame a nice lady."

"She's gotten to you, too. There's not a man alive that doesn't want a nip at a big bosom. But there's poison in there."

The bitterness of this man, the dignity he's squandered, infuriates Anthony. Nonetheless, glaring at Hildebrand, with shakes coursing through his arms, he suddenly finds pity for him. "Go home, Hildebrand. Sleep off this drink. I won't say a word about your drunkenness."

"Maybe I will. More likely, I won't. I feel I need to be here."

Anthony shrugs. "Becoming known for being sotted can't be good for you or Drury Lane's reputation."

"Then maybe Sheridan should find a way to keep control and not lose it to those less worthy." He knocks Anthony's pages off the table. They float like snowflakes to the floor. "If the swindler turned manager can't recognize greatness, then things should stay as they are."

"Leave, Hildebrand, or I'll make sure you never set foot onstage again."

The actor wobbles and turns. "Fine. I'll go. Maybe I should go grovel to Barbara. She'll convince you to keep me."

"Leave the lady alone. She has enough worries."

At the threshold, he turns back. "Perhaps you should take your own advice. No one likes a woman scorned."

Hildebrand leaves and slams the door, but it bounces and rattles back open.

Anthony will close it after picking up his pages. Hunched over on the floor, he claws at the papers, gathering them one by one, and listens to the actors above.

Hinges whine. The door shuts.

The sconce light is snuffed out.

Before he can stand and relight the candle, a sharp point hits his back.

Before he can punch at his attacker, the metal drives deeper into his flesh, near his spine.

Before he can utter a sound, the spear slices through his heart. Anthony Danielson has run out of time to reform his life.

Chapter 1

June 7, 1806, London

I tried to catch my breath, not think of the past few hours. Putting my head back against the sturdy theater seat, I waited for Drury Lane's magic to calm me, to aid in my pretending nothing had changed.

My godfather chattered about the latest bills in Parliament as we waited for the final act of *A Bold Stroke for a Wife*. I wasn't much for vote counting, not when my thoughts were consumed with violence.

Slashed pictures.

Stabbed pillows.

Shattered windowpanes.

"Lady Worthing? You've gone quiet. It was agreed you'd seem festive tonight."

Blinking, chasing away the tension in my chest, I fanned myself and forced a smile. "Is that what peers must do, Mr. Vaughn? Pretend?"

Sitting forward, looking straight ahead and in command, as

if he were the Prince of Wales, my godfather patted my arm, wrinkling my poppy-red satin glove right at my sore wrist. "The world is our theater. We shall act as if nothing out of the ordinary has happened to you or your residence."

Nothing?

Was *vandalisme*, wanton destruction, nothing?

By the time Neil Vaughn and the magistrate arrived at Two Greater Queen Street, all the shattered glass had been swept up. The mirror stained with dried wine, or what I hoped was dried wine, had been cleaned.

I'd worked hard, wiping and scouring off the stains, then tossing the rags into the fireplace to burn them.

"Abigail," Vaughn whispered. "Duncan said there hadn't been anything out of the ordinary reported in the neighborhood. He didn't—"

"Didn't want to cause a panic in Westminster. It was only my home, the home of the lone Blackamoor and absent baron, that was attacked."

"Abigail—"

"Hurray. My street is not experiencing the beginning of a wave of crime, merely me. A disturbed individual targeted me because of my race or fears the abolition debate might be won."

"Someone could be after Lord Worthing, Abigail. He has enemies."

"That doesn't help, Mr. Vaughn."

A noisy conversation coming from the hall behind my box beckoned my attention, then disappeared. At least it wasn't laughter at my life.

"When the final act is done, I'll go home and soak in lavender. As I dressed for this play, I saw my tub was unharmed. But I'm certain my maid is scrubbing it to be sure."

Seeming to ignore my complaints, my godfather fingered the fob to his gold pocket watch. "Old Hildebrand's name was in the late paper. Too late to garner a bigger crowd."

Craning to listen for footfalls, I bristled. "Who makes a last-minute decision to return London's greatest actor to the stage?"

"Alexander Hildebrand is a legend. Once the word is out, more people will come. At least I hope it happens. I wonder. With Sheridan's money woes, enticing a man out of retirement, one who can bring the people, must be costly."

The audience did look thin. "If I wasn't forced to be here, even after my tiring journey back from Bath, I'd still come for Hildebrand. I do hope he'll be less shaky in the last act."

Vaughn checked his watch again. "Richard Sheridan is an opportunist. Given more time, every broadsheet or scandal page would bear the name Alexander Hildebrand." His hands came together. Steepled index fingers sank onto his lips. "Goodness. I wonder what arms the man has twisted to make this happen."

Of course, my godfather, Prinny's man in the know, an arm twister for peers, would have knowledge of Drury Lane's owner. "Is Sheridan one of your card-playing friends?"

His mouth lifted into a humorless arc. "I don't sit at tables with everyone, especially not with men who can't afford to lose."

Craning his head toward mine, he stilled my jittery fingers. "It's going to be all right. I'll protect you, like always. This will be fixed."

His whisper, those words, had always meant comfort.

To the girl trying to save her scandalized family from further ruin, it had been everything, everything I'd needed to be convinced to accept Lord Worthing's offer of marriage.

It was also everything I hadn't understood—I'd lose my family, and the baron I wed would always be away.

Now this *everything* might get me killed.

The dapper man, my godfather, fiddled with his white evening gloves, then checked his watch for the fourth time. "And you must be befuddled by being at the theater without my niece, your fellow thespian lover?"

His voice sounded loud. His hand movements were exaggerated. The maestro wanted London to see and make note that all was fine. It was his idea, blessed by the magistrate, for me to come to Drury Lane and pretend.

My dear cousin Florentina still plodded along with abacus and paper, working on calculations with her employer to meet a deadline. I was grateful she wasn't with me to see what had happened to my home.

"Smile, Lady Worthing. No one but those close to you should know your pain."

His whisper cut through me.

The despair lacing and strangling my lungs eased. Pretending to be invincible—not heartbroken and alone—was better.

Anyone watching or hunting Lady Worthing would see me interacting with my respected godfather, not how my limbs trembled.

Or how I mourned Two Greater Queen Street.

Burglarized.

Broken glass lying everywhere.

And none of my Westminster neighbors, not even the curmudgeonly military man and his guard dogs next door, had said a thing.

The nightmare visions that had made me flee Bath were becoming true. Like my mother, I saw my end. Disease had claimed her life. A crazed villain would steal mine.

"You're right, Lady Worthing. Sheridan will do anything to save his theater, even retrieve a retired legend. Then there's you, his most loyal patron. He needs more like you."

"If I live, I'm sure to oblige."

Vaughn chuckled, then he suddenly sobered. "This warning will be addressed," he said. "I have my ears open to all reports."

I should respond to Vaughn, say something clever about him not being able to hear well, lest I screamed. Instead, I focused on the closed red velvet curtains covering the stage and how they contrasted with the bright blue walls embellished with gold filigree. "The last act of the play should've started by now. Such an odd delay."

"Let me distract you with more politics. The voting has started again. We may get an abolition bill this year. The new Duke of Culver has set fire under everyone, even Wilberforce."

My brow furrowed. The notion of the world finally doing what was right, ending enslavement, should be cheered. "I heard his speeches when he was still a viscount. He's impassioned. Nothing like the old duke."

Shuffling my hands, shifting satin between my sweaty gloves, I turned my attention from Vaughn to the jostling noises coming from the adjoining box. My neighbor, Stapleton Henderson, crept into a chair there. He came late to the performance.

"Abigail, is steam fleeing your nostrils?"

"Great. What good is a busybody neighbor if he can't detect that something is wrong with the house next door?"

Vaughn peered over at Mr. Henderson, and I watched as the man swayed in his seat and promptly napped.

"Lady Worthing, does he get under your skin? Have you had any visions concerning what his scandalous sister is up to?"

My glare at Vaughn could set his black coat on fire. "Mary Henderson is doing better. The vision burning into my skull is of broken glass. Seat cushions torn. The stuffing tossed about like ashes."

"Did you sense this attack? With your second sight, you should've sensed something." He grimaced and clasped my shivering hand. "I know it doesn't work like that, but your mother . . . no matter. I'll get to the bottom of this. No one was harmed. Nothing was stolen."

"Just my peace . . . the sanctity of my home—"

"The home which still isn't in your name. I'm sure when this detail is fixed, peace shall be yours."

His peace maybe. "The man who has everyone's ear needs to know my marriage has finally secured my financial success."

"Sometimes that's all a marriage is. Money still rules the world. It won't change."

True.

Gold, no matter its source, fueled businesses on expensive Bond Street and paid for the politics of almost every lord making speeches in Parliament.

Picking at the tips of my gloves, I despaired, my thoughts flashing from shattered windows to my neighbor snoring in the adjoining box. "How much longer will my place of respite stay in business, Mr. Vaughn, before bankers decide Drury Lane would be more suited as shops?"

"London will not quit its theater. Spectacle is in its bones." He stretched in his seat and checked his watch again. "You're anxious. Relax. I rest well knowing you and my niece weren't there when someone . . . Lady Worthing? Are you seeing something?"

My eyes had closed, but only to block frustration and self-pity. I blinked at him. "I see doom for Drury Lane. *A Bold Stroke for a Wife* doesn't look promising. Drury Lane is so empty. It feels lonely."

"Abigail, are you lonely?"

Vulnerable was a better word for the emotions swirling in my chest. "Cut adrift is more apt, but I'm quite used to doing things without James Monroe."

I bit my lip and turned back toward the stage. I hadn't meant to utter those words and especially not in a bitter tone.

Hoping I sounded independent and forthright, not aggrieved or even frightened with my circumstances, I tried again. "I'm good. This last act should be better."

"Everything has a beginning and ending, Abigail."

I gawked at this man who knew secrets, and wondered if he knew this would be how my life would go—hoping for things that never quite happened, wishing for things to bloom when everything was dry.

Sighing, letting air in and out, I looked up at the floral medallions decorating the ceiling. "Mr. Vaughn, tell me what you know. I've done what you and Lord Duncan asked. Tell me everything of this burglary. I can handle the truth."

"I know nothing, Abigail."

Sitting back, I gasped, then sagged in my seat, as if a spring inside my spine had popped. Neil Vaughn having no idea who had attacked my home was the most frightening thing I'd ever heard.

It took at least a minute or two before the numb feeling in my fingers passed. I grasped the chair and sat up straight, looking down at the curtained stage. The last act was still delayed.

"Mr. Vaughn, I've decided I'm not a patient person."

"Never too late to develop new skills."

"Before I married, my sister and I used to attend Drury Lane as often as we could. We'd sit in the last row, among the crowds. We didn't have the pleasure of something as comfortable as a private box. Father's money was honest. He couldn't afford this perch."

"Nothing like a pretty parrot in a gilded cage."

"I'm surprised, Mr. Vaughn, you've not said, 'Guilty cage.' Many of James's investors reap profits from Caribbean plantations."

"*Guilty* is not the word I'd use." He sat up straighter and pushed at the pin in his snow-white cravat. "Your husband's money is through inheritance and sea bounties. I made sure before I encouraged your attachment. Your marriage to the absent baron has advantages."

Then he sighed, making a sound—a soul-escaping moan, a whispered prayer—I'd heard only twice in my life.

Once when his brother, my cousin's father, was beaten and left for dead by alleged street thugs.

And once when my mother died.

The sound—it always meant hopelessness. I hated what it meant, hated the way life always changed when I heard it.

"Say the worst, Mr. Vaughn."

"Elevation doesn't outweigh neglect. A woman can make wrong choices when she believes her loved ones no longer care."

I thought he'd utter something of the burglary, not a warning for my bungled heart. Staring into his dark, secretive eyes, I wished I knew what had happened between him and my mother, why they had separated, why she'd married my father, even though she'd loved Vaughn.

More so, I wished I knew the kind of love that refused to die.

"When will Lord Worthing end his travels and settle into domestic life, Abigail?"

"When he's done searching the world, I think." Smoothing the Mechlin lace on my bodice, tucking the flighty pleated pieces against my neck, I hid any honest thoughts about James and my dissatisfaction with my marriage. "As my father readily points out, I'm young. There's time for domestication."

"Starting a family would keep you home and remove you from danger."

"Not so sure, with Two Greater Queen Street being violated. And it wasn't but a few months ago that I found my neighbor's estranged wife dead on my lawn. That's a dangerous domestic situation."

"Abigail, a killer almost murdered you in Saint Margaret's Church. You're lucky your neighbor arrived in time."

I shouldn't have told Vaughn all the details of my last mystery, especially when it made the irascible Henderson sound like a hero. Well, he was a war hero, the navy man. But I might've escaped without him.

A quick peek at the adjacent box exposed the fellow startling awake. He looked around and winked at me, then nodded off again.

"Now you're definitely frowning, Abigail." Vaughn shook his head but began clapping when the rest of the audience did. I followed his example once I had confirmed Henderson wouldn't tip over.

"Lady Worthing, this isn't right."

"Exactly, Mr. Vaughn. Hildebrand hasn't returned. A new man, a horrible one, is reading his lines. Horrible."

He patted my fingers and offered a fatherly condescending grin. "Not what I'm talking about. You keep peering at your mourning neighbor. The man who lost his wife—"

"Not lost or misplaced like a pair of gloves. Murdered."

His lips formed a terrible pout. "I'll accidentally call you by your nickname in a most public manner if you don't confess to your interests in him."

Vaughn never made idle threats.

He'd announce the diminutive sobriquet, which only my father still called me. It would be at some inconvenient time, somewhere embarrassing, diminishing the credibility I desperately sought.

"The gift of patience is not in our bloodlines, Mr. Vaughn, but if you must know, I'm annoyed at him for invading my theater and then napping through plays. And I wonder if he knows anything about my house. Did he see it happen and not care?"

"Abigail?"

"Mr. Vaughn, he's typically up late walking his greyhounds. He's next door. He might have seen—"

He sighed again. "Abigail."

"You're right. He probably wasn't home. Too tired from all his paramours to notice criminal activities. Mrs. Smith says he moved one in right before I left for Bath, saying she's a governess. His sister's too old for a governess."

At this, my godfather turned and spied the new man-about-town with his head down, surely grunting like a pig.

"And *this* annoys you, and not the fact the widower has begun to live his life again while yours is in suspension."

I blinked at the absurdity of such a statement. "I'm not one to tell anyone how to live. That's your job. But he shouldn't be here sleeping."

Vaughn leaned closer to my ear. "Where should he be sleeping?"

Face fevering, I refused to look at my godfather's countenance, at his cheeky grin. "Anywhere but here. It's a theater. Some decorum is required."

"My dear, we're the last people to be concerned about who should or shouldn't be admitted."

This time I gaped at Vaughn.

His wizened eyes spoke of past slights, things he and my mother and others in the family had experienced. My father, too, had seen several doors slammed upon him for proudly having a Jamaican wife.

I put a palm on my godfather's arm. "Wasn't what I meant. And no, I'm not interested in Mr. Henderson at all, other than being his neighbor and watching out for his younger sister. He should pay more attention to Mary."

"Ah, you still wish to keep the almost scandalized lass in your company. You love secrets and challenges."

Turning his chin, I made sure Vaughn saw me this time. "I know what it's like to be left without comfort because of the death of a parent or for making my own choices."

Vaughn dipped his head and sighed. "Your mother would be proud of you, a baroness with the ear of the magistrate and mine."

"I want to help. I always have."

He pulled out his gold pocket watch again and fiddled with its lid. "Yes, and it's the best of Magdalena in you. But when will your husband sail back to London and determine where you're sleeping?"

As hard as I could, I tried to will the hot blush from my cheeks. "Lord Worthing is doing important work exploring the world."

"You realize you're important?" He snapped his watch closed. "I have an appointment."

"But the play's about to end."

"Not soon enough. Your driver, Rawlins, will see you home. All will be well there. Mrs. Smith promised me the evidence of the burglary . . . will be gone."

Suddenly feeling chilled, I crossed my arms. "Why come with me if you can't stay?"

"Spending any time with my goddaughter is important. Time is a gift. And you've played your part well. Respectable, unbothered Lady Worthing. Rawlins and your butler will be prepared if the culprit returns to cause more mischief."

"You do suspect someone?"

He stuffed the watch back into his fine jet coat and gathered his hat and gloves. "Not yet. But I will find the guilty ones, and they will pay. Debts are meant to be collected."

After moving to the rear of my box, he looked back at me. "You can always be honest with me. I won't render judgment, only help."

"I've nothing to confess. Other than broken things, I've no excitement."

"There should be, Abigail." The words leaving his lips resonated in my hollow chest like a bell's clapper, solemn and echoey. "I didn't know Worthing would abandon you."

My lids dropped.

My breathing slowed, and I wrapped my arms tighter about me. I had to contain all the dashed promises, all my discarded hopes. "I'm no longer under any illusion. James and I are a marriage of convenience. I'm not unhappy. Nor am I searching for anything."

"Then why do crimes keep coming to you? Maybe if you had a more traditional marriage and children, you'd be safe at home knitting."

"It's never safe to knit. Those sharp, poky things can gouge out an eye."

"Or you could use the needles to make socks." He put on his jet hat and smoothed the brim. "You definitely wouldn't be concerned about your neighbor's sleeping habits."

Vaughn bowed. His slick beaver-pelt hat held a sheen in the sconce's light. "Good evening, Lady Worthing."

He left.

My sleeping neighbor had vanished, too.

Was the play that awful? Or was he Vaughn's appointment?

Stomach turning, I focused on the stage.

The stand-in for Hildebrand stuttered his line.

Oh, this was getting worse. This performance might doom—

The lead, a blond woman, screamed.

She kept at it, her high-pitched scream piercing enough to shatter windows. Then she uttered, "Bleeding! He's dead! In the old-scene store! Dead!"

The curtains fell.

This didn't feel rehearsed or even part of the play.

It felt true.

People started running, climbing over chairs, disappearing.

I grabbed my reticule and went out into the hall, directly

into Stapleton Henderson's path. Seemed he didn't leave the theater, after all.

More patrons trudged around us, but my neighbor didn't move. His indigo eyes bore down on me like I'd done something wrong.

"Lady Worthing. What's the commotion?"

"I'm not sure, but I feel compelled to find out."

I marched to the left of my neighbor and headed for the exit, but he followed close behind me as a sea of people flowed past, streaming into the stairwell.

"Wait, woman." He seized my arm and pulled me aside, hovering over me as if to provide shelter. "Good Lord, it's a stampede."

He grabbed my waist and dragged me closer.

"Let me go, Mr. Henderson."

"Getting caught in a crowd fleeing to safety can get you crushed. It's dangerous."

Against his chest, with his heart thundering, I almost gave in to the impulse to stay there, to wish this comfort had come hours ago, when I'd stumbled into my assaulted home.

But I tore myself away. "I'm going to the trouble."

"If you think I'll let you charge into danger—"

"Then come with me if you must. Clues disappear if you waste time. We must make haste."

"Clues to what, baroness?"

"Murder. At least that's what it sounds like."

"In old Drury? An actor calling out murder? That doesn't sound unusual."

"Did you hear the screaming? See the souls fleeing? The panic is true. I need to find out what's happened."

Shaking his head, he grunted and caught my hand. "Shall we?"

"We?"

"As a trained physician, I might be able to help."

It wasn't as if I had a choice: the big man drew me near and entered the dark stairwell while holding me close.

I hoisted the edge of my celestial-blue evening gown and kept up.

My neighbor wouldn't get to the scene of a crime without me.

Perhaps the presence of this big navy hero would thwart the dangers my godfather feared.

Chapter 2

Patrons shrieked in the darkened stairwell.

Silent, pressing forward, Henderson seemed like an unflinching knight routing the enemy.

I wanted to say that he didn't have to hold my hand so tightly or my waist so close, but who told a raging bull anything?

Imprisoned beneath his arm, with my palm flat on his, I surrendered to the smell of cherry cigar smoke in his onyx jacket, the slight anointing of bergamot in his cravat.

His grip eased when we approached the next landing. Light shined down on his blank face. "Oh, the bloody thing is too crowded. Don't stop. Keep going!"

His order wasn't given to me but to the people ahead of us.

"They're not jumping the last stairs, Mr. Henderson."

The grimace on his countenance made me rethink expressing more sarcasm. The man hated small, tight spaces. His morbid fear of confinement, his sister, and his dogs were his only vulnerabilities.

I gripped a higher spot on his arm. "They're moving again. We'll be out soon."

With a nod and a breathy gulp, the man started, full steam ahead, dragging me like a limp satin doll. The closer he got to freedom, to the cool night air, the more his deathly grip lessened. We descended the final stairs in lockstep.

I'd never been so glad to trudge out onto Brydges Street. He led us away from the crowds. And in the shadows of the theater, he bent over, gasping.

Giving the man a moment of privacy, I focused on the flurry of linkboys, the youths bearing fiery torches as they directed carriages to pick up stranded theater patrons.

"Right in front of Drury Lane, chaos," he said. "It's good the performance was half-filled."

The gray in Henderson's cheeks had returned, despite his strident sun-kissed tan. Though he might've needed more time to recover, getting to the murdered man took higher priority. "How do we get backstage now that we're out of the theater, Mr. Henderson?"

He stood erect, as if his broad chest now had an adequate supply of air. "Formalities again? Even when we are alone, Abigail?"

"In a street crawling with escaping people, one is hardly alone."

"Well, I'll have to choose more wisely places to meet, particularly since you've avoided me—"

"Since I offered you sound counsel about a murderer in your household. You told me to be silent on the matter, and I have been. Then I went to Bath."

"Silence by leaving—inventive." Frowning at me, even as the odd compliment tugged a brief smile to his lips, he waved his hand as he gave an over-the-top bow. "Will you always be so compliant to my orders?"

Gaping at him would expose my irritation. Instead, I scanned the exit we'd come out of and the steady stream of patrons fleeing. "When the crowd lessens, I'm going back inside."

He wiped at his face, then took my arm again and ushered me around the building. "You were right. The guilty person was punished. Allow me to express my gratitude. I'm glad you care, Abigail."

What I felt, I wouldn't exactly call care.

Not sure what the draw could be when I wanted to box his ears. "Don't take me to the mews. I want back into Drury."

"Stay close to me."

Too dark to go back, so I truly had no choice. Only the starlight highlighted the broad shoulders of the tall man.

Was he always this big? Or was it that my no longer hating Henderson truly allowed me to see him?

We kept walking farther from the entrance but not toward the mews. "Sir," I said in frosty, arch tones, "the front of Drury Lane is the other way. That's where the entry doors are. It's how one goes inside the theater."

I stumbled, and he slowed.

"Careful, Lady Worthing. I suppose us not fussing about dogs or murderers for weeks has made us estranged again."

Why did he sound aggrieved?

Yet he steadied me with *care* on the uneven pavement. Then the man pushed on a door I'd never seen before. "This way to backstage."

How did the new theater lover know of another way inside? What secrets did I have yet to discover about my neighbor?

I followed behind, and we trekked down an echoey passageway built of masonry bricks but painted a sad gray color.

Henderson reached behind, as if looking for my hand. Not knowing what was ahead, I took the offering. I stepped near him and breathed more cherry and bergamot and safety.

"Be prepared. If there's been a murder, you may not be able to see the body. I'll find out."

"*I*, not *we*? You think I don't wish to investigate?"

"As a physician, I might be permitted to help. You're a

woman. As exceptional as you are, such distasteful things as a murder are kept from feminine eyes."

He took a left, then a right.

"That's how you feel? That women should be kept from viewing distasteful things?" Didn't need him offering compliments with our hands entwined, with his fingers slipping about mine, offering warmth through my gloves and his strange sense of care.

The passageway opened to the backstage. It harbored the same chaos as the front of the house, but with people crying.

Others paced.

One lady, the blonde who'd announced the death, wailed, "This can't be. He was too nice. He was writing a play for me."

She pushed away from someone offering her a handkerchief and hurried into a room.

The door slammed. More desperate cries could be heard over everything, including my raging pulse. "We're too late, Mr. Henderson."

He dropped my hand and stepped into a young man's path. He looked like a sailor and smelled fishy and sour like the Thames. "Where's the injured person? I'm a physician."

"The old-scene store. The room is there." The fellow pointed to a door at the far end of this area. "It's bad. Mr. Danielson's dead."

It might have lasted only a few seconds, but the blank expression on Henderson's face changed. His lips grew small, forming an O. Then his features relaxed, the emotion having faded.

Surely, he recognized the name. Henderson knew the victim.

Abruptly, he turned and stormed toward the old-scene store.

My favorite actor, Alexander Hildebrand, stood at the door. "Hark. Who goes there?"

"Let me in," Henderson said. "I'm a physician."

"No. 'Hark, Tranio, thou mayst hear Minerva speak.'"

Hildebrand's voice boomed the line from Shakespeare, but he slouched and kept blocking the threshold. "The goddess of wisdom will say it's too late. We need to wait for the authorities."

"This man served Admiral Nelson." I made my voice sound forceful. I'd salute my neighbor's rank if it meant we'd get into the old-scene store. "He should be allowed to enter."

Henderson peered at me, then moved forward and barreled past the legend. Over his shoulder, he said, "I need to see if I can help. If not, I'll be able to bring comfort to his family."

My neighbor definitely knew the injured man and his relations.

"There's no helping him, unless you're a minister," the actor said, his voice lowering. "He's quite dead. This play and the theater are doomed."

Henderson roamed deeper into the darkened room.

"Let me pass." My tone sounded pitchy, and I was badgering a legend. "Time's wasting."

"Pushy wench. Is she always noisy like this?"

"She's no wench, but yes, she's pushy." Henderson's voice sounded farther away. "Allow my assistant to come. Then send for the magistrate directly."

Weighing things, I decided an assistant was better than a wench. And the actor let me follow.

Drinking from a flask whisked from his coat, Hildebrand came, too. His footfalls were heavy. Did one of his legs drag?

My neighbor lit a wall sconce. It cast eerie shadows about the cluttered room, with its high shelves, its dozens upon dozens of canvases lying about.

I stepped on a broken bust.

Seemed things had been tossed about, like a search had happened. Like the way things were strewn about my house.

Shivers flooded my arms. My limbs stiffened. My mind was back at battered Two Greater Queen Street.

"Danielson's behind the crates. He made a makeshift desk,

where he worked on things." Hildebrand eyed me from head to toe. "Hope she has a solid stomach."

"Nerves of steel." Henderson trudged forward. His pace was slow, and he avoided the scattered papers covering the floor.

A wild fight?

A crazed, fast search?

Someone had definitely hunted for something.

Reaching the edge of the desk, my neighbor stopped. "Oh, Danielson. No."

I came to Henderson's side and glanced down at the pool of blood that had spread on the floor. The sea of red looked like spilled paint from a bucket, but paint never had this smell—acrid, ferrous, and deathly.

For a moment, I mopped red stains from my drawing-room floor, from James's portrait, his busted frame. The ferrous odor I smelled now…was that what the scent in my drawing room had been? No. Old shed blood was nothing compared to this—this was fresh and warm and murderous.

"Lady Worthing. Are you all right? The smell of death can . . ."

"I'm fine, Mr. Henderson." Lifting my hem, as if a scarlet tide rushed toward me, I held my breath and stooped closer to the man lying facedown, one arm under his cheek, the other clasping the pointy metal protruding through his chest.

"A spear?" Henderson said. "Death had to be instant."

Hildebrand drank more from his flask. "They teach you to be so clever, training to be a physician? 'What ugly sights of death within mine eyes!'"

Careful not to step in blood, Henderson slipped to the side of the murdered man. "No need to quote from Shakespeare's *Richard III*. Though the weapon looks sharp, it would still take a great deal of force . . ."

"Or anger." I stood up tall, wanting to get away from the putrid fragrance. "Anger can give a person incredible strength."

"It's a true African spear. I forget what play we used it for. It will come to me." Hildebrand threw back his head and glanced up to the low ceiling. "Nope, can't remember. But the spear is sharp. I cut . . ."

His left index finger looked raw from a fresh incision. Had he been party to the struggle?

The actor looked frail. I doubted a young man would be done in by him.

Henderson carefully peeled back the pin-striped waistcoat and shirt of Mr. Danielson. "The blade has been plunged all the way to the wings of the weapon. Any farther, the shaft would be in his lungs. He died within seconds of the penetration."

A black jacket lay folded on a stool. It looked orderly in the middle of chaos.

"Is it casual backstage?" I asked. "Mr. Danielson has no coat on. His waistcoat is unbuttoned. In a busy theater, during a performance, is this typical?"

"Could be. But one might be informal and not be expecting to be killed."

Hildebrand laughed at Henderson's statement.

For a moment, I wondered about my helpful neighbor. He knew the decedent, the back door to Drury. Was he here to help investigate or to make himself seem less guilty?

As if he could hear my thoughts, Henderson gazed at me with wide indigo eyes, hurt by betrayal.

Remembering everything he'd told me in secret, I knew Stapleton Henderson was too shrewd to commit a crime so soon after his wife's murder. Unless he had done this before arriving at his box, he'd not have had the time to kill Mr. Danielson.

Moreover, if my neighbor had, I understood him well enough to know that he'd be the first to tell me. Then would dare me to prove it.

Hildebrand hovered nearby. His breath smelled soaked in liquor. He pushed at a shiny flask sticking out of his coat. Something fell, pattered on the floor. A button? The floor was too cluttered to see what had fallen and I wasn't about to hunt for a notion coated in blood.

Downing what smelled like brandy, he quashed the idyllic notions I had of him. Men who let alcohol control them were to be pitied.

"Danielson was going to save Drury Lane," Hildebrand said, his hands lifting in the same manner as when he played Hamlet. "Woe to the true thespians when this great theater closes. Guess he isn't going to be rich, after all."

Swaying, the actor started to stumble toward the blood.

I tugged him backward, closer to the shelves, and made him sit on a crate. "Don't go toddling into the crime scene and leaving footprints. It will make you look guilty."

"We all have to die. The gallows for me would be a dramatic scene. But alas, I didn't kill Danielson. Yet death lies here 'like an untimely frost.'"

"You made a good Romeo. I saw you perform it here." I pushed him back when he tried to rise and take a bow. "Please remain seated."

"Black, but comely, O ye daughters of Jerusalem. Who are you, pushy woman? Hey, old boy, you know she's pretty. Not so bad to look at, at all. Very comely, even if you're pushy."

His head whipped toward Henderson. "Hey, physician, you still picking at the body? Can you tell how long my friend's been dead? I saw him earlier. He was quite alive."

"How many hours ago?"

"He had a busy night," the actor said, responding to my question. Then he put a palm under his chin. "A few people stopped by to see him."

"Who, sir? Be clear."

"Physician, is she never not pushy?"

Deep in thought, Henderson shrugged. "I'll let you know when I experience such a moment."

Devil, take him and the legend.

"While you're down there, physician, see if you can ascertain if he fell on anything."

My neighbor's lips opened, poised to answer, but Hildebrand offered an ugly belch, then topped it with a sotted hiccup.

Unable to stop myself, I gritted my teeth. I know my face changed. Vaughn would be disappointed I allowed my frustration to show.

"Can't move him until the authorities come." Folding his arms, Henderson gawked at me like I'd found something I refused to share.

What I couldn't voice aloud was my disdain for Hildebrand and others who drank in excess. My neighbor didn't need to know my thoughts—the disgust raging through me for men with debts and thirst demons.

When I was sure the actor wouldn't fall off the crate, I turned from both men and hunted for a clue to what Danielson's last moments must've been like. It became obvious with the papers scattered everywhere. "The foolscap is not in contact with the blood."

Henderson nodded. "Someone other than the killer has been in here. I wonder what they looked for. I wonder if they found it."

Broken things lined a shelf. Artifacts and more were on others. "If Danielson's limbs hide anything, it could tell us if a bigger fight occurred. Yet why would no one hear?"

"The room's pretty isolated." Hildebrand coughed. He clasped the sides of the crate, as if it would stop his hands from jittering. "Most would be near the stage, not here."

Frustrated, choking on memories and the ghastly smell, I moved to the makeshift desk.

An old door lying on crates made an unusual work surface.

A few pages sat neatly stacked near a bottle of ink. The clear vessel—a fanciful blown-glass orb—holding the dark ink seemed delicate. "This looks like India ink. That's used for calligraphy. Such an expensive item to be left behind as if it were nothing."

"A murderer, but not a thief. Interesting," Henderson said.

I spun back to Hildebrand. "Why did it take so long for the last act to start?"

The actor wore a guilty grin. "My fault. I wasn't feeling myself. They had to rouse my understudy. Seems he was a little tipsy."

More drunks. "The woman who ran out onstage and announced the murder . . . Who was she?"

"That was Miss Barbara Banyan." He waggled his brows. "She was friendly to Danielson. The woman hasn't stopped weeping."

My neighbor groused, "I suppose some men can't help but collect a harem."

Rich of him to say.

According to the butcher's gossip given to my housekeeper and personal maid, Henderson had begun his own.

After fumbling with the buttons of his own waistcoat, he moved closer to the victim's head. "I'll have to wait for the magistrate to arrive before better assessing his injuries. Then I will be more certain of the time of death."

When I stepped lightly over the blood and came near my neighbor, he waved his hand as if he wanted me to stay back, but I hadn't come here to be protected. Other than wanting my slippers to be free of stains, I cared for nothing but answers.

A few inches from the victim, from Henderson, I gasped.

All those brave thoughts flew out of my mouth.

Danielson's eyes were open.

His lips were pursed, as if he'd uttered a final word.

Then I saw something.

"There's bruising on his nose, on the left nostril. From falling? But he's on his right side. An arm broke his fall?"

My gaze sought Henderson's. He must have noticed it, too. His mouth opened, then closed shut.

The magistrate, Lord Duncan, along with the theater owner, Richard Sheridan, and a flood of runners stormed inside the room.

"Oh good." Hildebrand clapped, almost falling off the crate. "More people to watch Danielson's final performance."

I'd have to find out later what my neighbor knew of this man and what he had been about to say.

Right now, we needed to answer Lord Duncan's questions as to why the two of us and a drinking actor were swarming a dead body.

Chapter 3

The stacks of bright and exotic canvases the runners shifted and tossed, looking for clues, made the old-scene store more chaotic.

Yet I couldn't expect calm in the midst of a murder investigation.

Anthony Danielson had been ruthlessly killed, stabbed in the back.

His body, his blood, still lay where we'd found them. A sheet partially covered him. It was slowly becoming scarlet.

Who hated this man this much?

Who'd do such a crime in the middle of a performance?

And what did Henderson know?

He looked shaken, standing at my side in the corner of the room, waiting for Lord Duncan's interrogation.

The magistrate shook his head, left Richard Sheridan at the makeshift desk, and barreled toward us.

"When I asked you, Lady Worthing, to go to the theater, it wasn't to become involved in a murder. This is not how to avoid unwanted attention."

Henderson's brow rose, and then his gaze flitted to me. "Ordered to come? Surely the magistrate has better things to do than suggest a woman newly returned from Bath to go out?"

Fire could come from Duncan and burn us and Drury Lane to the ground. "You haven't told him?" the magistrate asked.

"Told me what?" My neighbor folded his arms. "Seems there's more than one mystery afoot."

"No. Not for you, too," I said. "I need you to—"

Richard Sheridan stepped to us with the papers from the desk in his hands. His gray hair was powdered, and his burgundy coat was quite wrinkled. "This is a shameful accident. The old-scene store gets too crowded. Now this Viking or African spear from some forgotten farce has claimed the life of a would-be playwright." He gripped the pages tighter. "This play, *A Daughter's Love*, would've made everyone in London know his name."

"Now they'll learn it because of his murder," I said. Instead of waiting to see what this man would reply, I added, "The *Morning Post* shall have an article about his death and Hildebrand's return."

When Sheridan's lips formed a flat tight line, I understood I'd angered a bull.

"Who is this, Duncan? And why is she back here? It's your job to protect an inquiry. I can see the awful rumors now. Women can't hold their tongue."

The magistrate's countenance became a deeper scowl. The affable man I knew was gone. In his place was the taskmaster and acute disciplinarian I'd met long ago, when he'd arrived at Vaughn's estate to certify my mama's death.

"This is Lady Worthing," Duncan said in frosty tones. "Unfortunately, she's a witness."

Sheridan eyed me from my silver slippers to the frilly, finely pleated collar of my tucker. "Oh, yes. James Monroe's new Blackamoor baroness."

Wasn't exactly new. It had been two years since we wed. And since I was his only baroness, was it necessary to qualify by race? "I'm a dedicated patron of Drury in my own right." I clasped my arms and returned his glare. "And I saw the actress come out onstage and announce Danielson's death. I saw—"

"Then you didn't see the crime being committed, Lady Worthing." Lord Duncan's tone felt sharp and dismissive. More than ever. Had coming to Two Greater Queen Street and viewing me as a victim of vandalism diminished my stature in his eyes?

My mouth felt dry. The panic of having to fight for my place rose in my throat.

Henderson stepped a little in front of me. "Lady Worthing's testimony can attest to the time of discovery." He shuffled his stance, with his gaze steady on the bloody sheet. "But the coroner's examination will yield more specifics."

Though the man was trying to be helpful, it just added to this uncomfortable dynamic. I didn't want to be quiet and let the men talk . . . and decide for me and control my sphere.

With a gentle push to his waist, I forced my way back into the conversation. "I also saw how long the last act was delayed. Mr. Hildebrand said they had to rouse his understudy, but I suspect his discovering the body shook him. Forced the need for a delay, and he blamed it on brandy."

The actor clapped. "The pushy one has a point. I did find Danielson dead." He lifted shaky hands. "But I didn't kill him with the spear."

"I wasn't suggesting you did, Mr. Hildebrand. I merely pointed out how my observations might help figure things out."

Sheridan waved his arms wildly. He looked like one of the linkboys trying to direct traffic. "I don't care what she observed. This was an accident. I don't need any bad press. Duncan, do something."

Fists balling and unballing, the magistrate stepped closer to the body, turning his back on all of us. "Lady Worthing. This is no place for a woman. I need you to step outside."

I wanted to complain, to do something to prove I'd earned a right to be here, but I was only a lady who leased a theater box in a world where women weren't supposed to have a say about grisly things or hold serious opinions.

Henderson looked at me and shrugged. "At least you're not a suspect."

Sheridan clapped Duncan on the back. "Good. I know I can count on you. Know you shall always have my vote of confidence. I'll make sure my fellow MPs in the House of Commons understand this, too."

Lord Duncan seemed to ignore the compliment or the backhanded threat Sheridan had issued. The owner of Drury Lane and part-time playwright could compel the members of Parliament to vote Duncan out of office.

"Secure the rest of the theater." The magistrate barked more useless orders. The murderer could've escaped when the audience fled. "Let no one else leave."

Other runners began slowly picking up paper like it was cotton and organizing the white parchment into piles on the desk. Duncan turned and pointed to me, for I had refused to budge.

"Lady Worthing, Commander Henderson, I need you both to step outside. I'll question you two later."

Before I could openly protest, Sheridan sneered. "No, a woman shouldn't be in here. Duncan, this has to be quieted."

Both sexes gossiped. And if Mr. Sheridan weren't such a womanizer, his exploits wouldn't be talked about outside the theater. Mrs. Smith and Miss Bellows regularly returned with news about who the man was pursuing, as if I hadn't seen his antics in the halls when I went to performances.

"Lady Worthing, outside." The magistrate raised his finger and aimed it at the door like I was a naughty child.

Taking off his tailcoat, Henderson stepped forward. "Lord

Duncan. I'm a trained physician. Let me help with your examination of Danielson. I can give notes to the coroner, and then we can get this body out of here sooner. The poor man should be at peace. His relatives have to be notified."

Duncan nodded. "Who knows when the coroner will show? Yes. Henderson, stay. But out, Lady Worthing."

My neighbor handed me his coat and whispered, "I'll share with you everything."

"'Out, damned spot, out, I say! One, two. Why then, 'tis time to do 't. Hell is murky.'" Hildebrand wobbled as he said his speech. Then he sang to Henderson, "'Fie, my lord, fie, a soldier and afeard?'"

Hell on earth was murky, and so was my position. Clutching the fine onyx tailcoat with silver-threaded buttonholes, a mourning band tacked to a sleeve, I walked from the room and didn't look back.

I didn't flinch when the door slammed behind me.

I sat in a chair off to the side in this wide backstage area. From here, I could see exposed metal wheels close to the ceiling and the magistrate's runners stopping four rough looking working men who handled these iron mechanisms to lift and lower scenery and move the long velvet curtains. Duncan's men asked lots of questions and gained useless answers—no one saw anything.

These fellows weren't in the room where it happened, where Duncan and Sheridan decided I wasn't to be of use.

Brooding, I hoped that my neighbor might gain more insight into a death that was no accident.

Unable to sit still, I stood and paced.

Wasn't used to being banished.

No, I was more accustomed to being left behind or given impossible choices.

Swallowing bitterness, I watched as runners disappeared into passageways.

When I moved closer to where these men went, I saw a tunnel that looked dark and smelled damp.

A slender fellow—ruddy face, sea-blue eyes—approached. "They go all the way to the Thames. Sailors come up from there to work the curtains. But the tunnel's long and scary. Wouldn't suggest a lady go."

Peering into the dark passage, I agreed. "Are you an actor, sir?"

"No. But aren't we all? 'Cuse me."

The fellow went over to Miss Barbara Banyan. He whispered something, and she began crying again.

Shifting Henderson's coat in my arms, I spun away from the emotional creature. It wasn't wrong to express one's feelings, but I hated how others used tears of women as a sign of weakness or to prove unwarranted points.

In this place, where men felt I should be emotional or ready to faint, I wanted steel in my gut. And it should remain hardened and battle-ready when I returned home, returned to my violated Two Greater Queen Street.

Yet, how could I not be emotional when I saw the damage to my house. Someone did this to warn me, to make me fearful. Who?

And why did I sob in front of Vaughn and Duncan?

How can I not be diminished in their eyes?

Focus, Abigail! I had to find clues to the murder, not remember the evils in my life wanting me to cry like a child.

The lady's tears ebbed.

When I turned back around, the man who told me of the tunnels, who'd spoken with her, had disappeared.

He'd left against Lord Duncan's orders.

Why should men feel as if they had the freedom to disobey while women had to stay in our places and hide our emotions?

Moving, listening to my slippers patter on the hard clay floor, I edged closer to the tunnel. That had to be the way the slender fellow had gone, but the mouth of the tunnel seemed too dark to know.

Focus, Abigail.

A vanishing man wasn't as important as trying to organize all the clues I'd gathered, including the faces that had appeared onstage with Hildebrand and then again for the first act and people milling around here backstage.

I counted on my hands, witnesses or suspects—Hildebrand, the understudy, at least three sailors still here, the slender one who'd disappeared, Miss Banyan, and Sheridan.

Paper. I wished I had pen and paper to jot down things while they were still fresh.

All the foolscap on the floor, on the desk, which the runners had collected—it had to mean something.

The door to the old-scene store vibrated but remained shut.

In my heart, I rooted for Henderson to find something, anything, to show Sheridan this was no accident and to give Duncan the courage to prosecute the investigation to the fullest extent.

I also hoped the physician wasn't rusty. He'd retired from the military about six months ago. Couldn't be out of practice so soon.

A hinge whined.

Turning, I spied Hildebrand coming out of the room.

He seemed a little steadier as he headed for me. "Have you found ways to amuse yourself, Lady Worthing?"

"No." I paced, but the actor swept in front of me.

"Now, little woman, your physician friend said you might be curt. I hope you won't be that way. I want to be your friend, so I might hang on your words. Let my eyes follow you around."

Wanting his stupor to make Hildebrand go sit somewhere and be quiet, I strode around him.

"You don't notice it, do you? From Duncan, and especially Henderson. What's the hold you have on them?"

His grin was obvious. Not even subtle.

But instead of angering him with several choice words, like *fool* or *arse*, I decided to defang the beast by acting sweet, like how Mama would be to soothe foolish, asinine clients at my father's firm. "Alexander Hildebrand, why not show me how magic is made here? Drury Lane must be special for an actor of your caliber."

Though only a few inches taller than me, he drew himself up, with one hand clutching his coat. Then his smile beamed, like he'd just caught sight of the audience clapping for his performance. "Well, you're now familiar with the old-scene store. This is where old backdrops and props for the stage go to die."

He bit his lip. "I didn't mean to imply . . . Danielson was always talking with me."

"You're Alexander Hildebrand. Who wouldn't?"

He chuckled; the notes were low, hollow. "You'd be surprised about how many respect nothing of the past."

"Well, sometimes the past is wrong. And if a thing is wrong, it should be said."

"Lady Pushy, nothing is ever simple. One must weigh the consequences of taking positions. The costs . . ."

"The costs to you? What of others? People suffer from your cowardice."

"What if it gets you to live another day? Sometimes one has to make compromises just to see dawn's light."

His bloodshot eyes held purpose. Had he lived a life of making choices? Ones now turning him, the great actor, into a bumbling drunk.

"Ah. No answer. You haven't lived long enough."

I definitely hadn't. I just wondered if my vandal had taken it upon himself to make sure my days were numbered.

I still clutched Henderson's tailcoat, seeking comfort in the bergamot fragrance my folding it about my arm had released. "You sound as if you have regrets."

"Many. In a different world, I'd have a wife and child. I'd be a tanner." His arms spread, like he'd hung himself on a cross. "Then I'd miss out on all of this."

"What? The backstage of an empty theater?"

"Come, Pushy. Let me show you my world." The actor led me to more rooms and areas in which they staged canvases, though none were as big as the old-scene store.

"And this passage behind the stage is where an actor moves to suddenly appear onstage or assume the mantle of an apparition."

"I don't remember you playing a ghost."

He stopped and pivoted to face me. "I have. I've paid my dues."

"Does it irritate you when newcomers who haven't earned their stripes come and take the spotlight?"

"Lady Worthing, I've had a long career. I've seen everything. But Anthony Danielson was special. He'd run lines with me. I'd hide in here and hear him and Barbara Banyan read parts. I know in my soul the young man's words would've made him famous. He'd have risen like a star."

"Something bright and casting light upon the dark?"

"Once he made his life calm, I'm sure he would. The man was talented. He had ideas on how to save Drury Lane."

"Was the rowdy, unsettled part of him why he was in the old-scene store?"

"He had to start somewhere, even if it was taking inventory. He'd shown Sheridan his smarts."

I looked up at the shadow of ropes the actor pointed to: the iron mechanisms near the ceiling, which I'd seen earlier.

"Up high, sailors work the hoists, the ballast, the heavy metal winches to raise and lower scenery, even people."

"The winches?" Those were the metal contraptions I'd seen before, hanging above, and since there were no barmaid wenches suspended from the ceiling, I was confident in this assumption. "The gray contraptions ... sort of like heavy spindles with ropes linking to the curtains ... does it take many sailors to work them?"

Hildebrand took my hand and pointed straight up at one of the iron wheels then down to one of the dangling hanging ropes. "Depends. They make the curtains go up and down. I've been attached to them and four or five men held the supports and allowed me to hover in the air."

"Mr. Hildebrand, no one floated during *Bold Stroke for a Wife*. How many sailors worked here tonight?"

"Four, I think, but maybe someone should've floated. That might save the theater."

"Save it from this tragedy or debts?"

"A little of both, Lady Pushy. Floating always draws a crowd. And busy hands don't have the time to shove a spear through a man."

So Hildebrand suspected as I did that a sailor could slip in, commit the murder, and disappear with little effort or notice. The slender man left by the tunnels.

But that was too easy.

I glanced at the heavy metal winches, the three remaining sailors still answering questions from the runners, and then back to the actor. "Did Mr. Sheridan take kindly to Mr. Danielson's plan to save the theater? Or did he think him a threat?" I shrugged and wondered about my own foolish questions. "It would be silly to think a man who owned Drury Lane, a member of Parliament, would feel threatened by someone trying to save his theater."

Hildebrand rubbed under his chin. "But you don't know Sheridan. He can be a bit of a brute when it comes to women or not getting his way. I suspect Lord Duncan is acting out of character for him in order to keep Sheridan from making his life—and, I suspect, yours—more complicated."

Hadn't considered this.

Hadn't thought of someone who'd been a mentor having to act a certain way to keep his position or to protect mine.

The tightness in my chest eased a little. "Has Mr. Sheridan ever been violent?"

He thumbed his lips. "Don't know. One hears rumors. Not everyone gets along all the time."

"And you came to know these rumors so soon. You just came out of retirement."

Hildebrand smiled. "Old ears still hear." A shaky finger flicked a part in his all-over-the-place silver hair. "I've played a few villains. Some victims deserve their comeuppance."

"You think Mr. Danielson deserved his killing. Is this gossip?"

"We all have to die sometime. I'm sure a young, brash fellow could gain enemies . . ."

A dark-haired woman came out of a closed room. As she walked closer, I saw it was the same screaming blonde who'd announced the murder.

Her face was red and wet.

With his gaze seemed pinned on the lady, Hildebrand coughed, then cleared his throat. "Where was I? Oh, yes. A fellow can gain enemies and friends. There's one now. Barbara Banyan."

One what?

She looked lost. I'd have to say friend. The force needed to impale a man through his back had to be substantial. Could a woman do it? Especially a dainty one like this Miss Banyan?

Hildebrand took his flask from his jacket, passed the woman, and went to the tunnel entrance on the far side of the backstage area.

Did Miss Banyan find the body before the legendary actor? Had her discovery led to Hildebrand going into the old-scene store and seeing the lifeless Danielson?

The answer to who had found the victim first was in there. I had to wait outside the room where the murder had taken place.

Chapter 4

My index finger traced Henderson's buttonholes—stately, stitched with fine silver threading. My pacing began anew.

Runners gathered at the center of the backstage area.

My gaze turned to the closed door of the old-scene store. My neighbor had had more than enough time to examine Danielson. If there were clues under the body, in the tailcoat or shirt of the victim, he should've found them by now.

The material of Henderson's coat, the worsted wool, felt smooth. The lapels were flared. It was new and stylish. The widower was taking more care with his appearance, more than when we had first met. I thought he still had on his uniform.

His newly won bachelorhood must be appealing to him. Wondered if he had to abandon evening plans. The gossip my maids had chattered about before we traveled to Bath had to do with his growing popularity.

The raven-haired woman walked up to me. Her footfalls had been completely silent, like Henderson's on my creaky floor. "Beautiful tailoring."

"Miss Banyan, are you feeling better?"

"A little. You can always tell a gentleman by the refinement of such things."

"Miss Banyan, were you blond earlier this evening, or is this another costume?"

She touched her dark, curly tresses. "It was a wig. I have many costumes in my dressing room. People often confuse me with the parts I portray. It can cause difficulties."

About my height, but more petite, she seemed youthful in her features, until you sought her eyes. They were clear blue and sorrowful, with distinct lines of distress around them.

"Did you know Mr. Danielson well?"

"Yes. He was my friend. He joined the theater in January and was well liked by all. I can't believe he's gone. Such a good man. I'll miss him."

Her gaze went over my head. Her cheeks became fiery red. I turned and spied the man who'd shown me the tunnels. He must be one of the sailors Hildebrand had mentioned who helped out with the curtains.

When I turned back, the sweet face of Miss Banyan had hardened. Her expression directed at this sailor was either frightened or frightening. I wasn't sure which.

Examining the actress more carefully, I determined that the white powder and rouge on her countenance hid years. I believed her to be older than me by ten years or more.

"Have you had a long career in theater, Miss Banyan? I suppose you haven't always worked under that name?"

Tears leaked from her eyes.

"Excuse me." She ran away, down the hall, like a frightened hare.

I turned and saw that missing sailor flee.

The door to the old-scene store opened.

"Everyone out of the way." Lord Duncan appeared first, followed by a few runners. On a cot, these men carried the sheet-covered corpse.

The wound still oozed and had stained the cloth a deep scarlet.

Mr. Sheridan and my neighbor exited next. Henderson looked solemn. The grief on his face seemed genuine and had thinned his lips to nothing. But maybe it was just the nature of murder—to think on the sorrow of a life lost.

Yet what was Henderson's relationship to Danielson?

Had he come tonight to see him?

Were they friends or enemies?

Was it possible to be both?

"It's an accident, Lord Duncan. Tell the authorities." Mr. Sheridan slammed a fist into an open palm. "If word gets out about anything else, it will spell disaster for the theater. I can't be ruined."

With my neighbor's gaze beaming at me, drilling a hole into my skull, I sensed he was warning me of something.

Nonetheless, he should never expect me to stand still. So much wrong was done by good people saying and doing nothing.

"Lord Duncan." I stormed toward the men. "How can an accident occur when a man is impaled from the back, with him lying forward? Bad luck would have him falling the opposite way. Mr. Danielson appears to have been surprised, perhaps even tried to get away. Don't you agree with this assessment, Mr. Henderson?"

Sheridan turned to me with an eyebrow raised. "Lady Worthing, as a patron, I do hope you're not one given to gossip."

"I might enjoy hearing a bit, but I'm not a gossiper. And I'm merely stating my observation. Anthony Danielson was murdered."

"Well, you're wrong." He plastered a false smile on his face. "Your husband is one of my great patrons. He made sure to implore my assistance in assuring you had access to the theater with no difficulties. Lord Worthing understands how things can be made difficult by misunderstandings."

He threatened me in front of Duncan and Henderson and everyone lurking backstage. I couldn't back down. I loved theater, but I loved the truth more. "Sir, Danielson was murdered."

"No. No. No, milady. The box that you enjoy so much, for it to stay—"

"Mr. Sheridan, this is hardly the time to threaten loyal customers, when it's obvious your business is light." Henderson came closer and retrieved his tailcoat. He slid it on in one fast motion. Then adjusted his cuffs, taking the opportunity to look down upon the man. "Lady Worthing and I, and many others, can understand the peculiar circumstance in which you find yourself, but a man's life has been taken. His loved ones will want justice. Idle threats make you sound guilty."

The color drained from Sheridan's face, leaving it ashy and gray, like the color of the backstage floor. He wiped at his mouth. "The man was a loner. There are no others. I'm probably the closest thing poor Mr. Danielson had to a friend."

Clapping.

It came from the corner.

Hildebrand came toward us, pounding his hands together. "Bravo, Sheridan. You almost moved me, but you were no friend of the young man. You exploited his genius. And his death makes you more secure, doesn't it?"

After swiping at his neck, Sheridan waved at Hildebrand. "Quiet, you drunken fool. Go home. Sleep off the brandy. Leave before you give the magistrate and his friends the wrong ideas."

Sheridan pivoted to Lord Duncan. "This was an accident. Murder doesn't happen at Drury Lane unless it's in a script."

Duncan, who hadn't uttered much, fumbled with his white dinner gloves. Who knew from which ball or rout he'd been summoned? Probably something formal. Tonight the politically astute man had shown he was more than capable of toeing the familiar political lines than I had thought.

He smashed on his hat. "It does look like something dastardly has occurred. But I can assure you, Mr. Sheridan, nothing will be said in the papers . . . yet. I can investigate things quietly. With the debate raging over parliamentary bills, I'm sure there's enough gossip about votes to occupy you and all the members of the Houses of Commons and Peers. I'll make sure this deadly incident can remain off the scandal sheets until there's an indictment."

"Indictment? That means an inquest and more questioning?" Sheridan pointed to me. "You have a nosy Blackamoor back here, asking questions. It's bound to get out."

I swallowed gall. I was a lady. I didn't deal in gossip. I had maids who did such for me. Well, it was what I wanted to say, but I was in a room of men who didn't think I belonged there.

Maybe they were right.

This was backstage.

I was Lady Worthing, occupant of a gilded perch.

"She's pushy," Hildebrand said, then hiccuped. He pulled out his flask and doused his throat with liquid fire.

Clenching his fists, Sheridan seemed wound up like a spring. "What type of shoddy investigation are you doing? You let customers from the theater inspect the body."

Hildebrand groaned. Then laughed. "I'm sure Danielson didn't mind. Not now."

The tease made Sheridan more incensed. His cheeks were as red as the blood spilled in the old-scene store, the same blood that now stained Henderson's slippers. "I think you're no longer competent, Lord Magistrate."

Sighing like a wall of bricks had spilled upon him, Duncan smoothed the brim of his hat. "Retired Lieutenant Commander Stapleton Henderson is a trained physician. He was Nelson's man. He's quite capable, in the absence of the coroner, to examine the dead. I did assume you wanted the matter handled quickly, not spread out over days. The newspaperboys you fear would love the intrigue."

Sheridan drew his arms behind him and marched a little. He peered at Duncan and then at Henderson, as if to find a new flaw to gain the advantage.

Then, gawking at me, he stopped. "Those same newspapers would love to know the magistrate of London has to rely on chance and a *woman* to do his job."

The way Sheridan said *woman*—it was worse than a slur.

He sneered and did everything but call me names under his breath. "I think Parliament should review your office, Duncan. Perhaps London needs a new magistrate, one who takes his position more seriously."

"Please don't threaten Lord Duncan. This man is more honorable than you." My rebuke was clear. I wanted my words to pierce Sheridan's pompous heart. "His record of convictions is impeccable. What are you hiding, sir? Did you want Mr. Danielson dead?"

"See? Now the *woman* is doing the talking." Sheridan stepped directly to Duncan. "I don't care what you've done in the past. I don't need you or anyone else causing problems for Drury Lane."

"This is an official investigation," the magistrate said. His tone was again hard, again final. "Mr. Henderson, please see Lady Worthing to her residence. My men will solve this crime without either of you. No more assistance. That's an order."

Unlike my godfather's and the magistrate's earlier words to me, this *order* wasn't for my safety but for Duncan's self-preservation. My mentor wouldn't risk his position for me.

A "kicked in the gut" feeling made me vibrate. I was a hollow gong. Time was up for me to help.

Duncan stepped away, flicking a finger toward the hall, the way to exit Drury Lane. "Leave this one alone, baroness. There are plenty other mysteries for which I can make use of your special talents. Not this one."

Holding my breath, I lifted my head and went into the hall and hoped to disappear.

I didn't gasp for air until the night fell upon my face.

Outside of Drury Lane, away from Duncan and Sheridan, I wanted to cry, to sob at being dismissed as if I were nothing.

Walking aimlessly toward Brydges Street, I kept going until heavy footfalls overtook mine.

"That's the wrong direction, Lady Worthing."

"Henderson?"

He stepped in front of me. "Yes, I'm here."

"You haven't abandoned the pushy woman."

"No, Abigail, I haven't." He pried at my arm, then tucked my hand against his side. Gently, he turned me around. "This way. Come with me."

In silence, I heeded his request and headed with him to the front of the theater.

The street was dark and still. The lively visitors frequenting Covent Garden had disappeared. They must know there was a murder at Drury Lane.

When we passed the front entry to the theater, Henderson came to a stop. His hold on my hand tightened. "Lord Duncan had to do that. He had to be dismissive. Sheridan's in Parliament. He has the ear of many. He's the type to cause trouble. With the way vote counting is going on all issues, enemies, for any reason, aren't needed."

"Why are you telling me this? Is this how you gloat at my shame?"

"Rejection is never easy, Abigail. Never."

It was too dark to see his face; I could only go on the charity, the warmth in his low voice. He understood.

"What do I do now? Hender . . . Stapleton, I can't just let this go."

We stood toe to toe in the silence.

Clouds parted, giving me the light of the moon.

I saw my neighbor looking down. The planes of his face, the chiseled line of his jaw, softened and offered the comfort of a small smile. "You can't investigate, but I made no such promise. I intend to find Anthony Danielson's killer."

"Because he was your friend. You knew the man?"

"Not well, but his wife is a dear friend to my family. The couple just wed a few weeks ago. Come with me to tell her the news. I don't know how."

"Oh, no." I gripped his forearm tighter. "Yes, I'll go. Where is she?"

"Hiding at Eleven Greater Queen Street."

At Henderson's town house.

The one next door to mine.

The woman my staff had snickered about as my neighbor's newly moved-in governess. They had ridiculed her as his paramour. She'd become a widow.

"Then you must know why someone wanted him dead."

He took his time buttoning his coat. "The marriage wasn't favored. Her parents were very angry."

"Angry enough to have Danielson killed?"

"Honestly, yes. But I don't know. I'm honor bound to find out. Will you help?"

"Of course. My driver's at the mews."

"Mine too. I'll send my carriage on and accompany you."

We started walking again, but the dray with the sheet-covered body crossed our path.

Both of us stayed still, stayed with his hand about mine, offering respect to young love, doomed love.

When we started again, Henderson's steps became shorter and shorter. The walk to the mews seemed like an eternity.

"I know your thoughts, Abigail. I'm delaying. I am. I don't like to be the harbinger of bad news."

"Together, we'll say what must be said."

With a nod, he led. I followed, and I wondered how one prepared to tell a newlywed filled with hope that her married life had ended.

Somehow, I understood the dark words would come. I knew intimately that hollowed-out feeling of when dreams died.

Chapter 5

My driver stopped on Greater Queen Street, right between number two and number eleven, the oddly numbered but adjacent town houses. The ride from Drury Lane seemed short. Rawlins, who commanded my yellow bounder, was too efficient.

My guest in my carriage never said a word. I reached for his arm. "You think Santisma and Silvereye are up and need walking? Teacup might. I think he might miss you."

His soulful eyes rose to mine. A penny for his distant thoughts.

"As much as it pains me to say, I missed your scruffy little terrier while you were away. Teacup has grown on me. I let good bacon go to waste. Well, not to waste. Santisma gobbled it all."

Not moving toward the door of the yellow bounder, he stared straight ahead. "My greyhounds will wait. I can walk your dog, too."

Two adults, not moving—at first, I was at a loss as to why. Why we hadn't inched forward. Why our hands remained close on the seat. Why each of us seemed frozen.

Then it hit me.

This woman in Stapleton's house had lost something neither I nor my neighbor had—a partner who had risked all to be with them.

"Mrs. Danielson loved her husband a great deal," I said, "to go against her parents."

Stapleton nodded. "The match is not looked upon well. It ruined her guardians' trust. I'm not sure there's any protection for her, something a proper marriage contract would've erected. The marriage has stood for less than a month."

"You didn't answer me, not directly. Did she love him?"

A slow chuckle left his lips. "Such an impertinent question. You are pushy."

"I'm sorry. I just like actual answers."

Still not budging, he folded his arms and set his head back on the seat. His slow breathing wasn't labored. My small vehicle didn't bother him much tonight.

I suppose death can change perspectives.

"I'm not one to know a woman's feelings on such matters. I can only judge by actions. If I were her, I'd wonder if a moment of happiness was worth the harm she's done to her relations. It's hard, Abigail, to *unburn* a bridge."

Now it was my turn to sit and stew. My marriage had set fire to many things. I had a new, honorable name. My family's financial ruin had been stopped. Though I was the wife of a peer, I rarely saw James. My sister had run away. I hardly spoke to my father. He hadn't forgiven me for having my own mind.

Glancing at Two Greater Queen Street, knowing the window glass in my parlor had been shattered by rocks thrown by someone upset with my husband or me or both, I knew I could rally. My changed life and the lives of my staff were unharmed.

Nonetheless, for good or for naught, I threw a bonfire to my former existence. I accepted that. "Stapleton, some things need to burn."

Rawlins wrenched open the door to help me down, but I wasn't ready to unleash more sorrow. "A moment, sir. We'll descend in a minute."

His bronzed face looked surprised but then he nodded. "As you wish, Lady Worthing. But I must say bad news doesn't go away, no matter how long one waits."

'Twas true, but I still needed time.

He closed the door again.

Stapleton sat up, filled his lungs, then turned to me. "Abigail, this business has upset you more than I feared."

"I'm fine."

"You look miserable. You don't have to come."

He moved to descend from the bounder, but I caught his hand. "I'll see this through. I might be able to help. I need to feel I'm good for something tonight."

His fingers wrapped about mine, and he settled again on the seat. "Why?"

"My theater."

"You don't own it. Sheridan does."

"Sort of feels like mine. It's my respite. And it's been violated. I have to know who did this, for your friend as much as for myself. I haven't met Mrs. Danielson, but how could I not ache for her? Her husband was brutally murdered . . ."

"Are you quite certain, Abigail?"

"You're a physician. Tell me how he falls forward and has a knife jammed through his back."

"Through the heart, Abigail. Through the skin and scapula and ribs to pierce the right ventricle and beyond. It was intentional, with great force. This was done with pure rage."

He dropped my hand and rubbed at his tense neck. "Sheridan wanted us to believe Danielson was acting out a scene in some play he was writing and something went awry." Stapleton seemed shaken, frowning wide, groaning lowly. Then he coughed. "No accident."

"Shall we follow this notion? Danielson was writing a play. According to Hildebrand, the budding playwright had been hired for inventory but had plans to fix Drury Lane."

"Odd." His response sounded performative. He wasn't paying attention. Grief addled him. He must be close to Mrs. Danielson. For one moment, I was jealous. Though Vaughn had said he'd take care of things with this vandal, I wanted someone to make me feel they'd hunt down the guilty person or persons and make them pay, pay for shattered windows, the scarlet stains on my sofa.

With neither of us moving, and my heart slowly breaking for him, for what tonight's news would mean to the young woman at Eleven Greater Queen Street, I surrendered. "We could wait until morning. Let's all sleep. I'll come at dawn. I don't even rise early, but I'll do it . . ."

"For me?" He captured my palm, squeezed it a little, offering a tiny bit of pressure. "Abigail, bad news is served better cold."

"That's revenge, sir. Or are you saying her guardians will take matters into their hands, even though they didn't like Danielson? Or will you?"

"I'll not lie. The Mathews could very well be behind the murder. And if they aren't, they may take action to avenge it. They're as close to me as blood family. Mrs. Mathews is the woman who's like an aunt, the one who lives in Mayfair."

"She established an alibi for your sister when she needed one."

"Yes."

"And you might feel compelled to seek revenge, too?"

My heart thudded in my chest.

He didn't move or answer.

What had Henderson seen in the old-scene store to lead him to believe his friends could be guilty? "Why are you telling me this? You want me to look the other way? Let the guilty go free?"

"No. I'll not ask you . . . I won't make you an accomplice. But you . . . I trust you. I want you to trust me. I understand if I ever deceive you, I'll never have it."

My fingers slipped away from his, and I clutched the lace of my neckline. It had deflated, becoming sweaty and wrinkled. "You make me sound unforgiving. That's not me."

"You're a seeker of truth. You're uncompromising in your pursuit. This is not a complaint, but something to admire." His head slumped. "It's late. I'm not saying things well."

Stapleton opened the door and popped out of the bounder. "Coming?"

Wasn't sure how this man had done it, moving me from hating him to merely being annoyed by his presence to trying to understand him and his demons.

But former commander Stapleton Henderson had.

What was worse, he'd looked into my soul and found it lacking. Yet he still wanted my trust.

After seizing his offered hand, I descended from the bounder. "Let's go find Mrs. Danielson."

As if he . . . we'd become self-conscious of our fragile connection, we dropped each other's fingers.

Rawlins climbed back to the top of the yellow bounder, my speedy carriage. "I will find a closer mews. The thought of you walking the streets after a murder is unsettling."

"I'm fine, sir. I have my neighbor, the honest war hero, to keep me safe."

Rawlins looked at me with eyes forming tired slits. "Send a linkboy to fetch me next time. It isn't safe for a lady, even with an escort. With your house being burglarized, it's too much. We need to keep you safe."

"I'll keep that in mind for the future, Rawlins. Thank you. Go get some sleep."

I'd forgotten to tell my driver about Vaughn's warning not to mention the trashing of my house.

I couldn't look at my neighbor, whose growing fury heated the night.

Rawlins started the horses. My carriage disappeared.

Westminster Abbey chimed, distant and mournful.

Midnight.

"Someone attacked your house?"

I wouldn't look at him, not when it felt like I'd lied. We'd just talked about trusting one another.

"Abigail, answer me."

"Duncan and Mr. Vaughn said to say nothing."

"Abigail, you came back from Bath to find your home violated?" The rage in his clipped tones was as if I'd been struck.

"Sometime when I was gone. I don't know when."

"Must've been when I was away, taking Mary to Paris for her summer with friends, or when I chased to Gretna Green to retrieve the newlyweds. If I'd been here, I'd have seen something."

"Then you might have been . . . hurt."

I wanted to close my eyes, to not see him draw back and punch at the sky with his fist.

"Abigail, I swear—"

"No. Tomorrow, Stapleton. We can discuss this tomorrow. Tonight we have someone who has experienced a loss that a good cleaning and a glassman can't fix. Let's do this."

Stone jawed, anger leaking from his pores, he nodded, then pointed for me to lead.

The fury of the man, I felt surrounding me, making me want to go still and linger in it. He cared, but this felt different from Vaughn's or Duncan's admiration. It was seconds ago that I had wanted someone to act as if they'd do something. Yet, with that person being Stapleton Henderson, it terrified me.

When we arrived at his steps, the doors to his house immediately opened. We dashed inside.

The hall sconce admitted an uncomfortable truth. I did have

someone ready to fight with me and for me. Henderson . . . no, Stapleton, cared.

Eyes wide, readying to pop, he pumped his hand and waved away the groom reaching for his tailcoat. He wiped at his mouth, let out a steamed gasp. Then asked his taller servant, "Where's Mrs. Danielson?"

"The parlor, sir. She waited up to see you."

Silvereye, one of Stapleton's, I dare admit, adorable greyhounds, approached. He crossed his paws in front of me and stretched, as if awakened from a long sleep. When his sleek jaw lifted, he went straight to his owner.

The man stooped to him. "Yes, my boy. You remember Lady Worthing. Seems I might have a task for you. Santisma gets too distracted sometimes with the ladies to be effective. Your terrier, is he well?"

"Yes. He was with me in Bath. My household was away. I hate to think what would have happened if I'd left him or any of my people . . ."

Stapleton turned the fire in his eyes from me to his dog. He smoothed the sleek creamy fur along the dog's head with a light touch. "Mrs. Danielson is babying Santisma again? Feeling left out, boy? Feeling lost, not knowing what's happening or what to do? I understand."

With a snap of his fingers, the dog stood and looked ready to march. Then Stapleton rose and led me and Silvereye to the parlor.

From the burgundy chair tucked close to the mantel, the shadow of a woman snuggling with the other greyhound appeared.

She leapt up and came toward us. "Have you seen Anthony? Did you give him my letter? Did he send another one for me? I love his steady hand. It's so beautiful."

My world slowed to a crawl.

This woman.

Trimmed in a blue and gold gown, the styling of a wealthy young woman, she frowned as Stapleton's no resonated.

Then he whispered the evil. His lips formed the silent word *dead*. He wrenched at his cravat, then said, "Your husband . . . He's been murdered."

First, the young woman squinted. Her eyes dashed between me and Stapleton. My heart pounded, as she surely waited for one of us to say this was a mistake, a horrid joke.

No one made a sound.

Then one of the dogs whined.

Mrs. Danielson shrieked. It cut through my soul.

She fainted, but my neighbor caught her.

I stood off to the side, unable to say a word, not capable of calling for water or smelling salts.

Stapleton Henderson, the man ready to protect my property, had forgotten to mention this friend—this ward of his pretend aunt, one the Mathews might kill for—was a Blackamoor woman like me.

Chapter 6

Suspects in Anthony Danielson's Murder
Alexander Hildebrand
Richard Sheridan
Lanky Sailor
Unknown Sailor(s)

Sinking deeper into my bronzed tub of hot water, I nodded to Miss Bellows to pour the sudsy water down my back. My bathing chamber had not been touched by the vandals. It had to be *persons*, for the damage wrought. Thankfully, this room, my oasis of blue tiles with a delicious copper tub, hadn't been touched.

"So clean."

"Yes, Lady Worthing. We had everything finished about an hour after you left. It went quicker. Probably 'cause . . ."

Her lips flattened.

She mumbled her reasoning, but I knew it was because they weren't attached to Two Greater Queen Street, not like me. James left me as its mistress. The town house was a woman, one with secrets and deeply personal beauty. Each room I'd refreshed, hoping my husband would return to a warm and cozy house and think me accomplished.

I'd made Two Greater Queen Street special, but it would be for me alone.

"Let me shampoo your hair, Lady Worthing."

"Yes, please."

I was tender headed, but kindly Miss Bellows had learned to handle my thick, curly locks quite well. Once dried, my tresses dressed with coconut pomade and lavender would be wonderful.

It was probably too soon to offer my maid to help the widow next door.

The sloshing liquid covered my shoulders, warm and wet, as suds ran down my neck.

To be at ease in the bathing room was a blessing.

And though my husband wasn't here, he still lived.

The heartbreak from Mrs. Danielson was palpable. She truly loved her husband. I hoped he loved her, too.

My maid set down her bucket. It offered a hollow clang against the tiled floor. "Ma'am, you seem so tense. It's understandable with all this going on. Let the good water talk to you."

That was my wish.

And I prayed to be of more use than I had been last night. From Lord Duncan demanding I leave to my barely being able to mouth hopeful platitudes to a woman in pain—I'd been useless.

"Miss Bellows, tell me what you've heard about the woman next door. I know it's been a few hours, but I put nothing past your ability to gather news."

She laughed, then parted and lathered another coiling tendril. "Not much more than I told you. The butcher at Covent Market is talkative."

"Yes, I know they made a jest about this woman being employed for Mary Henderson, but anything else unusual . . . more unusual?"

When I tried to look at Miss Bellows, she pushed my head forward. "Now hold still."

"Yes. Of course."

The tugging began. I held the edges of the tub to steady myself, to brace for the worst of the tangles. "You were going to say . . ." My voice became a series of squeaks, but I managed to get out, "Unusual woman."

"Well, when I walked Teacup . . . You know he's a lot easier now, with the Henderson bacon thing."

"Miss Bellows, concentrate." The dear was an easy soul, unless faced with knots.

When the brush ran into some, I tried to hold in the tears forming against my lids. I fought crying. It had never been easy for me, not since Mama left us and Papa grew so angry if Dinah and I were upset. "Start again, ma'am?"

"Oh. The maid from two doors down. Well, she was so happy we're back. The woman had heard nothing strange happening here and said her employers were happy the fence was down between us and the Hendersons."

Was it good to know no one had heard anything? Perhaps my house was old news, with Stapleton's abhorrent wrought-iron monstrosity gone.

My finger tightened as it drummed on the curved rim of the metal tub. "That's all? Doesn't sound so unusual."

My teeth gritted as she worked a final section.

Then it was over, but for the oiling and braiding.

I released a breath and thanked the Lord my eyes had watered only a little.

"There you are. Good and brave bearing this." The fiend chuckled, then massaged the salve smelling of the best coconut into my raw scalp. "The governess—I think Danielson is her name—and Miss Henderson, before going to Paris, were asking the maid for the best place to get baby clothes. The governess said it was for a friend. I suppose she didn't want any rumors spread about the young lady at Eleven Greater Queen Street about to go away on holiday. I wonder about Miss Henderson."

"Mary Henderson is healing a broken heart. I know she's not . . ." Oh no. Mrs. Danielson was a widow and would have to be a mother alone. Parenting by oneself must be terrible.

"You came in late from next door. Is all well with Miss Henderson?" Her face was cheery and curious, as always.

I hated having to say anything. Miss Bellows participated in the gossip circles Vaughn and Duncan were so fearful of. "The governess, Mrs. Danielson . . . Her husband was murdered at Drury Lane. I went with Mr. Henderson to tell her the news."

"Last night? At the theater, you went . . . We sent . . . you to another murder?"

Mrs. Smith sauntered in with fresh, fluffy white towels. "Murder. Is this what you're saying about getting ya hair washed? We have to get all the sea air out of it. Ya spent far too many days walking on the coast in Portishead and Clevedon on those day trips from Bath, getting sand in your curls."

"You know she can't help it," Miss Bellows said as she towel dried my hair. "The sea is where she feels closest to the baron. I think it romantic."

Didn't need to look at my housekeeper to see her thickly curved lips form a sarcastic pout. While Miss Bellows saw things as beautiful and innocent, Mrs. Smith understood the truth. A marriage of convenience, with one partner always away, was paper, a mere contract.

She put the towels by the tub. "Lots going on next door. Commander Henderson was up early. Dressed in more mournful solid black, he came over and browbeat Mr. Rogers about the break-in. I suppose you told him."

"He what?"

"Ya, he said you told him all about it at the theater." She looked at me as if I'd done something wrong.

I wanted to stick my face below the suds, wanted to purge my anger, but there wasn't enough water in the tub or the world to drown this feeling of betrayal and fury over his heavy-handedness. "Did the busy man tell you I was under duress? A man was murdered at my Drury Lane."

My housekeeper mouthed the word *murder* while Miss Bellows helped me stand and begin drying off.

"I forgot to tell him to keep it a secret." *Like I've kept his.*

"When did ya take possession of Drury Lane? The husband buy it for ya as a gift to make up for his absence?" Her Jamaican wit stung worse with her upturned nose. But she'd been so proud when I accepted Lord Worthing. "You know what I mean."

The glance she gave me stabbed through my heart. James had been attentive when he was here. He had gifted me Teacup, but I hadn't seen the baron in almost a year. "I love Drury Lane. It was violated. I must find out who'd do such a thing. And the young woman next door is now a widow. I'm compelled to figure this out."

"What?" She paled. Her warm brown skin seemed to become ashen. "I was teasing ya. Please say you've been teasing me."

Peachy-faced Miss Bellows gasped. "Lady Worthing isn't joking. Oh my. Newlywed and now a widow."

"Yes." I stepped out of the warm tub onto a fluffy white towel. My bare feet would have to touch a couple of cold tiles before returning to the wood and warm carpet of the hall and then my room.

I started to escape, but then I stopped and turned to Mrs. Smith. "Have your say, ma'am."

"Seems the man next door is followed by death."

"Same could be said about me, Mrs. Smith. And last night I comforted the poor woman who eloped and was hiding with the Hendersons until her husband smoothed things over with her family. Seems the Mathews, friends of the neighbors, are upset."

Shaking her head, Miss Bellows wrapped up my hair. "Seems the poor man didn't live to do it. You think the family killed him?"

"Miss Bellows, I don't know. I don't want to think Mr. Danielson was murdered by his in-laws."

Yet it was a horrible possibility.

Mrs. Smith shook her head, added another towel about my neck. "The Mathews of Mayfair. They've got the money to hire someone to do it."

Could someone be so cruel as to kill to keep a young couple apart?

The sober dark brown eyes of my housekeeper found mine. She said, "I'm sorry to hear this. How did the young woman take the news?"

"At first, she was stoic. Then she sobbed like a newborn . . ." Like a girl who'd lost everything that mattered. "I need to find out all there is to know about the Mathews."

Mrs. Smith tsked her teeth. "Aren't you forgetting to ask about the obvious?"

"What, Mrs. Smith?"

"The man's family might've killed him for taking a wife of a different race."

Mrs. Danielson, formerly Miss Joanna Mathews of Mayfair, was a Blackamoor woman like me. "I'll research the particulars of all involved. But if the young lady has money, his family might not have much of a problem. Riches trump race."

"It can't be ruled out. It's very much a possibility." She and Miss Bellows picked up the towels discarded by the tub.

Was everyone in my household becoming a sleuth?

When I stepped foot on the tile, I recoiled. It was cold. Shivering, I caught a glance at my housekeeper's guilty eyes. "You knew who she was," I said, "and her background, but you let everyone think she was Mr. Henderson's paramour."

My accusation was met by her knowing smile. "I know better than to get in the way of good gossip. If she was hiding next door, she had good reason. With her new husband dead, seems she was entitled to keep her secrets."

Her logic couldn't be discounted. I rushed to the hall, planted my feet on the warm, creaking pine planks. "Next time, tell me your secrets. We're supposed to be on the same side."

"Of course, ma'am. Let's get you dressed. Your cousin should be here any minute."

Florentina was someone I deeply missed, but her work on the naval compilations with Mrs. Edwards couldn't be delayed. I wished she'd gone to Bath. Being alone, awaiting word of my husband's ship, could have been borne better with my dearest friend. When I had kept driving out to the close shores and had seen nothing, I'd given up and returned to Westminster.

The thought of Mrs. Danielson at Eleven Greater Queen Street, not knowing whether the people who had raised her had a hand in her husband's death, made me tremble.

Miss Bellows came from the bathing room, but she dropped the pile of towels in her arms. "Let's get you warm. No catching a cold."

Allowing her to lead, I went on the short journey to my bedchamber. After dressing, I sat at my desk and made a list of suspects. It wasn't long. The notations were quite vague. Many questions needed to be asked and answered before I'd have a clearer picture of the person or persons responsible for the murder.

Once Florentina arrived, I'd convince her to go next door with me and we'd try to be a comfort to the Widow Danielson.

Then my investigating would resume.

Despite Mr. Sheridan's and Lord Duncan's wishes, I'd gain justice for a woman who appeared to have lost everything, the love of her life and her family. I had to solve this crime and offer a fellow independent spirit a measure of peace.

Chapter 7

Suspects in Anthony Danielson's Murder
Alexander Hildebrand
Richard Sheridan
Lanky Sailor
The Mathews
Unknown Sailor(s)

Dressed in my black carriage dress with shiny brass buttons on each cuff, I descended my stairs and pretended the carpet beneath my feet hadn't been scrubbed of blood.

Never did figure out if the stains belonged to man or beast.

A pit in my stomach opened, and a hole filled with pity tried to suck me inside.

The nightmare I'd had in Bath played again in my head. I saw myself running. Then a knife blade pricked my neck.

Barking. Loud, persistent yowling woke me from my dream state. I clutched the banister.

Then I sank to the steps and grabbed my terrier.

He kissed my face, licking at my cheeks.

"You know I needed that, boy." Hugging him, I remembered I had too many things going on in my life to wallow in sorrow or to be haunted by a stupid vision, a stupid nightmare that meant nothing.

"Teacup, I'm a pretty parrot, just not in any cage. I'm free to go and come. No one is chasing me."

I said this aloud, but I sat on a carpet runner stained by some bandit.

My breathing became shallow again.

I put Teacup down and staggered to my feet.

After lightly nipping at my heels, he began to run around my ankles. Then he stopped in front of me and sat on his hind legs.

"That's a new trick, boy."

He sniffed my gown, maybe smelling the lavender Mrs. Smith used to scent the wash. I stooped to my beautiful boy. "I wish I had some bacon for you."

He leapt at my fingers, then seemed to track something. Since Florentina hadn't arrived, I followed. He went into the parlor where my butler stood.

I hesitated at the door, looking at the missing windows. "Rogers, when will the glass be fixed?"

"A service is currently arranged for next week. 'Twas the soonest it could be arranged. We'll cover the holes until the repairs can be made."

With a nod, I left him and went into the drawing room.

Not sure why the destruction in there made me feel so scared.

Remembering how James's portrait was on the floor, the frame busted and gouged by a knife, the gold leaf scraped off in places, made me realize how much hate someone had for me and my husband.

Slowly, I gazed around. Seeing my husband's face devoid of its gilded border hurt.

Why did this violence seem so personal?

My stomach clenched. There was a person I knew who overflowed with anger.

One person who'd target a house James owned.

One person who'd traipse their venomous soul up the stairs, stain and cut up curtains, even my clothes.

Could my sister have done this?

Dinah Carrington hated that I had married James. She had run off because of it. Would she come to Two Greater Queen Street and do this?

Dinah. Did she think this hateful act would cause me to run from Westminster, to go back home and stay with our father? She wasn't even living with him.

No. Not her. She was angry and hurt, but not this cruel, never this cruel.

This wasn't sibling rivalry gone amok. This felt evil and obsessive, even murderous. Thank goodness, no one was here.

The scent of the bleach solution used to scrub the blotches from the walls remained. Miss Bellows had said they'd finished cleaning an hour after I left for the theater. I doubted that was true, figured that was something the staff, at either Mr. Rogers's or Mrs. Smith's insistence, said to give me comfort.

My doggie abandoned the parlor and trotted into the drawing room.

"Hey, Teacup. Remind me to tell our people to not be so noble. I don't cry for things I can't change. Right, boy. Let's celebrate our motto."

After picking up the heavy portrait of James, I whirled it around, as if I were performing a dance. Something faster than the minuet, slower than a country dance. The pace should make me dizzy, make me forget I thought my own sister capable of such destruction.

"Lady Worthing. Lady Worthing?"

My cousin's voice. She'd arrived to save me from this thing called pity.

"In here, Florentina."

She came to greet me.

Her finger went to her nose. Her gaze swept to the wall with the lighter bleached patches of pink.

"Wow. What happened here?"

"Late spring cleaning. I'm so glad you've gotten a chance to get away."

"It's only for a few hours. My head and eyes are filled with numbers. I want a nuncheon with you, and to be swept away as you tell me all about your reunion with Lord Worthing."

"Swept away? You? When did you become a romantic?"

"Life is not all about numbers. And for you to go away abruptly to Bath to await the baron, it is the things one dreams of."

Putting my back to her, I labored to set the portrait down, taking extra time and care, hoping words would come to respond to her rare enthusiasm.

"Do you remember Lord Worthing? Salt-and-pepper hair, high-bridge nose, beautiful silver-blue eyes. My husband's eyes, those were the first things I noticed about him. Wonder what you think has changed about him?"

My terrier craned his neck, then stretched his nose away from the wall and headed from the room.

Obviously, Teacup was unprepared for this conversation and my awful confession.

"I don't, Abbie. More silver hair. Maybe a scruffy beard. Probably lots more jokes."

Nodding, I stepped to her. Folding my arms, I tucked one palm under my chin. "I can't quite tell, either. I didn't get to see him."

"No Worthing?" Her gaze shifted to me. After examining me up and down, her mouth snapped shut. The beautiful golden-brown bonnet shadowing her eyes came off and was tossed to the floor.

"Abbie, I'm so sorry." She ran to me and drew me into an embrace, tight and hopeful, everything I'd craved since yesterday, since forever, since the day James sailed away.

I held my cousin, breathing in the jasmine my aunt used for Sewell hair wash days. So comforting, so honest, so missed.

"You poor girl. I'm so sorry. You've had to face this alone."

"Face what alone, Florentina? You're not late."

"Look at you, being so brave." Her arms tightened about my neck. I grew lost in her comfort. Knowing someone loved me, didn't judge or leave me for my choices, meant everything.

"Oh, Abbie. How did they tell you Worthing has died?"

Stepping back, almost tripping over the painting, I gawked. "James is alive. He's well, for all I know."

"But the black dress. His picture is off the wall. The sour smell in here. Did you have them cleaning for a wake or party with the dead . . . the Scottish thing they did next door?"

"The lichwake?"

My cousin's mathematical mind had added up all the clues wrongly. I picked up her glorious bonnet, then moved back and topped her head with it. "Lord Worthing is doing what he always does, exploring the world. And I'm doing what I do, finding a guilty culprit."

The light shifted about her luminous olive face. A series of emotions darkened her cheeks—relief, grief, fear. "Abbie, I'm glad you're not a widow, but I don't know what you have in store. I came only to eat, talk of Bath, then go home alive. I have three more days of calculations to do with Mrs. Edwards. Can you try not to get me killed?"

"I'll promise to keep you safe if you come with me next door."

"Next door doesn't sound dangerous. What are the Hendersons up to?"

"Providing comfort to a friend who became a widow last night."

Her soft mouth opened, then closed, then opened again. "I guess I need to calculate the odds of surviving this and eating at Olive's."

I locked my arm about hers. "Oh, silly goose. This shouldn't require a sacrifice. I merely want to see if she's doing better, and—"

"And get her to talk about the deceased, thereby telling us something to help us be targets of a killer."

"Well, not exactly, Florentina. But I can hope."

She shook her head. "I just wanted food. Now my odds of living past the day have dropped five percent."

I'd argue if my house hadn't been abused, if I didn't have visions of being attacked. "Come, let's hurry and face these odds and then hurry to get the best Stilton and port."

My cousin shrugged, but walked with me.

The light pale-pink silk of her gown contrasted with my heavy bombazine one. We were oddly matched.

Yet she was right. I did hope Mrs. Danielson wouldn't mind receiving us and talking about her late husband. Who, besides her parents, wanted Anthony Danielson dead?

There was no waiting a decent mourning period to make inquiries of the widow. Sitting around thinking about James or the vandals or awful visions shouldn't be borne, not while a murderer who struck at my beloved theater remained at large.

With Florentina by my side, I entered Eleven Greater Queen Street.

Footmen in silver took our bonnets, Florentina's beautiful brown one, my jet-black one with a dark egret plume fluttering at the brim.

On the outside, I appeared calm, serene, as easy and as light as a feather. On the inside, I was a storm pounding along the rocks. The mourning and weeping that happened here last night returned, flooding my head, drowning me in hopelessness. Mrs. Danielson's sorrow could've been, would've been mine had the bandit found anyone home next door. I was convinced my vandal sought someone to murder.

Breathe, Abigail, I told myself, but my voice was shaky when I said, "We're here to see Mrs. Danielson. Is she being attended by Mr. Henderson?"

My irritation at my neighbor lessened. He still shouldn't berate Mr. Rogers, but Stapleton had sensed the danger.

The taller of the two footmen stared at us, then shook his head. "He's gone to town, Lady Worthing. Seeing after Mr. Danielson's remains. His widow is in the rear parlor."

He pointed, but I knew the way. That was where the lichwake was held for the late mistress of the house. Clasping Florentina's hand, I guided her to a room with pale blue walls and gilded molding, the place where I and others had mourned Henderson's wife months earlier.

The room felt cold.

The notion that death was waiting here gripped my chest.

Why was I acting like this? Like I was still in a nightmare?

The woman looking out the window didn't turn to greet us. Dressed in an expensive bombazine gown with velvet ribbons, she seemed calm, very different from last night.

Perhaps she'd cried out her emotions.

Perhaps, as my father would say, she was getting on with things.

"Mrs. Danielson?"

"Say it louder, Lady Worthing." Her gaze stayed pinned on the glass. "Yell it if you can. I was in hiding as long as I was married. Never got the chance to be announced in public. I think a bride should have the privilege."

Sneaking a low breath between my lips, I enunciated, "Mrs. Danielson. Mrs. Anthony Danielson, do you mind receiving us?"

With a slow swivel she sat in a close chair. The elegant woman faced us. Her countenance was blank; then a muscle in her cheek twitched. "Say the name again."

"Mrs. Danielson." I led my cousin deeper into the room, the

room with the creakless floors, then stopped midway. "Mrs. Danielson, do you feel like talking?"

"Well, I don't want to dance. Though Anthony, he was a good dancer. We met while dancing in Mayfair. He'd pretended to be a landowner from Antigua."

"Pretended?" Florentina folded her arms. "Did he pretend to own slaves?"

The temperature in the cold room dropped to ice cold. I glared at the girl as if she'd lost her mind; then I turned back to the widow. "Mrs. Danielson, this is my cousin, Florentina Sewell. She can be rather outspoken."

The lady nodded. "Anthony could be callous, but he'd been a swindler for most of his life. He thought the lie would impress my guardians. Didn't work."

The financial ties between His Majesty's colonies in the West Indies and Mayfair were dubious and insidious. The rich depended upon the *investments* to maintain their lifestyles. Most with those connections failed to associate the money with human misery.

"Why weren't they impressed?" Flo kept at it. "Are they rallying for Parliament to do the right thing?"

Mrs. Danielson's face didn't change. Still, she seemed to look at me and Florentina as if we were necessary distractions. I didn't blame her.

"Just talk." I pulled my palms together as if I prayed. "We . . . I'm listening."

Mrs. Danielson lifted her hands, hands of light gold skin, much lighter than mine. In some respects, if not for her flared nose and tight curls, she could blend seamlessly into the Mayfair world and merely be accused of spending too much time in the sun.

"They were appalled. His scheme fell apart. The Mathews are abolitionists at heart. They forbade me to have anything to do with him, but the man made me laugh, laugh quite a lot. I think they were wise to see an attraction before I realized it."

Florentina edged forward. "And he courted you to take revenge. How awful."

"Awful, maybe. Exciting to my spirit." Glancing at me, she stood. Her immaculate dress hovered over onyx slippers boasting a beautiful sheen. "He apologized. Admitted everything. Then wrote me incessantly. Anthony was a playwright. He would've been a good one. He'd finished it to make Drury Lane a fortune. Now his play, *A Daughter's Love,* will never be performed."

Finished? Didn't Sheridan allude to the work not being done? "If it's completed, as his widow, you could make it happen somehow. Represent his work. It would be a fitting memorial."

She shrugged. "I don't know. It's all so wretchedly new. I was waiting to start our lives together. Now I have to think of being alone."

The gossip about baby clothes . . . Did that mean she had something lasting of the man she loved? Nonetheless, bringing a babe into a world his father had departed must be heartbreaking.

Florentina squinted at her, then at me, then back at the parted curtains, billowing like they'd allowed in ghosts. "You fell in love with a known swindler? You married him against your parents—"

"Guardians. The Mathews are my guardians. They are good people. They have given me so much."

My cousin put her hand on her hip. "But you chose to discard their wishes. You married a criminal. In what world does this make sense?"

"Florentina, please. She's in mourning."

The young woman crossed the room to us and stuck her finger in my cousin's face. "You didn't know Anthony. He was brilliant and passionate and—"

"And you chose him against your guardians' wishes. You'll

inherit a play, pages of meaningless words. That can't be worth much. How do you expect to make it?"

"Flo, please. Stop."

Sighing loud and long, Mrs. Danielson half turned to the window. "It's nothing I planned. I often think if I hadn't read his first letter, if I hadn't met him in Saint James's Park, if so many things hadn't led me to him, I wouldn't feel like this right now."

"But would he still be living if he hadn't married you?" I said it. I hated that I had, but I did.

Her cheeks became red, like fire. "That's a horrible thing to voice."

"But is there any truth to it? Some families can hate their daughter's marriage so much they implode. Others might resort to murder."

She groaned and went to the window again. The curtains enveloped her like a hug.

Feeling awful for pushing this woman who had fresh wounds to her heart, I waved at Florentina to stay back and went to Mrs. Danielson. "The grounds are lush. You can see Henderson's garden. Next spring it will be beautiful."

"Yes," she responded. "Anthony would come here. These past few weeks. He wouldn't tell a soul. He'd come, and we'd walk in the park. We'd talk for hours. We even danced once in the rain. Do you know what it's like to truly be heard by someone?"

No. Didn't know what this felt like, their magic.

My godfather appeared to listen, but there was always an angle or line of reasoning he'd steer me to. My father never tried. He refused to hear me out. With James, maybe I didn't hear what he said. I wanted to be advanced in society and loved. Missed the part where it was two separate choices.

Then it struck me. Mrs. Danielson was hiding in plain sight. "The Mathews and the Hendersons are closely connected. This would be an obvious place to go. You didn't fear your guardians would harm you. Who were you hiding from?"

Her eyes darted. "I still sit here waiting for Anthony. I keep hoping this is all one of his jokes. He should be coming here."

"You want this to be a scheme? Mrs. Danielson, I saw him last night. He's very much gone. His murder is true. Who did it? I know you suspect someone."

Like rain clouds, she burst. Tears leaked. Her reddening cheeks became so wet. "I don't know. Someone he defrauded in the past. Or someone who didn't want Anthony to make an honest living as a playwright. That play would change things."

Florentina sucked her teeth hard.

Making eyes at her, I needed her to quit, but I wondered why my cousin was angry at a woman she'd just met.

I made hand motions for her to settle down, then turned back to Mrs. Danielson. "I want to help you. I want to find the killer, but I need names. I must have the truth. Who do you think killed your husband?"

"It could be anyone from his old life. His parents were angry at him, a third son who didn't want to be a vicar."

"And your guardians?"

"*Non, ne sois pas une oie stupide.* I don't think them guilty. Maybe someone at the theater. Richard Sheridan owed Anthony a lot of money."

"Did he sell him the play?"

"I'm not sure. I . . . I didn't ask."

This she said with a clear voice. The violent tears of a moment ago, before she said in exquisite French that I was a silly goose, had disappeared. Maybe the budding playwright had found an actress and married her.

Folding my arms, resisting tapping my foot, I gaped. "Help me understand why a smart, educated woman wouldn't ask a reformed man why someone owed him money, money you both would need to live on since your guardians didn't approve of the union."

Mrs. Danielson turned from me to the sparkling clear panes.

Florentina shook her head and left the room.

"Excuse me, Mrs. Danielson. I'd like to talk later," I said.

She sighed. "I think I'm going to be tired for a long time. Please leave."

I did. This woman wasn't ready to confess what she knew.

Florentina was at the door, retrieving her bonnet.

"I'm coming, Miss Sewell. Slow down."

She didn't listen. She barged outside.

Clasping my bonnet, I charged after her. "Will you wait?"

"No, Abbie, let me be. I wanted to come have a nuncheon with you before I have to get back to work. I'm busy night and day, and we're next door, poking into business that's not ours, with a woman who's lying."

"Flo! I have to know what happened. And yes, I believe she's hiding something."

"Abbie, she's lying. This woman in there is finely dressed. Her mourning outfit could rival those of your mantua-maker. You think Mr. Henderson has these stately things lying around? Or has she been in contact with her guardians? They provided those garments."

"It's possible, Flo. But why are you upset? Are you terribly hungry?"

"I work hard for everything. My parents are decent but not rich. She tossed away all her advantages on a schemer." She pointed back to Eleven Greater Queen Street. "Mrs. Danielson wants you to believe she was so in love, she didn't know how her hubby would pay their bills. Lies."

"Florentina Sewell. You're being rude. This woman just lost her husband."

My cousin balled her fists and headed behind the town houses toward Saint James's Park. "Come on, Abbie. Let's find the tree under whose arbor the Danielsons committed their love to each other."

Florentina moved quite fast. Before long, we were deep into a grassy knoll close to a row of black mulberry trees.

"Will you stop? Let's head back and get Rawlins to take us

to Olive's, or I'll have Mrs. Smith get the cook to create something fabulous. Like bourbon biscuits or chocolate short-breads."

She parked herself at a tree with thick limbs like an octopus's and pounded on the rough bark. "Biscuits can't fix everything. Cheese can't, either."

"Tell me what's going on with you. This is not about Mrs. Danielson."

"No, it's about you. I walked into Two Greater Queen Street, and everything felt different. And then I thought you a widow."

"I'm not—"

"And I was relieved. I feel so guilty. I'm sorry."

My mouth dropped open. A bug or hummingbird could have perched on my tongue.

"Say something, Abbie. I'm sorry."

"So, you're not in my corner?"

"Abbie, you risked everything for a man of means, one who had a spotless reputation, until he was framed for a crime. You saved Lord Worthing from the gallows. Marriage to him elevated your family. You made the best choice. You're not reckless. You did what you did because you respected the baron and yourself and knew it would benefit your family. But Mrs. Danielson used her privilege of being in rare spaces, accepted and loved, and squandered it. A thief wrote her fancy notes, and she turned her back on everything."

"We can't judge her circumstances. And one can't help who they love."

She lifted her hands, dark, beautiful hands. "I don't get into places of such privilege. I have to leave when certain admirals come by to check Mrs. Edwards's progress. The poor woman has to fight for her position just because she's female. If I were fair like Mrs. Danielson or even had your complexion, I might get to stay and help present our numbers."

"Flo . . ."

"Look. I love my deep olive skin. I think you are lovely but too pale, but I'm not ignorant of the advantage you get from being mixed with Scottish blood."

"The world needs to change. Mr. Vaughn says the voting is looking better. New people are stepping up to help Mr. Wilberforce."

"It's not changing fast enough. The world has people who still want the three of us in chains. Like you, she should be trying to use her privilege for change."

Didn't need to say Florentina was right.

But she was.

Didn't want to agree that everyone had to fight.

But if not us, who would risk their position for fairness?

Yet where was the opportunity for us with tint in our skin, from gold to coffee to jet, to be frivolous, to live in the moment, to not always be strong? Why couldn't we be foolish and not be weighted with the regrets of all our race?

That world didn't exist, not when people wore chains. Not when the right legislation failed to pass from lack of courage.

"Maybe this play might—" I began, but Florentina cut me off.

"Ask Wilson Shaw. He'll tell you how hard the theater business is and how long it takes to make steady, decent money."

Didn't need to, for I'd learned from Dinah's experiences that an actor or anyone dependent on the theater wasn't what one wanted in a husband. "It might not have been smart, but perhaps love requires blind leaps of faith."

"Not this blind, Abbie. Mrs. Danielson will be made into gossip. She'll either be a jezebel or a fool. London will make her another Blackamoor who is an example of low behavior."

"Even a fool in love needs justice. And a woman, regardless of who she is, needs to be brave enough to follow her heart, to make choices, even bad ones. We need to be fools and brave. We have to be allowed to be everything, to be fully human."

She leaned back against the tree and closed her eyes. "I

know. But I still feel awful having these thoughts. Guess I'm human."

I put my hand on her shoulder, then straightened her gorgeous bonnet. Its brown color brought out the flecks of gold in her eyes. "One day, it will all be righted. Haiti's ruling their nation just fine. London's headed for progress. Peers in the House, men of conviction, are standing up. I think the paper mentioned that Lord Lauderdale, Lord Sidmouth, the Duke of Culver, and even Lord Ellenborough are actively taking the lead. Wilberforce doesn't have to be the only one. He's brought more to the side of right in Parliament."

"That's good, but why does it feel like one wrong move by a Sewell or a Danielson, or even a Lady Worthing, and everything good will be torn away?"

Having no answers, I held her.

Pulse slowing, I took a half step back. "I'll ask you once. Please tell me why you were relieved when thinking Lord Worthing dead."

She gazed at me, then maybe through my skull. "Because I know you're suffering. I see the hurt when you don't get letters. I watch the sadness grow in your face when you finally get one and it's the baron writing of another delay in his return. I want that pain to be over for you. Yes."

That tension in my gut over trying to make a difference or solving mysteries filled my emptiness. I was creating Lady Worthing, not the Worthings. When I'd received James's last note in Bath, in which he said he'd changed his mind on coming, I'd returned to London, only to find our . . . my home wrecked. I did everything but violently sob. Maybe I should've.

"Say something, Abbie. Please forgive me."

"Of course."

She went into my arms again and wept.

My eyes stayed dry. I didn't know what to think, and I wasn't here to assess my choices.

She swiped at her eyes. "I'll go back and apologize to Mrs. Danielson."

"Let's send a note. She seems to like those. We'll go to Olive's and get you fed."

A personal letter was a start, but finding out who had killed the woman's husband would be the best way to make amends.

With a smile and a nod, we ran back to my house, to my awaiting terrace.

Florentina stopped and gaped at the windows missing from the parlor. The big opening, with a sheet anchored over it, exposed the assault on Two Greater Queen Street.

She looked at me and knew I'd forgotten to tell her something important, but I'd had enough honesty for one day. I needed Stilton cheese to make the pain go away.

Chapter 8

My carriage took the slow journey through the crowded streets of London. I stared out the window as my cousin calmly explained the difficult calculations she and Mrs. Edwards had been working on. Something about a cosine, I thought, but I needed a sign.

Though our nuncheon of Olive's best cuts of cheese had restored Florentina, I remained disturbed. Mrs. Danielson's choice to marry a known swindler had begun to make less sense.

She seemed a calm, logical woman. With her guardians' willingness to lie for Mary Henderson to protect her future, surely they'd have conveyed how her life would be made difficult by marrying such a man?

For Mrs. Danielson to be hiding next door prior to the murder and not to be with her husband hinted at a level of danger.

"Mr. Henderson will have to tell me more about his guest," I said.

Florentina sat back, with her head up. "He does make me want to ask some highly inappropriate questions, but that seems to be my role today."

Her chuckle drew me to her. "What type of questions, Flo?"

"Oh, I don't know . . ." Her gaze sharpened upon me. "Like why do people he knows keep getting killed? How do these Mayfair types actually treat darker members of their families? Not that Mrs. Danielson is that dark."

"Let's leave the subject alone for now."

"Which one? Henderson, Mrs. Danielson, proximity to whiteness?"

"All of the above, especially where I'm heading."

"Where are we—"

"You're going back to work. Some lovely numerical thing is waiting for you. I need help puzzling out the Danielson business. To chase who killed a schemer, I need a charmer. However, the man who fits the bill is in the place that causes me to rethink everything in my life."

"You're going to see Wilson Shaw. But he's at your father's . . ."

I sighed.

She sighed.

"You couldn't send for him, Abbie?"

"Summoning the busy man last minute? No. I need information about the money—Sheridan's, Danielson's, the actors', even the guardians', the Mathewses'—now. That's a lot of digging. Last time Vaughn asked for me, and Wilson was almost killed. I'd rather do so in person. It will convey how much I need the information and I could warn him to be safe."

"It's fine if you want to see your father, too."

Every little girl grew up with the desire to be the apple of her father's eye. And I was, and so was Dinah, until she was of an age to be presented. Two years older, and untouched by mother's, her stepmother's, hushed-up scandal, I believed she even had an invite to Almack's, but mine never materialized. My father's hopes for the family's advancement were upon

Dinah, a mantle she didn't want. That was when she first rebelled.

"If my father's there, I'll say hello. It should be civil."

"Wish things could be different."

Wishing didn't change things.

"Abbie, why don't you come to my parents' house tonight? It will be safer. Nothing happens in Cheapside."

"What of my servants? There's not enough room, and I don't wish Mr. Rogers or my housekeeper or maids to be in my house without me, to face who knows what alone. I won't run. Lady Worthing needs to be strong. I must fend off who did this."

"Then you expect them back? This is an ongoing threat?"

I didn't answer her, because I was still figuring it out. There weren't clues left behind, just evidence of rage. Maybe I needed a list of suspects for my break-in.

"Abbie, what say you? Will you come?"

"I can't live in fear."

She grasped my hands tightly again and rubbed the cold digits. "But you have to live."

"One mystery at a time. I'll figure that one out. Then Lord Duncan or Vaughn or someone will make him or them pay."

"To be so confident is a gift, a foolhardy gift, Abigail Carrington Monroe. Your husband should be here to help."

My name sounded mighty fine, mighty special. And it hid a woman terrified of the message the vandals intended to send with their violence. "Someone wants to frighten me, to make me run. I can't. I won't. This stance doesn't require my husband to be here. It's my right."

Hoping to dismiss her concerns, I spoke in platitudes, wishing them into existence. If one said something enough times—I was fine without James—it should become true.

Florentina released my hands. Her head shook like it was

hooked to a spring. "You're brave, Lady Worthing. I just wish you weren't alone."

Is that how she saw me? With a house of servants? With her and old friends and my godfather in my life, the absence of a husband still made me a loner?

No. It had forced me to learn my strength.

"I won't hurry him home, not again. Being in Bath showed me I can't rush him into deciding he wants more from our marriage."

"And do you want more of one? I've always thought you did."

The girl who married a baron had had stars in her eyes. The woman who'd been alone for two years no longer saw night as a wonderment, just as a time that was pitch black, painted with intrigue and danger. "Let him come back and commit to staying, and then we'll see if he can still dazzle me. Mr. Vaughn looks forward to my domestic bliss and to seeing me knit. He wants that for you too."

"Uncle Vaughn wants us knitting, as in baby bonnets and blankets? Hardly, Abbie. You'll buy them. I'll get my mother to make something."

She laughed, and I did, too, but it reminded me of Miss Bellows's gossip. If Mrs. Danielson was with child . . . My heart went to her.

My cousin stretched, even yawned. I guessed making me sentimental had tired her. "Today's selection of cheese was fabulous. Perhaps the baron can send some. A wheel of Stilton or some exotic fare could dazzle you."

"I can procure my own cheese when I need it," I answered.

Her lips curved sarcastically, like she doubted me, but I'd become a regular at Olive's. Mrs. Smith was a wizard at shopping at Covent Garden.

Florentina sat back, her head bobbing along the seat back. "Well, Mrs. Danielson is enchanted by notes. You like tales of exploration. You'll both be dazzled again."

Catching myself, preventing my shoulders from shrugging, I craned my neck to gaze at my reticule, a satin blue wonder with many pockets. I had had the seamstress make it to house my theater glasses so that it would be convenient to retrieve them. Fine workmanship, but I wasn't settling for cheese and satin— the costuming of a life or privilege. I wanted everything, even love.

"Look at the traffic, Abbie," she said. "More time to change your mind."

It was almost as if she had reasons not to go to Carrington and Ewan, my father's firm.

"Flo, the closer to Bond Street, the closer to our charmer. Mr. Shaw is Mr. Carrington's greatest asset."

My cousin rolled her eyes, then chattered more about her work. Yet my thoughts drifted to the schemer, the reformed playwright.

What about Anthony Danielson other than his talent with words had made the former Miss Mathews wish to be his wife?

Her Mayfair family had means. There had to be a dowry for her if she hadn't eloped. And how could they be duped into letting a schemer, a scoundrel no less, be near their ward?

"We're getting really close to a final set of numbers. I feel good about the Navy presentation."

Florentina answered a few of my questions about procedures, then chattered more about longitudes and latitudes and places by a reef.

The passion in her voice warmed my chilled feet.

Glancing over her shoulder, I spied Saint Bride's Church out the glass window. "You know the well-to-do had to court architect Christopher Wren to build that church? So many houses of worship were destroyed in the Great Fire of London, but Wren felt one here wasn't needed. Grandfather Carrington was part of the effort to sway him. Papa used to tell me so many stories like this when we were children." It was when he wanted to inspire Dinah and me. That was when he and Mama were happy.

"It's a pretty building," Florentina said. "So calm and stately."

Did I look calm, stately . . . preparing to see my father?

"What are you thinking, Abbie?"

"How men are congratulated for marrying well. Mrs. Danielson said her husband was a third son. Though indicative of a peerage, the heir's spare's spare typically means no money."

"Must be a Vaughn-Magdalena type of love. Something to defy logic and what we're taught to look for in a partner."

My godfather and my mother—I couldn't say anything, except, "Mr. Vaughn has always had the means to protect anyone he loves."

"Uncle Vaughn was never a poor man. And Aunt's vows offered no caution. They didn't stop her from leaving your father."

Florentina's voice was low, as if she offered a rebuke, but she stated fact. The love my parents had was nothing compared to what my mother and Vaughn possessed. Their hearts defeated all obstacles. Again, I was envious of Mrs. Danielson for knowing what that passion felt like, and I was also frightened at what the loss of it meant.

Florentina stretched again. "A third son is set for the church, but since the widow acknowledges him as a scoundrel, albeit reformed, I don't think that was the victim's calling. His family held a peerage. Do you think their objections to this marriage might've gotten Danielson killed?"

"Titles and scandal go palm in palm. But whose helping hand shoved a spear through Anthony Danielson's back?"

"Ghastly." Her nose wrinkled, as if she could smell the scents plaguing my nose yesterday—those of blood and bleach. I still could. And I could see those stains on my sofa, on the walls.

"Abbie, do you truly think love could make a woman so reckless?"

I could see her mind spinning and accepting that James and I had no such feelings.

"Sorry," she said, looking away. "I haven't experienced passion so deep it makes me abandon my principles or my work. Not sure I want to."

"My discontent must be as obvious as a linkboy waving a flaming torch."

Florentina said nothing.

The silence, the absence of any type of reassurance that I was fine, that Lady Worthing was doing well, filled the carriage like a fog.

Some things must be owned, even choices not going as intended. "I was flattered when the baron proposed. I saw the opportunity to help my family, and I foolishly thought he might love me."

"He might. Absence. Doesn't it set a heart to missing people?"

It would be grand if James returned knowing it was me he wanted, choosing me over adventure or a bachelor's freedom. Yet as weeks had turned to months, then years, I had doubted it would happen, had doubted him. "A man not in the military, not serving king and country, does what makes him happy. Staying here with me . . . I'm not what makes Lord Worthing happy."

She dug into her reticule, produced a handkerchief, and lifted it to my dry eyes.

There was no need to take it. In privacy, I had cried out everything in Bath.

Waiting for James, only to receive word he'd changed his mind about returning this year, had unlodged something in my spirit, something I hated—the realization I'd failed.

Rejected, I'd walked the beaches and cried for days. It was why I had had so few tears for my trashed Number Two Greater Queen Street, why Vaughn and Duncan had thought me the calmest of women.

I wasn't.

I was just a person who understood her position.

"Abbie, I'm sorry."

"Don't be. I'm under no illusions. None." Not anymore.

She said nothing.

Neither did I. Why voice disappointment in doing what I wanted?

In our foggy silence, we progressed up Fleet Street.

I had the battle ahead of me. I was moments from stepping inside my father's firm.

The carriage stopped. Florentina proceeded to descend.

"No." I held the door latch closed. "I've entangled you enough in my problems today. I need you to go, rest, and attack those numbers in the morning with all you have."

"Abbie, I wish to help with the mystery. Let me come with you. I know visiting your father's firm upsets you."

"Lady Worthing can handle this. You'll not be drawn into any new conflict today. No thoughts of anything but numbers. Yours and Mrs. Edwards's."

Straightening my new bonnet appointed with a silver bow, I filled my lungs and climbed down to the pavement.

The open carriage window exposed Florentina's fretful expression. Nothing made her generously formed lips look so sad as a frown. "Abbie, no."

"I'm fine. I'm in no danger here, other than of getting an undeserved dressing-down from Mr. Carrington. I can handle words with my father, and he still cannot say he was right, that I shouldn't have wed. He's benefited too much from this union."

"Abbie, are you sure?"

Rawlins's gaze went from her to me to the door of Carrington and Ewan, Proprietors. "What would you have me do, Lady Worthing?"

"Take Miss Sewell to her home, and then return for me. This visit is overdue. It shouldn't take too long."

My cousin shrugged and released her grip on the open window. "Tell Mr. Shaw I'll miss annoying him. And offer my regards to Uncle Carrington."

Dread knotting and twisting in my gut, I went to the door, imagining what the former Joanna Mathews had faced when telling her guardians of her intentions to wed Danielson, and wondering if she had known marrying him would be murder.

After a nod to my driver, a wave to my cousin, I held my breath and went inside Carrington and Ewan.

Crisp white walls.

Dozens of yellow and green and black canvases of Port Royal that my mother had painted still hung about the entry.

Then I siphoned that first bit of air. The ginger scent coated my tongue.

Magdalena Carrington's special candles.

My throat felt hot.

One series of blinks sent me running, though my slippers didn't move.

A blade shining. Raised high, it swept toward my neck.

Heart pumping, skin pulsing, I gasped.

More ginger and vanilla beeswax painted my tongue.

My vision cleared, but my fear remained.

I couldn't do this today.

"Ma'am, may I help you?"

Wished he could. Wished someone could make sense of these notions.

After half turning, readying to leave, I watched Rawlins power the yellow bounder down Fleet Street.

Too late to flee with dignity, I turned and marched to the clerk's desk.

Head up, like I hadn't let my imagination frighten me, I approached this new face, someone who'd been recently hired to the firm.

His blank gaze assessed me, or it felt like it did, as he manned a stack of papers. "May I help you?"

"I'd like to see Mr. . . . Shaw. Let him know Lady Worthing must see him."

The man shuffled the pieces of parchment like they were a deck of cards. "He's busy. If this is social—"

"He'll see me." With my assured tone, I let him know the urgency of the matter.

He raised his head, and his gaze flicked over my tidy curls, my gold carriage dress, and the brass buttons, which denoted a woman of means. Carrington and Ewan specialized in women with means. The young fellow left his chair and went to the back.

Minutes later the handsome Mr. Shaw appeared. No jacket, but he had donned a brilliant white wide-collared shirt and a check-patterned waistcoat over tight jet breeches. "Lady Worthing, here for me. This is unexpected. You've come to see me before my holiday?"

"You taking time away from work? Who is she?"

He started to laugh. "Fillies. I'm going to the races in Gloucestershire, village of Bibury. Then a little rest in Bath. You just came back. Pleasant trip?"

"Tolerable."

His black eyes sparkled, then settled on me. "Anything the matter . . . dire?" The look of concern framing his high cheekbones let me know Vaughn had told him of the attack on my home.

"I just had an early meal with Miss Sewell, not too far away. She wishes you well, but I wanted to speak on business matters."

"Business? Well, anything for my favorite wealthy baroness." He held out his arm to me. I took it and walked with him to his office. My slippers paused in the long hall, and I stared at my father's door at the end.

Images of Dinah and me running in here as young girls filled my head.

"He's not here, Abbie. You know he'd want to hear about the danger you're in."

"No, Wilson. I don't want him concerned or gloating."

"Abbie." He held my arm closer to his side. "Mr. Carrington has difficulty expressing himself. He does love you very much."

Letting the comment exist as a thing in the air, as a partial truth or a wanton wish, we headed into Wilson's office. He helped me into a chair and then went to his on the other side of his desk. "He's with the politicians today."

"Which side? The abolitionists?"

"Lady Worthing, never doubt him on where his heart lies."

Maybe since Wilson wasn't related but had become like the son my father wanted, he could be generous. I had my father's blood and pride. Everything between us became a battle.

My forgiving my mother's and Vaughn's betrayal was an unpardonable sin.

"Lady Worthing, it's been a while since you stopped in."

A year, four months, five days—but who's counting? "I came to see you. I need—"

"Oh, couldn't we pretend you came to see me to ask about the weather? Some pleasantries before I must risk my position or my life."

"Your art, Mr. Shaw. It's lovely."

He swiveled his head from side to side, his smile blooming, as if he hadn't noticed the yellow color of his walls or the new painting of a seascape.

It was unlike my mother's colorful canvases, but the waters seemed blue and true.

"Bland, but soothing. My clients enjoy it. Gets them in the mood to allow me to handle their investments."

"Perhaps you're the artwork, with your colorful waistcoat."

The ebony and bottle-green colors of the check pattern contrasted with his tanned skin and made him seem so vibrant.

"A gift from a friend." His smirk widened. "A patient one. But I assume the bland start to your compliment means you're not here to give me what I want, access to all the wealthy women on Greater Queen Street. So how bad are things?"

"Not terrible. I've come for your help on another matter."

He sighed, then recovered his laugh. "I assume my only purpose is to give you information."

"I don't know other wealthy women in Westminster whom you with your special influence haven't already discovered." I waited for the pretend rooster to settle down. "Information, sir, is your specialty. But aren't you busy managing my husband's money?"

"It's a blessed portfolio, Lady Worthing. The numerous naval bounties, the generational wealth, the occasional rare artifact sold . . . interesting means."

This was the first I'd heard of artifacts and interesting means. I kept my smile even and pretended to know all of James's business. Inside, it was another piercing of my soul. Men outside my house knew more than I, the wife, did.

Studying me, maybe waiting until I spilled what I knew and complained about what I didn't, Wilson sat back and folded his arms behind his head. "This elevation does work for both of us since I manage your money. And we should call it yours, as in your investment. You saved Worthing's neck from the gallows. He'd not be able to spend another dime if not for you. Some miserly relation would enjoy Greater Queen Street and more."

He lifted his palm and waved a circle. "And your father would be ruined."

"I found the clues. I let Lord Duncan know the baron was innocent of embezzlement."

"You could've said nothing. Another rich man gone, one with no heirs, doesn't impact the world."

"Wilson? That's cynical, even for you."

"Sorry. One of my widow friends, with custody of heirs, was just defrauded by the late husband's family. The worthless earl had never thought to improve the terms of his will from his first marriage. Now my friend will have to fight for everything, just so her sons can have what's their due."

Fire raged in his stormy jet eyes. Children not being protected was a sore spot for him.

"I'm sorry, Wilson. But I know you will get her everything she and the children are due. No one is smarter when it comes to such things."

"We will be updating the terms of the baron's will. I'll not have you left at the mercy of the courts if something unfortunate happens."

I swallowed and forced my mind from my circumstances. With my dreams coming as they were, it was I who was in jeopardy, not a husband an ocean away. "Knowing you'll fight for me is a great comfort."

After a mirthless chuckle, he pulled closer to his side of the desk. "What else am I to do but protect the girl who snuck me food and gave a wayward boy a place to sleep when I needed it?"

"You were never wayward."

"Depends upon who you ask. I'm the ton's chameleon. If I'm direct, I'm intimidating. If I'm solemn, I'm plotting something. If I'm reserved, then I'm leaning too much into my bastard's blood. Seems a duke's by-blow is not to have airs. But if someone is supposed to be full of hot air, shouldn't it be someone set adrift with the well-wishes to fly?"

"Wilson. I'm—"

He held up his palm. "Nothing to be sorry about. It's my life. For good or bad, it's me. Of course, I'm not allowed to express the angry parts of my existence, not as a man, not as a Blackamoor. That's if I wish to keep existing."

"Why are you saying this?"

"Regret is in your eyes. Your father is a good man, but losing everything but this firm to Vaughn has made him bitter. Bitterness kills all the good."

It was rare for Wilson to be this honest or openly vulnerable. I could quibble about his rights as a man versus mine as a woman, but we both still lived in a time that didn't always treat us as what we were—bright, ambitious lights trying to glow in a dark world.

"You're a brother to me, as dear to me as any could be. You never have to pretend. I think you and I understand being caught between worlds better than any. But has something else happened?"

He twiddled his fingers. "Seems my father has summoned yours. The duke wishes to talk investments. He's checking up on me or trying to get me fired. I'm not sure which."

Sitting up straight, I offered a confident stare. "My father will never fire the fellow keeping him in business."

"Such easy praise."

"It's true. My confidence in you is complete. You're brilliant, good at your job, and wonderful at setting people at ease. You slip into rooms and gain everyone's confidence."

"Especially women. Don't leave that part out when you're trying to butter me up for something."

This time I laughed. "I have a widow, and I need you to discover everything of interest about her family and her late husband's."

"A widow, you say." He brought his hands together, fingertips touching, like an evil henchman. "Keep talking. Do not leave me in suspense."

"Joanna Mathews, now Mrs. Anthony Danielson. She's a ward of the Mathews, a Mayfair family. I need information on the family as well as Richard Sheridan, Alexander Hildebrand. And Barbara Banyan. Also anything on Anthony Danielson. How did a third son and reported schemer end up working in the theater?"

He flicked his quill in indigo ink and jotted down the names. "I should be able to get you something before I go. Anything else?"

"Start with those names and chase anyone you discover who you think would want her husband of a month dead. You understand what I'm looking for."

The white vane of his quill swept under his chin. "Another murder? Oh, Lady Worthing. I don't need to tell you to be careful."

"Can't help being curious about her. She's of mixed heritage. She could almost pass. Miss Sewell seems to wonder why this woman would marry a poor playwright. Help me prove it was a love match."

A clerk knocked, then stuck his head inside. "Lady Worthing's driver has returned." The fellow dipped his head and scurried away.

I stood. "I think I need to go to the theater again. I'm sure I'm missing something. I'm seeing . . . I mean I just feel like there is something obvious there."

"Lady Worthing, it might be too dangerous."

When I didn't retake my seat, Wilson left his. "I suppose this means you won't be waiting around to console me if the duke has secured my termination? You won't convince your father to keep me around?"

"You believe in my father. You're more loyal than I or Dinah. He'd never want to lose you."

"He didn't want to lose you, either. Sometimes a man is so set in being right, he'll do a lot of wrong things."

"Wrongs add up to a great deal of hurt."

Wilson escorted me all the way to my carriage. "Stay. See Carrington. With you and your sister gone . . . he misses you."

Part of me wanted to challenge Wilson to do the same, to ride to his father's ducal residence and talk with a man who might be reaching out for him. But I'd seen the hurt Wilson hid in jokes. At times, it mirrored mine. Some pain was impossible to ease.

"Get me answers that help me make sense of my current investigation."

"Well, stay safe and alive. Come back in a few days. I'll have gems for you."

I wanted him to bring the information to Greater Queen Street. A second visit to Carrington and Ewan in a week would mean seeing my father.

It was a high price to pay, but Wilson always found diamonds—the bright, shiny kind highlighting a killer.

Chapter 9

It was a quick decision to return to Drury Lane. The gnawing in my spirit about things hidden or hiding in plain sight wouldn't relent. Another examination of the crime scene was in order. This gnawing wouldn't abate until I saw the grand theater before me. It was several stories in height, with brightly colored doors and sharp gating to keep people from the king's entrance and the one for the Prince of Wales.

Grasping my blue reticule, I stepped out of my carriage into the brisk wind of the afternoon.

Rawlins helped me down. "How long will you be here? Don't want you caught in a rainstorm."

Before I could answer, a familiar carriage stopped beside mine. Out popped a cross-looking Stapleton Henderson. He glanced at me, then at my driver. "Lady Worthing, where have you been? I stopped at your house. I thought we'd be investigating together."

"You've been busy making arrangements for Mrs. Danielson. How did you know I'd be here?"

"Drawn to you, I suppose. Or a sense of you walking into danger."

My mouth dropped open.

But then he offered a short smile and tipped his hat. "A jest. I'm not good at this, but I'm here to pick up Mr. Danielson's things. She was insistent upon having his letters and such."

"Ah. The letter lover." My heart broke for her anew. Despite what Florentina had said, despite my own doubts, I wanted to believe Joanna Danielson married for love.

"I've settled things with her guardians. The Mathews want Mrs. Danielson to return to Mayfair. She's not ready."

"All the ill will is gone? Just like that?" I shook my head, cutting my eyes, over his naivety. "I believe your friend is smart enough to avoid the people telling her she's wrong, even in her grief."

I covered my mouth. Mrs. Danielson wasn't me, but I knew the pain caused by disobeying or defying a family's wishes.

Stepping closer, I saw Stapleton's gaze had hardened. His cheeks had reddened, as if he had remembered he was cross with me.

A foot away, his indigo eyes narrowed. "The magistrate asked you not to come. It can be troublesome if you're here alone."

"Lord Duncan cannot bar me from the theater. I lease a box."

"You know what I mean, Lady Worthing."

Rawlins must not have liked the harsh tone. He stepped down from the box. "Is everything well, ma'am?"

My neighbor groaned and rubbed his jaw. "It's not. This woman may have *forgotten* to tell you Lord Duncan has reservations about the baroness being here. I'm frustrated she doesn't take care with her safety. And she omits or fails to communicate the risks."

"Hypocritical banter? Adorable." I folded my arms. My reticule, the thicker one with the heavier lining, slipped to the crook of my elbow and hung like an anchor or a weight. "It's a greater omission to allow a killer to go free. Riskier too."

"Your safety means nothing? Impatience wins?" He turned and motioned to his driver to head to the mews; then he moved to Rawlins. Hat in hand, he said, "I apologize for my tone. I'll see Lady Worthing is returned to Two Greater Queen Street unharmed and not in trouble with the magistrate."

Rawlins squinted at me.

Eyes rolling, I nodded my consent.

Stapleton Henderson was a confused soul. His changeable moods, from friendly to cold to overprotective, made my head hurt.

But I'd learned he could be counted upon. My tight inner circle of friends might've inadvertently increased by one.

My driver stood still. I guessed I had to express verbally that I was certain. I was. My neighbor, the curmudgeon, was stiff and honorable and occasionally right. "Yes, Mr. Rawlins, Mr. Henderson will see me to Greater Queen Street. You can turn in early today."

"If you say so, ma'am, but I will remain in the area for an hour. Send a linkboy for me at the mews on Long Acre Road if you decide you need other transport."

Henderson's glance, blank but heated, hadn't changed. "Shall we, Lady Worthing?"

Like he had the night of the murder, he held out his arm, expecting me to be at his side. With fewer and fewer reservations, I took it. We walked away from my yellow bounder.

Our silent footfalls, the small whistle of a breeze seemed eerie for a late summer day.

Then the vision I'd tried to suppress returned. I stumbled.

The blade shining in the moon's light.

A swing at my throat.

I gagged as Henderson steadied me.

My eyes finally focused on the backstage door to Drury Lane.

He stopped. "Abigail, did you hurt your ankle?"

"No, Mr. Henderson." I pulled away and folded my arms about my quaking middle. "Don't be concerned."

"Concerned? You shouldn't assume what I am or what I do. You should ask. You can always ask me anything."

Blinking, readjusting to a darkening sky, I gaped at him. "I think you misjudged what I'm trying to say."

"What is it, then? We're supposed to do this together."

"I know you've been busy. I met with Mrs. Danielson. She seemed *torn* by her grief. You have to take care of her."

"Well, Santisma has been helping with her welfare. They go on long walks, even stay in my garden for hours. Mrs. Danielson, for the most part, has always been levelheaded. Joanna Mathews, now Danielson, is like another sister to me."

This disclosure sounded like a defense, as if I'd accused him of something. "Then, you're definitely busy. Sisters can be handfuls. Mr. Henderson, I don't think you're guilty of being up to something or untoward toward the widow. I don't think of you at all."

He swallowed hard, then held the door open.

I regretted what I'd said. Well, more so how it had sounded. I grabbed his arm and pressed the door closed. The hinges rattled with my slam, but I kept hold of him and my composure. "I didn't mean that. I'm frustrated today. My words aren't coming out right."

"There's no need to babble. And there's nothing to apologize for. You haven't been rude, just honest."

"What I meant is I don't think ill of you anymore. I've assigned no dastardly motives to you. Though I may listen to gossip, it doesn't mean I believe it. I know men and women can be friends without it being anything more. So read nothing into my tone. I'm more and more discounting yours."

He looked down at my hand locked on his arm. "You don't sound rude or cold, Abigail, just distant."

"Is there a difference?"

"Yes." Nodding, he looked away to the street, to a passing carriage. "There is. *Cold* would mean you don't care. *Distant* means you're frightened. I frighten you."

"You don't."

"I must. You've switched again to being formal, and we're alone. Is acknowledging anything but disgust between us problematic?"

"Old habits. I just came from a visit I had to steel myself to endure. The man who required me to be formal and perfect, or at least pretend to be, wasn't there. I'd worked myself up for nothing. And I remain filled with tension."

"What a heavy burden, to be perfect, to always say and do the right thing." When he glanced at me this time, his jaw had slackened. A sense of something wrong or the opposite of distant possessed his eyes. "Then why, Abigail, does it feel as if you're waiting for me to prove your first instincts right, that I can't be trusted?"

"Mr. Henderson . . . Stapleton, please. We've been shot at before. Survived more than a bumpy road together. You even saved my life. I think I can trust you."

"Still feels like you're wary and waiting for me to do the wrong thing."

Not knowing what to say, I took my fingers from his sleeve. I'd still been holding on to him.

He rubbed at his neck. "Perhaps you can't fully trust me, not now or ever. But I'll correct rumors or gossip. If I fail, it will be on my merit. I'll earn your condemnation fully."

Not sure what that meant. Or why his low voice had become prideful. Was my approval some sort of prize?

"Sir, I'm sure if you set your mind to something, you can bring it to pass. Shall we . . . Stapleton?"

With a grunt, he opened the door, and we entered Drury Lane.

Shoulder to shoulder, we walked into the den of thespians. This time, I hoped I'd find the missing clue that would break this mystery open. I needed this done, needed to prove who had killed Anthony Danielson before I had to depend upon Stapleton or one of my few champions to save my neck.

In the old-scene store, Stapleton and I searched the shelves. My gloves became soiled with dust. The shelves were thick with artifacts, including a section of bronze gating and a bust that looked similar to the one of the poet John Donne in my neighbor's study.

Squeezing through a tiny aisle, with my reticule slapping shields, a suit of armor, pieces of a broken chair, I felt my frustration rising. "We're missing something. I know it."

My neighbor followed me to Danielson's makeshift desk.

"The body was here. There was a stack of papers up here. Another set littered the floor. Why not all the pages on the floor?" I said.

He drummed on the old door tabletop. "And nothing, not a piece, was in the blood."

"As a physician, is it possible the bleeding would be so selective?"

"No. When blood courses, it spurts in all directions."

"What a ghastly concept."

He moved deeper into an area with stacked crates. "You asked, Abigail. Dying can be nasty business."

I set down my reticule on Danielson's cleaned desk. Today it was one devoid of the papers we'd found the night of the murder. "Was there one or two stacks here before?"

"Not sure, Abigail. Is it important?"

"I'm not sure, but where do you suppose the papers went? Sheridan had them, but did he give them to Duncan's runners as evidence?"

"I thought they were left here on the desk. Neither man left with them." Stapleton reemerged on the other side of a stack of canvases. "Surely, no one would throw them away. Maybe Sheridan took possession of them, after all. His theater. His commissioning of a play."

A noise rustled.

Henderson put a finger to his lips, slipped to the far aisle, then banged on the shelves.

Hildebrand popped up. "Must you be so loud?"

The man had been huddling in a corner. Was this where he slept?

"Sir," I asked, "are you well?"

"Oh, the physician and the pushy assistant. Wasn't the woman banned from here?"

"She has a reprieve." Stapleton cleared a path for the actor. "Have you been sleeping in here awhile?"

"It's comfortable and near the action."

The action of what? I watched him stumble toward me, noticed how one foot sort of dragged. "You said you were here in this very room the night of the murder. You did see Anthony Danielson alive before . . . the unpleasantness?"

He started to shrug; then he beat at his chest like a wild man. "Yes. I saw him alive that night."

Tugging on his soiled gray waistcoat, Hildebrand walked over to me and put his fists on the makeshift desk. One edge flew up, then flipped down. The motion coughed up dust. "As I told the magistrate, when Danielson was alive, he was working on his play and comforting women. He had high hopes for his actions."

For a moment, Stapleton's face held a bemused look. "From comforting women or writing the play?"

"Both, I guess. But you and I know there's no hope in a woman, only trouble. Unless, of course, you're one of those 'lucky in love' types."

"Hardly." My neighbor's voice was low, grumbly. "You mentioned women and a woman. Which is it?"

After stepping away, moving closer to a wall sconce, Hildebrand turned back fast, as if to shock us. "Alas, poor Danielson. I knew him well. The women he enjoyed too much. But then the past two months, he seemed a changed man. Must have been the afterglow of falling into Barbara Banyan's web. As Shakespeare would say, love was his master and he was yoked by a fool."

Though I had my doubts about love, the urge to correct this pressed on my throat like the point of a knife. Someone needed to defend Mrs. Danielson unless Hildebrand's words were true.

The actor reared up. "Now, don't go getting cross because I said *master*. I didn't mean it in a plantation, exploitive sense."

Unsure if my admiration of Alexander Hildebrand would ever recover, I decided to set him at ease before more nonsense spewed forth. "I'm familiar with Shakespeare's *The Two Gentlemen of Verona*."

"You know Shakespeare, not Donne." Stapleton shook his head. "How depressing."

Hildebrand clapped his hands. "Oh, good. With all this slaver talk happening in Parliament and the young bucks constantly criticizing the older ones, one can never be too careful."

"Too careful?" I asked. "Does right have to be careful?"

"Yes. Wrong hates to be called out." Stapleton said as Hildebrand groaned.

"Or made into legislation," the actor said, then strode back to the desk. He pounded upon it like he was gaveling in a session of the House of Peers. "Oh, you, mister physician, could be a rabid speechmaker, like Sidmouth or Culver."

A gasp came from the doorway. "What's the fool telling you?"

"Nothing, witch," Hildebrand replied. "But give us another lame performance. Show off your bosom, Miss Banyan. You have men here to entertain."

"I see one gentleman and a beast."

Hildebrand clapped again. "Next time say what you want with more feeling. I was telling the physician and the pushy assistant how you drew in our poor Mr. Danielson."

Barbara Banyan spun to leave but then stopped and squinted at me or the makeshift desk, as if it was her first time being in the room.

Perhaps it was unsettling—us being here where her lover or friend or close acquaintance once worked.

"He lies. Men who run from responsibility, who mock people in love, are all liars." With a hand to her hip, she left.

Overly dramatic but sadly true, her statement took all the air out of my growing resentment of Hildebrand. "Why are you so bitter? You harass a woman trying to better herself. Men seek gains through relationships. Haven't you, before turning sour, been linked to a number of ample talents?"

This made the fellow guffaw. The rich, deep chuckles boomed like an orchestra's drums. "Yes, you are right. Though Barbara reminds me of a hateful nobody of long ago, I've become a hypocrite. It's hard sometimes when everyone abandons you. They all do when the performance ends."

I flinched. My thoughts sailed to my father. Was that what he believed? Was this where his anger had originated? In feeling abandoned? And like Hildebrand, had his regrets turned to bitterness?

"What's this?" The actor bent to pick up a piece of something but was so drunk he had to catch the edge of the desk to keep from falling.

Before Stapleton could help him, Hildebrand recovered and grabbed a page, which seemed to have come from nowhere. "Oh, more of the fool's foolscap. God, I'll miss Danielson. We used to talk. I gave him a few pointers on shortening or expanding a line or two. But everyone wants to believe they're Shakespeare."

"Was the play any good?" Stapleton's monotone voice gave an air of disinterest. He'd moved from us to a corner bearing a tiger's pelt. "I had heard it was. And where is the full copy?"

Taking note that he didn't mention Mrs. Danielson had told him this information, I decided to do the same and not mention her name. "I'd heard the same. But you know women and gossip. It can't be relied upon, but you . . . you should know."

Patting his pockets, Hildebrand seemed to search for something. "Ah, you must be one of his private funders. Seems Danielson thought his winning play would save Drury Lane. Now nothing will."

Wilson's information would definitely clarify the money situation for Sheridan. Yet was it realistic that one play could right whatever debts the man had amassed?

Hildebrand leaned against the desk, tired, like his hopes had been dashed.

Though he'd been erratic and even mean, I felt for the creature. He talked as if his good days were spent. Was this pitying demeanor an act?

"A man such as you, with over forty years in the theater, would know a good play, something that had merit. I don't know about Mr. Henderson, but I do invest in worthy gambits from time to time."

"It was amusing. His early farce about killing a politician who was stalking another man's wife seemed a little far-fetched for my tastes, but this new one, *A Daughter's Love*, it had the raw passion that would have the crowds eating out of the hero's or, more so, the heroine's hand. Very lovely."

"Wait? He wrote a play about someone after a politician and his wife? What?"

"Oh, Henderson, the little assistant is getting things wrong. Stick with making bandages, ma'am, or whatever the big man has you do. Danielson wasn't married. And the way Miss Banyan was always on him, I think she'd know it. She has some morals."

My eyes went to Stapleton's. His face remained stiff, but the twist of his mouth, the parting of his lips meant he could spew fire. "Are you certain he and Miss Banyan were involved?"

"Don't know for certain, but a man championing her, writing a play so she'd be the talk of London . . . listening to her in the quiet of this room, steadying her as she weeps . . ." Hildebrand stopped and gulped a breath. "My, it's hot in here." He staggered and swayed until he was out the door.

Henderson's fingers balled behind his back.

I felt his tension.

Knowing Mrs. Danielson may have been cheated on by her new spouse must tear into a man, a widower, who'd experienced the same deceit by his late wife.

"Stapleton, I know I shouldn't ask, but . . ."

"Say it. Hold nothing from me."

Biting my lip didn't retract my hunger to know. I filled my lungs, then asked, "How did you find out about your wife's infidelity?"

He stared at me. I felt the passage of time whirling in his indigo eyes.

I had to know.

It was a real possibility that while James was away, he took lovers and enjoyed a pleasure-filled life, while I twiddled away, abandoned in Westminster.

Still, Stapleton was quiet.

Covering my mouth, I felt embarrassed. "Sorry. I'm ridiculous and nosy, the pushy assistant."

"Pushy sleuth. There were signs, even obvious clues. No endearments in the rare letters. Rumors. Missing passion in our bed."

It was a more honest answer than I had expected.

He journeyed closer. "Then I asked, and my wife told me. It

wasn't a dagger plunged into my back, but it hurt. Betrayal always does. Then it didn't. She was happy, happier with others than she was with me. Life is too short to dwell on such squabbles."

"Her admission made it better?"

"No. But it was something I could understand. Her adultery was easier to live with once I knew I wasn't crazed, that jealousy had not driven me to see things that weren't there. My retirement meant the distance between us caused by my naval service or the seas could no longer be the cause of our estrangement. Her admission let me forgive her."

I dipped my head. "Thank you for your honesty."

"I told you, Abigail, I understand what you need. I shall always give you the truth."

Those words, his tone held both an ominous and luxurious feel. I had to be careful about what I asked of Stapleton. Some truths didn't need to be known.

Before I straightened to catch his gaze, I saw a corner of a piece of paper protruding between the undersurface of the door, the makeshift desk's top and the supporting crate.

"Hildebrand's theatrics may have given us a clue." I bent farther, grasped the stationery, and yanked it free, then put it near the page Hildebrand had picked up and put on the desk. "What is this?"

Unlike the other page, which had words from the play and beautiful script, this one was blank. Yet when I stood upright, I saw that the candlelight from the sconce glowed through the vanilla paper, revealing imprinted dates and maybe amounts. "It's a copy of something, or more so, it absorbed the writing of a top sheet. I can't quite tell, but it may be the same author's script. You transported letters between the couple. Can you confirm it's Danielson's script?" I picked up both pages. "What do you think?"

Stapleton stood beside me, looking over my shoulder. Was that cedar in his tailcoat?

"It looks to be the same paper. And the same hand. Danielson's. The tally seems like debt markers."

"The surface of the old door is rough. He must've written on a stack of papers. If I had ink—no, charcoal—I might be able to smear it on this and clearly make out the numbers drafted."

"When I came to deliver correspondence, I remember piles of neatly arranged paper." He took the pages from me, folded them, and put them into his pocket. "We'll find out tonight. Joanna can clearly recognize her husband's handwriting."

"What if we find these scribblings have mentions of another woman? Should we find out first . . . ?"

"No. We need answers, especially if they are debts. Mrs. Danielson might now owe them."

Studying the notations, I did see how they could be debts, but they could also be winnings. "If these are IOUs—or vowels, as my father would call them—to Danielson, the numbers are sizable. Someone owing him this much money could've gotten the playwright killed."

Stapleton nodded. "I'd automatically assumed the so-called reformed man was the debtor, but this could be a reason for murder."

"Yet why would this be left here for us to find? The night of the murder, it seemed as if the papers were searched. Did the murderer find the original markers?"

"This place was clean when we entered, Abigail. Our shifting the door must've dislodged the page from its hiding place. I suspect the killer wouldn't have destroyed it if they'd found it."

The need to find some charcoal and see exactly what was scribbled on the paper made my fingertips itch.

"Let me look at the note again. I'm asking, so as not to rip into your pocket and ruin the lines of your slate-gray waist-coat. Nice to see you dressing in something other than mourning black."

He half smiled and pulled the page out for me. "I'm still in the mourning period. The colors are a sign of respect, even if there was no love."

Not wanting to dwell on his words, I burrowed into my reticule and found my lorgnette and inspected the foolscap. "No inky prints from any fingertips, but there are definitely numbers and words impressed in the weave."

Then I saw it. "Look."

Stapleton hesitated, then came closer. The tall man could put his whole head atop mine. "What, Abigail?"

"The smudge. Something spilled, or it got wet. But it's not blood, is it?"

"No." He grunted. "A puzzle upon a puzzle."

Instead of handing it back, I shoved the page and my magnifying lenses into my reticule. I turned to look around at the shelves and banged into Stapleton's shoulder.

"Sorry, sir."

"Quite all right, Abigail. You'll get more used to me being around."

His indigo eyes bore down upon me, and I backed up. "We need to ask Duncan what became of the papers. We need to find all the pages that were here last night. And anything else of Danielson's writing. There has to be more clues impressed on the pages."

Something that sounded like a shout made us move to the door. Peering around the doorjamb, I didn't see anything but the actors and seafaring men who had begun to gather.

Stapleton tugged me back into the room. "Perhaps you should go speak with Miss Banyan. She might confide in you the nature of her friendship with Danielson. I'd hate to convict him and break Joanna's heart. Taking gossip to a woman who's mourning a murdered man is unacceptable."

It would be horrible to depend on rumors and innuendo as truth.

My old neighborhood had been rife with tormenting whispers when my mother left my father. Thinking of Hildebrand's bitterness, my father's . . . I wondered if I should offer John Carrington more sympathy.

The heavily drinking man had sought the bottle more to cover the pain of his broken heart and the embarrassment that a woman had chosen to live the final years without him. Mama had sought peace. She left us to be with the love of her life. Poor Dinah and I had been abandoned and left to pick up the pieces—to salvage our broken father and to keep our reputations clean and without scandal.

"Abigail, do you disagree? You're in deep thought about something. You don't feel confident in asking Miss Banyan? Or are you having a vision?"

I clasped my temples, then tried to rub myself free of the headache that was forming. "I don't know why James told you of my silly dreams. They have no meaning, nothing I can decipher. I have to puzzle out this crime by good old logic and the hope that the guilty made a mistake."

A loud cry shattered my ears.

Then another shout.

Then another.

Stapleton looked at me, and I at him. We ran from the old-scene store into the crowd of sailors sitting on benches, joking with each other.

"No one seems panicked, sir. The shouts must be acting."

Stapleton's brows rose and hung neatly over his dark eyes. "I'm not convinced, but no one else seems concerned."

Mr. Sheridan came from an office. "It's getting late. Move the cables to the corridor behind the stage. Start counting the links." He said this to the sailors who began rushing into positions with the ropes and iron blocks hanging above the curtains.

My neighbor pulled me to the side. "Let's go and come back another time."

Before I could agree, Hildebrand wandered toward us. "The riggers are prepping everything for tonight. They'll inspect the ropes and winches for each scenery drop. Then things will calm down a bit. You should stay and watch how things ramp up in an hour or so."

"It seems many sailors arrive from the tunnels." I said. "No one cares that they just walked up from the Thames."

Hildebrand shushed me, placing a hand to his blueing lips. "The magic and indifference of the theater."

"Don't tease Lady Worthing." Stapleton stepped between us. "We're not physically that far from the river. It's easy for men to come and go. Proximity is no magic. It's an opportunity. Indifference is everyone's misfortune."

Used to my neighbor's dry pronouncements, I chose to turn and focus on the actor. Hildebrand looked pallid. "Sir, you don't look well."

"Good. I shall be a ghost tonight." He clapped his hands together. "Now that the nosing around is concluded, will the physician and his pushy assistant stay for a proper performance? Tonight shall be my finest."

Before I could agree, Hildebrand began to walk away and bumped into Stapleton. The actor fell back a little. The fellow appeared worse for wear—disheveled, smelling of more brandy. Waving his hands, he said, "Stay. See the magic of Drury Lane."

"The night he died, did Mr. Danielson come out of the old-scene store at all?" I asked. "It's a little secluded. It's the far-thest room from the stage."

He staggered in front of me and slurred, "I don't recall."

Stapleton steadied him. "Do you ever give your liver a rest from polluting it with liquor? The organ works as hard as the heart."

Hildebrand offered a drunken chorale, but the ice in my neighbor's voice reminded me of our first arguments over our dogs, when I thought Stapleton Henderson guilty of the worst crime.

"Wait," the sloppy fellow said. "Let me think."

The fussing from before became loud, louder than all the various conversations happening backstage.

Craning his ear, Hildebrand went toward the angry voices. We followed him.

"Oh, the noise is coming from Barbara's dressing room," Hildebrand announced. "The witch is practicing a new part. I wonder if that's Danielson's play."

Did Miss Banyan have the pages? How did she get them?

Hildebrand grabbed at his chest, his sagging cravat. "Perhaps she'll take it to another theater. That will sink Drury Lane. It will draw people away." He coughed something awful and dry.

Stapleton went to him and pushed his head down lower than the man's chest. "Take a deep breath. How long have you been struggling to fill your lungs?"

"No struggling, busybody physician." Hildebrand pushed away; pills fell out of his jacket.

Stapleton picked them up, held them for a second, then of-fered them to him.

With an exaggerated hand motion, Hildebrand snatched the white dots and placed one in his mouth. The man plowed for-ward. "Give chase. Something to see."

We did. The man wanted us to follow.

"Slow down," Stapleton said. "You can hurt yourself."

After stopping in front of Miss Banyan's room, Hildebrand banged along the entrance. The hinges whined. The door moved, and he fell inside.

Stapleton knelt to give Hildebrand assistance. Before I could help, think, move, I froze. A fellow had his hands around Miss Banyan's neck.

She glanced in our direction. Her screams shook me, freed me from my fright.

"Sir!" I started to charge forward.

With his back to me, the fiend pulled away from her. Then he tossed his greatcoat about his head, clearly intending to escape.

But it was too late.

I saw him, saw his face, gawking at me as if I'd done wrong.

And I became paralyzed, unable to move.

The Duke of Culver, the hero renewing the abolition fight in Parliament, passed beside me, knocking me with his shoulder into the wall.

Arm hurting, mind tormented—why was he here, and not in the halls of the legislature, lobbying other politicians?—I watched him flee.

"Abigail, are you hurt? Don't move." Stapleton's voice. Behind me.

Couldn't heed his advice. Had to know if what I'd seen was real.

Why was the duke trying to kill . . . ?

Too many questions. No answers. I picked myself up and gave chase.

"Lady Worthing, wait!"

That was Stapleton again, trying to caution me to stop, but I refused to stay still, to submit, to be weak or confused.

A murderer was escaping.

He tapped down his hat and went down the hall and then disappeared.

The lanky young man, one who'd been at Drury Lane the night of the murder, stood in the shadows, but he pointed. "He went into the tunnels, miss." Doffing his cap, the young fellow held the door open to a blackened passage.

Leaving any bit of sense I had behind, I chased the Duke of Culver into the dark.

Chapter 10

Into the old-scene store, Alexander Hildebrand lets the mad physician drag him. Henderson props Hildebrand's head against the crates, the base of the makeshift desk.

"I'm fine," Hildebrand says to Henderson. Unsure if the man can hear him over the low curses he utters, he shakes a finger at the physician. "Go on. Go after the busybody."

"You better hope she's unharmed. You did that on purpose. Fell into the doorway to expose Banyan's attacker."

Smiling wider until it hurts. "I thought it was a dramatic performance. What better way to expose the hypocrites?"

"You mean hypocrite. Just one fool attacked a woman, and in public."

"Two fools. An actress not understanding the dangerous game she's playing with men and the second fool, the Duke of Culver. He's in all the papers, professing to be a champion of rights. Hypocrites. I'm sure His Grace doesn't want people to hear his sins. I guess everyone loves to act."

"A paradox, to be sure." Henderson snaps up Hildebrand's wrist.

"You truly are a Donne fanatic."

"Two. Three." He counts Hildebrand's raging pulse. The veins in the actor's arm want to explode. From the unchanged expression on the physician's face, it's obvious that things still beat, even if this man may want them to stop.

"To hurt anyone is to be tarred and feathered," Henderson declares. "Last I checked, the duke fought unfair taxation and pushed for abolition. Neither are prerequisites for moral living."

"I didn't say he needed to be a monk, but the irascible duke is a big hypocrite. The other wants to make a name for herself. Banyan thinks she can be the greatest on the stage, bigger than Elizabeth Inchbald. Now, that was a legend."

Henderson tosses Hildebrand's hand away. "Still not a crime. Sit and catch your breath. No more faking false attacks."

Henderson moves to the door; his hand pries it open but his part is not done.

"Then back to you, hypocrite." Hildebrand forces his voice to bellow, to beckon the fellow. "Did serving Nelson help you outrun your father's name?"

Those words make Henderson stop, release the door, and kick it shut.

"Well, I still know how to deliver a line that punches at the gut. What say you, physician?"

Ramrod straight back, eyes possessing a lethal, narrow stare, Henderson marches back to where he'd left Hildebrand at the dead man's makeshift desk. Fitting.

"What else do you want me to know? Your last wish needs to be good. This delay could be deadly for my colleague. If one hair in her chignon is harmed, I'll kill you, even if you are already dying."

With a sleight of hand, he palms a pill from Hildebrand's pocket. "Dover's? These opium-laced poisons are supposed to subdue wretched pain. They also can have the effect of making one look drunk. You must be in agony, the way you've been swallowing them."

Grabbing the pill back, Hildebrand gobbles it. He wipes spittle from his lips and greedily awaits relief.

Henderson stoops and demands his gaze. "Talk. You obviously have something to say."

"Be assured your family's secrets are safe with me. I'll say nothing of it as long as you say nothing of my condition. I don't want my last performance to be today. Seems a rumor of my ill health might shorten my tenure. Sheridan needs the income my name draws."

"Does he know of your condition?"

Glare disappearing, Henderson stands up, but puts his palms flat on the door Danielson did all his writing on.

Hildebrand can still picture his friend doing so. Such a shame for the desk to be empty, devoid of his piles. With the pain in his chest easing, he sits up a little straighter. "Does the fetching Blackamoor know you want her? Does she even have a clue?"

"Be careful. Don't besmirch the good woman."

The man in front of Hildebrand is big. With his years in the theater, he's seen brutes, people who bark threats or offer poignant rebukes. It's the doctor's cold stare that unnerves.

But fool that he is, and a gambler, like his lost friend, he has to poke. "Does the pushy little baroness know you fancy her and will hurt anyone that troubles her? Oh, the lust of the flesh is strong. Like the taste of a fresh biscuit, one that's warm and brown and delicious."

Henderson adjusts his cuffs. Sparkling fobs, which are probably solid gold, catch the light, making them linger about his powerful hands. "Dover's pills addle the brain. Makes one see or say crazy things. Makes them do foolish things, too."

"Abstaining from pleasure is foolish? Nothing, not even the morrow, is promised. What's making you forgo what you want?"

"Currently, it's my oath to save lives. You're not dead, so if you excuse me, I must go after Lady Worthing." He starts to the door again.

The tightness, the lingering tightness in his chest, makes the actor not want to be alone. With Danielson dead, that's how he passes the time, alone.

"How disappointing," Hildebrand says in a renewed voice. "I thought that's what Hendersons do. Get everything they want."

The physician spins. The caustic gape, his dark, burning eyes make Hildebrand grateful that Danielson's spear is in the custody of the magistrate.

"You want to die sooner than when your heart stops? The tongue is the deadliest weapon. Once something is said, the damage can never be undone."

Hildebrand claps shaky hands. "Fine performance. Go after her down the tunnels to the Thames. That's how His Grace visits."

Blinking, Henderson again adjusts his cuffs. His expression becomes somber, removed. "Culver comes here often?"

"Yes, he didn't take too kindly to Miss Banyan spending time with Danielson. He should just up and marry the chit. Who wouldn't want to be a duchess? Apparently not her."

"If she's not inclined to be roughed up, I don't blame her rejection. Culver seems rather stupid to risk his political name by harassing an actress."

"But she's an actress. A rather good one. Looks can be deceiving, physician."

"Hardly."

"Well, some want to be deceived. The risk and the chase can be gratifying. Consider this a push to make you go after the pushy lady."

"Forthright and honest, that's what Lady Worthing is. It's a pleasure and a pain to know her better. Now if you'll excuse me, I must go, whilst hoping she possesses the mettle to stay alive while I dawdle with you."

"The pushy, wily ones always live unharmed. Just churn a wake of destruction behind in their path. Such happy strolls. Then they leave and take what matters with them." He laughs. "But that's another thing the Hendersons are known for."

Shaking his head, the physician leaves.

And Hildebrand stretches out on the exact same spot where Danielson died.

When the pain in his chest subsides, Hildebrand sits up and stretches. He takes another Dover's pill for good measure. His taunting of the physician continues to amuse his soul.

Men are all fools for smart women.

There's no doubt in Hildebrand's mind who the hypocrite with the plan is in the Danielson-Banyan affair. The question in his head is, Why did the savvy actress want the unpredictable playwright dead?

Or did someone wanting Miss Banyan free from her entanglement need Danielson dead?

No matter the reasoning, it all centers around the hussy and the dead.

Outside the old-scene store, he steadies himself by holding on to the doorframe. "It's always a woman."

The lull of the dinner hour has begun. Once this break is done, everything will become magic again—with people buzzing and readying for the performance.

Hildebrand steals a deep breath. The fresh paint from touchups on the canvas scents the warm air. This smell and the fiery candles are the things he loves most about Drury Lane.

Noises come from behind. Something or someone has advanced into the crossover space, the area behind the stage where he's walked hundreds of times, to suddenly appear in the background of a performance.

Thinking of following and perhaps looking out toward the stage, Hildebrand hears Danielson's old partner. The man is in the shadows, talking to Barbara. She acts to some as if she doesn't know him, but Lucas Watson's just another bee hunting the actress's nectar.

Did the hate this sailor had for Danielson end his life? Watson had threatened Danielson with a knife the night of the murder. "I should tell the physician and Lady Pushy about the sailor."

Hildebrand covers his mouth. The walls have ears. Speaking ill of someone shouldn't be done.

The two have stopped their chatter, but she glances at Hildebrand. Why does Miss Banyan always look angry, like Hildebrand has done something? Maybe he should admit she has talent.

Then she'll believe he's after her, too.

Barbara Banyan is young enough to be his daughter. That might not matter to most, but it does to Hildebrand.

There's a locket of jet hair he keeps on his person, from the only woman he's ever loved. A child and a bride that disappeared at the height of his fame. Her family didn't want her to wed an actor. And Hildebrand was too prideful and boastful to tell her he loved them more than the applause.

Pity. They left, and Hildebrand still wonders what that life would've been like.

Barbara swivels her hips and comes toward him. Her neck is up, her shoulders back, and she passes Hildebrand as if he's nothing. Then she turns. "Go home, sir. Sleep off the stupor. An understudy can perform your few lines. I want to shine tonight. Can't happen if you're a stumbling fool."

"Shine with practice, witch. Shine after years of performances." He drums his fingers together. "Keep working. You'll actually be good. But don't ease your troubles with some new fool."

"Should I choose an old one?"

"That duke doesn't look that old, but he bothers you, Barbara."

She blinks her sassy blue eyes, ones that at times seem familiar. "For a fellow who used to be one of the best in the theater, how can you not tell the difference between grief and someone rehearsing for a part and someone trying to rid herself of an obsessed man? Please stop with the fatherly advice. I don't need it to get rid of a rich man sending flowers."

Tears dampen her lashes.

How can she do that? Look so innocent when Hildebrand is sure she's evil.

"Maybe you're a better actress than I thought. I almost believe you, but I know losing Danielson ruins your plans for taking over Drury Lane. Suppose you'll have to ride something else. A common thief like Watson is not it. Maybe give His Grace another go."

She rolls her shoulders as if they have tension, as if his foolish words have stabbed something deep inside. "Despite your venom, I do care for you, Hildebrand. You're a legend. But all lores end. Go home. Rest. Be a mean drunk another night."

"Back off with those eyes, she-devil. You can fool the young bucks, even old Sheridan, from time to time, but not me. I'm staying. I need to see this through."

Coughing, he grabs at his soiled cravat, which has spittle and a few unfortunate drops of crimson on it, and wipes his mouth. "I'm not fooled by your concern, either. No one pays attention to what I know."

"Are you sure? It's hard to fool a fool."

Barbara folds her arms and goes back to her dressing room. The sailor, Watson, has disappeared.

Again, Hildebrand is alone at Drury Lane.

No one listens or cares anymore. If he doesn't do well tonight, even old Sheridan will reconsider having him here.

Then what will that mean?

Sighing, wobbling, he thinks he hears a noise. Slowly spinning around, he sees someone go into the crossover space. "Chasing ghosts is as good as chasing a pushy assistant."

Wonder if the physician caught up to her and Culver. Hope he did. The duke is mean to pretty women.

"Halt. Who goes there?" His voice sounds raspy from coughing. Hildebrand clears his throat and prepares for a direct address. "Halt! Who goes there?"

Nothing.

No one responds.

He wanders into the crossover space. Dimly lit candles expose parted burgundy curtains.

After stepping forward, he looks out at the rows and rows of empty seats. Tears form as he remembers the past: the packed crowds, the thunderous applause, the benefit nights when the tickets collected made him rich, reaffirming this was all he had, money and memories.

The coughing starts. When he opens his eyes, he's not alone.

"You came back? No need to apologize." Hildebrand waves his arm and points. "If only you could see it. This place full to capacity. People were on their feet clapping as I gave the best performance of Shakespeare's Clarence London had ever seen."

He sways a little but reclaims his balance. "Oh, to be young again and have that moment in the sun. Alas. No more bows, not even for a performance of *Richard III*."

A creaking noise sounds to his right.

He squints at the apparition, which is surely Danielson's ghost.

"I let you down. You were crying out to be saved. But I knew you were dead. Sorry."

To find a body and ruin the performances when Sheridan needed every ticket to pay his gambling debt was suicide.

"I won't be banished from Drury Lane. This is my home. Nothing will harm it, especially not the truth."

A whine sounds from above. An iron block and pulley drops at his feet.

Hildebrand hops out of the way. "Sorry, Danielson. Don't tear up the place."

Wandering deeper into the crossover space, he traces his steps, remembering the moments he surprised the audience.

His heart begins breaking. Fear of never returning to the stage, the place where he's been adored and loved, has caved in his chest.

Perhaps that's what Sheridan wants to tell him. Has Sheridan asked him to come early to dismiss him?

"You convinced him, didn't you? You convinced Sheridan that I'm good for nothing. I still have something to give Drury Lane." His voice rises as he repeats, "I have something. I know something."

Panting, he beats on his ribs. Then he searches his pockets.

Empty.

Empty like the past years of his life.

Empty like the choices he made that abandoned love.

"Hope the doc gets his pushy baroness before death comes."

It has for Hildebrand.

He flees up the stairs the sailors use when they hoist and anchor ropes to raise the curtains and position heavy scenery drops.

"Death," he says, "wait another moment. Let me have my last memories." Clasping the rail, feeling his passions racing his pulse, he declares, "I was here, Death. I was Clarence from *Richard III*."

Holding on to the ropes, he weaves his arms through loops and stretches the jute wide. "'Who sent you hither? Wherefore do you come?'"

The murderer in the shadows doesn't answer.

The blackness shifts. Men must be lighting Drury's sconces. "Always the best light here."

Yet Death made them open the curtains so far back that Alexander Hildebrand could see the seats and all the boxes. This is the place to go.

"You come to kill me, aye? Is it for what I know? Or like my youth, has my usefulness fled?"

Death stands at the bottom of the stairs, moaning. The pounding of his pulse blocks the words. Death must want more of the scene.

"Oh, my brother hates me." Hildebrand lets his voice boom. "No, Sheridan, Danielson . . . whoever. Should they hate me, hate me for what I've done. I let go of my first and only love. That's a crime indeed."

Hildebrand waits for the response, but the ropes about his arms feel tight. He can't let go; the scene must be finished. "'Tis he that sent us hither now to slaughter thee. 'Make peace with God for you must die, my lord.'"

Those words of Shakespeare are slurred in his mouth and make his heart slow.

That feeling. Dover's pills in his pocket will ease it.

Death races up the stairs. Reaching for the intruder entangles Hildebrand more in the ropes.

Then the words the murderer said to Danielson ring out. "Look behind you. Take that, and that."

A push.

A slip.

A fall.

With him caught in the net, the rope becomes a noose. The ropes stretch but become taut about his throat.

But Death is not finished. It laughs. It cries. It threatens to drown him "in the malmsey butt within."

Claps ring out.

And on the last beat, everything stops.

The famed actor falls over the stair rail and hangs at Death's feet.

Chapter 11

Suspects in Anthony Danielson's Murder
Alexander Hildebrand
Richard Sheridan
Lanky Sailor
The Mathews
Unknown Sailor(s)
Martin Simpkins, Duke of Culver

The scent of seawater became heavier in the stone passage. Unable to see, too foolhardy to turn back, I kept edging forward, hoping to see the light. The chiseled bricks I fingered felt moist. I must be getting closer to the exit, which had to be near the Thames.

Hoped I didn't have to swim.

No longer hearing the Duke of Culver's footsteps, I slowed in the darkness he'd forced. The fiend had extinguished the torches as he fled.

The pitch black chilled my soul, but I couldn't turn back and be exposed as a fool.

But I was one, running after a man in the dark.

Inching along, not knowing if he had stopped and was waiting to strike, I realized this wasn't my brightest moment. I could only hope the duke was more desperate to escape than to turn back and do me harm.

I wished Stapleton had followed me.

I wished I had those knitting needles Vaughn had talked of to protect myself.

Seeing only a few feet ahead made the passage feel like an eternity. This by far was the stupidest thing I'd ever done.

Remembering I was young, I figured it probably wouldn't be the last.

The sounds of waves lapping ahead became loud.

Finally, a ray of light broke before me. I quickened my pace, then stumbled into the sunshine.

The docks of the Thames spread before me. The call of gulls filled the foggy air. Ships and workers were everywhere.

But no Duke of Culver.

I shadowed my eyes and searched, but the man I'd chased, one guilty of certain treachery, was nowhere to be found.

There had to be an explanation. Did all powerful dukes look alike?

No. That was me hoping I hadn't seen what I saw.

If Culver wasn't guilty of something—violence against Miss Banyan or, worse, the murder of Mr. Danielson—why had he run?

My lungs filled with the wetness of the low clouds. The stench and sourness of the polluted Thames filled the air, but I gulped heavily.

I'd made it.

I hadn't faltered so badly.

I could recover from this blunder.

Looking this way and then that, I lowered my hand. No one was running or hopping into an awaiting carriage, none that I saw.

My gaze became fixed on a ship dead ahead. Black and white dots scattered along the ship's deck. Those dots worked together, hoisting goods, tying up crates.

Too far away to know for sure, but I assumed these men were worked hard. These sailors shared common days, sweating together in the sun, joining in honest free labor.

Nearby, drays held stacks of barrels containing rum or sugar or indigo.

Most of Britain cared not about where these goods originated or the enslaved labor that created them. The current bills in Parliament would change this. Yet, the man I saw in Drury Lane who was one of the main voices fighting for abolition could be a murderer. A scandal involving Culver would jeopardize the heated debates about slavery.

If I was somewhat wrong in what I saw, I'd be adding to gossip, and this gossip would ensure these shipments would never originate from freed labor.

My heart thundered.

I had to believe in a logical explanation for the duke being at Drury Lane, interacting with Miss Banyan.

The feeling of being watched, threatened, struck me in my spine.

Heat flooded my neck.

Slowly, I spun around.

Stapleton Henderson stood behind me, huffing and puffing like a fiery chimney, an angry dragon. "If you ever run off from me down a dark corridor, after a potential murderer, so help me I'll—"

"You'll what? You were in more danger following me. Tight spaces are problems for you, not me. And last I checked, you're not my husband or the magistrate. You cannot command me to do anything."

His mouth pressed open, then shut, tightening to a line. He walked around me, then bent over and clasped his knees. "We can both agree that it's best I'm not Lord Worthing. Though

I'm the last man ever to control a wife or diminish her free-doms, I believe you'd be my demise. And you'd relish it. For both our benefits, limit your abandon. Stop behavior that can get you killed."

I wiped at my sweaty, sticky brow. Tar had smeared on my forehead. Must have come from the tunnels. "I, ah . . . I know what I'm doing."

He tsked his teeth, stepped within throttling distance, and pulled a white cloth from his pocket. "May I?"

My neighbor had asked, but before I could answer, he began mopping my forehead. His touch was gentle. He didn't have gloves, so his skin, his fingers trailed my face.

"There. All clean." That indeterminate look on his face had changed from a grimace to intense study, then to nothing.

As he stuffed the cloth into a pocket, Stapleton said, "You're putting yourself in places where you could be hurt or attacked or worse. Can't you see that? Is that why Worthing's not here? Is he so unable to bear stopping you from your investigations that he'd rather be on a ship, awaiting news of your luck run-ning out? No, he can't be here and witness this."

I'd slapped Stapleton before. Sort of wanted to now, but how could I when he might've spoken the truth.

I swallowed. I'd rather believe that James's fearing for me, due to my puzzling, kept him away than think that he was in-capable of loving me.

"I need you to take more care, madam."

Flinging my arms about me like I was affronted, and not try-ing to hold my insides together, I nodded. "Say no more of this. Take me home. Stapleton Henderson, take me home."

"Fine." With a head shake and a sigh, he said, "Let's—"

"Wait. My bag. I left it in the old-scene store. I have to go back and get it. Lead the pushy woman back to Drury Lane."

His arm lifted, then snapped to the side. Stapleton marched forward, away from the tunnel and toward the side streets. "For my peace, come this way."

There was no need to fight. I didn't want to head back into the tunnel, either.

In the dying sunshine, I could at least see Stapleton as we took the long walk back to the theater.

He gritted his teeth. I'd made him mad by being me. Yet those blank dark eyes weren't so blank when he looked back at me. "Come along, Abigail."

Filled with fury, my neighbor hadn't abandoned me. He was still here. Not looking to send me back to Greater Queen Street in a rented hackney or letting stubborn me find my own way, this man was determined to see me home.

That was something.

I caught up to him and paced at his side as he started up Brydges Street.

"Did you catch Culver, Abigail? Did he answer your questions?"

So Stapleton had seen that it was the duke, too. It hadn't been my imagination.

"No. He was fast, and he stunted my progress in the tunnel by dousing the lights."

"Bastard." Stapleton grunted something else, and I was glad I couldn't decipher it. "Another mystery, my lady? At least you're unharmed. Taking risks and being no closer to solving this crime seems foolish."

Stapleton was right. It just felt like the thing to do. "We have a new suspect. A man who runs and has things to hide."

"You could've stayed and found out the same information from Hildebrand. He's fine . . . recovering from his fall. Thank you for asking."

My head dropped for a moment. "It's good he's better."

"I left him to recover in the old-scene store. If we hurry, he might still be there. You can ask him more questions about Culver." His hand fisted. "It would be a shame if Culver's guilty. He's a needed vote in the current debate."

The route to solving this murder mirrored my life, becoming

murkier and murkier. My feet slowed, then stopped. "Here's to hoping the man is just a lover, not a killer."

Halting, Stapleton offered a slow chuckle. "I suppose it would be terrible for him or any man to be both."

When he lifted his arm and waited for me to grasp it, I couldn't help thinking he was attempting to train me, as if I were one of his greyhounds.

Nonetheless, I went and put a palm on his forearm. There was something reassuring about walking next to a man who was confident and angry and respectful—traits I admired in Vaughn.

"In the morning I'll send a note to Mr. Wilson Shaw. He's doing some research for me on the finances of the theater and our current persons of interest—Hildebrand, Sheridan, Banyan ... the Mathews. I'll ask him research Lord Culver too." That name should be added to my suspects list.

A muscle in Stapleton's sleeve tensed beneath my palm. "You could've asked me about the Mathews. They are my friends." The heated glance he offered said what I feared: Stapleton would protect them even if they were guilty.

"I don't want to compromise you. We are developing trust. You're right about how I respect the truth, but it's hard to stay objective with people you think of as family."

A minute or more passed. He said nothing, and neither did I. The wait for him to admit I was right in my logic seemed like an eternity.

His head dipped. "Tracing the money makes sense. It's the root of evil." He started moving faster. "Thank you." His tone was so quiet that the words almost disappeared beneath the din of the busy streets. "Thank you for allowing me to be a part of your confidence, despite my misgivings or censure of your approach."

"We're on the same side. In this matter."

His jaw softened. There may have been an audible chuckle.

"Let's hurry and gather your reticule before the theater begins to fill. We can attack this mystery tomorrow."

"Once we get a full report from Shaw, we'll better understand our suspects and their motives. Or even a lack of one. I hope Culver ran only because of a fear of being caught in a scandal. Who'd want their name bandied about as an abuser of women?"

"Abuse is so horrid. Men can behave atrociously toward women, but many in the public won't care because Miss Banyan is an actress."

"If someone I admired in politics could be so dastardly in private, how exactly can anything in this world survive?"

"I suppose we'll have to hope for logical explanations or a fast vote in Parliament before a murderous Culver would stand trial. That is if he is guilty of killing Danielson."

Reflecting on the Black and White dockworkers unloading ships together or even on Stapleton and me puzzling out a mystery, I had to believe there was hope.

But this was London, where hope could be as easily extinguished as a young bride's future.

After slipping in the back door of Drury Lane, I noted that people were crying.

I looked at Stapleton's stretched eyes.

He knew something.

When he took off his hat and held it to his chest, that confirmed it for me. Then he stashed it again on his thick black hair. "There should have been more time."

My stomach knotted. "More time for what?"

His arm lowered; his hand slipped to mine for a moment. "I didn't have a chance to tell you. A heart condition."

"He's dead," Miss Banyan wailed. "I cannot go on tonight. This is too much."

Mr. Sheridan had arrived. His round face looked red and

sweaty. He spied us but offered no reaction to Stapleton or me being again backstage.

My neighbor stepped in front of me and went over to this powerful man, who'd been boisterous and threatening. "Where?"

"The crossover space," Sheridan answered.

My neighbor went in the direction of the stage. I followed, keeping directly on his heels. We turned the corner. Expecting to see a stranger or even the missing duke, I felt I'd run at top speed into a wall.

Alexander Hildebrand, the famed actor, a former favorite of mine, hung by his neck among the stage ropes. His body dangled above us, swinging like a human pendulum, hovering over my reticule.

Flat, devoid of contents, the thick blue satin sat on the floor like a beacon to announce my involvement.

Henderson groaned softly.

When he glanced at me, his countenance expressed everything. It was as if he was shouting at me not to utter a word or claim ownership of the reticule.

He didn't have to say a thing out loud.

I knew him, or had come to know him. He saw the clear threat.

To implicate me, the killer had placed my bag as evidence at the site of the murder.

Chapter 12

Hours spun by as Lord Duncan and his runners scoured Drury Lane. Their boot heels made heavy pounding noises as they searched the building, very different from the sounds made by those in evening slippers the night Danielson died.

Stapleton said the actor had a heart condition. Did that mean he wouldn't have the strength to murder a healthy younger man?

I supposed that Hildebrand being strangled by ropes and discovered before sunset had brought these men from their daily activities. Unlike the mixing of races at the docks, Duncan's runners were white-faced fellows who seemed eager in their jobs to be instruments of justice.

I highly doubted that any would be concerned with my alibi: I'd been walking down a long, damp tunnel to the Thames, going after a man who'd disappeared.

One runner passed in front of me while heading toward Miss Banyan's dressing room. She'd gone back to it. Sullen face, red eyes—she had seemed truly upset at the loss of a man she hated.

Perhaps, like me, she knew better than to seem too engaged. No one wanted to be dragged to Newgate Prison tonight.

Pacing, again holding tightly to Stapleton's onyx tailcoat, I stood out of the way, sequestered in the corner, waiting to be questioned about the reticule, my reticule, being found under Hildebrand's dangling feet.

The image of him, eyes half shut, face blue gray, devoid of air, would stay with me. It had taken forever for Duncan to have the body cut down.

Why would someone do this, hurt a harmless old man?

Had Hildebrand's sharp tongue said too much?

Stepping from the corner, I wanted to peek into the crossover space. Part of me feared doing so, but my gut knew that I'd miss clues by skulking far from the action.

After getting close to the stage, I peered into the crossover space. Though runners had the curled body of the esteemed actor lying among tangled rope, about his neck was an 'awful pirate's cravat.' That's what one called it.

Hildebrand's brandy-sotted cheeks were purple.

How long had he struggled?

Had he fought until he couldn't?

Had the killer, who had taken the time to place my reticule under Hildebrand's body, waited with him, or had the fiend allowed this legend of the theater to die alone?

Those eyes, which no one had closed, had they captured Danielson's murderer as well as his own?

It didn't matter anymore.

That voice, which had wowed thousands, was forever silenced.

My thoughts had me addled as I wondered about the humanity of a murderer.

Rubbing my skull, I wanted to punch my fingers through my temples as punishment for being so careless. I could be entangled in this death, and by extension, I would draw Stapleton into it. Again, we could be suspects in a suspicious death.

At least this time, neither of us had a motive.

Lord Duncan took his hat off and fanned his salt-and-pepper hair.

Every sconce in the theater was lit. The heat of the flames, the ire of the scrutiny, the hope of catching the guilty made the temperature feel as hot as fire, fleeting fire.

Duncan asked, "Do you see any signs of struggle?"

"None." With his hands pointing to Hildebrand's bared arms, Stapleton stooped down. "Nothing under his nails. No bruising anywhere but where the ropes wrapped about his arms and neck."

When Duncan took possession of my reticule from a runner, I wanted to turn away. He shook it. I held my breath, waiting for a slight of hand to make my lorgnette appear and fall, smashing to the floor, pronouncing me a suspect.

But nothing dropped. The killer had absconded with the contents. Or Duncan or Stapleton or theater magic had saved me.

"The papers." I covered my mouth.

Stapleton glanced at me, unbothered. "No paper or anything else to identify the culprit. You'll have to search for clues later." His voice sounded confident.

I should be, too, but I couldn't explain how my bag ended up with Hildebrand. I'd left it in the theater when I chased after the duke. Would that be believed? Wasn't sure, but my trust in the politically wary Duncan to listen was low.

Nervous, I went back to the old-scene store. Staring at the makeshift desk, mourning the missing pieces of foolscap, which might illuminate motives or even the murderer, I felt sick.

The clues Stapleton and I had found, which I'd put inside my reticule—the piece of script and the foolscap with indentions that charcoal could make decipherable—were gone.

My fault.

There needed to be another clue here. I began rummaging through the shelves, searching among the piles of old paintings, the re-creations of buildings and landscapes I'd witnessed from my pretty perch in the theater. A great deal of work had gone into these.

A velvety pelt on a higher shelf, was this once worn by Hildebrand? Was it from Shakespeare's *Richard III*?

My eyes felt a little sticky.

Must be the dust. The costume cape had been finely crafted. Small stitches perfected the seams. So many seamstresses and other artisans would lose their livelihoods if Drury Lane closed. With two murders days apart, how could it continue?

I pounded the makeshift desk, where my reticule and lorgnette should've been.

Nothing made sense.

If I were to be framed, why not have my lorgnette in view? Who didn't know my signature glasses?

Perhaps the murderer wanted me frightened.

I should be.

My carelessness, my need to have the foolscap in my possession over Stapleton's tailcoat, could allow the guilty to go free.

One person needed to confess right now. I was woman enough to accept the scrutiny for my actions. I'd hate if it would cause me to be banned from any further investigation. Stapleton had said I was honest. I needed to prove him right again.

Pushing out of the room, I held my head high, not low, as if I knew I'd be detained.

The immediate shock I'd witnessed in fellow castmates and staging crew had lessened. They'd moved on to celebrating Hildebrand's life, offering sundry bits of conversations about his greatest roles.

As I reached the crossover space, Barbara Banyan was leaving it. We stood face-to-face. Her countenance had dried tracks of tears. Seeing her visibly moved touched me.

"I'm sorry, Miss Banyan. I'm also sorry that you won't perform tonight. I know how important that is to you."

Anger, hurt, and something else flashing in her eyes, stiffened the corners of her pouty mouth. "We lost a legend."

The hurt in her voice pricked my heart. The animosity I'd seen between the two actors replayed in my mind, as did their final scene.

Hildebrand hit the entrance of her dressing room.

The door flung open, breaking his fall.

Lord Culver pulled his hands from the actress's neck and fled.

I ran after him, leaving Stapleton to deal with Hildebrand.

"Death has a way of putting things into perspective," I said, hoping my words made some sort of sense. Miss Banyan had experienced a great deal today.

"Hildebrand and I, as actors . . . Our paths go back some ways. Theater life. I wished he'd seen my brilliance onstage. I wished he could've acknowledged I was good."

The heat in her words, words stewing in sadness and pity, felt familiar.

"You never did wish him ill, Miss Banyan. You wanted him to understand you?"

"I'd not wish him ill. How could I? He was the best."

Such an honest confession from this woman, but was it so? Was it a message? If I weren't drained, I'd play along, but I was spent.

"Tell me what you want me to know. What do you think I should tell Lord Duncan?" I said.

"Hildebrand and I may have quarreled, but I did admire his work."

Her voice sounded lyrical again. The woman wished to sway me, but I'd have to forget all I'd seen.

"I remember the first time I saw him perform. It was as

Clarence in *Richard III*. He was magical. Such a marvelous actor," she said. "That's what we should focus upon, not gossip or jealousy."

"His career was outstanding, so many roles, so many farces. Now you have the lead in *A Bold Stroke for a Wife* at Drury Lane. Then Alexander Hildebrand returns, and his name overshadows yours. Isn't that part of the animosity you had for him?"

As she drew away, her mouth quivered. She seemed helpless and under attack. I'd become her villain. "I welcomed him. I looked forward to working with him, showing him my talent."

Thinking fast, not wanting this woman to cry and call attention to us, I offered praise. "I was here opening night. You were lovely. You made Anne Lovely feel bigger than life."

She batted her lashes. "I wasn't expecting a compliment. I thought you were trying to insinuate I had something to do with his hanging."

The woman raised her thin arms. The big velvety sleeves of her medieval costume slipped down her wrists. "There's no way I can lift a man or do anything of the sort."

"I'm not suggesting that, Miss Banyan." That would be like saying, "Because a woman's bag was near the body, a female was involved." "But you're connected to both men who were murdered. Could someone who didn't like Mr. Danielson being your friend or who mistook your troubles with Hildebrand want to do something about it? An aggressive peer perhaps?"

For a moment, she looked away, toward the riggers and the dozen runners circulating in the crossover space. Lord Duncan's men were moving, too, hunting. Her finger twirled a loose blond curl of the wig she wore. "I cannot control others' emotions or actions. I think that's too heavy a burden for me or any woman."

Her tone had again become haughty, but she spoke the truth.

"Lady Worthing, some call us the weaker sex, but I think we have to be the smarter one. If we lack the physical strength to charge through a wall, there's nothing wrong with harnessing a mule who can."

"Is that what you did? Did a mulish duke claim two lives?"

Wide, angry eyes settled on mine. "That reticule near Hildebrand seemed expensive. It doesn't exactly match your outfit, Lady Worthing, but the price point might."

"Many things go with silk, Miss Banyan. The reticule could be a present from a gentleman of refined tastes, a mule from a popular stable."

Her lips pursed. I believed she understood my point. Two smart women could match wits.

On the rare occasion James and I played chess, my words might be called a check, something to stop an aggressive move. I wasn't going to take the blame for this, and I wouldn't quiver or scrape or cry to give anyone power over me.

Nonetheless, my godfather had taught me one could gain more by being polite than combative. "I'm not accusing you, Miss Banyan. I'd like to help. The hold a passionate politician had about you seemed possessive, not warm or loving. I heard you scream. Others thought you were practicing lines. Are you in trouble? Were Lord Culver's attentions unwarranted?"

"Lady Worthing, are you concerned because you have an interest in His Grace? I hear he's a favorite, championing abolition. Many bored wives of peers seek him out."

"Yet, he's here, sneaking about you. Do you have his attention?"

She folded her arms about her like armor. I'd pushed her to battle.

"I'm sure some want titles like that of baroness. I'd rather have stability, my own fortune, my own way to control my destiny, independent of a man. In the end, most men abandon their responsibilities for something more pleasurable than their housekeeper with modiste bills."

And that would be checkmate.

Miss Barbara Banyan, great talent of the stage, had slaughtered me. James's title and a young lady's crush of feelings were enormous inducements. To accept his hand meant righting my family's finances, saving my father's Carrington and Ewan, and gaining my elevation.

Well, until the attack, I did keep a neat house. The tally for my tailored gowns was high.

"Lady Worthing, do you have any more questions? I'd like to change and ready for another of the magistrate's series of questions."

Half turning, with a fully frozen smile, I bolstered myself. "Just one. Do you think with Danielson's and now Hildebrand's deaths, the theater is doomed?"

"Don't know about Hildebrand, but Danielson and I were close friends. He was writing a play for me. It won't be finished. What I saw was good. It would've saved Drury Lane and brought me acclaim. I don't know what to do now. God, I wish I could honor him. He was pure."

The reformed swindler, with a wife and mistress, that gambled, pure? "I would still like to help. If you think of something to shed light on these incidents or if you need protection, find me. I'm on Greater Queen Street."

"Greater Queen Street?" Her brow wrinkled, more of the slight jealousy we'd exchanged. "That's a nice neighborhood."

Women needed to move beyond these feelings. We needed to lift each other up. "My invitation is open, Miss Banyan. I wish to help."

"Thank you, Lady—"

Men carrying a sheet-covered stretcher went past us. Barbara bowed her head to the fallen man, then went to her dressing room.

Duncan followed, then stopped in front of me with my reticule under his arm. He shook his head at me. "You can't resist investigating, can you?"

I swallowed and opened my mouth to confess. "Lord—"

"Tragedy." Sheridan wailed this over and over. He flew out of the crossover space and rushed at Duncan. "Someone is trying to ruin me, killing anyone who could save my theater. Duncan, help."

"This will be solved," the magistrate said. "The guilty will be punished."

"Hurry on with it." Sheridan trudged past us, scowling, cursing.

Stapleton came over and took his tailcoat. "Sorry for you to hear such, but grief looks different, even coarse."

Duncan juggled his hat and gloves with my reticule. "Find out what you can, Lady Worthing. These crimes are proving more difficult. Innocent people can be hurt."

With a quick glance at a red-faced Sheridan, I lifted my brow. "You're no longer concerned that my asking questions will trouble you?"

At this, Duncan offered a mirthless chuckle. "Mr. Henderson told me of the Duke of Culver's appearance. I think politicians will be consumed with much more than the likes of me or finding replacements for my position."

The wily smile on Duncan's face dimmed, and he followed his runners.

"Shall we go, madam?" Stapleton asked me.

I wanted to ask him why he'd disclosed the duke's appearance to the magistrate, but when he lifted his arm to escort me from Drury Lane, I felt compelled to comply, and refrained from questioning my friend as I clutched his forearm.

"Is this why you are so good with Teacup and the grey-hounds? Patient training?"

Offering a shrug, he said nothing and led me outside into the cool night air. It was dark. How many hours had passed?

We walked toward the mews. Then he stopped, looked over his shoulder. "Had to give Duncan something to distract him from the reticule. Culver was a good substitute. It calmed Sheridan's tirades. Neither will bother the duke or rush accusations upon anyone now. Duncan will wait for you to put together the clues that will lead to a true conviction."

"But Culver may not be guilty."

"Perhaps not, but it buys time. We need time. We can't be so careless, ever."

His admonishment was correct. I accepted that. The man I thought Stapleton Henderson was, a curmudgeon, was so different from who he actually seemed to be, a blessing.

"You probably have a big, obnoxious carriage that can't be hidden."

"It's spacious, Abigail. It will give you plenty of time to noodle over a new clue."

Clasping his crossed elbows, I jumped in front of him. "What? I got nothing from Miss Banyan. You took the paper from my reticule?"

"No. I wish I'd thought of that. One of the runners shared a list of people who were here the night Danielson died and again tonight. There's a new common name. Lucas Watson. Apparently, he's a petty thief and an old partner to Danielson. He had a confrontation with the playwright the night the fellow died."

"A confrontation? Was he angry enough to want his old partner dead?"

"Not sure. But one stupid enough, according to Sheridan, to supply Alexander Hildebrand with Dover's pills. That's an opium . . ."

"To ease pain, even that caused by dreams."

"You've heard of it."

I dipped my chin. I had.

Vaughn had procured some for my mother when her end was near. I thought back to Hildebrand's coughing, his seeming to be drunk, and having problems being lucid.

"So Hildebrand was dying, Stapleton?"

"Yes. But he wasn't going to die yet. Someone might've helped him. There were no marks on his hands except from the ropes. I can't help but think that someone could have tried to free him. The time taken to place your reticule at his feet seems to indicate there might have been a few minutes to save him. It might have made a difference."

That murky, sinking feeling that we were missing the obvious, that we were running out of time, consumed me.

I clung to Stapleton's steady arm, hoping we'd find our way.

Walking unnervingly along Russell Street toward the mews made my pulse race. I stopped and peered behind us. The streets were naked, devoid of another soul. Just us.

"So empty. You suppose word has already leaked?"

"It's odd, but for a big city, London's infamous for thrusting news into every nook and cranny instantly."

"Two murders in a week might be enough to dissuade revelers."

He tugged at his cravat, the wilted, limp thing. "Perhaps it's better we're alone on these streets. Two neighbors walking from Drury Lane into the heart of Covent Garden late at night could be the start of rumors."

"You're afraid of gossip, Mr. Henderson?"

Peering up at the cloudy sky, he said, "No. But your Mr. Vaughn is."

What?

My godfather had struck again.

My heart pounded at what he might have said to my neighbor. I stopped walking and pulled my hand from Stapleton's. "I apologize for anything he might've said or implied."

He laughed, then captured my nervous gaze. "'Twas nothing out of the ordinary. More of a question of my choice of theater boxes and a hint at something more." He licked his lips as his eyes darted beyond me. "You don't have a problem being near me, do you, Abigail?"

"I . . . ah. No."

"When the fence came down between our properties, I told you I wouldn't keep myself away. That includes Drury Lane."

His piercing indigo eyes held steady, but his classic unreadable expression was on full display.

There was tension between us, and I wasn't ignorant of the attraction, at least on his part.

But was he becoming more handsome and dear?

I'd admit none of that. But the sense of camaraderie, our shared knowledge of this investigation made me tolerate . . . look forward to engaging with him and learning his thoughts.

Glancing up, seeing why my maids gossiped about his comings and goings, I refused to admit he might be more handsome than James. Stapleton was definitely younger, no matter how much my neighbor was set in his ways.

Nonetheless, he was here. And my neighbor came from family with baggage. Mine did, too. And I think we both owned and dealt with those heavy portmanteaus.

That had to be the bond.

"I want no misunderstandings, Abigail. You say we are friendly. Is that true, or should I find some trivial thing to argue about?"

"No trivial pursuits. Nothing to find fault in. No wish to fight."

He looked straight ahead, as if he were waiting for lines in a script. "The late Hildebrand told me to claim what I wanted. I want you . . . to have no doubts in my admiration. I want the assurance that as I let down my guard, you'll do the same."

"Sounds like a big, dangerous ask."

"Oh." He pulled out a handkerchief and dabbed at his neck. His gaze shot to the full moon. Then he trudged ahead. "Well, your honesty and avoidance seem on par tonight."

My flippant response to ease the tension had done the opposite. Had I hurt him? I'd done nothing . . . but refuse to be honest. "What is it that you want, Stapleton? Does not my presence on your arm prove my comfort?"

My neighbor slowed his motion but still maintained his distance in front of me. "You said I was training you, as if a woman could be made to be a certain way by a lecture."

Lifting my skirt an inch, I sped up to him. "I'm sorry, Stapleton. We don't seem to get on for more than a few moments."

"Why do you seem flummoxed in private? Is it purposeful to be confusing? I fear you'll always keep me at a distance."

Though I'd admit being inexperienced in dealing with men, I wasn't stupid. I had to let Stapleton know I had no designs upon him. I didn't want more than friendship. No lover. That would be the opposite of peace.

"I stand beside you. We're not fighting. I'm not building a fence. That should be proof we can get along. You purposely kept Duncan from discovering the reticule to be mine. Is this not proof we've progressed?"

His head whipped over his shoulder. He stilled, then forged a slower path down the street. "Let's take this shortcut by Crown Court. It'll cut down our time getting to the mews."

"We can take time. It's a pretty night, as if stars have emerged to bid respect to London's late actor."

His chin craned up, then lowered, his gaze settling on me. "Shortcut. We have plenty of time to stare at the firmament in the safety of my carriage."

The solemn path didn't look any less safe than the main road through Covent Garden, a place known for its vices.

"You've taken my sister's confidence into your bosom," he said. "I'd rather you not hate me. That's all."

"I don't hate—"

A twig snapped along the cobbles. I startled and stumbled.

Henderson caught me and drew me closer, holding me tightly to his chest. His heart drummed, and so did mine.

"You must take care, Abigail." This whisper felt soft on my face. He continued to shelter me in his arms. "We need to pick up our pace, but I can't have you falling."

My hands felt small and weak in his. He hadn't let go.

I needed to be free before I remembered how nice it felt to be in a man's arms, ones that gave a damn about me.

Commander Stapleton Henderson did care.

Sticky, sweaty, I slipped free, pried off beige calf gloves, and stuffed them into my pocket. "We're not too far from Anderson's Eating House. It's on the corner of Clare and Drury. Let's stop in and send someone to the mews. My cousin and I dined there after a show when I felt someone following me. Last time it was you."

"Curiosity of two women in Scottish tweed got the better of me. Now I'm just wondering about you."

My heart raced.

It shouldn't.

Was he teasing? And if he was, what was this manner to accomplish? "Anderson's does have good Stilton cheese."

"Are you hungry, Ab-i-gail?" My name lingered on his lips, dangled in the creases of his generous mouth like an invitation.

Then Stapleton shoved me hard to the right, flinging me to the pavement.

I tumbled.

Flat on the ground, shoulder stinging, I saw a knife. Then it struck, and I was dragged.

Blinking, I grasped at my neck. I was unharmed, but Stapleton wasn't.

He took punch after punch from a blackguard.

This sighting was true.

My neighbor battled with a knife-wielding attacker.

Chapter 13

The cobbles beneath me felt cold and slick. How long I'd been helpless, I wasn't sure. But I lay on the street as my neighbor fought a fiend.

A pop to the jaw—the sound of the bloke's fist hitting bone—made me shudder. This man cloaked in black struck Stapleton in the face again and again.

"Get away, Abigail." My neighbor sounded like a ghost.

But I'd not take orders from a soon-to-be dead man, either. My visions had me convinced he or I would die if I left.

Even as the knife sliced his coat, Stapleton punched back. "Get away, Abigail. Now."

He'd been hit in the head if he thought I'd leave.

I crawled and grabbed a loose cobble.

"Go, Lady Worthing," Stapleton said. "Go!"

With a *thwack*, I hit the attacker between his shoulders. After getting the stone again, I hit him in the temple. Red washed his face.

Then my protector brought our fiend to his knees, but he still had a hold on my friend.

Stapleton's indigo eyes, ones I thought cruel, glazed over to perfect mirrors—black and powerful and deadly. He surged and kneed the assailant in the gut.

They flopped onto the cobbles and rolled, fighting.

The shiny metal appeared again. The blade caught the reflection of the stars along its ragged edge and brought them to the pulsing vein along Stapleton's neck.

After grabbing the cobble again, I smashed it against the fiend's skull.

This distraction gave Stapleton an advantage, and he flung away the knife. Then he knocked the man headfirst against the ground.

Crack, boom—the sound of a nose bouncing on the street was drowned in curses.

Stapleton had the assailant under control.

But those dark eyes wanted more than just subduing evil.

Wham. He drove his knee deep into the man's chest.

Bones crunched.

He lifted himself up from the man and stomped on him again and again.

After scrounging for the knife, I picked it up and handed it to Stapleton. "Here. Now you won't have to kill him. I suspect Mr. Watson may want to live."

Smiling, or more so sneering, he took the weapon. "No. No, I don't want that."

Stapleton dropped and, like in my dream, pushed the steel into our attacker's neck. "Tell me who sent you, and I'll make your death less painful."

I held myself back; I dared not stop him. I had to trust this was a jest, but I knew in my gut that Lieutenant Commander Stapleton Henderson had killed in the line of duty and would kill to protect himself and now me.

The man squirmed. From my cobbles and Stapleton's fists,

the man's face held bruises. A fine line of scarlet streamed down his throat.

Blue eyes wide as plates begged. "If you must kill me, tell me why you killed Danielson and are trying to set me up for the blame? I know you been comin' to see him here."

"I didn't kill him," Stapleton grunted, then cut a little along the man's neck. "Who sent you after us?"

More crimson flowed.

Into my stomach, nausea flooded.

My light head spun.

I thought I was used to such things, but I was actually used to seeing death, not dying. "Please, Mr. Henderson. Stop, please."

"Why, Lady Worthing? He'd have no mercy for us. Speak, Watson, while you can. Get right with your Maker."

"I'm Watson. Lucas Watson. Danielson was my friend. But you killed Danielson. Stabbed him with a spear through the heart like he was a pig. You go to hell."

"Time for you to join—"

With my palm on Stapleton's shoulder, I sought to calm him, to draw him back from the dark place into which he'd sunk. War and mortal combat, even instincts, controlled him. "You don't need to kill this one. Please."

Blinking, my brooding neighbor glared at the night sky, maybe even growled.

"You have him subdued. He . . . We see that you have everything under control. Let him live."

Breathing hard, like he was having a panic attack, Stapleton looked down at his stained hands.

Balled fists shoved to his sides, but with his boot staying on the man's chest, my neighbor rose. "The lady chose that you keep your life. I suggest you talk before I change her mind. Start with your true name."

The fellow gasped and then rubbed his chest. "I'm Watson.

Lucas Watson. Danielson was my friend and my business partner. You murdered the poor bastard, like you did Hildebrand. I heard you talking my name up to the magistrate. I'll not go down for this. Clever to stash that purse underneath him."

"You came at us." Stapleton pulled a cloth from his pocket and wiped the knife and his palms clean, then tossed the cloth to the man. "Hold this to your neck. A superficial wound can bleed a lot."

Of course, a skilled physician would know how to do such to scare someone without killing them.

I breathed a little easier . . . but that wound did look deep.

Stiffening, perhaps pretending he hadn't lost control, Stapleton shoved the knife to me.

I took the bloody thing. This was what I saw in my vision. The gold handle made my heart slow. It was done. The visions would be done. "Why do you think Danielson was murdered, Mr. Watson?"

"You mean if the physician didn't kill him? The past. One of our schemes. Yes, Danielson ran rackets in cards and forgeries. But I saw the doc snoopin' around when Danielson died. Then he talked to that fool Hildebrand, and he ended up dead. You're cozy with the magistrate. Sheridan would prefer the likes of me blamed to protect his precious theater."

Stapleton grimaced. Pretty sure he wanted to kick Watson again. "Hildebrand was alive in the old-scene store. Did you give him too many Dover's pills? Was he already dead when you hung him in the corridor?"

"No. I didn't kill him. I left when the crazy woman chased the duke down the tunnels."

Holding the knife loosely between my fingers, I wanted to toss it away. "The old-scene store is at least twenty paces from the corridor. Someone would've seen you or Mr. Henderson walking with Hildebrand or carrying a body that distance. You both couldn't have done it."

He pointed at Stapleton. "The doc would visit Danielson at Drury Lane. He was here the day before he died. You're more of the new rich friends he took up with. Your filthy money changed him."

"That's rubbish." Stapleton jerked like he'd stomp Watson into the cobbled street. "I visited to deliver notes from his wife."

Watson didn't seem disturbed or shocked by the news. He must know that his friend had wed Joanna Mathews.

I wanted to give Stapleton back the knife. It would be better in his hands, but he still seemed so angry. It was different seeing him so animated.

"Mr. Watson," I asked, "did you speak with Danielson before his demise?"

The fiend or friend kept patting at his neck. "I don't feel so well."

"Hold the cloth tighter against the cut." Stapleton backed away.

The fellow looked at the cloth, which was quite red, and cursed. "At the middle of the awful play, he was still alive. I think you set me to bleed out."

"That's the least you deserve for coming after us." Stapleton stooped, took a handkerchief and white evening gloves from his pocket, and held them to Watson's neck. "More pressure. This area will be incredibly sore for the next couple of days."

I believed in my neighbor. I wouldn't doubt him, even though I had a feeling this type of wound could be fatal. "You and Danielson were friends a long time?"

"From the streets. When his father didn't care nothin' about him, I was there for him. Taught him everythin'."

My neighbor rose again, but he resumed the same defensive, ready to attack if necessary pose with fists raised. "You sound quite angry, Watson. Are you sure you two were friends?"

"Why should I help you when you're trying to set the blame on me?"

"It'll go a long way toward keeping this attack upon us secret," I said as I moved closer to Watson. He wasn't dressed like a gentleman. The heavy jacket, nankeen shirt were what the sailors and dockworkers wore. "Who would the magistrate believe? Two people who help with his investigations or you? Someone who may have carried out schemes on the people Lord Duncan is sworn to protect."

Stapleton glanced at me. The tension in his arms was as if he wanted to wave me back. "Lady Worthing, take care."

"Should've run you both off when I had a chance," Watson growled. "Or struck this one better."

This foolhardy statement sent my neighbor spiraling. He hauled Watson up off the ground. "I should just kill you now. That would take care of my concerns permanently. I don't like loose ends."

"He's joking, Mr. Henderson. Mr. Watson, tell him you're joking," I said. "He sometimes lacks a sense of humor."

His feet kicked as my neighbor held him in the air. "Joking, Doc. Sorry."

Red spurted from the wound anew. My neighbor tossed him away.

"Here." Stapleton tore off his cravat. "Hold it tight to the wound. You will be in trouble if this isn't under control." His emotionless voice, monotone and deadly, made his words feel dark. I'd be afraid if I were Watson.

"Did you take the vowels from the room, Doc? You were in there with his body a long time when Danielson died."

Balling up the soiled handkerchief and gloves, Stapleton hissed, filling his chest. "That's why you came after us? Gambling debts?"

"Those marks were Danielson's win. He earned that money. It was going to set him up good. That new wife would be kept in the manner she was accustomed to. Then he'd repay me. That's what he said."

Was that what was on the paper missing from my reticule? "Who owed him money? Answer, Mr. Watson."

The man swore as he sat all the way up. "I think my rib is busted."

"It will grow strong." Stapleton's tone rang cold and unfeeling, controlled—he was back to the normal man I knew. He shifted his stance and stuck his stained hands into his coat pockets. "She asked you a question. And as I'm out of things to help stop you from bleeding out, I suggest you answer."

"Tell me the truth, Mr. Watson," I urged, "before my dear friend gets upset again."

Those dark eyes of Stapleton's glinted—dangerous, delightful mirrors bringing the stars and sky close enough to touch. I supposed he liked that I'd called him friend or dear or both.

"Danielson got one of you in your old game. Gambling with marked cards. That was our . . . my gambit. I taught him that." I noted how Watson's face changed. He seemed prideful, with his cheeks puffing; then his speech slowed, becoming wistful and sad. "Yes, I taught him everything. Poor bastard."

"Your friend moved on without you. He changed his life, and you haven't. That makes you angry, doesn't it?"

"Oh, no, you don't, miss." Watson waved his hand, but then returned it to all the cloth that was stopping him from bleeding. "Nah. Don't let this chit twist things." He staggered to his feet, looking like he'd swing at both of us.

Stapleton drew forward, but Watson retreated.

"I didn't kill him, but half the people at Drury Lane wanted him gone, even Sheridan. I heard him cursing at Danielson, trying to get out of the debt." Watson's eyes went big. I didn't think he meant to say that.

Before he slipped away, I stepped closer. "How much did he take Sheridan for?"

Watson took his hand and acted as if he was sealing his lips.

"Fine. I won't ask you about the debt. What about the Duke of Culver? How did he feel about sharing Miss Banyan with Danielson?"

"Ah. I don't know. But I don't think my friend wanted her, well, not for anything but a bed. He'd found his love in Mayfair. He wasn't going to get caught in something stupid. I even heard him telling her they were just to be friends."

This was getting more confusing. Had Danielson told Miss Banyan he'd married? Was the actress jealous enough to do Mr. Danielson harm? If the friend knew of the wife, wouldn't the actress?

"Miss Barbara has her own troubles. From the jealous old actor to greedy Sheridan to the politician who won't leave her be. Take your pick of them. Anthony Danielson wasn't one of them. Well, not after he'd reformed."

He edged to the side, his weight bearing down on his left foot, readying to flee.

A carriage rolled by. It looked like more of Duncan's runners. Who knew what disturbance they could be heading to?

I grabbed Stapleton's arm to keep him from waving them down. "We're having an enlightening conversation with Mr. Watson. No need for additional interruptions."

The fellow nodded, staring at me. He knew I'd done him a favor. He was better off with us, answering questions, than being interrogated by the magistrate's men.

Maybe we were saved from answering questions about that visible wound to Watson's neck. Yet in 1806 London, Stapleton's version of events, the words of a military officer, would be readily believed.

Once the runners could no longer be seen, Watson turned his back to us. "What do you two want, especially if you didn't want my friend or Hildebrand dead?"

"The truth, sir. That's all." I nodded at Stapleton and continued, "We must find out who did this. We can get justice for both men. And that doesn't require us to turn you over to Lord Duncan."

"And you owe us, Watson," Stapleton added. "Now be gone. Find me if you learn anything."

In a flash, Watson grabbed the knife, then ran off into the night.

"Abigail, you let him . . ." Stapleton wiped at his mouth. "Dangerous." He stopped and stared. "Are you hurt from my roughhousing? I didn't mean to . . . but the fool. The knife—"

"It's over." Brushing dirt from his sleeve, I rejoiced that we were unharmed and had overpowered and outmaneuvered Watson.

I was grateful for the loose cobbles of town streets. "You would've been justified in slicing through Watson's throat."

"But I didn't."

The control to refrain from killing had to be as strong as the desire for someone to survive.

With his palms to my shoulders, then to my neck, Stapleton assessed me for injuries. Slowly, he lifted my arm, and I howled.

"So sorry, Abigail. Nothing is broken, but you'll be sore."

"It's fine. I'm alive."

"I hurt you. You need to tell me when I do that." He wasn't merely talking about my shoulder.

"I'm jostled but unharmed. Next time, just say 'move'."

"Actions are easier than finding the right words."

The heat of his tone, the sweet vigor of his concern wrapped about my frayed nerves like gauze to a fresh wound, binding my fears—the vision of my dying and the newfound knowledge that Stapleton Henderson would've killed for me tonight.

"I see why Mr. Vaughn wants me and my cousin to knit rather than investigate."

"Let's get to the mews. This night feels long, Abigail."

"Yes, lead the way."

"No. Side by side."

Seizing a deep breath, he lifted his dusty coat sleeve. I clasped his arm, and we headed again along Drury Lane. Staying close to Stapleton until we reached his carriage, I thought of nothing. I became nothing surrounded by his scent of bergamot, cherry cigar, and blood.

Chapter 14

Suspects in Anthony Danielson's Murder
~~Alexander Hildebrand~~
Richard Sheridan
Barbara Banyan
Lanky Sailor – Lucas Watson
The Mathews
Unknown Sailor(s)
Martin Simpkins, Duke of Culver

After updating my suspects list, I prepared to ease my way downstairs to an early breakfast. My sky-blue carriage gown appointed with shiny brass buttons and a fabric-matching reticule, which would never leave my arm, seemed a good choice to wear for a busy afternoon on Fleet Street.

It wasn't perfect. I needed to remember that this was fine, too.

I clasped the banister; a finely carved pineapple tickled the soft curve of my palm. But even raising my elbow a little sent a tremor down my side. Three days had passed since Stapleton and I were attacked leaving Drury Lane, and my arm remained sore.

In the mirror at the top of the stairs, I saw a confident woman looking back, not a lady who could've been more seriously harmed or even had her reputation in tatters by being suspected of murder. It had taken several nights of hot tea, liniment, and reflection to forgive myself the potential chaos I had caused by being careless with my reticule.

From up here, I could look down at the cleaned carpets, the sparkling floors. My visions were done and once the glass in my parlor was replaced this nightmare would be over.

Except for catching the vandal—my arm and insides hurt anew.

"Lady Worthing." My housekeeper's cheery voice met me. "See, rising with the sun won't kill ya. Ya might even find it refreshing."

"I find it early, Mrs. Smith. But with a noon appointment to see Mr. Shaw, these things can't be helped."

"Oh." Her lips had pushed out, making her look like a startled duck. "Twice in one month you're headed into Carrington and Ewan? Couldn't believe it when ya told me last night. Ya think going early ya might not see your father? Ya cousin would tell ya the odds are low a second time."

"No, Florentina would tell me I had a fifty percent chance. Sort of like heads and tails when tossing a pence."

She stared at me from the side with her hooded lids. In this moment, I decided I'd leave all numerical explanations to my cousin.

"Mr. Shaw can't come here. It's a busy day for him. I'm grateful he can fit me into his schedule before he goes off to the races."

Pretending nothing was amiss, that my aches had been relieved in the heat of my bath, I slowly descended the stairs. My mind needed to be focused on the murder suspects. I had to hope money was the linking factor. Watson's disclosure about Sheridan's gambling debt could be the clue we needed.

Mr. Rogers met me in the hall with another large bouquet

in his hands. "This one is bigger than the flowers from yesterday."

Mrs. Smith stopped on her way to the kitchen and eyed the huge arrangement. "Mr. Henderson must still feel awful guilty making you vulnerable to the streets. Couldn't believe how ya dragged in here hurting. All black and blue."

"I take it those aren't from Mr. Vaughn?"

My butler shook his head. "The neighbor, like yesterday's daisies."

"He saved my life." I said this out loud. I wanted it to echo, so that nothing would stir rumors of there being anything more. "He's kind and has good taste in flowers. And I'm only a little bruised."

Shaking her head, Mrs. Smith traipsed down the hall, whistling like a Jamaican fairy of sunshine.

"And Mr. Henderson took the worst of it," I added. Well, Watson had probably been hurt more. Hoped he had staunched the bleeding.

"I'll put these in the drawing room, ma'am." Rogers left with the bouquet. I supposed my parlor was already full.

It was a sweet gesture from Stapleton, but unnecessary. Watson had been rendered harmless. But the attack had been dangerous, though I'd kept Stapleton from turning him in. We needed Watson to owe us.

Well, those were my thoughts now. Then, it was pure gut instincts. Something I was learning to be more assured about trusting.

A footman announced, "Miss Sewell."

Florentina came to me in a lovely chocolate bonnet and a matching carriage dress with ivory buttons.

"You look as if you are ready for a celebration. My dear Florentina, does this mean you have finished the calculations? Have you and Mrs. Edwards saved the king's navy again?"

She brought her arms together, as if to pray. "I think we are.

Final checks are being done, but I think we have performed our best."

"A good performance is all one can ask for."

Mrs. Smith came with a tray of cream and biscuits. "Ah, Miss Sewell has come to play, so ya don't have to dally so much with the neighbor. Good to see ya, miss."

"Thank you."

My cousin gripped my sore arm, and I hollered. She immediately released me. "You have five minutes to tell me what has occurred and how much you . . . we are in danger."

"Nothing more than usual." I hoped I sounded cheery. "And Stapleton Henderson might've . . . well, did protect me from a street thief."

Florentina stared through me, piercing me in the gut with the shock in her eyes.

I clasped her elbows. "I'm fine. Not very injured. Stapleton took the brunt of it."

She cocked her head to the side. "Stapleton is it? Abbie, tell me all that has occurred."

When in doubt about saying too much or too little, I decided to change the subject. "Let's have tea in the parlor."

She followed me down the hall.

"Then come with me to see Wilson. I believe numbers are at the heart of this mystery. You love numbers. You might be able to add up why two men have died."

Her footfalls stopped. "Two, Abbie? Two."

"A great deal can change in a short period of time."

After we stepped into my sunny parlor, my cousin headed straight to the urns of daisies and tea roses that decorated my mantel.

My gaze went to the curtains affixed to glassless windows. It felt so naked and vulnerable in here.

My cousin stroked a creamy petal, then turned an accusatory gaze on me. "I doubt these were sent by Lord Worthing."

"No." I took my seat and poured a generous cup of tea. Soft chamomile smelled lemony and calming. "Mr. Henderson felt I was rather shaken by the street attack. These are meant to express his anger at the situation. He took responsibility for it, as if it were his fault. It wasn't."

"But it is this mystery's fault. Your chasing a villain at Drury Lane has made you vulnerable. Well, more vulnerable."

"What am I to do, Flo? I can't help myself. I work with charities. I support the abolitionists as much as I can. But my heart is in puzzling out circumstance. Don't you understand this?"

I sipped from my cup and waited for her to take a seat or storm out of the room.

She crossed her arms, looked toward the flowery mantel, then to the open door to the hall. Then toward the curtain-covered holes, where my windows once sat.

It seemed to be taking forever for glass cutters to come fix this. Was glass for my house special or rare?

She moved and sat beside me on the sofa, which had been re-upholstered in a joyous straw color. "I like numbers, and you're drawn to crime. Maybe together we'll find an illegal game of Hazard."

Our chortles and crumbs grew, and we kept eating currant scones from the large platter freshly baked by my housekeeper.

"Ma'am." Mr. Rogers entered, smiling. He seemed so happy.

Grabbing a napkin, I wiped my mouth, then clapped my hands. "Has your daughter had her baby?"

"No, ma'am. Any day, though." He beamed. The man was a proud father and a soon-to-be loving grandfather. "But the workers are here to set the glass. I can move you and Miss Sewell to the drawing room to finish your visit undisturbed."

"No, Rogers. I want to see the restoration. I need to see this room made right."

He nodded, left, and returned with three men. They looked

like the salt of the earth type workers, like the men unloading the ships. They went about their tasks as if this was the thousandth time they had repaired such things.

Perhaps it was.

Windows were such a luxury, they were taxed.

Rogers stayed and even directed where these men laid their tools. All three of us stared as the workers put the rectangles in place, as they spread fresh glazing into the corners to secure the glass.

A couple of nails were tapped securing jambs and rails, reanchored mullions. In no time at all, it was done. I doubted anyone could tell the original windows from these new ones. Now if I could only forget the bits of shattered glass covering my favorite room like diamonds.

When all the men had left, Mrs. Smith entered with a fresh pot of tea. She stopped and stared at the windows that looked out onto my patio. "Ah, Lady Worthing. It's as good as new. Mr. Rogers has been championing this. I know his mind will now be at ease."

"It is a good job." Florentina stretched for a treat, but they were gone. "Has Lord Duncan mentioned any progress on finding out who did this?"

"He's been busy," I said. "Once the murders at Drury Lane are solved, I'm sure he'll have a suspect."

Mrs. Smith tsked her teeth, then set down the new refreshments. "He'll find him when this fiend strikes a different neighbor."

I understood what she implied, that a victim who wasn't me—meaning racial motives weren't a possible factor—would garner more attention. As things stood, Lord Duncan could dismiss this as someone thinking I needed to be set down for marrying outside my race. I might be a target because of the progress the abolition movement had made in Parliament. A dozen other reasons which all led back to hate.

Yet the way my house was vandalized, I couldn't dissuade him. It was hate to do this—but hate for me, James . . . I didn't know.

"Ma'am, Mr. Rogers won't ask, but he needs to go see about his daughter, you know, with the new baby coming and all. He's quite nervous."

"Tell him to take the rest of the day or even the week off. Caring for family is important."

The warmth in Mrs. Smith's wonderful face felt good. "I'll tell him." She dipped her head as she gave a small curtsy and left the parlor.

"This room will be warm again. The fresh paint will happen next week. It will be a lively yellow. I feel safe," I said.

Gingerly easing her palm about mine, Florentina replied, "I'm glad. This is your home, Abbie. You've respected how Worthing kept it, but use this as an opportunity to make it more of your own."

"Who doesn't love decorating?"

My question didn't take the sting from her eyes, take away her concern about me. I'd lost bits of myself by trying to be James's wife.

I went on. "I like yellow. Perhaps a brighter shade, but all I did was refresh and reupholster in the same styles in the two years I've lived here. I hate that an attack spurred me to action. Perhaps, I'll find something other than dead-salmon pink for the drawing room."

"Abbie, we need to find out who did this, so they won't do it again. Then you can become fully comfortable and own this space."

This was a nightmare, but with the windows fixed, it had to feel more distant, more away from me. "One thing at a time, Florentina. Lord Duncan . . . Well, Vaughn is looking into this. I trust that one or the other of these well-connected men will find the culprit. The guilty will be brought to justice."

"I hope you are right, Abbie."

Happy barking sounded.

"Teacup? Flo, you think he sees the new glass?"

We went to the new windows, and I spied my doggie and the greyhounds accompanying Stapleton and Mrs. Danielson on a walk.

I waved at them. "They must be heading to Saint James's Park."

"You think he gives her flowers, too? The widow and widower make a handsome couple."

The tone in Florentina's voice irritated me. I pushed away that feeling and allowed my heart to be joyful that my neighbor had come out to inspect the new glass.

He tipped his hat. Then he and his party, my dog included, began to move. From the appearance of things, it seemed my new friend was as invested as Vaughn and Florentina in my safety.

"Come along, Flo. We have to go see the man with the numbers. I hope they add up to murder."

"Please, Abbie." She shook her head at me. "No math jokes. At least not for a while. I heard them enough when the admiral came to collect the data from my employer."

"You got to be in the room where the calculations were reviewed?"

She beamed. "Mrs. Edwards took a risk. I was in the back, observing the admirals, as my brave employer discussed the numbers."

Hugging her, embracing her joy, I wanted to enjoy a moment of progress. "Let's celebrate after meeting with Shaw. For now, let's be on our way."

With a final glance at the neighbors and the dogs, I knew it was time for me to get cracking. Before I met with Mrs. Danielson and, in a quiet room, asked her my final questions about her husband's murder, I had to be sure. Stapleton wouldn't take kindly to me questioning the innocence of his dear friend.

*   *   *

Humming a tune, some blessed hymn, Rawlins handed Florentina down from my carriage. He'd expertly guided us from Westminster to Fleet Street. When he helped me down, his grin seemed larger than any I'd witnessed.

It was infectious.

I needed that kind of contagion as I headed into my father's firm.

"What is it, sir? What's causing this glee?"

"It's in the post this morning. It's happening, ma'am."

With my hands ensconced in cream-colored kid gloves, I crossed my fingers and delayed entering Carrington and Ewan, Proprietors. "Tell me."

"Yes, Mr. Rawlins," Florentina said, almost holding her breath. "Please say."

After almost doing a little dance, the tall man stopped and straightened in his crimson mantle. "The best vote counters think it's going to happen. It'll be tight. Every lord will be needed to cast their affirmative vote, but Parliament will pass a transport bill. The first since Haiti's independence. The world is beginning to be made right again."

So wrapped up in mysteries, I'd forgotten that Britain, the country of my birth, a place that made it possible for my mother to marry a Carrington, for me to be a citizen and now a baroness, still had the capacity to do just things. I put hands to my cheeks to contain my grinning.

Florentina straightened her bonnet, a lovely chocolate brown one that made her wetting eyes and warm skin look rich. She clapped her hands. "It's going to happen. Mama talks of her hopes for Jamaica. It could help so many if Britain does this for the colonies."

"And it hasn't taken years," Mr. Rawlins said, "as the naysayers and even I thought."

This was good news. Locking arms with my cousin to keep

from frolicking, I wanted to dance. Here on busy Fleet Street, it wasn't appropriate to do a jig. "Haiti doesn't have to rule for a thousand years before realizing free Blacks being political and governing is not a threat."

"Lady Worthing, Miss Sewell, this is the beginning of a whole new world." He shut the door and climbed to his perch. "That Duke of Culver has made the hypocrites writhe. That young man will get it done. The old duke must be turning over in his grave, or more so roasting in hell."

My heart went into my throat. It wedged there so fully, I couldn't speak. Culver was awful. Unless some mistake had happened, I'd seen him sneaking about Drury Lane, threatening Miss Banyan. He wasn't heroic.

Now it felt wrong to celebrate something he led.

"Lady Worthing, shall I return for you in an hour?"

I managed to nod, then wave. My pulse still hammered. A duke who threatened women was at the heart of the politics of good.

"Abbie, come on," Florentina said. "We have to discover what tidbits our gossiping solicitor has found."

"Yes." It was all I could manage.

Then I prayed the news Wilson Shaw would share about the money connections to Drury Lane didn't expose the abolitionists' newest star as a brutal killer.

Chapter 15

Suspects in Anthony Danielson's Murder
Alexander Hildebrand
Richard Sheridan
Barbara Banyan
Lanky Sailor
The Mathews
Unknown Sailor(s)
Martin Simpkins, Duke of Culver
Joanna Mathews Danielson

In the lobby of Carrington and Ewan, we waited for our appointment with Wilson Shaw. Florentina moved about the front area, glancing at my mother's artwork as if she'd never seen it.

"Aunt Magdalena loved watercolors and grassy pastures. I remember her painting in the summer."

"Yes. In Bath and the close coasts. She always loved the sea."

My cousin touched one of the rosettes that formed the corner of a gilded frame. "It's so lovely. I hadn't remembered that there were so many paintings."

It had been a long time since Florentina had visited Carrington and Ewan. When my mother abandoned my father, the family left behind had had to choose who was right or whom they wished to be in the right. The Sewells, Vaughn's half brother and my mother's sister, had sided with Magdalena. My half sister Dinah had chosen our father. I had tried to be the peacemaker, loving every flawed person.

That had ended up pleasing no one.

Pity only Florentina, Wilson, and Vaughn, to some extent, had offered the same grace when I made choices that others didn't like.

Wilson, the man of the hour, swept past Florentina at exactly two minutes to noon with a red-haired beauty fastened to his arm like a bracelet. This woman, dressed in burgundy and wearing an exquisite hat of egret feathers, laughed at his whispered jokes.

"Next month, madam," he said, as if addressing a crowd or his fellow solicitors in the firm. "I'll have a list of properties for you to invest in or, shall I say, use your late husband's funds to acquire. You'll not be disappointed."

"And supper, Mr. Shaw? Will you disappoint me again?" The woman's invitation to mix business and pleasure couldn't be hidden by her waving fan.

"You're too kind." His face turned sad with a deep frown. "But my work is infinite. Another time. I want to do my best for you, and that can't be when my mind is on so many other things."

"No, Mr. Shaw. You should concentrate. I feel well taken care of at this firm. I'm glad they have assigned you to be my solicitor. I love being in your hands."

He kissed her gloved fingers and sent her to her awaiting carriage.

The door closed with the softest thud.

Wilson released a long breath.

Then he turned, with a humored look on his face. "The things I do for Carrington and Ewan," he laughed. "And I love it."

The flamboyant man bowed before standing tall and straightening his bronze-green waistcoat, which hung smartly over buff breeches. "Come this way, ladies."

Not quite a dandy, but Wilson's intellect matched with his charm was a potent combination.

Florentina rolled her eyes at his over-the-top act. "Must you always play the buffoon?"

"Everyone loves the stage, Miss Sewell. Don't you act like a mute servant when the navy men visit Mrs. Edwards?"

She bit her lip and looked down. "I was in the room this time. Next time I may get to say something."

He lifted her chin with such care. "Hey, pretty lady, I'm not faulting you. We all do what we must to survive in our roles."

She offered him a small smile, and I gazed over them to look for a light or signs of life at the end of the hall. My father's office seemed dark. I supposed this was the good version of the odds.

Wilson made Florentina laugh about something. He defanged her claws when it came to unserious things. Yet this was his gift, a definitive part of his performance.

He was fit and fine and full of himself—the makings of an easy flirt. It was one of the things we loved about him, and this power enabled him to slip into all kinds of places and social situations where we Blackamoors weren't easily allowed or wanted.

"Wilson," Florentina said, "you don't have to be the wittiest man in the room to secure invitations."

Sequestered in his office with the door closed, he allowed his expression to change from mirth to simmering sadness. "Then everyone, clients included, would be concerned with my pedigree, tailor, or skin. I don't share my tailor with anyone. The other things cannot be helped and shouldn't be discussed."

This dance that Wilson had perfected had restored the reputation of Carrington and Ewan and kept its coffers filled with commissions.

He held two chairs for us. When we took our seats, he moved to the other side of his desk. The sadness had faded. His gaze sharpened on the paper on his desk. "I think I've found the information you want. But I don't know if I should give it to you. It's somewhat disturbing."

That sounded bad. And if Wilson didn't want to say something, it had to be awful. The man prided himself on getting useful information about people's finances, things he could leverage for the firm and that he used to draw more clients.

"Money is the root of all evil and often the cause for murder. Just tell us, sir. We are prepared," I said.

"Ladies, I don't know. Sometimes it's better to let the magistrate figure things out on his own."

That didn't sound like the brash Wilson Shaw.

"Don't you relish confounding people in authority?" Brow lifting, eyes shifting, I tried to see if a name was written on one of these piles of papers, but then I returned my gaze to the man with the answers. "We've been friends for a long time. Give me the good, the bad, and the horrid. Let me make up my mind on things."

Florentina folded her arms and sat back. "If Wilson Shaw doesn't think we should know, then the information must be terrible. He is a lot of things—puffed up and so on. But I trust his judgment when it comes to information."

"Why, Miss Sewell, that almost sounds like a compliment. What will a fellow do?"

"You will spill, Wilson." Tugging off my gloves, I shook my head. "Things won't get any better by you being silent. The truth is freeing. Two men have died. Attacks . . . have been threatened. It's too late to keep secrets."

Stopping myself from admitting what had happened to Stapleton and me, not wanting Wilson or Florentina to second-guess my advice to let Watson go or cause greater worries about my safety, I made silly hand motions, as if I could draw the facts from the solicitor.

Wilson shuffled papers on his desk and then proceeded to uncover a financial ledger. He flipped a few pages and then stopped. "Well, if you insist. We'll start with the easy, then go to difficult."

I waited, and he added another dramatic pause. "Please," I said, "don't keep us in suspense, sir."

"Your victim, Anthony Danielson, was the third son of an aristocrat. He had a falling-out with his father, the Earl of Montz, and was turned out on the streets." Wilson rubbed at his chest as if something burned inside. "Is this the only thing these men with titles do?"

Flo asked, "Wilson, are you well?"

"Quite." He adjusted his cravat. "Just hate cruel rich people." He became quiet, staring at his notes as if they were written in another language.

"Sir." I tapped the desk. "How did Danielson survive?"

My friend didn't respond, not for a long time. Finally, he said, "The fellow got on with the wrong element. I found links to a man named Lucas Watson. Petty crimes and scandals involving threats, bribes to keep quiet."

Florentina, who seemed enamored by the fretwork along the legs of Wilson's desk, fingered it and asked, "Any convictions?"

"No. All I have is rumors from other clients or potential clients who've been defrauded. The lady leaving here, her husband was one. Watson knew the limits to victimize his marks. No charges were ever made for Danielson, either. Seems being a peer's son does have its advantages."

His gaze cut above me. It radiated with unspoken things — anger, pain, maybe even regret.

"If doing these searches for me is costing too much, Wilson—your peace, your dignity—you don't have to . . ."

"No." He shook his head hard. It would fall off if not so well attached. "I do benefit. It gave me a new client. For that I'm grateful. I also take pleasure in thinking my small act will keep you and the mathematician from getting in trouble."

One glance at Florentina's nodding chin showed she agreed. "Thank you and continue your briefing."

After turning another page in his ledger, Wilson creased the corner. "That didn't belong there. Now let's talk of Drury Lane and the suspects."

His actions made me curious, but I had enough mystery to solve. "I'm hoping you have information on Danielson, Sheridan, Miss Banyan, and now the late Hildebrand."

Florentina shifted in her seat. "Late, as in never being on time again?"

"Yes. Yesterday. Hanging."

She gasped.

Wilson took out a cloth and dabbed at his mouth. "Well, let's start with the recently departed. Nothing. Not even a lease of something. I suspect he was living . . . Well, he was living at the theater."

That sounded as if the fussy Sheridan was being charitable.

"Any relations?" I asked.

"If he married, I found no proof. Was rumored to be involved with a fellow actress, Paulette Falls. She disappeared from the theater for years. Last she surfaced, she, her husband, and a daughter lived in Surrey."

That sounded normal. A dead end.

"What of Miss Banyan? She didn't seem to like Mr. Hildebrand."

"Barbara Banyan, or Lady Barker, is an interesting character with plenty of secrets. A baroness like you. Widowed and finding her way in the theater."

"That's heroic, Wilson. Not what I expected."

"No one is what you expect. It's the theater. And Lady Barker is also from Surrey."

How curious. "Let me guess. Lord Barker left her with debts. That is why she is working as an actress."

"No. Quite the opposite. She doesn't have to do a day of labor. The woman has chosen to keep her path and money a secret. Wonder if she needs a solicitor."

"That's not helpful." I drummed my fingers along the blotter, this time closer to his stacks. "What of the Duke of Culver? Have you heard of their names being linked?"

"No. But I'm told the old duke had high debts. The new Culver is trying to clear these debts, keep his lands, and promote abolition. Busy man."

"You don't think him sincere."

"His father owned plantations in Jamaica. That paid for his education and their Mayfair home. No, he's not sincere. I think his fight is convenient. The gentleman wants to be a star, even if he's as broke as a church mouse."

Florentina had leaned forward. Her palm was as if she readied to count debts. "Mayfair? Then there has to be money."

"Not as much as you'd think. A poorly run abomination yields no fruit. And the man, as a viscount, was on the outs with the old duke for courting what his father considered the help. I'm checking, but there seems to be odd provisions and entailments on what money there is."

"Do we have the names of these unsuitable women?" Florentina said in a syrupy voice. "Was one an actress from Surrey?"

"No." Wilson smiled brighter than the sun. "One is staying with Lady Worthing's neighbor. The former Joanna Mathews. Everyone's shocked she wed someone other than Culver."

I thought I'd never been as stunned by news Wilson had uncovered. "But she claims to have been so in love with Danielson."

"Ladies, love is a splendid thing. It covers many a sin. It can also be confusing and as toxic as poison."

The conversation with the widow took on new priority. Perhaps it wasn't money at the root of this mystery, after all.

My cousin shook her head. "Well, at least we know his push for abolition is true."

"Do we, Miss Sewell?" Wilson picked at his perfect waistcoat, as if a thread had suddenly pilled. "People do a lot of things in the dark they never want seen in the light. With his ascension so soon after Mrs. Danielson's elopement, we'll never know if he had the stones to marry her. Timing is everything."

I sat back, tapping my nose, staring again at the calm watercolor. "The Mathews, her guardians, are prominent. Were they at odds with Culver and their ward's attachment?"

"A duke is rarefied air," Wilson said. "Most will bow and scrape to have access. Her marriage to Culver would solve his liquidity issues. She'd come with a lot of money. Her marriage to Danielson cut her off from the Mayfair gold."

Florentina glanced at me; her eyes dared me to say it. But I opened my hand to coax her. "You say it."

"She obviously had waited too long for the duke to come up to scratch. Yet none of this matters. She's a widow. There could still be a marriage once her mourning is over."

That wasn't what I was thinking, but it was true.

"The Mathews are interesting people," Wilson said. "They'd enjoy Mrs. Danielson becoming a duchess, after all. But they are no one to cross. Just rumors, but people imply they believe in an eye for an eye in business. Be careful with them, Abigail, by extension the Hendersons. Your neighbor's late father and the Mathews are linked to philanthropy and controlling the ports. It's an incredible blend of blessings and strong-arming. Don't get twisted."

"You and Florentina are overprotective. Stapleton Henderson is a documented veteran, a war hero. I think he's quite safe . . . Now we know he didn't kill his wife."

It was a comfort to know the man next door wasn't a murderer. And yet I understood he'd use his strength to keep me safe.

"Please tell us about Mr. Sheridan," I said.

"Now the worst news. You probably know that Drury Lane is in trouble, but you don't know Richard Sheridan is heavily in debt, as well. Your happy place may close. Sorry. I know how you love it."

"A world without Drury Lane." I shook my head. "No. Can it be saved?"

"Word is Sheridan was attempting to take loans out on everything to pay a large debt last Friday. No one was willing to lend to him. Then suddenly, he no longer was in a rush for the money."

"Because Danielson died before the markers could be called." I clapped my hands. "Timing is everything."

"My gambling buddies said the debt was for half of Drury Lane. I think the Mathews may not have had rarefied air in their former son-in-law, but one with the potential to make a fortune from hot air spoken to thousands in a theater was not a bad position."

"There you go, Flo. A second reason to marry a reformed man, a potential fortune. Wilson, if the vowels are in possession of his wife, is the debt still viable?"

He sat back in his chair. Whenever he either delayed saying something bad or stalled, he thumbed his chin. After a moment, he leaned forward. "A gentleman would honor it. Sheridan is a member of Parliament but is also a heavy gambler and a heavy womanizer. Weigh that against Mr. Danielson and his old partner, a Mr. Watson's, criminal past."

The ever-dramatic Wilson fingered something in his notes. "Mr. Lucas Watson is known for cheating at the table. But if

Mrs. Danielson had the IOUs totaling around twenty thousand pounds, I'd press on her behalf to make Sheridan pay or give her half of Drury Lane."

"Half?" Florentina did imaginary calculations in the air. "The theater should be worth more than that. The income continuing to pour in—"

"From a brilliant new play would stabilize a Drury free of debts," I interrupted. Danielson's play, the pages scattered about the old-scene store. Where were they? Who had them? They could be as important as the vowels.

Florentina shook her head. "Giving up half of Drury Lane is insane, Mr. Shaw. It doesn't add up."

He smirked as he looked at my cousin. "I do love how your mathematical mind calculates, Miss Sewell. But I comprehend simpler things, like a braggard, a fool, and his money, plain old-fashioned stupidity. Never gamble what you can't afford to lose."

His eyes gleamed when he said this. Wilson Shaw's access to meaningful gossip was pure fire.

"Are you implying Sheridan killed Danielson to keep from paying or from having to give him half the theater?" Florentina scowled. "You enjoy being the smartest man in the room."

"Oh, come now, my number lover. Never the smartest. That's Abigail. But being in the know, that's a safe place to breathe."

She scowled and counted sums. "You, fretting about safety, such a hedonistic thought."

" 'Happy the man, whose wish and care a few paternal acres bound, content to breathe his native air, in his own ground.' That's Alexander," Wilson replied.

"Pope, his 'Ode on Solitude,' " Florentina said, with eyes as big as my newly installed glass windows. "I didn't think you fond of poetry."

"Or capable of reading, Miss Sewell. I'm capable of finer thought and dwelling on things that bring meaning to life."

"Before you two battle with dead poets, can we focus again on the life and death of Alexander Hildebrand? He was murdered and my reticule was found under the body."

Wilson leapt up and waggled a finger at me. "Abigail Carrington Monroe, you can't be so careless as to leave your bag. Do you want to be implicated in murder?"

"No, and I didn't do it on purpose. So many things were happening. But someone moved it from the old-scene store and put it under the dangling body."

Wilson put his back to us. "Lady Worthing, this is not fun and games. That's a warning. Someone doesn't want you solving these murders. Give the magistrate your thoughts and let's be done with this before you are a target."

"I'm already targeted." I made him turn and look at me. "Wilson, I am. You both know that."

"Abigail, I'm sorry." His voice was low.

The pity stirred me to say my new truth. "I wasn't looking for trouble. I was trying to solve my domestic situation. I was working to be a wife." Tears choked my throat, but I swallowed them whole. "My husband didn't come. I don't know if he ever will, at least not anytime soon. But trouble is here whether he's by my side or not."

My cousin covered her mouth.

Wilson turned and offered me a handkerchief from his drawer. "I keep a ready supply for all my clients. It's emotional in here, sorting through what's left after the husband's gone."

The door opened, and in came John Carrington.

My father, the man I'd barely said two words to after my wedding, stood at the threshold. High brow and nose lifted as he glanced at me, then at my cousin and Wilson. "Helping another destitute widow, Mr. Shaw?"

"No, sir. Your daughter's happily married, and your niece is happy, as always, with her numbers."

Shoving the cloth into my pocket, I glanced at my father, his slacked cravat, the stain from his favorite pea soup on his lapel. "Good to see you, Papa."

"Squidgy. I didn't mean anything of it. I just saw you crying. And, well, Shaw here is good with widows."

The horrible nickname I'd earned in my childhood from having a whistle-like sound, a lisp when I spoke. It took years of concentration and practice to be rid of it. My embarrassment still lived in my father's memories as something endearing. It was just another way of making me feel like a disappointment, far from perfect.

"You do look good," my father noted. He offered a quick lift of his lips, the anemic smile he saved for clients, then went away.

Seconds later, I heard his office door slam.

How long I stared out at the empty hall, I wasn't sure.

How long my cousin and Wilson remained silent was also a blur.

When Wilson pushed another fresh handkerchief from his pile into my palm, I knew quite some time had passed.

In front of the two people who knew me best, I didn't voice a response or dare to sob aloud. I merely let tears roll down my cheeks until Rawlins returned with the carriage.

Chapter 16

Rawlins took the long way from Fleet Street back to Westminster, taking Blackfriars Bridge.

Florentina clasped my hand as if I'd escape and leap into the Thames. Nothing but the best swimmer could defeat the river, that is, if they survived the jump.

Sitting back, listening to the yellow bounder, its wheels clacking against the cobbled surface, I stared out at the water and the beauty of the huge elliptical arches that supported the bridge over the Thames. "The bridge is made of the finest Portland stone, Florentina."

"That's strong, Abbie."

"I suppose the architects and builders meant it to last forever, like a father's love."

"Uncle Carrington will come around."

"When? When this London bridge comes falling down? I think not."

Florentina drew her hands to her lips, as if that would soften or dampen what she said next. "You need cheese. Something creamy, with a tang. I asked Rawlins to stop at Olive's." That meant we'd cross Westminster Bridge, the most efficient route. "Or we can go back to Fleet Street, and you can talk to your father."

"And say what to him? Should I tell him I'm sorry again for wanting to save the family's fortunes? You can't possibly think he was right."

"James Monroe asked you to marry him. He asked you to be his baroness, knowing you had no dowry, and he paid off the Carringtons' debts. My uncle gets to be respectable. If your sister had stayed, she would be respectable."

We held hands, and I looked in her eyes. "I'm a respected wife of a peer. How does that make me the villain?"

She shrugged and then scooped me into her arms. "Abbie, I don't know what to say. You made your decision, but my uncle has a right to his opinion."

"Florentina, you said I was doing the right thing. Were you just saying that to save my feelings? Do you believe like my father?"

Her embrace tightened. "I think you did the best you could do. Without the baron's money, you'd not be in a good match. Carrington and Ewan would be shuttered. Who knows where the angry Wilson Shaw would be?"

"He's resourceful. But he could've been in the streets, using his brains to pull schemes, just like Mr. Danielson before the man met his wife and reformed."

With a pat on my back, she released me. "That's why I told Mrs. Danielson she had a unique opportunity to make a match with a respectable man. If she'd waited, she might even be a duchess. Can you imagine? Someone like us a duchess."

That was the heart of this mystery, the one about Drury Lane. What would one do for respectability? Everyone had different answers, and perhaps would even be willing to die for their beliefs.

The carriage turned onto Margaret, the street before Olive's.

"We should walk to Parliament," I said. "We should see if we can gain an audience with the Duke of Culver. He's the only one I haven't spoken to."

"Abbie! The duke is a bit busy. Remember abolition."

Wanting to punch the seat, I let my frustration build. Yet I sat back and simmered. Too much today had caused my tears. "I know. I know that."

I took a breath and glared out the window, hoping for the words to express what I thought. There was nothing but the truth. "He might be saving the world with needed legislation, but does that excuse his personal flaws? He could be a murderer. I saw him at Drury Lane, threatening Barbara Banyan. Him being there, of all places, has to be pivotal to the mystery."

"And for Joanna Mathews . . . for his former love to have married the first man killed is too much of a coincidence." Florentina had spoken the truth.

"The duke might be the murderer."

She again put her hand to her lips, and I swiveled my stiff, tired neck from side to side.

"Abbie, tell Lord Duncan your suspicions. You can't go after Culver. He's too powerful. You think life is crazy now? If you chase after a politician who is being called a saint by everyone, you must have undeniable proof, not gossip, not innuendo, and definitely not a vision, which you yourself said is faulty."

"Second sight has nothing to do with this. Culver was at the theater. He knew about the tunnels. Danielson married the woman he loved."

She dipped her head. "You *suspect*, not *know*. You will do what you want, but you can't go after a man like the duke unless you have ironclad evidence."

My cousin, the mathematician, was a hundred percent correct. A baroness with a scandalous lineage couldn't make trouble for one of the ton's select few, one of its dukes.

I blew out a breath and surrendered. "Florentina, we're

going to have a nice meal. Hopefully, Olive's will have the best Stilton today."

"A nice claret, too. That will go well with good cheese."

I wished tasty food made all the bad go away, or at least released me of this feeling that if the Duke of Culver wasn't guilty, he knew exactly who was.

Florentina and I walked into Olive's. Revelers crowded the dizzying place. I had had Rogers arrange with the staff to always have a table ready for me. It was sort of like having my own box, but at the theater of Olive's.

Jacob, the waiter who always served us, an adorable redhaired young man, knew my face, my name. "This way, Lady Worthing. Busy day today."

Most tables were filled. A few men stood around with ale tankards.

"Oh," Jacob said. "Your table's not clean. Wait here."

We allowed him to proceed and stayed close to our usual spot. Gazing at the assembled patrons, I saw many peers of Parliament. It wasn't quite five. Had they broken from debate early?

Whatever the situation, these men were festive, eating Olive's fare and drinking, drinking a lot. Clearly, one could hear hearty belly laughs, a few obscenities, many lusty jokes.

For a moment, I couldn't breathe.

It was as if my mind was trying to sweep through the eye of a needle. My face became flushed. I was running again. Things were shifting, moving about me.

The knife appeared, shiny gold handle. Lucas Watson's. It came toward me. The moon again glowed on the blade.

"Lady Worthing? Your table is ready." The squeaky voice was Jacob's.

When I could focus, I felt Florentina's hands on mine, drawing me from my terror. I shook. I couldn't stop.

My cousin attempted to guide me to our table, but I was stuck waiting for that knife to cut at my neck.

A dark voice, familiar and foreboding, called my name.

Stapleton Henderson stepped in front of me. Like he'd done in the streets about Drury Lane, he lifted his hand. "Take it, Abigail."

His whisper broke the hold the nightmare had on me. Yet it took everything for me to clasp his arm. When I did, his warm palm covered my icy fingers. He hurried me to the table.

Against the hard seat, I collapsed.

I heard the small talk he and Florentina had about the weather.

"Lady Worthing," Stapleton said. Did his head turn to see if anyone stared? "Had I known you would be stopping in here today, I could've driven you and Miss Sewell. It's the neighborly thing to do."

My lips parted. I wanted to say this was a last-minute decision, but fear had my tongue glued in place.

Florentina wove her fingers about mine. "She just needs some tea. Hot tea makes everything better."

"And biscuits." My whisper was small. I felt embarrassed and nauseous. "Something with ginger."

"Yes, Lady Worthing. Something sweet for her stomach. I believe the baroness likes treats."

"I'm not Teacup. Please stop with the feigned niceties. I'm no longer fragile."

"Perhaps I am," Stapleton replied. "You've seen me on numerous occasions not at my best. Is it wrong for a friend to help?"

He was helping, wasn't he?

"Sorry."

After a few blinks, I peered up. Stapleton's indigo eyes and Florentina's gray-brown ones bore down on me.

"What did you see, Lady Worthing?" My neighbor shifted in his seat, as if the fate of the world would change because of what my foolish mind had conjured.

"I keep seeing the night we . . . had the confrontation with Mr. Watson. The shiny knife. I wish you still had it in your possession."

He nodded as Florentina hissed, "Abbie, you said you were attacked and saved by Mr. Henderson, but mentioned nothing about a knife? You were almost killed, weren't you?"

"Flo, it was nothing. A petty thief who came after us."

"Don't Flo me. Petty thief with a knife sounds serious."

Stapleton chuckled. "Lucas Watson took the worst of it. Seems Lady Worthing is good with cobble-throwing. And I'm well, too. Thank you for asking."

My cousin's mouth opened and snapped shut and opened again. "Sorry, sir. I'm just so shocked. My manners . . ."

He glanced at my cousin with a less than thoughtful expression. "Yes, Mrs. Danielson said that your manners are sometimes lacking."

"Like her judgment." Florentina sipped at her claret Jacob delivered.

Our server also brought bread and a large chunk of Stilton.

"What about her judgment, Miss Sewell? Do speak up," Stapleton said.

Even as I tried to stare at my cousin and hoped for once she'd say less, I knew she'd be herself. That was a testament to her bravery.

"I've consulted Lady Worthing on the matter, and I'd love to hear a man, one born of privilege and responsibilities, tell me how someone can be so swept away in emotion they lose reason and marry someone substantially beneath them."

Stapleton crumbled a bit of Stilton and added it to a slice of the fresh bread. "It happens."

"What of duty?" Florentina shrugged. "I do owe Mrs. Danielson a note of apology. I said what I thought, but I needed to refrain from inflicting my opinions on a stranger."

That wasn't as bad as I thought it could go. Stapleton and Florentina were getting along.

When Jacob brought the ginger biscuits, I liberally helped myself.

Florentina's harping began to make more sense.

And Mrs. Danielson's decision, less.

Why would a woman of her background be taken in by a schemer, even if said schemer had suddenly changed his life?

Clapping sounded all around us.

Looking to the door, I may have seen the reason, the Duke of Culver. He and Wilberforce had entered Olive's. I'd been given the opportunity to be as brash as Florentina. I simply needed to find a way to outwit the celebrated man. It wouldn't be easy to get him to confess to why he'd killed Danielson. Was he jealous of the man for marrying the duke's love, or was it to stop being blackmailed over His Grace's antics with an actress?

Or worse, could he have been sent by a woman who wanted to be a widow, in order to later become his duchess?

Chapter 17

Suspects in Anthony Danielson's Murder
~~Alexander Hildebrand~~
Richard Sheridan
Barbara Banyan
Lanky Sailor – Lucas Watson
The Mathews
~~Unknown Sailor(s)~~
Martin Simpkins, Duke of Culver
Joanna Mathews Danielson

Our waiter brought another cut of Stilton, more port, and a new pile of ginger biscuits as I updated my suspects list in my mind. Like the smell of victory the buttery cookies were fragrant and delicious. Not as fine as Mrs. Smith's, but beggars couldn't be choosy.

I needed something sweet for my souring stomach. Watching Culver get patted on the back and bask in Wilberforce's admiration felt wrong, stomach-churning wrong.

"Abigail, you look upset. You're crushing your biscuit."

"Sorry, Florentina." I put down the treat and wiped my fingers on my handkerchief. "But I saw Culver manhandling Miss Banyan."

"I saw him leave, not the roughhousing," Stapleton commented. "Hildebrand fell on my feet. As I helped the old man, you and Culver tore off down the tunnels."

"His hands were about her neck." Craning my head to gaze at the ceiling, I sighed. "At least you did see it was the duke. I don't have to doubt myself on that."

"I believe you," Stapleton said, "but we need more proof."

His simple words resonated. How did one get evidence when the actress didn't seem willing to confess to the duke's misdeeds?

Florentina glanced at the commotion, at the men chanting and celebrating. "They seem confident. Didn't Mr. Rawlins say the votes were still close?"

I nodded. "He did. And that every peer needed to vote."

My crazed visions probably might not make me the most reliable witness. Could I be convicting a man by mistake? Culver was crusading for right.

"Lady Worthing, are you going to keep stuffing biscuits in your mouth?"

I was, and I offered Stapleton a smile full of crumbs.

Florentina laughed, but then her attention drifted to the revelers.

I glanced at my neighbor while I chewed and savored the spicy ginger of the biscuit. "How are the Mathews? Have they seen Mrs. Danielson?"

My neighbor's eyes darted. His relaxed posture became tense. "She won't see them. They may be sorry for her loss, but that doesn't repair the pain they inflicted in rejecting her husband."

That sounded like the advice Florentina had shared in the carriage. "I suppose they hoped she'd fallen in love with someone else, like a viscount now elevated to a duke."

He put a hand to his mouth. "You're good, Lady Worthing, at digging into people's pasts."

"I have friends, Mr. Henderson. They help. They also tell the truth."

He picked up his glass and poured a little of the port. Swirling it, letting the candlelight reflect upon the sloshing ruby wave, he answered, "It has to be my truth to tell. Joanna's heart is not my business."

"What is it you two are whispering about?" Florentina interjected. "That Culver and Mrs. Danielson were in love? We just found that out. Why are you two talking in code?"

It did sound as if we possessed state secrets. Lowering my head into my hand, I laughed.

Then Stapleton did, too.

"Well, at least you're not fighting," Florentina said. "Perhaps it's time for you two to divulge what the other knows. That might lead to us figuring out who the killer is and stopping him."

"She's right, Mr. Henderson. Let's have a moment of complete honesty."

"What does that entail, Abigail?" he asked.

The way he said my given name this time was as if we were alone. Not only did he wish for me to respond to his overtures of friendship, but he also wanted my cousin to hear.

Blatant, manipulative, but oddly sweet, his wanting an acknowledgment of our changed status, but I should remind him this closeness came from us merely being neighbors. Or his invading my theater, the dog truce, or the fact that I adored his sister.

But wasn't I done lying to myself?

I kept my gaze on him. "I ask a question, and you answer it as quickly and as directly as possible. Then I'll do the same. We reciprocate."

He took a sip from his glass. "Agreed. Begin."

"What do you know of Culver and Mrs. Danielson?"

"They seemed to be courting. It was intense. Rumors of an engagement went about for years. It was an utter shock she ended up with Danielson. When they eloped, I tried to catch them in Scotland, but it was too late. I brought them back to Greater Queen Street to give them time to fix things with her guardians."

"And the Mathews?"

He waggled a finger at me. "That would be two questions, Abigail. You've forgotten my turn."

"Go ahead. Ask."

"Do you know the amount of the debt that Sheridan amassed?"

"I heard it's close to twenty thousand pounds. It was to be paid last week, or he'd forfeit half of Drury Lane."

Eyes getting big, he looked down, broke a biscuit in half, then in half again. "That's a lot of money."

"My turn. Would the Mathews forgive Mrs. Danielson if she became the half owner of Drury Lane or the owner of a celebrated play and the twenty thousand pounds?"

"Clever." Florentina crumbled some of our favorite cheese onto a slice of the fresh bread. "Three questions in one."

"Drury Lane is prestigious, but they couldn't care less about any play. They made threats to Mr. Danielson, the playwright, when an attachment was suspected. You can imagine they had higher ambitions for Joanna than a reformed thief. This young woman is highly talented on the piano. She has the voice of a goddess. She speaks four languages. Paints. Too accomplished for who she wed."

I hadn't sensed it before, Stapleton's disappointment in what Mrs. Danielson did. Nonetheless, he stuck by her. The man possessed great loyalty to those he cared about. Could that be what this mystery was truly about?

Stapleton lifted his glass and drank fast. "Fine. Now my—"

"What we know is very much on the surface and might be unrelated. The angry actress without the strength to impale a man. The dying actor hung. The—"

"Everyone, take heart." Culver stood on a chair, making a speech for his supporters. "We are on the side of right."

"Lady Worthing? Abigail."

Stapleton's voice pulled me away from the theatrics. "Sorry. Gloating or speechmaking only yards away."

He sat back, with one hand clasping a buttonhole of his midnight-blue waistcoat. "It's understandable. And it's difficult to know the debate hinges on Culver."

For Stapleton to say that, did he know more about the man? He probably did but couldn't say. It wasn't his truth.

"You should truly just say what you know." I motioned to Jacob for the bill. "When you're serious about puzzling things out . . . you know where I live."

"Abigail, stay." Stapleton ran a hand through his hair. "Let's look at other clues. Have you added to your assessment a man with a scandalous background possibly tricking Sheridan into the debt?"

"It's gossip unless we can find the actual vowels or we gain a confession from Sheridan."

Florentina put down her glass and offered a soulful gape. "Hildebrand's tale sounds sad . . . being alone."

"But he might've witnessed Danielson's murder," Stapleton said. "He was always hiding in the shelves in the old-scene store."

With his intense eyes beaming down at me, brighter than the candles and the sconces over our table, he dipped his chin. "We should check the letters I retrieved from Drury Lane from Danielson for his wife."

Culver stepped down from the chair, but the crowd stayed with him. "Gentlemen, we must never lose sight of our humanity. We must cleanse our soul."

Florentina dusted her fingertips of toasted bits. "Does one gain this zeal all of a sudden upon ascension to being a duke? I mean, we've been helping the movement for years. We've never heard his name."

Stapleton's gaze went from me to above my head. "Well, this devil has hold of the movement."

I stared at the foul woman-handling duke. "I hate that things are so tenuous that no vote can be missed."

Culver's voice, boastful and loud, rang like church bells. "Follow me. Don't be fearful in doing what's right. Our reward both here and beyond is worth it."

People clapped and cheered the duke, as if he was the Second Coming of the late prime minister Pitt.

The hard expression that my neighbor formerly saved for me came over his face. Then I realized Stapleton hadn't been completely honest.

He knew the duke on a personal basis, so much so that his voice raised the man's disdain.

"How could you?" I said.

"How could I what?"

"Just when I think I can trust you, I realize you've been lying."

"Excuse me?"

"Lying, omitting. Same thing."

"Not the same thing."

"You've seen Culver and Mrs. Danielson together. You have an opinion. By definition, the opinion is yours."

"Yes, I did. But everyone has a past. I saw no bearing—"

"I chased after the duke."

"Of your own foolhardy design."

"You could've said something about him or his nature during your lecture at the Thames."

"Abigail, I was more concerned with your safety. Then we found another murder victim. All this while helping a friend bury the man she loved."

"You're assuming she loved Danielson."

"Do take care." His grousing tone had returned. "She's like a sister."

"What if this sister was using a nice, reformed fellow to get out of a bad situation? I saw Culver with his hands about Miss Banyan. What if marrying Danielson helped her escape the poison of a philandering duke?"

"Speech!"

"Speech!"

The crowd drowned out Stapleton's reply.

Culver again popped up on a chair. "Now that Lord Sidmouth has arrived, I can announce the slave transport bill has advanced to a second reading."

Lord Sidmouth nodded and raised his glass as he stood near the wall. Tall Lord Ellenborough and Lord Lauderdale, each also good at making speeches, clapped.

Lord Lauderdale motioned to Sidmouth. "Go on, Siddy. Don't let him steal all the thunder."

"We are almost there," Lord Sidmouth said. "But even as it passes, the fight is not over. We must keep at the good work no matter how hard."

Sotted fellows shouted the peers down with a barrage of boos.

"Why? Why change things?" one yelled.

Culver waved and hushed the crowd. "Vote our conscience. Convince every old man that his sins must end. That what is right is freedom. Burn down all things wrong. London . . . the world is wrong on enslavement."

He turned in our direction. His gaze soared, then fell upon us like a feather. "The world is full of sinners," he said. "Of good people stuck in the old ways. Of people who make mistakes in the heat of the moment. It's time to forget the past and move forward in unity. Our time is now."

The clapping erupted like thunder.

Like my favorite actor, this man took a bow and came down from the chair.

Burning in my seat, I had to leave. I knew the duke was

guilty. His rhetoric merely replaced a full-throated confession. He had killed Danielson and had just said it was a mistake. And I could prove nothing.

Lord Lauderdale, Lord Sidmouth, and even Lord Ellenborough sat at a table across from ours at Olive's. Culver was on the other side, chatting with table after table.

I stewed, seated with Stapleton and Florentina.

"Abigail," she said, "you're turning red. Breathe."

"These peers who've been slow to act are being led by a charlatan," I said. "Why celebrate this?"

"Abigail," Stapleton sighed. "Not everyone has the courage to act alone. It's why I admire Joanna's courage. She knew the trouble it would bring to elope but did so, anyway. That's brave."

As much as I wanted to agree, the sour noise of Lord Lauderdale's pitchy voice and Wilberforce's confident tones as they congratulated Culver's leadership made me ill.

Before I became overwhelmed by nausea, I rose and started in their direction.

Stapleton stepped into my path. "No, Lady Worthing. While you are every inch as bold as one of the king's soldiers, this is too much. I think you ladies should be going. We don't need a scene tonight. Nothing to draw attention to you."

He tugged the reticule, which was up to my forearm. "You've been targeted. We can't afford mistakes."

My neighbor was right, but that didn't stop the gall swirling inside me. "Sir, I'm not the one who's guilty."

I turned to let my cousin pass from the table and found myself eye to eye with the Duke of Culver. His gaze swept over me, chilling my limbs on a warm summer evening.

"In some ways, aren't we all guilty, Lady Worthing?" he said. "Though my father's vast resources didn't originate from the plantations or habitations of the West Indies, I'd be negligent not to acknowledge my mother's family built fortunes in Aruba and Jamaica. Money they used to control people, places, and relations was built on sin."

Culver folded his arms and stepped closer. "Many of the old families invest funds into firms like Carrington and Ewan. Does one consider the interest tainted?"

"I'm not one for calculating interest." I said this softly while cutting my gaze at Florentina. No math. Only I needed to battle with the snake.

"Then what do we do?" he asked. "How do we all gain absolution for our sins?"

It hadn't struck me until this moment that this man knew my name, my family, knew my father's business. I swallowed hard.

Stapleton slipped between us and used his height to force the duke to step back. "I'll send our waiter for your carriage," he told me.

I nodded. "Yes, Mr. Henderson. Do so. You can return with us."

The duke coughed, as if he'd taken issue with my party ignoring him. "You both live in Westminster. Such a lovely district. One wonders about the sourcing of funds, and even the crimes committed by kings and queens, to get us to the open society that Britain is now."

"Open in some regards. But whether enslaved in a cane field or appearing in the Old Bailey among peers," I replied, "someone always pays."

Culver's gaze narrowed. "True, but some sacrifices can't be helped. If they stand in the way of the greater good, they must be cut down."

Stapleton took a half step toward the duke. "Too much has been lost to fools venturing where they needn't go. One could say they tried, stuck around, and found out."

Dark silver-blue eyes darted. "Always a pleasure to see you, Commander Henderson."

Not smiling or looking any less brooding, Stapleton folded his arm across his onyx tailcoat, the black mourning band about his sleeve. "Keep making good speeches, Your Grace. But leave the sacrifices to the bishops."

"Well, I welcome every peer who may have guilty hands to vote with me. And every gentleman should persuade his friends and patrons to vote. Together, we can end enslavement. Excuse me."

Florentina dipped her chin, but neither I nor Stapleton did.

One shared glance told me Stapleton, too, thought Culver guilty, yet we had no proof.

The duke went back to his party as if nothing had happened.

That was exactly what he wanted.

When I spun around to take Florentina's hand, Stapleton's blank face again met mine. Then I realized his countenance wasn't so emotionless.

He seethed.

Stapleton didn't just want the duke charged for murder. He wanted revenge. How did one do that? Without solid evidence, we'd have to leave Culver alone, knowing the man who battled to end enslavement fought with dirty hands, hands stained with Danielson's blood.

Chapter 18

My cousin looked out the window of the yellow bounder as we headed away from Westminster. "Abigail, the evening is long. You told Mr. Henderson that we'd retire. Doesn't that require we head to your home on Greater Queen Street?"

"We dropped my neighbor there but now we have to make one stop."

Florentina flopped backward, as if all the air had drained from her lungs. "Must we go seek more danger tonight? And why didn't we take Mr. Henderson? He could offer protection."

"No, Flo. This won't take long."

"I think we should go read in your parlor and admire your windows."

"This cannot wait. I need to protect someone. It's all about the motive for why the Duke of Culver murdered Anthony Danielson."

"Abigail Carrington Monroe, are you sure? The celebrated duke seems to have his hands full. You know, saving the world, fighting for the cause, which puts us at risk. Shouldn't that be encouraged?"

"I'm sure the duke is guilty. I merely need to figure out why. Did he kill for jealousy over losing Joanna Mathews, the present widow Danielson? Or did he do it because of his affair with Miss Banyan, to keep the news from spreading to the press? It would be a distraction from his serious fight in Parliament."

"How is it a scandal when unmarried men have relationships with women all the time? Having a mistress is a leisurely pursuit for gentlemen. Culver has the influence to keep the scandalmongers at bay. Remember Uncle Vaughn used his influence to keep Aunt Magdalena's name and your father's out of the broadsheets."

His actions had protected my godfather's name, too. It was meant to keep my and my sister's futures untarnished. Looking up at the smooth creamy ceiling of my carriage, I wondered aloud. "Did keeping the truth of my mother's leaving save anyone? The knowledge may or may not have kept Worthing from marrying me. The gossip would've kept any eligible suitors away from Dinah. Yet I know she wouldn't have wed to save our fortunes. Then she'd have found another reason to run than my becoming a baroness."

Florentina rubbed at her brow, then pushed her chocolate bonnet back into place, high on her dark chignon. "All I'm saying is that a duke having an affair with an actress wouldn't actually disparage him."

The rules for men and women were so different. "Culver threatened Miss Banyan. Maybe Anthony Danielson slipped back into his old ways, blackmailing the duke to protect his friend, and the duke decided to eliminate the threat."

Florentina bit her lip and shrugged. "So you think it is a crime not of passion but of punishment. To contain the scandal, the duke had to eliminate Danielson. But then that means—"

"That means Miss Banyan would be the next target. She's flamboyant and sympathetic. She could cause the duke problems. The papers would love to use her to discredit Culver and, in so doing, kill the abolition movement."

"But, Abbie, you proving him guilty of murder will do the same."

I couldn't look at her and admit what my thoughts were, how I was about to surrender the honesty Stapleton claimed was my foundation.

Florentina clasped my hand to her heart. "Say it, Abbie. I'm with you for better or for worse."

That was a marriage vow. "If we let one guilty man go free, we may gain legions of people their freedom. Won't that help me to live with myself?"

She drew her arm about me. "Let's go save a woman who is in danger. That has to be the right thing, that and ending enslavement."

I listened to my cousin breathe. Then I relearned to breathe as I accepted that the only thing I could do was save lives— Miss Banyan's and those of the enslaved oceans away.

Scenery being painted backstage at Drury Lane scented the air with a tart smell. Florentina held her nose, but my house had smelled of this and bleach for many days since I'd returned from Bath so I was unbothered.

Not as many actors or sailors were about.

Standing close to Miss Banyan's dressing room, I spied Watson. Navigating around scene boards, my cousin and I went to him.

"Mr. Watson."

"Who've you come to harass, Lady Worthing?"

Heart beating a little fast, I stepped beside him. His face held bruises, but I couldn't tell if this was from my stone or Stapleton's fists. Chanting to myself that he'd not attack us in the theater, I said, "I see you got things contained."

He glared at me. "Well, no runners have come for me, so I guess you did what you said."

"Are you here painting? Getting things ready for the next performance?" I asked. "That will be next week. I believe I heard Mr. Sheridan will reopen Drury Lane then."

Barbara Banyan popped out of her dressing room, and the open door blocked me and Florentina.

"This looks like his hand, Lucas," she said. Sounds of paper being slapped into a palm made me want to peek at what was happening.

"Just make this one. Like the others," he told her.

The door closed.

She hadn't seen us, and Watson looked dead at me, as if I knew what had occurred.

He stuffed the pages into his coat, a thick, short greatcoat as if to brace London's chill from the river. The man turned to leave.

It was now or never to get my questions answered. "I hear your friend truly changed his life."

Watson stopped. He seemed to be heading to the tunnels. Then he turned back to us. "Anthony Danielson was a rogue and a fool and a brother. He understood me. And though I thought he was leaving me behind, I think I get how he tried to protect us, get us a new life. He said he wasn't going to forget about me."

"Then why are you helping people erase him?"

His head tilted. "What are you talking about?"

"The play he wrote. That would have brought him fame and fortune. It's gone. Don't you remember coming here and spying him writing it?"

"Yeah. I saw him working so hard on it. It became his obsession. I came down here, thinking he forgot about me. Don't think he had, but he loved that play and that woman more."

After getting close to Watson, I held out my hand. "Then why are you helping people steal his work?"

The petty crook started laughing. "No one's stealing his work. You know you really had me. I thought you were on to something."

I covered my mouth. "I'm so embarrassed. Come along, Miss Sewell. I don't need to take up this man's time when it's so obvious I am mistaken."

Trying to sidestep him, I did a Hildebrand epic stumble. I fell toward Watson and caught his coat, causing the pages to fall.

The stack fell floating about the floor in the same way the foolscap had been strewn around Danielson's desk.

"Oh, I'm sorry. Let me help you pick this up." Before he could object, I gathered a page here and there.

The longhand on the paper was familiar, but the words, the lines weren't from the play Danielson had written. This page, with its words and numbers embedded in the weave, resembled the paper that was taken from my reticule.

Florentina finished scooping up the pages. We handed them to him.

"Sorry, Mr. Watson," I said. "It just feels as if someone is trying to steal your friend's legacy. Don't help Miss Banyan steal what Danielson worked so hard to accomplish. You loved Danielson as a brother. Remember that. It's not worth making quick money."

"Easy for you to say, with your expensive clothes and fancy blue reticules."

"My reticule is here. It's emerald green."

His face sobered. He clutched the papers and ran.

* * *

Deciding it was unsafe to traipse after Watson, I turned and almost knocked on Miss Banyan's door.

My fist was inches away when Mr. Sheridan ventured toward us. "Lady Worthing. To what do I owe the pleasure? Please don't tell me someone else is dead."

"I'm sure there is some part of Britain where a soul has departed, but I've seen nothing here today."

He gripped at his chest and blew out a breath. "Good. I want to reopen next week. I don't need any other problems."

"She's not looking to cause any, sir."

His gaze traveled up and down my cousin's hips. "Who is this?"

"She is a human abacus. I bring her with me when I need calculations made," I answered.

"Didn't think women were good for that." He folded his arms over his potbelly, pulling his coat lapels forward. "What you need that for?"

With Florentina's eyes widening, I hatched a plan to test what Wilson had said. "Sir, I have it on good authority that you may be looking for investors. I hear a great sum of money may be due shortly and that you may be in need of assistance. As a great lover of the theater, I would never want anything to happen to Drury Lane."

The amusement in his countenance disappeared. "What is it that you are proposing, Lady Worthing?"

"I'll propose later if the rumors are true. You, sir, can help me make an intelligent decision."

His mouth drooped, like he'd stuffed it with cheese. "Is that a lot of fancy talk to determine if you wish to invest?"

"Lord Worthing left me in control of his considerable portfolio. I'm to look at things with reliable returns."

This was true. Wilson had invested the pocket change and

other allowances, as well as all of James's money. I could make sizable investments.

He thumbed his lips. "Putting on a theater is expensive."

"Even more if you gamble away the receipts." Florentina's tone was not subtle. "There are rumors about that, too."

With his face turning beet red, Sheridan nodded. "Gentlemen of leisure do take wagers. We live by cards, ladies. Sometimes fortune is with us. Sometimes it is not."

He stared at us for a long moment. "You're sly, Lady Worthing. You must be representing Mrs. Danielson's interests. Tell her that time is not up. She must understand that Drury Lane closing is out of respect for the great Hildebrand. I'll have the funds to pay the vowels her husband extended to me."

He walked away, humming to himself.

And I turned to Florentina, who had a bemused look on her lips. "He's the first to acknowledge your neighbor's friend as Mrs. Danielson."

I held my gloved hands up and even clasped my cousin. "And he thinks we're in league together. How interesting. What would make him think that you and I and Danielson's wife had something in common?"

Florentina started to laugh.

Before I could join her, Miss Banyan charged toward us. "Wife? Anthony had a wife? No. That's a lie. He was writing his play for me." With her face turning scarlet, she seemed angry.

"Can you show us this play, Miss Banyan?" I asked.

"Why?"

"I know you've been rehearsing it in your dressing room. I believe you have been acting scenes from it. When Sheridan left the play in the old-scene store, you gathered the pages, both stacks. Both as in the pile on the desk and the one flung about the old-scene store when someone was looking for something as Mr. Danielson bled to death."

Tears began to fall. "Stop it. Must you be so cruel? Anthony and I were close."

"Of course, because you understood his playwriting soul."

"Do you know how hard it is for an actress looking for her big part? And it never matters what you've done in the past or who your parents were or their acting talent. You have to make it every single time. So, yes, Anthony Danielson was drafting a play that would make me a legend. I could be as good as Alexander Hildebrand." She was visibly upset, even shaking.

I dug into my reticule for a handkerchief, one with no initials or identifying marks. I'd learned my lesson. "Here. I didn't mean to upset you. I can see how it is easy to do so when we learn unexpected things."

Florentina crossed her arms and squinted at the actress. "How could you be so close to Mr. Danielson and not know he was newly married?"

The waterworks lessened. She gaped at Florentina. "I have a lot of admirers. They lie about wives all the time. But Anthony was special. He only wanted to be my friend. He knew how hard it was to sustain this type of career. I think his mother was once an actress, before she married his father. He was trying to do something special for me. He cared that much."

Florentina stepped to the side of us. Her gaze looked toward the crossover space. "You were in love with Mr. Danielson. And when you saw he couldn't love you back, you decided to be his friend. That's why you are crying. You didn't have the chance to tell him. Or maybe you did, and you didn't have the chance to win his love."

My cousin didn't sound as if she was acting. This story of unrequited love sounded true.

Tears drizzled down Miss Banyan's face. "I think we met at

the wrong time." Her shaky voice, quivering hand made me believe her.

"Anthony was a gentle soul," she said. "He was trying to fix things he'd done in his past. He was trying to be a good man. I didn't care much about his yesterdays. We all have them."

"I didn't . . . we . . . Miss Sewell and I didn't come here to upset you. We came to warn you. I saw the Duke of Culver in your dressing room."

"Men come at me all the time, all the time. But only Anthony was special. He only wanted me to smile. I understood his alienation from his father and yet his wanting to be someone who that man would respect."

The temperature backstage felt twenty degrees higher. My chest felt full. "Wanting a father's love—"

"No." Swatting at her face, she shook her head. "None of that matters. If Anthony Danielson had a wife, I feel sorry for her. But we shared his heart." There was defiance in her tone amidst the weeping.

"I know this is difficult, but I want the play," I told her. "It should go to his wife."

Miss Banyan swallowed hard. She went into her dressing room and then returned with a handful of foolscap. "There are a few pages missing, but she will see it's brilliant. It would've been marvelous to perform this at Drury Lane. I would've been Anthony's perfect Jasmine."

Though she said she was giving us the play, the papers were clutched in her hands, held tightly against her chest.

"Please, Miss Banyan," I said as gently as I could.

She gave them to me.

"Thank you. And I do suggest that you take care. I believe Culver is vicious. You have to stay safe. How will you ever get to perform this work for your friend?"

Sobbing now, Miss Banyan dashed off to her dressing room.

"Well, you've done what you came to do," Florentina announced.

Had I?

I wasn't sure anymore. Neither was I so sure of Culver's guilt as I was before.

"We need to leave and get this play to its rightful owner as soon as possible."

"You have that look, Abbie. Did you find your motive?"

Flipping through the pages, looking at the clever lines, the expressive handwriting with extra curly loops, I felt I needed to start all over.

"No, Flo. I don't have an answer, but I suspect there is one person who does. My dear cousin, you were right all along. Why would a woman of privilege marry a man that only recently reformed, one that had told only Mr. Sheridan of her existence?"

Clutching the pages, I towed Florentina out of Drury Lane and into my carriage.

"Where to now, Lady Worthing?"

"Eleven Greater Queen Street, Rawlins. We have something for the neighbor, but after we drop off Miss Sewell."

He closed the door and got the carriage speeding along.

"Abbie, I want to come."

"No, Flo. She already knows you disapprove. I believe I need to see her alone. Let her think I'm sympathetic."

She crossed her arms. "I hope you know what you are doing. That Watson guy looked scary. Mr. Sheridan isn't a threat. He's merely looking for more time."

"At least we have confirmation from Sheridan the vowels are true. I wonder where those are."

"Well, if Mrs. Danielson carried a reticule, it would be in there. It would have to be someplace secure."

"Exactly, Florentina. You are a genius."

She sat back, smiling, not realizing I had two people to question, not just Mrs. Danielson but also my new friend Stapleton Henderson.

Solving this mystery would prove to me several things about whether I could trust my instincts.

And, after all that had been said and done between us, I'd know if my neighbor was someone I should trust.

Chapter 19

The weather had turned bad, rainy and foggy, by the time Rawlins drove onto Greater Queen Street. I changed my mind about going over to my neighbor's tonight. I'd save the questioning and potential disappointments for tomorrow.

It had been a long day. Dashing into Two Greater Queen Street, I was soaked. After pulling off a dripping bonnet and gloves, I hurried to my stairs.

Miss Bellows was there with a blanket. "Here you go, ma'am. The sky opened up and hasn't relented."

My maid looked red in the face.

"Are you well?"

She hugged herself, then turned as the loudest sneeze left her. "Got caught at the market, ma'am."

"Go to bed at once. I'll have Mrs. Smith bring you tea."

"She can't, ma'am. She went with Mr. Rogers. The baby's due."

Oh. My heart rejoiced he'd be with his daughter during this special time. "Then I'll get you tea. Go on to bed."

Miss Bellows sneezed again. "Are you sure, Lady Worthing?"

"Quite. I need you healthy. My mother believed in warm blankets and mustard plasters and lots of chamomile tea."

"I don't like mustard. It is so smelly."

Well, I wouldn't know where the ingredients for a good plaster would be in this house. Nevertheless, I waved my maid up the stairs. "Go on to your room. Get in bed. And after I change into dry things, I'll bring you tea with lemon and lots of honey."

"You are too kind." Miss Bellows trudged up the steps, coughing.

If that persisted, I'd have to figure out where the mustard was or I'd have to send a footman to fetch it.

Thunder crackled in the distance. I moved quickly to my room to change and warm myself. I had no time to be ill. A killer or killers were still at large. If the storm cleared before it became too late, I'd go next door. Once I talked with the widow and the widower, I'd have the guilty sorted correctly.

A few minutes before ten, the weather changed from a heavy downpour to a trickle. Upstairs in the servants' quarters, I made sure the fireplace in Miss Bellows's room blazed. The dear woman's complaints of being cold and her sneezes subsided once she had drunk her tea. When my maid remembered where Mr. Rogers kept the key to the private reserves of brandy, an ounce or two of the fine liquor in her hot beverage teased her spirits. When I was sure she'd sleep off her chill and the brandy, I ventured downstairs.

The house was always quiet, but the weather and the lack of people made it feel isolated, even eerie.

Teacup nipped at my heels. I stooped, ran a finger along his cold nose, then scooped him up. "Guess I'm never alone if I'm with you. Right, boy?"

He put kisses to my chin, and I carried him to the parlor. Mr. Danielson's play sat on the table next to the sofa. The title, A Daughter's Love, didn't make me curious. After seeing my papa this week, I wasn't sure I'd fare well reading someone else's heartache.

Once I released Teacup, I climbed onto the sofa and wrapped my mama's blanket of quilted patches about me.

Sitting, staring at the play's beautiful penmanship, I touched the pages. "Not afraid of paper." I flipped through several, then I sank into the world the words created.

When I finished, my wetting gaze went to the window glass. The rain had stopped. Stars peeking from ribboned clouds dripped shine like candles dropping wax.

I couldn't believe Danielson's words affected me. I'd smear charcoal on this side to bring out more letters, more of his curly hand, but I'd not destroy this, this masterpiece. "It would've done well, sir."

I'd tip my glass to him if I had a goblet or some of the sweet claret from Olive's.

Barking softly, Teacup charged toward the new glass pane, a low one he often pressed his nose against.

Halfway there, he sat and whined. My doggie seemed hesitant to go any farther.

Perhaps he had headed toward the window, hoping to find comfort, to enjoy the nice, soothing feel of cold glass on his wet nose, but then he feared he would discover netting and nothingness.

"Go on, boy. Trust your . . . instincts."

Then I realized my terrier was me—hesitant to trust something new, finding it almost impossible to try again once proven wrong or betrayed.

"How about we both go at it again tomorrow? You and I." I'd hear out Stapleton and hope I was wrong, that he'd not withheld a clue from me. The omission, as he'd call it, might be one of the reasons a man had died.

Glancing at the pages, I realized that the theme of *A Daughter's Love* was haunting. In order not to become like the lead, Jasmine, whose quest for significance and joy was never manifested, I'd need to unlearn old habits and retrain my thoughts.

From my parlor windows, I saw the glowing lights in Stapleton's office. This was a sign to go have a chat and complete the puzzle in my head of who killed Anthony Danielson and Alexander Hildebrand.

With my lantern lit and Teacup at my heels, I pulled on a long sarcenet pelisse. The thick burgundy coat may have been too warm, but London storms typically ushered in strong winds.

Opening the door, I braced for the night. A chill definitely filled the air. A distant bell of Saint Margaret's chimed.

The darkness seemed thick, like pitch. It wasn't far to the neighbor's house. We shared a yard.

Yet the way my heart pounded at the sounds of an owl hooting or even a bush shaking its leaves, my body seemed ready to shatter as if I were miles from safety.

"Nonsense," I chided myself. I even swung my lantern liberally to pretend I wasn't afraid.

Teacup must have thought my actions were a new game. He scampered about and chased the moving light. His happy moments, the way his little furry body scurried along the wet grass, calmed my spirit. When he stopped and wriggled his little bottom as he shook water off his coat, the metaphorical rope binding my chest loosened.

Halfway to the rear of Eleven Greater Queen Street, I heard a noise. It sounded low, like a thud, ten feet or more away.

Lifting the lantern, trying to cast its brightness on whatever was there, I saw nothing but puddles and fallen leaves.

Reminding myself of good things, such as easy, playful pups, not the bad—the surprise attack on the streets or the killings at Drury Lane or the marring of my poor house—I traipsed a little faster.

Something large shifted.

The corner of my gaze caught it. But the low fog, which kissed dew on my cheeks, obscured everything.

Movement. Heavier and faster than before.

Run back. The warning rang in my skull, but fear gripped my boots.

Teacup growled.

Something was there, coming closer.

"Show yourself."

Nothing answered or obeyed.

I picked up my skirt, the muddy hem of my pelisse, and tried to find a sure path to the Hendersons.

The visions I'd had, the nightmares that had drawn my tears—my house being vandalized, that shiny blade slicing—all the horrid emotions tightened again about my chest. This fear like curtain pulleys could hoist me from the ground and hang me in the deepest shame.

Reckless. I had chosen to leave the safety of at least a footman and my fevered maid, to venture outside and get killed.

A footfall dropped too loudly to be imagined.

I ran fast.

Teacup stayed behind and barked. Something was out there. I just couldn't see it.

Scrambling from the edges of Stapleton's garden, I knew safety was on the other side, the door to my neighbor's study.

But I couldn't leave Teacup.

As fast as I could, I headed back for my pup. "Teacup, come to me. Go away, trespasser."

My dog didn't heed me. He charged into the mist. Then his chirping bark died.

Praying he was well, I stood my ground, waving my lantern, as if the light was a weapon.

A rushing figure swept in my direction.

Forgive me, Teacup. I ran.

Along the ground my lantern showed a shadow behind me growing, then overtaking mine.

Before I could scream, an ebony glove covered my mouth as an arm grabbed me about my middle. My feet left the ground.

I fought and fought. Hit him with my lantern.

"Argh. I got you, Abigail. Don't wake the dead. Just calm down."

"Stapleton?"

"Yes." He turned me within his embrace. "Now, stop hitting me."

I did. I dropped the lantern.

The light went out.

It didn't matter that he kept secrets. He may've omitted something out of loyalty or pride or whatever.

I needed him, needed to count on his protection when I was daring or foolish or threatened.

So I melted against Stapleton and allowed him to hold me, hold me close until my fear died.

Chapter 20

Stapleton guided me into his study and made me sit in a chair next to his desk. Then he moved back to the door and flung it open. When he snapped his fingers, his greyhound Silvereye came inside, along with jolly Teacup. My terrier's gait was as if nothing was wrong.

"Something's out there," I said.

He glared at me and stripped off his greatcoat, then tossed it over his desk, almost slapping the bust of Donne. The marble holding court in the corner might have to referee for the next few minutes.

Stapleton glared at me, then fell back against his bookcase. "You shouldn't have been out there. It's too dark. Bad weather. And a fiend attacked your house. He could still be searching to harm you."

"We don't . . . it could . . . The weather eased, and I had to get to you."

"You got to me, Abigail. You got to me."

He pulled forward a little and glanced down at his palms, as if he needed to trace where his hands had fallen.

The man knew where they'd been.

And I still felt warm from his caress.

"Abigail, how many crimes have you solved for Lord Duncan?"

The question was unexpected, but I supposed it was a safer subject. "A few."

"In how many haven't you found the guilty party?"

Squinting at him, I couldn't figure out if we had veered to safety or back to the fire. "None. I've been able to puzzle out the clues. That's when I have all the clues. Typically, I find them."

He sighed and peered up at the ceiling. "I suppose your reticule isn't often stolen."

"And my friends don't often hide something important."

No banter returned.

No protests.

No denials.

Nothing.

Silvereye stretched and lay at his feet.

At first, tiny Teacup did the same at my boots, but then he popped up and went to lie next to the big greyhound.

"Stapleton, are we friends, or has this been more manipulation?"

"Abigail, don't." His voice died. In its place, the tinkling of a pianoforte could be heard.

The tune grew and filled the empty, yearning, turning space between us.

"Someone's playing? Mary?"

"Joanna is." Though his words sounded monotone, his fiery gaze never left me. "Mrs. Danielson's talented."

Listening to the innocent tune, noting the contrast to his brooding eyes, I started to laugh.

"What's funny, Abigail?"

"Us. In this room. We've argued here. Maybe even shared a joke. But have we ever been completely honest?"

The mesmerizing stare between us broke. He glanced toward the floor. "If we haven't, then it's my fault."

"No, Stapleton. Don't do that. Don't be magnanimous. Be truthful. Trust me. I'm smart enough to understand and capable enough to empathize with a difficult situation."

Clasping my palms like I wanted to pray, I mumbled into my knuckles what had to be said. "Tell me what you took from Danielson's body the night of the murder. I know you did."

"What?"

"You heard me." I stood and went toward Stapleton, stopped inches from him, the bookcase, the dogs. "The vowels. The IOUs he had from Sheridan, you had to know about them. You took messages between the couple. You're like a sibling with Joanna Mathews Danielson. Of course, out of concern, you'd want to know her finances. You couldn't have not known and be the man I've come to respect."

"Abigail. Please—"

"Please what? Please don't feel stung by you asking the amounts of the IOUs when you knew. You want to protect her. I understand. And now you want to protect me from knowing the truth. How can this be when anything keeping us from finding this killer keeps us all unsafe?"

I rubbed at my brow. "My visions haven't stopped. It's hunting me, a knife still comes for my throat. If we solve the murders, perhaps I might recover some control. And if you can't trust me . . . It's like you said. You know I've let my guard down, but walls will be built again, bigger than any you tore away."

"I can't."

"I was outside, afraid. I couldn't even enjoy your garden or look at the new plantings in the moonlight. I was fearful of everything but you. I won't be the same after tonight. Lies make me terrified."

His face hadn't changed. The candlelight showed nothing different. Perhaps everything—respect, friendship—had been imagined.

"You stay there. Since this work of Beethoven is ending, I'll ask Mrs. Danielson what you took to protect her."

"Some things can't be helped, Abigail."

"And some omissions aren't for the best." After putting my hand on the door and opening it, I started through, but he caught my fingers.

"Wait."

With the gentlest of care, he led me back inside his study. Then he sidestepped Teacup and Silvereye and went to his desk. After opening the top drawer, he removed a folded paper, paper stained with crimson, lying beneath his quills. "Take it, Abigail."

The bust of Donne quietly looked on as I picked up the familiar foolscap. Unfolding it, I saw a list of debts, the familiar curly hand emphasizing the zeros in the huge sum. "This is the mate to the page stolen from my reticule. This is why you knew what it said without smearing it with charcoal."

"Why charcoal when it's coated in blood? Performing the examination for Lord Duncan afforded me the opportunity to retrieve the markers. Where would be the safest place to keep your insurance to riches, your ability to provide for the woman you love? On your person, stashed in a hidden pocket of your waistcoat."

I handed the vowels back to Stapleton. "Quite a sum, as well as the provision for half of Drury Lane. Right now, the debt's in default. Sheridan has extended himself an additional week."

Putting the markers back into the drawer, he bit his lip for a moment. "How did I fail?"

"Did you? You were protecting your friend. And with

Sheridan waiting to see if these vowels are found, those debt markers or the new holder, Mrs. Danielson, isn't safe."

"You think Sheridan may have had a hand in the murder?"

"Perhaps, but wouldn't he have searched for the vowels before the body was discovered? I'm not convinced this paper is why Danielson was killed. Mrs. Danielson knows. I must ask her."

He reached out to stop me but then lowered his hand. "I have obligations to Joanna and to the Mathews. They are old ties. Mine to you are new, developing."

His heated stare warmed my cold hands. Perhaps I was greedy, but I would've mourned the loss of Stapleton's friendship, too.

"What happened outside—"

"Was outside, Stapleton. Just two friends finding each other." I said this, then left before he saw I didn't know what that moment was either, only that I couldn't let myself need him like that again.

I headed the short distance to the music room where Mrs. Danielson sat at the grand pianoforte. She didn't cease playing the grand pianoforte when I entered this place, with its wall-to-wall paintings of ancestors.

Old men of wealth. I could assume all had had power, could imagine it beaming through the artist's rendition of the blue or gray painted pupils.

How many would be scandalized to see Mrs. Danielson and me here—women with color in our skin, women who could trace our lineage to enslavement—as honored guests?

She looked up. For a moment her expression seemed startled; then her eyebrow cocked, and she did a run along the keys. "A little late for you to visit, Lady Worthing. Is all well?"

"I suppose it all depends upon perspective. Lovely music."

"Beethoven. His An die Hoffnung, something he composed for the widow Deym. It seemed appropriate," she said.

I moved closer to the polished box. "It was urgent that I speak with Mr. Henderson."

Her fingers kept moving across the keys. "Did you find him?"

That I did. "We met. Now I have a few questions for you."

"Still rather late, Lady Worthing."

"Time is a gift. I've learned never to delay."

With my hands on the side of the beautiful, polished instrument, I cleared my throat for a direct address. "No moment should be wasted." I waited for effect, then said, "That's a line from Mr. Danielson's play. I think the sentiment is true."

Nodding, the widow continued making sweet music. "You read it, *A Daughter's Love*. I think it would've been phenomenal."

"I think you're right. Mr. Danielson seemed to have lived an interesting life, turning from being a discarded third son to a common thief to a playwright."

The music became louder; then Mrs. Danielson relented. "He changed his life. Perhaps he needed someone to believe in him."

Drumming my fingers along the edge of the pianoforte, I quite agreed. "My cousin was rude to you, questioning your choice in men."

"You don't have to apologize for her."

"Why would I do that when I think being upset over your decision can help explain why a woman of sophistication and elegance who'd been courted by a rising politician suddenly marries a man she just met."

The melody began again. Mrs. Danielson's fingers stroked the ivory keys with such lightness. "Love explains it."

"Convenience does, too."

She hit a wrong note, then drew her hands to her lap. "What are you accusing me of?"

"My staff seems to report you've inquired about baby clothes, about where would be the best place to get blankets and baby clothes made."

Mrs. Danielson looked down at the keys. "I thought I might've been with child. I was mistaken. That is a hard loss with my husband dead."

"You've been married a month. It seems a bit early to think one is with child."

She huffed. "You're ignorant. You must know things happen between a man and a woman that can lead to unexpected consequences. But Stapleton says your husband is often away. Perhaps you know nothing of desire and marital love."

"I'm not ignorant of such things. Seems to me those consequences of yours may have been the responsibility of your former lover. A viscount waiting for ascension left impoverished because of a difficult relationship with his father. And now his lover, a Black woman, is to have his child."

She folded her arms. "You insult me."

"Just stating the facts of our world. It's common knowledge in the abolition circles that the viscount's father, His Grace, did not appreciate anyone of mixed lineage or ebony skin. A woman who believes she might've been compromised, whose fellow won't marry her while his father lives, needs someone's name for her child to come."

Mrs. Danielson rose. Her motion was slow. "I think I might retire."

"How did it feel tricking Anthony Danielson into eloping, only to find the joke was on you? You weren't pregnant, and the viscount's father dies not a week after your wedding."

She spun around. Her golden cheeks were scarlet, as if she'd been slapped. "Who are you going to tell this rubbish to? Stapleton thinks you are a fine, honorable woman. Does he know you peddle gossip?"

"Mr. Henderson knows I deal in truth. I will do everything in my power to right wrongs."

Fist balling, she shook her head. "We've been friends a long time. We have a lot in common, and now we share equally in the loss of our spouses. He'll believe me."

Since I knew Stapleton didn't love his late wife, I wanted to state this commonality.

Of course, my husband could join this tardy club.

"Mr. Henderson will protect you. And I think you're in danger. The man who killed Danielson did so out of jealousy and to have you free again."

She put her hands to her face. "No. Martin wouldn't."

Mrs. Danielson had volunteered her lover's name, even the intimate forename of the present Duke of Culver, Martin, as in Martin Simpkins.

Her face scrunched. Her eyes became glossy.

I'd offer her a handkerchief if I had one but, of course, I wasn't done with my questions. "You hid here on Greater Queen Street, not just to hide from your guardians. You're hiding from Culver. You didn't want to be discovered by him."

Turning away, glancing at the portraits, she sobbed. "He's a possessive man, His Grace. Goodness. After all these years, he's finally been elevated. The things his father would've denied him, he has it all. And I was now married."

Walking to her, I witnessed a broken woman. All the control, the poise had disappeared.

"Did you ever love Anthony Danielson?"

"I could've. I had to believe we could've. He was funny. He wrote me such notes. The man had the finest script." She smeared her cheeks with salty tears. "He knew I might be with child. He didn't care, and his gambling winnings would keep us well provided for until his plays became talked about all over London."

"You didn't want Culver back, did you?"

"The passion one has for politics can be overwhelming and

volatile. And those volatile emotions can turn violent. Danielson always made me feel special, something worth protecting. Martin did not."

She began to breathe heavily. "Then it is possible to love two different people at the same time. It's possible to meet the right man at the wrong time and the wrong man at the right time. I don't know who I wanted, but hiding from Culver would keep me from making another mistake. Then Anthony made a mistake."

My heart ached a little for her. Then I grew angry for her.

"Mrs. Danielson, from everything I've discovered, I'm fairly certain there was nothing but friendship between the actress and your husband. He wrote a play for her to portray a role, but everything was to make you financially secure."

"He didn't betray me?"

"No. I don't think Mr. Danielson did. But that's what the duke wanted you to believe. Probably sent word through your parents. But someone else knew of your relationship with the duke and your marriage and told the killer your husband would be in the old-scene store at Drury Lane the night of the murder."

Her face paled. "That would mean I had a hand in Anthony's death."

"You cannot control what someone else does or feels, or even when they come home. Has the duke sent word to you stating his hand in your husband's murder?"

"No."

"Have you been in contact with the Duke of Culver?"

Mrs. Danielson glanced away as if the portraits on the wall would come to her aid.

"The duke still wants you, but he had to make you free to be with him. He eliminated his rival, your husband."

She shook her head with such violence. "I can't believe this.

Martin's fighting for abolition. I mean he's a champion." She fisted her hands and plunked the keys. "He's going to get the bill to its third reading within days. I have to believe in him. I can't think he killed Anthony."

I didn't have proof of the duke murdering Danielson. The confession I thought I'd hear was more of a conflicted heart than her being complicit in the killing.

Santisma rose from his nap in the corner. He came and licked her palm.

"You need a walk?" she asked him. "And you, Lady Worthing, should go home."

"Mrs. Danielson, at least two men have died at Drury Lane. How can you expect me to look away? If Anthony Danielson meant anything to you, you should want his murderer caught."

She raised her wet palm and slapped me.

Teacup wandered into the music room. He looked at her but went to me. Loved my loyal boy.

Then Stapleton slunk into the room. Silvereye was on his heels. Santisma picked his head up but didn't move from Mrs. Danielson. He curled his gray body about her leg.

Didn't blame him.

There were too many sides to choose.

"Is all well in this room, ladies?"

"No." Mrs. Danielson moved closer to the threshold. "Your bothersome neighbor has just accused me of aiding in my husband's murder. She's so focused upon being proven right, she'll come to you in the middle of the night to gloat over her notions."

"I'm not gloating. I seek the truth. Someone said that . . . truth's important. It makes things equal for women, giving us the chances and opportunities we deserve. It's the only thing we truly possess."

Mrs. Danielson folded her arms. "That's not all. Sometimes

you have moments in the sun. Sometimes you have memories of passion. And then there are days where the memories keep you from feeling insignificant. Nothing will bring Anthony back. But everything will remain horrid if Martin Simpkins, the new Duke of Culver, is not able to fight for abolition. So if you don't have any proof, I suggest you stop causing upset and let him change the world."

She snapped her fingers the way Stapleton did. Santisma unfurled like a waving flag. "I'm going to take him for a walk."

With my palm nursing my cheek, I let her go.

What did you say to a woman who hoped both men she loved were innocent?

"Joanna," Stapleton said, "it's too late to go outside. I just warned—"

She began to laugh, dry, angry chuckles. "Yes, that's why your neighbor has come from her close property to accuse me of things in your house."

"I'm right, Mrs. Danielson. The Duke of Culver is behind all of this. He killed your husband."

She threw her arms over her head. "I can't hear any more. Come along, baby." The widow spoke again to the dog, but Santisma stood at attention, awaiting Stapleton's orders.

"Go on, boy. Protect her. Don't leave her side."

As if the greyhound understood, he lifted up his snout and disappeared with the angered widow.

The slam of his study door echoed. Mrs. Danielson and the greyhound had gone outside.

I pivoted to Stapleton. "I should be going, too."

He stooped and picked up my yawning terrier. The fact that my dog might fall asleep in the midst of chaos was amazing.

"Giving up so easily, Abigail?"

"Not giving up, but I don't know how to prove the duke guilty without a witness."

"Mrs. Danielson doesn't believe Culver did it. Shouldn't she be the judge?"

"Not when I sense there are things she doesn't want to say out loud like he's abusive. He hurts women."

"I don't believe she's involved, but that's not what I'm questioning." His sharp indigo eyes shifted from a harsh stance to a conciliatory one. "Are we still good, Abigail? I don't want to build another fence or be away from you . . . like before."

"You have an odd way of asking. Or even apologizing."

He stepped closer. His lips parted. "We are connected—"

A high-pitched scream came from outside.

Stapleton shoved Teacup to me, but we both ran back to his study. From his desk, he pulled out an old sword. "Stay here, Abigail. I mean it."

He grabbed my lantern, which I'd placed on his desk, but my fingers were already on the handle.

With no time to argue, he let me join him, and we ran out into the night.

Swinging the light, I saw nothing.

No one running.

Nothing.

Then I saw . . . her.

Santisma whined. Loud was his cry as he stood guard over Mrs. Danielson.

She lay in the flower garden, eyes wide open. Her throat was slit.

A gold knife, like the one Watson had had, was in her hand.

I stumbled. Began to shake, then sink.

But Stapleton grabbed me and held me up. The man shook. "No! This wasn't supposed to happen to Joanna."

"My dream. I saw this. I thought it would be me. I could've warned—"

He put his hand over my lips. Then held me by the shoulders.

"Not you, Abigail. Not this time. Never, if I can help it."
His voice had tears.

Some leaked down his face. Then he knelt beside his friend
and shut her brown eyes, whispering words of vengeance.

I didn't realize this stoic man could care so much.

Teacup and I pulled Stapleton away from the body.

Wrapping my arms about him, I became his comfort and
waited with him until Duncan and the runners came.

Chapter 21

Suspects in Anthony Danielson's Murder
~~Alexander Hildebrand~~
Richard Sheridan
Barbara Banyan
Lanky Sailor – Lucas Watson
The Mathews
~~Unknown Sailor(s)~~
Martin Simpkins, Duke of Culver
~~Joanna Mathews Danielson~~

Stapleton and I and our dogs sat on my patio, watching Duncan and his men investigate the crime scene. The wrought-iron chair beneath me felt slightly damp from the former rain.

My neighbor looked distant as runners trampled all over his newly planted garden. "I could've handled this myself. You should be inside your home, locked away, safe from this, from me."

"Not many are here. A lock or barred door doesn't stop a motivated killer."

"It has to be safer if Santisma couldn't . . ." He bit his lip and turned again to our mutually trampled lawns.

Miss Bellows was inside my house, but she could sleep through all noises, with or without the brandy I had put in her tea. "Tell me how you are. Mrs. Danielson was close to you."

"Oh, God. I have to tell Mary. She's with the Mathews." His voice sounded anguished. "If Duncan thinks you had a part in this—"

"Nonsense. He knows well enough I have a talent for being in the wrong place at the right time. Besides, we are neighbors. Where else would I be?"

"Bath." He stared straight ahead, not at me or the doggie asleep in my lap. "You left for Bath. You didn't give me the chance to apologize. Perhaps you should've stayed. Maybe you need to return. Joanna could well have been you."

He didn't have to say it for me to think it, to feel that fear rattling in my chest.

"Stapleton, you want me to go away because you are afraid for my safety or because our friendship makes you vulnerable?"

His jaw stiffened. He hadn't looked into my eyes since he'd openly shown his feelings of loss over the death of a woman he had said was like a sister. "You didn't speak with me before you left. Maybe this was best."

"I think we are beyond disagreeing over the past. Justice was done. We're speaking again."

Sitting back in the wrought-iron chair, he pushed out his legs. He seemed so defeated.

"Was Bath a holiday?" he asked. "I'm sorry. I'm babbling. Waiting for Duncan to say his piece—that he doesn't think you or I had anything to do with Joanna's murder—is causing me pain."

Pain was an apt way to describe my humiliation. What did I say about the most humbling time in my life? "The Worthing town house there is lovely. I took several trips to the beach, just to walk. When the solace became unbearable, I came home. All in all, Bath was uneventful."

"Suppose London has saved the excitement for your return." He rubbed at his chin and kept looking to the sheet-covered body. "You still think the duke is guilty? Did Culver do this crime?"

"I don't know. The duke was in love with her. He was never free from his father's control, so marriage was impossible. She couldn't wait forever and married Danielson. With him gone, why kill her?"

"Joanna's neck was slit wide. She was slaughtered like an animal. I can't see a man who claimed to be in love doing this."

"Exactly. Why kill her, especially since his handiwork had already made her a widow? She would've been free to be with him after her mourning period."

With Culver's ascension, I doubted he'd face any repercussions from their relationship. Since he was a hero to the abolition movement and had been fighting to save lives by ending enslavement, could anyone disparage his choice to be with a Blackamoor woman?

Yet a volatile man like Culver would probably have a volatile reaction upon learning the woman he loved was dead.

"We should beseech Lord Duncan to keep Mrs. Danielson's death as quiet as possible. She's obviously a threat to someone," I said.

"Are you, Abigail, a threat to someone?"

Stapleton was a man of few emotions. Before I'd seen angry, angrier, and bemused. Tonight I'd witnessed grief and regret, and now there was this cross thing, where his lips were pressed tightly closed and his eyes shifted between conveying care and displeasure that he'd expressed his pain.

"A threat to someone, Stapleton, or a threat to you? I must be. In one year we've had two deaths on our lawns."

"Nonsense. And technically, my fence and now my garden. Is it bad luck for me to build?" He put his hands behind his head. He gazed at the sky.

I did too. There were thousands of stars out tonight.

"The clouds have cleared, Stapleton, but before, with the mist . . . Do you think the killer truly saw whom they murdered?"

"Clouds? Mist? I hadn't noticed. I don't know what to say to the Mathews. Joanna was under my protection."

When Stapleton's wife was murdered and we found the body, he was saddened but not openly emotional. This death had cut into his armor, armor our friendship seemed to be breaking, too.

"My fault, Stapleton. We'd argued. I drove her out the door with my insistence for the truth. I wish I . . . we could've . . ." I pulled my hands together and prayed for the lost Mrs. Danielson and the guardians, who would be devastated.

"If we'd stayed in my study, we might've delayed this. The murderer wouldn't be deterred. The passion to do this is too great."

I squirmed in my chair. Had this person been out here before? If Stapleton hadn't met me and taken me inside, would it have been my throat slit?

Santisma came to me and nuzzled my palm. Poor boy. He must be mourning, too.

Growing more sentimental, I stroked the sleek fur along the back of his head but forced my mind to be logical, to think of what had changed with this death. "Mr. Shaw would be concerned with the property of his widow clients. Who will have custody of the markers or even the play now?"

"The way the IOUs were written with both the Danielsons'

names, I don't think they are transferable. The Court of
Chancery would have to decide. Then they'd need to gather
proof that they were legally married. Since they were so against
the union, I doubt the Mathews would fight even for half of
Drury Lane."

The Mathews had money. If I were them, I'd be concerned
only about justice. There were protections in courts for
women, even Blackamoors. But it still required jurymen and
judges to see us as human, to believe that tinted or dark skin deserved protection.

Santisma whined. Teacup didn't seem to stir. Silvereye was
up on all fours, ready to pounce.

Stapleton was motionless, gaping as runners tracked up and
down our lawns.

My nervous chatter had to come out. "Sheridan will win,
after all. I suppose that's a win for theater lovers. Well, the play
should go to Miss Banyan. I believe she was the inspiration for
the characters of the king and his misplaced daughter."

The notion struck me, the familiarity of the theme of fathers
and their children, just as paternal Duncan walked over to my
patio.

He waved a gold knife. "Tell me this doesn't belong to either
of you."

"No, sir. But I wonder . . ." I waited for the magistrate to ask
me to finish. I also hoped dour Stapleton would follow my
lead.

Duncan frowned. He stood half in the muddy soil and half
on my cobblestones. "What is it, Lady Worthing? Spit it out,
lass."

"I believe I've seen that knife before. The fellow . . . I think
one of the fellows who helps with the rigging at Drury Lane . . .
He had a knife like this."

Stapleton stood, snapping at his dogs, causing Santisma to

stop growling at Duncan and come to him. The greyhound should have known him by now, given the many times the magistrate had been here.

Over the man's shoulder, Stapleton's stony countenance showed. "Lady Worthing, let's not waste the magistrate's time unless we're sure."

He and I both knew it was Lucas Watson's knife. Nonetheless, why did the answer to the question of the identity of the criminal who had attacked us seem too simple? I wasn't convinced that Watson had killed Mrs. Danielson or that he had a motive to do so.

Then I forged a plan to entrap the guilty party.

Looking at his notes, Duncan nodded. "Lady Worthing." His tone sounded as dreary as the night. "Do you think you would be able to identify this person, Lady Worthing?"

"Yes, I believe I could. Mr. Henderson and I should head next week to the theater for its reopening. I have to give Miss Banyan a play written by Mr. Danielson. I'm sure the person I saw with this type of knife might be around when Drury Lane reopens."

Duncan put his notes in his pocket. "I talked with Sheridan earlier today. He's reopening this week with a tribute to celebrate Alexander Hildebrand . . ."

"And to line his pockets with the proceeds from a packed audience wishing to pay respects." Stapleton's teeth clenched.

If I had a fan, I'd impatiently flutter it at him to try to calm him. Instead, I settled into our familiar role of antagonist. "Mr. Henderson, that's ungenerous. As a growing theater patron, you haven't quite felt the draw, the desire to be in our box seats as soon as those curtains open."

The bemused, sarcastic expression, the shrinking of his lips started. "Will it be a good thing to honor Hildebrand so soon? Not even a week since he lost his life."

Whether he was acting the part or being truthful, I was not sure, but Stapleton couldn't hide his sadness.

"I guess my neighbor is a stickler for protocol, mourning rituals. Aren't you. Mr. Henderson."

His mouth disappeared; not even a line formed. He groaned, as if in agony.

At first, I thought it was for dramatics, but it was for death. We'd become accustomed to finding its victims.

He sat up straighter. His gaze was again anchored to the runners. I watched, too, as these men surrounded the sheet-covered figure.

An audible count sounded as they lifted the body in unison from the budding floral bushes. It seemed to take them a long time to carry the stretcher to a dray.

She didn't deserve this. It wasn't a crime to love two men. For her heart to choose one over the other wasn't worthy of murder.

"Let me go with you, Duncan," Stapleton said, "or meet you at the Mathews'. I must be there to break the tragic news of their ward's passing."

"Of course," Duncan said.

Stapleton bent to Santisma and cupped the dog's sleek chin. "Stay and redeem yourself." He rose. "I'll go get my hat and gloves."

Then he turned with dark, vengeful eyes to me. "Lady Worthing, bolt your doors. Don't let a soul inside. We don't know what this is. And you won't find out alone tonight." He glanced at me, maybe hoping to beseech me with his steely expression.

I was scared. He didn't have to coax me.

With a nod, he charged off to Eleven Greater Queen Street.

Fanning his top hat, Duncan shook his head. "Lady Worthing, you have one concerned neighbor. And he must think Mrs. Danielson was killed by mistake."

If I wasn't sure the knife found by the body belonged to Watson, I'd think the same. Guessed I couldn't ask to see the weapon one last time.

Teacup stirred, and I let him into my parlor. The fellow headed for the sofa and Mama's blanket.

Stepping back outside, I shut the door and filled my lungs. The cool, wet air made my chest feel heavy. "Lord Duncan, the person who vandalized my house stayed for hours, taking his revenge in multiple rooms. He wanted to show me how angry he was. The person who killed Mrs. Danielson ran away too quickly. I don't believe it's the same criminal."

"Oh, lass, if you're expecting a fiend to be logical, you have more to learn. A husband and wife killed a week apart is too convenient not to be linked. This was no random crime, but I do agree with you. This murderer is not your vandal."

He peered at my wall of windows, the sparkling panes flanked by sheer curtains. "Good to see things repaired."

"Fixed glass doesn't make it all go away. Mrs. Danielson's murder is unlike the two deaths at Drury Lane. This was quick and not elaborate, unlike stabbing Danielson with a prop or hanging Hildebrand with scenery tethers."

"I don't agree with the assessment. But why would a bloke who'd been so clever leave an obvious clue?"

This logical person was the man I admired, not the political one who'd banished me from Drury Lane.

"Lord Duncan, did you see any signs of struggle?"

Santisma growled when the magistrate stepped toward me. I bent and soothed him. "I guess Mr. Henderson's talk energized you, huh, boy?"

Duncan rounded the other side of the patio table. "To answer your question, no. And the wound wasn't self-inflicted. That's not what you're suggesting?"

"No, sir. Not at all."

Vaughn rushed up to us. He was breathing hard, as if he'd run from whatever party his snow-white tie and formal tails required straight to Two Greater Queen Street. "Lady Worthing, you're well. I'm so relieved."

Santisma reared up. My godfather's arrival upset him, but he didn't growl. I put the greyhound inside the house. The poor pup pressed his nose against the glass like my dog did.

I turned back to Duncan and the man who I thought was unflappable . . . unless the circumstance had something to do with my mother. "What's happened, sir?"

Vaughn looked truly disturbed. There were even beads of sweat dampening his beautiful ebony brow. "I've just come from Windsor Terrace. The crowd is all abuzz. Everyone in abolition circles is preparing to celebrate the passage of the first slave transport bill. No one, no one thought it possible with Pitt's death."

"Celebrating impending legislation without all the votes being cast is foolhardy." Duncan guffawed, then sobered as I folded my arms.

Peering at the magistrate, I said, "It's a good thing, Lord Duncan."

"To be sure, it is, but this is politics," he said. "Don't get happy until all the votes are counted. I've seen things change by a simple speech or someone not showing to cast a vote. The good and the expedient are two separate things. And Culver, the blowhard, may lead his temperamental following to nowhere."

Vaughn glared at me and then at Duncan. "That's a little cynical, even for you."

"And for a man who has so many people's ears, you sound naive." Duncan looked over his shoulder as Stapleton headed out of his study dressed in a black coat, the armband of shiny satin still tacked to a sleeve.

"Well, now to the next part of my duty, as murders are still occurring." The magistrate dipped his hat, then walked off toward the dray.

My godfather didn't correct him.

We remained silent, watching the horrid dray and the runners' carriages leave and head toward Saint James's Park.

Vaughn dropped into a seat at my patio table as if the stars had fallen upon his shoulders. "The talk at the party of a young woman who doesn't know her place being taught a lesson was quite prevalent."

"That could be anyone."

"The noise started with Sheridan. He was at the party. It buzzed throughout the room. I was meant to hear it. They wanted me to."

"They, Mr. Vaughn?"

"Those who've taken notice of how freely you move about at Drury Lane, at public places like Olive's."

"Do they expect me to be a hermit? Do they want me to hide my face so the mixing of races, by choice or otherwise, isn't seen? Let them know that one of Leah's daughters who wanted to assimilate has died."

He threaded his fingers together. "I suspect you're talking about the King James story of Jacob's daughter. Foreigners raped the poor girl, and then she's given in marriage to her attacker, until her brothers subsequently murder the rapist and his family. Couldn't come up with an easier Shakespeare allusion?"

"It's late, Mr. Vaughn. A woman I'd argued with, who could be me, is dead."

My godfather came over to me. "Just before leaving this party, I heard Duncan and the coroner had been called to Greater Queen Street. I came as quickly as I could."

"So the theater owner and the rest of the ton are celebrating my demise? Guess Sheridan doesn't like paying customers."

"Abigail!" He ripped off his cape, a deep onyx wool trimmed

in black satin, and slung it on a chair. "You're not listening. Perhaps if your maid is up, she can get me something to drink. I think I'm going to need something stronger than tea."

"Miss Bellows is ill. Mrs. Smith is with Mr. Rogers for the birth of his granddaughter."

"So you were virtually alone when a murder happened next door?" He leaned on the table, rubbing imaginary stubble on his clean jaw. "Do you know where Worthing's private collection of wines and spirits is? I require something strong and dark."

"I found the key to the liquor cabinet earlier. Will brandy do? Would that quench your thirst while you prepare to lecture me?"

When I started for the door to my parlor, he grabbed my hand. "The gossip . . . I had to come and know you were well. I'm thankful, so damn thankful you are."

The care in his voice, fatherly and soothing, made me sniffle. "I'm quite fine."

"Abigail, your property was vandalized while you were away. Whoever did it was hunting for blood. Yours. So excuse me if I hear gossip which sounds like threats to my bold goddaughter. I don't want you under attack. And I don't take kindly to people threatening my family."

I stretched my palms to him, bypassing his strong, weathered hands, and clasped his neck. "I'm alive and well, well shaken. But Mrs. Danielson, she's dead. And if we hadn't argued, she might be alive."

"The Mathewses' wayward *daughter* has met a foul end? And so soon after her husband?"

"The rumor is he was wayward, too. Sounds like a match."

"Abigail, the young woman had such promise."

"You mean she might have been wed to an abusive duke. That's her promise?"

He sat again, murmuring something like "Intense bastard."
"How did she die?"

"Her throat was cut. Ear to ear. Like in my dream."

He clasped the table tightly, shifting it like it had a wobbly
leg. "Sorry, Abigail. It hurt your mother when she couldn't figure out what a vision meant. But it's a powerful gift."

"This gift, or curse, I don't want it. Mr. Vaughn, I saw the
blade. I witnessed the terror, but I thought it was for me. Had I
known, I could've—"

"You didn't. This isn't your fault. You don't know where a
spark will fall. You don't know if it will smolder or light or if it
will start a fire at all. It takes practice and leaning into your gift
more than your intuition."

"I'd rather use my intellect to puzzle things out and merely
sleep well at night."

"You will be haunted by these visions. Magdalena was tormented. Then, at other times, she mastered it. Perhaps you
should accept your hidden talent."

"Mr. Vaughn, I do not want this talent. It drove my mother
crazy. It made her make decisions, choices, that had such dire
ramifications."

"It made her choose herself. Her happiness was worth more
than her suffering."

"But what of everyone else who suffered? Me, Dinah, even
my father."

Picking up his cape, he stood and laid it over his arms. "You've
done well. Carrington's not in ruins. Your sister has chosen her
own path. I would've helped her, but I'll not regret one day of
making Magdalena happy."

"Sit, Mr. Vaughn. It's too late for judgment. I merely wanted
to say it did hurt that she didn't choose us. I suppose I can understand a little more why my father . . . saw my choices as betrayal. Like mother, like daughter."

Vaughn put his cape back down over a chair. "Magdalena

was fearless. Most will always remain trapped in others' expectations. That factor helps me provide influence for my friends, terror to my enemies. When I find who did this to hurt you, they will pay. I can assure the Mathews will do the same."

The prospect of more violence wasn't exactly what I wanted to hear.

"Abigail, our days are not promised. I think you should respect your mother's decision to leave for her sanity, to live another moment in the sun, even if it burned."

I heard what he implied, and I wanted so much to disagree but couldn't. I hadn't wished for my home to be broken, but it would have been broken whether Magdalena had stayed or not. Her walking out of Carrington and Ewan and never coming back hadn't changed my father. He had drunk the same or more. He'd gambled and taken bigger risks. He'd created chaos, all the things my mother's leaving was supposed to fix.

"Mr. Vaughn, I never spoke up about what happened."

"If you had, you would've suffered his wrath. She couldn't take you with her. The Court of Chancery would never have awarded custody of a child of color to her Jamaican mother, not when her Scottish father claimed her."

"It gave her peace, her choice to be with you," I said. "But seeing my mother suffer and decline, that must've been horrible for you?"

I reached out and grabbed his hand. I held it in silence until all the torches illuminating the yard had been extinguished.

Then I let go.

"Let me get a new candle for the lantern and find the brandy." At the door, I waved Santisma back, but then I returned to the patio table.

Some things needed to be said directly, not mumbled, not while heading into another room. "Mr. Vaughn, my mother loved you, and I know she never regretted her decision. I have peace now. And I'm still learning to choose me."

"Abigail, she wanted to show you and Dinah that you could choose your happiness."

His wide nose wrinkled; then he lifted my palm and kissed my fingers. "Find a tall glass, provide a generous pour, and tell me what you wish me to do with these rumors. I'm ready to be more aggressive at finding whoever is trying to harm you."

I had ideas. They mainly focused on me playing dead.

Chapter 22

Suspects in Anthony Danielson's Murder
~~Alexander Hildebrand~~
Richard Sheridan
Barbara Banyan
Lanky Sailor – Lucas Watson
The Mathews
~~Unknown Sailor(s)~~
Martin Simpkins, Duke of Culver
~~Joanna Mathews Danielson~~

The rumors of my demise didn't change much of Westminster. Window curtains were drawn closed, which was such a shame to cover the new glass. My maids abandoned their checked gingham for black. And my cousin and I abandoned luncheons at Olive's.

Florentina, dressed in an onyx gown with a high collar, came down from my upstairs bedchamber. She plucked at the shiny jet buttons adorning the front. "Lady Worthing," she said in a formal voice, "how long do we have to pretend you're dead?"

"Long enough for the Mathews to force Richard Sheridan to consider the debt on Drury Lane valid."

"That could take a long time and a dead woman can't go to the Court of Chancery. Though I do look stunning in this dress, I don't intend to be in this color forever."

"None of us will, my dear. I just want everyone to think Mrs. Danielson is alive and the killer has claimed the life of the wrong person. Well, actually everyone who is not the killer will believe this ruse."

She shook her head and stepped around Santisma. For Stapleton to agree and get the legal things moving for the Mathews as if their ward lived, his greyhound watchdog had to be my guest.

Florentina stroked Santisma's chin. This dog was a ladies' man. Not a single person in my household had received a bark.

Well, Mr. Rogers had garnered a few. But the fellow was so excited about his healthy daughter and new grandson, he had no cares.

My cousin sat on the sofa. The hem of her gown floated, then settled about her ankles. "Will you resurrect yourself today, after the bill in Parliament is debated, or after the Duke of Culver kills again?"

I shuddered and held onto the simple bookcase in the corner of the parlor and avoided my habit of drawing near the windows and throwing open the curtains. "If debate finishes today, they vote for a third reading. If it survives, then it will be in a red box on King George's desk. He's still well, right?"

My hand flew to my mouth. I didn't want to sound flippant, but everything happened to stop progress—a mad king, a murderous duke.

"Abbie, as a dead baroness, must you go about in black, too? I would want to be buried in a lively color." Laughing, she poured a cup of tea, then stuffed a piece of cranberry scone in her mouth.

"My demise should be serious. And this gown is very serious." It was jet crepe, with double-breasted buttons and gorgeous puffed sleeves. "I have it on hand for formal occasions to attend with Lord Worthing."

Turning from her to the fireplace, I wondered about him, wondered what he'd think if I had died—regretful, relieved?

"It was a joke, Abbie. Please don't be sad."

"I know. I was just wondering how my husband would react if he heard I was no more. Would he mourn?"

Florentina came to me and put her palms on my shoulders. "He would be hurt at what he lost, at what you two might've built."

Pulling the dear closer, I held her against me. "If I wasn't expecting a delivery, we could go find an expensive lichwake to attend. Make the mourners try to figure out what side of the family we represent."

"Abigail, keep a good sense of humor about being dead and all."

Mr. Rogers came into the room with more condolence cards. "Ma'am, I heard from the fishmonger that the vote today out of the second reading didn't go well."

"Why? I thought things were going well."

"The brash Duke of Culver missed the session."

Missed it? "Is he well? Has something happened to him?" I asked.

"Not sure, ma'am. The talk was he was distracted yesterday. The side for abolition delayed the vote until tomorrow. Hopefully, he'll be there. It's obvious. If he isn't there, the bill won't pass."

I gripped Florentina's hand. "Yes, let's hope he will be ready to fight tomorrow." My voice sounded hollow.

When Mr. Rogers left, I sank onto the sofa, barely able to lift my eyes.

Then we said the worst together like an awful refrain.

"He knows Mrs. Danielson is the one who was murdered. He knows I'm alive."

Florentina's eyes went wild. She lifted her fists, then dropped them and looked at the patio door to see if it was barred. "Then he'll figure out this ruse is a trap. He could come any night. You're not safe, Abbie. Let's go to my parents' house. He'll not look for you in Cheapside."

"No, Flo." I shook my head. "I'll not bring this level of danger to my aunt and uncle. They've done enough, standing up to the Carringtons. Won't put them through the type of worries my mother's troubles caused."

"Then how does this end, Abigail? How does this all end?"

"This whole ruse is for naught. Mr. Vaughn is even bringing a coffin."

"He's what?"

"Yes, your uncle procured one. We're going to set it up in the drawing room."

Mrs. Smith came in with a tray of strawberry tarts. She was stiff. She dropped the silver platter with a clang. Her arms folded over her white apron. She was the only one in the house in gray.

Frowning, I waved at my housekeeper. "Out with it. Please tell me of your disapproval."

"Me, ma'am? Ya want to hear what I think, mocking death? No. I don't think ya seriously want me to say such."

Scooping up a tart and preparing to sink her teeth into the woman's fine pastry, Florentina chuckled. "As long as you didn't take offense with your treats, I think all is well."

"It's not funny, Miss Sewell. We have death running rampant in the neighborhood. You don't want to invite the evil into your home."

Mr. Rogers popped his head into the parlor. "Mr. Vaughn is here with a rather large delivery."

"The drawing room. Tell him I'll be there shortly," I said.

"Very good, madam." A little red in the face, he seemed upset, too.

"If we are faking my death, for what good it is now, we need to go through all the steps. Mr. Vaughn said he'd help."

My godfather swept into the room and bowed. "Yes, my dear. I want to help. I see you're disapproving, Mrs. Smith?"

My housekeeper went to him, swinging her dusting rag at him. "You put her up to this. Instead of just—"

"Just what, ma'am? Waiting for the person who broke into Two Greater Queen Street to come back right away, even more incensed Lady Worthing is unharmed?"

"A fast talker is what ya are."

"You know I'm right. My grooms are setting up the display now. Why don't you ladies come?"

I looked at Mrs. Smith and then at Florentina. My godfather seemed to be serious in this playacting. I pinched myself underneath my cuff to ensure I was awake and this was part of our plan.

Pretending to be bold, I stood and followed Vaughn.

He held the door, then ushered the three of us inside the drawing room. Refreshed, painted in bright blue, the drawing room was as regal as ever. Though the gilded-leaf fixes weren't as smooth as I wanted, the antique frame had again been placed on James's portrait. Off the floor, the painting hung in its proper place over the mantel. The room held not the scent of bleach now, but of roses. My godfather had had two large urns placed about the pine coffin.

"I'm beginning to think this is a bit much, Mr. Vaughn," I said. "I don't want to make a mockery. I just wanted to fool people for a little while. At least through the vote facing Parliament."

"Normally, I'd agree with you. But after I left here, I went to visit some old friends. The Mathews are in deep mourning."

My head tilted as Vaughn drummed on the coffin's lid. It didn't give a hollow sound.

The grooms whom my godfather had with him, I'd not seen before. They were tall and muscular and not the norm for typical household hires.

"What surprise do you have?" I asked.

His glaring, accusatory stare made me feel small. "Mr. Henderson told me of a little difficulty you had in the streets about Drury Lane."

Gawking at the coffin and then at my godfather, I felt faint. "We were attacked, but I received nothing more than a bruise."

"Nothing?" His fist pounded the top of the pine-lidded box. "It's not nothing. How can I keep you safe if you don't tell me everything?"

"We were fine. Mr. Henderson protected . . . What's in the coffin?"

He waved to the grooms to open it.

They took bars and wedged off the lid. The smell of fresh-cut wood scented the room. The noise of nails being ripped away sent a tremble through me.

Mrs. Smith began making the sign of the cross. She had retained her Catholic faith even though she had been transported from Port Royal to London.

"Please leave, ma'am, while I inspect my present from Mr. Vaughn," I told her.

She began to back away. "Told ya about fooling with such. Makes ya all crazy."

"Mrs. Smith, please, and have no one else come in here," I said. "Take Miss Sewell, too."

Florentina looked as if her calculations had broken on one-hundred-percent-we're-dead. We were coconspirators to what was in the box.

"No, I'll stay, Abigail. My uncle is a good man. He'd not do something terrible."

"You know I've done a great deal to protect my brother, your father?" He punched the coffin's side. "I do not deal in idle threats. And if someone has tried to harm either of you, they will pay."

My eyes widened. "That's why you agreed with Lord Duncan to keep things quiet. You played on his fears of causing outrage in the neighborhood so you could handle it yourself."

His smile was slow. "Maybe your intuition is as great as your gift. I almost thought my delay had cost you your life last night. And when Mr. Henderson offered a name, I knew what I had to do."

The door slammed behind us after Mrs. Smith ran from the drawing room.

The grooms flung the lid to the side. It fell on the floor in the shadow of James's portrait.

Vaughn reached in and forced a beaten and bound, but alive Lucas Watson to sit.

In my drawing room, I tried to catch my breath.

My godfather, I knew, was a powerful man. London was his town. He had allies reaching all the way to the Prince of Wales.

And Vaughn acted. He'd delivered the thief in a coffin to my home.

"Sir, this man did attack us on the streets," I said. "But he didn't kill us. I don't think he meant to. He wanted the missing markers."

Watson shook his head, but no one seemed convinced. The gag in his mouth prevented him from uttering lies or truths, so I decided to keep speaking.

"This man has a violent past. He was a former partner in crime to Anthony Danielson. They were close, committing all types of crimes, thefts, rigged games, even forgeries. That's what Mr. Shaw says they've done."

"Nod if it's true," Florentina said. "The truth might set you free. I'd risk it."

Watson lifted and lowered his chin like that of a crazed doll on a spring.

Still begging my godfather not to kill Watson, with my eyes, I said, "And though this man was mad at Danielson, he didn't kill him. Isn't that true?"

Again, Watson nodded.

Vaughn glared at me, then him. My godfather seemed angrier at these answers.

"He attacked us only because he thought Mr. Henderson and I were trying to frame him for Danielson's murder. He recognized my neighbor taking notes back and forth between the newlyweds and assumed there was another scandal happening." I gawked at Watson. "Am I still telling your truth?"

I stepped closer and pulled the gag free. "You didn't kill Mrs. Danielson last night. And you had no reason to try to kill me. I'd convinced Mr. Henderson to let you go. And though you blamed Mrs. Danielson as one of those rich people who tried to take away your friend, I highly doubt you'd risk everything to kill a woman who'd lost everything."

"Everything but those vowels and the play."

I could understand the debt markers being important, but why the play? Then it all made sense. "Mr. Watson, I will again beseech my friends here to let you live, but I need for you to understand something. Your knife was used to kill Joanna Danielson. Someone you think you can trust is setting you up to be arrested for murder or to be killed by someone wanting revenge."

He shook within his restraints, as if this would free him.

"The knots will tighten if you keep it up. You do realize circulation is needed in your hands if you wish to keep them?" Vaughn pulled me aside. "You want me to let him go?"

"Abigail?" My godfather gripped my arm right at the spot I'd bruised when Stapleton pushed me out of the way to safety.

I winced, and his eyes glazed over. "You kept saying you had visions of a knife."

"Yes, Mr. Vaughn, but I don't want Watson killed for a mistake, not when I need him to come to Drury Lane tomorrow. Lord Duncan will be there, and we'll solve this mystery."

"You want me to go to Drury Lane and walk into a trap?" Watson shook his head. "You must think I'm stupid. Rich people."

"No. It's not stupid to see who's been behind your friend's murder. Mr. Watson, you will make sure that Anthony Danielson's life mattered. You can make sure his killer won't go free."

Flo held up a finger. "I'm not sure you recognize your odds, Mr. Watson. Those gentlemen there already found you once. They'll do it again if you don't comply. Or they'll keep you until tomorrow. I don't think those look like good odds. I suggest you bet on Lady Worthing. It sounds as if she's saved your life twice. That's a decent record."

"Fine. I'll be there. But I ain't lying on no one." Watson rubbed at his wrists. "I'm not turning anyone in."

"You will. I need you to hear the truth," I said. "Tell Anthony Danielson's story. He has been horribly maligned. This could be a moment to change your life."

"I give you my word. I'll be there, but I'm not promising lying or turning in someone."

I nodded. "That's enough. But I know you will feel differently when you hear the truth of your friend's murder."

Vaughn's grooms cut Watson free.

"Do you need a ride back to Seven Dials? My men and I can provide it."

Watson leapt over the side of the coffin, shook his head, and ran from the room.

When the outer door of my house rattled shut, I spun around to Vaughn. "Was that necessary?"

"Yes. Watson may not have had anything to do with the break-in here, but I need London's dark side to know you have friends who will protect you. They need to understand I can be ruthless and merciless. Word will filter to every part of the underworld. They shall think twice before bothering you again."

"Vaughn—"

"Your husband isn't here to protect you. I am. You're in this position because of my advice. I don't take things lightly. I know you'll not stop trying to puzzle out crimes. I have no intention of stopping you. You refuse to knit."

"Knitting needles might be a good weapon to carry on my person." I wanted to make jokes, but it felt scary and powerful to know Vaughn would do this for me. "You're crazy, Mr. Vaughn, but I love how much you care."

My cousin seemed a little frazzled. "This is highly unusual. I think mathematics is a safer profession than mystery solving. We should go find Mrs. Smith and let her know all is well."

I let them go ahead.

Florentina almost leapt ahead of them as Vaughn instructed his grooms to help Watson return to Seven Dials alive.

That part made me breathe easier.

Yet my eyes lingered on the open coffin. I wasn't sure what this stunt would do. It could surely continue to escalate things. Nonetheless, a great sense of relief coursed through me. My pulse sped. My side had done something.

The sooner Drury Lane was solved, the sooner the abolition bill was done, the sooner I could again feel completely safe in my own home.

Chapter 23

Suspects in Anthony Danielson's Murder
Alexander Hildebrand
Richard Sheridan
Barbara Banyan
Lanky Sailor – Lucas Watson
The Mathews
Unknown Sailor(s)
Martin Simpkins, Duke of Culver
Joanna Mathews Danielson

Sitting in my parlor after Vaughn had departed and Florentina had gone upstairs until dinner, I awaited my last mourner. The sun began to set. The slight crack in the curtains allowed a little of the fading light inside. I didn't realize how much I loved the sun, the way it felt on my face, until I had to pretend to be dead for no reason.

I thought if it was believed I was out of the way, the duke would proceed with the vote. Somehow, he knew I wasn't deceased. I didn't believe he or Watson had killed Mrs. Danielson. But what if I was wrong and the duke had killed her?

Sinking upon the sofa, my doubts began building. I wasn't sure I'd be able to prove anything now that the woman who could say the Duke of Culver was guilty was dead.

Depending on Watson to admit to anything was risky. Merely thinking him innocent of Mrs. Danielson's murder had no bearing on his innocence concerning Anthony Danielson's death.

A tap on the glass set my heart racing. I didn't move until I heard Stapleton's voice.

He called my name again. I rose slowly and peeled back the heavy shrouds Mrs. Smith and the recovered Miss Bellows had hung.

"Abigail, it's only me. Let me in."

With Santisma at my side and Teacup in my arms, I stood at the door, glaring at him, refusing to unbolt the lock.

Tapping again, he demanded, "Let me in, Abigail. There's nothing to fear, even if I think your plan is odd."

"You haven't arranged a way to enter Two Greater Queen Street through my godfather? He helped Watson here today. Quite an efficient transport."

He grimaced, the lines in his jaw darkening. "Mr. Mathews hinted at it. He wished Mr. Vaughn had followed through."

My gaze darted from his. Vaughn had said that Mrs. Danielson's guardians wanted vengeance.

"Let me in, Abigail. You have my dog."

"I don't know. Santisma is a ladies' man." I stooped and hugged the greyhound about his spotty middle. "See, he's comfortable."

"Don't do this, Abigail. You know Teacup loves me more. One snap of my fingers and a bit of bacon and it's over. I'll even change his name to something less delicate."

The way my terrier whined and looked at me with traitorous eyes, it was probably true.

"Fine." I unbolted the door and let him inside. "His name will always be Teacup."

"I take it you're upset." He closed the door behind him and proceeded to tower over me.

I craned my neck and captured his befuddled gaze. His countenance, typically blank, mirrored how I felt—angry, disappointed, questioning. Why was I seeing all of this now, when I wanted to box his ears? Why was he becoming more open the more I fumed, the more I wanted to shut him out?

"Tell me what great sin I've committed today, Lady Worthing."

"You told Mr. Vaughn of our attack."

He rubbed his ear, and his eyes traveled to the ceiling and then back to me. "The last time I checked, that was no secret. And you managed to invite the magistrate to Drury Lane to point out said attacker."

"That's what I said, but not what I meant."

He combed a hand through his hair. Dark curls coiled about his fingertips. "Excuse me. Maybe it's me. I seem unclear. When did my friend, the beacon of truth, the lecturer of omissions, take to lying?"

"What I said to the magistrate was for him, not you."

"So you will lie to everyone else but not to me, Abigail?"

"I wasn't exactly lying." I bit my lip and tried to calm down, rid myself from this out-of-control feeling that arose from having to explain myself to a smart man pretending to be obtuse.

Taking a breath, I tried again. "Lord Duncan needs to feel as if he's coming up with the answers. I believe that on Friday the person who murdered Mrs. Danielson can be made to confess. Mr. Watson being there will help ensure it."

"This seems like a complicated plan. Why would Duncan want to claim any part of that?"

"Are you trying to be helpful, or will you muck up things more?"

Shrugging with an almost hurt look on his face, he moved from me and went to the mantel. Clasping the poker, he straightened it in the collection of tools to move coals. It was too warm for a fire. The sun would have to set and a few more hours would have to elapse for temperatures to drop low enough. "At the Mathewses', I mentioned to Vaughn I believed the fellow who'd attacked us near Drury Lane might be Joanna's killer."

"My godfather doesn't take kindly to people threatening his family."

"Vaughn's an honorable man."

Stapleton didn't seem to understand my godfather might've had no problem removing Lucas Watson from the streets forever. "Mr. Vaughn has an interesting code of ethics and his own rules on loyalty. He doesn't need information that could make him wish for bad things to happen."

"Wish?" The hurt look dissolved, and his countenance became amused. His eyes sparkled. "Bad things. Hmmm. I think I'm in agreement. Watson almost stabbed me. I hope I broke his nose."

"Well, he's nursing those bruises from our encounter and rope burns from today."

"You went and saw him? You're supposed to be playing dead."

"Stapleton, you're not listening." I rubbed my tired brow. "Vaughn delivered him here in a coffin. Luckily, the thief remained alive."

"Inventive, Abigail. Your godfather has an imagination and can get things done. I like it."

"Mrs. Danielson's murderer used Watson's knife and left it to put our street fiend under suspicion."

"Means the murderer knew of him attacking us."

"Yes, he might've even hired him to do it to run us off. I don't think he was going to kill us. A good scare that went too far. You surprised him with your vigor. You surprised me, too."

His glance settled on me and felt heated, but he turned his attention to Santisma, stroking his thin tail. "You've been babied again?"

"He's been good company. He cries for Mrs. Danielson. The attack must've been quick and unexpected. I don't think by Watson."

"Great. You've absolved a thief in one mystery, but not the original one. He could well have killed Anthony Danielson."

With a long sigh, I said, "You are right. We may have one or two different murderers."

Stapleton rubbed his brow and looked as if he'd take all the dogs and leave. "Just tell me why you're angry with me."

"Your casual conversation almost got Watson killed."

"That's not it."

"Of course it is. My godfather is heavy handed."

"Why does it make you angry with *me* that he'd kill for you . . . too?"

I couldn't say anything else. How could I when I knew in my bones Stapleton was serious?

He turned away from me and the dogs. "If anyone should be furious, it's me, me with myself. My dear friend was killed outside my door. You felt something when I encountered you. If I'd taken the threat more seriously . . ."

Giving chase in my comfortable parlor, I moved to him and put my palm on his shoulder. My fingers became tangled in the pleats of his finely pressed shirt. "I wasn't the target. If the killer was there, they awaited Mrs. Danielson."

"She never hurt anyone. Culver hurt her."

"The man is volatile, but I don't believe he touched Mrs. Danielson, not last night. Like Santisma, he's mourning her. That's why he missed the debate on the second reading for the bill he's championing in Parliament. Why would the man, either fighting for his convictions or wanting power by leading the charge on a deeply political and divisive issue, miss the moment? He knew the woman he loved was gone."

"If you are so confident, why are you frustrated? Powerful men get away with what they want until they cross men with more power."

"Are you speaking from experience?"

His eyes narrowed, burning a hole, if they could, through my skin. "I know that's a true question from you, not a sarcastic or rumor-based one. And since you ask in earnest, I'll answer in truth. Yes. My father, the admirals I served, knew how to use power. And no one could do a damn thing to stop them."

This man was grieving hard, but he wasn't shying away from the truth.

I didn't budge from his side. I'd stay in his sphere if it could lead us both to peace. "I'm frustrated, Stapleton. One killer will probably go free. Another may never be caught because I have to depend on the thief who attacked us, one who's been threatened by two men who are trying to protect me. I'll be the cause of the guilty going free. I feel horrible."

"You're not." His palm covered my hand. Rugged and warm—something to enjoy. He was someone to forgive. He cared maybe as deeply as he mourned.

"Abbie." Florentina stood at the threshold. Her mouth hung open.

Stapleton didn't move, didn't feign embarrassment for being too familiar. He kept his hand atop mine.

"Excuse me if I'm interrupting."

"No, you're not," I said slowly, parting from my neighbor. "Come in. Mr. Henderson was telling me why he tried to get your uncle to murder Watson. He's partially responsible for today's theatrics."

"Oh," she said.

My cousin didn't move from the threshold until I sat on the sofa. She joined me, with her beautiful gray-brown eyes staring at him and then me.

Stapleton stayed on the other side of the room. "Lady Worthing, again, I deeply apologize. I'll share my concerns for your welfare more directly with you in the future."

"What does that mean, sir? Abbie, what does he mean?"

Before I could say anything, something equally ambiguous and teasing or slightly menacing, Rogers entered the parlor. "More condolences have arrived, ma'am. Must we continue this much longer?"

"No, Rogers. Open the curtains. Seems my scheme has fooled no one."

"I don't know, Lady Worthing. It seems we have a note from Carrington and Ewan." He handed me the note.

But I struck my forehead. "I meant to tell Mr. Shaw. I hope . . ." The script on the notecard wasn't Wilson's. His hand was slanted. Very in a hurry.

"Isn't he supposed to be traveling on holiday?" Florentina squinted at me. "Are your escapades known as far away as Gloucestershire and Bibury Races?"

Popping the seal, I recognized the familiar script. I closed the note and dropped it on the sofa table.

Stapleton came closer and looked over my shoulder. "Abigail?"

"It's for Lord Worthing. The firm wants to know how to handle the accounts that have been set up in my name. Rogers, send a response letting them know that I'm alive and will be spending the funds on bright, bold colors to make sure I'm seen. I want no troubles at my modiste."

"Yes, ma'am."

Rogers left, and I kept breathing. In and out. In and out. A supposed death didn't change things.

"Abbie, you don't look well," Florentina said.

"Fine, I assure you." Spreading out my mother's blanket and letting Teacup, who'd been patiently sharing me with Santisma, stretch out on my lap, I thought I seemed remarkably adjusted for having had my teeth kicked in.

"Lady Worthing!" Rawlins shouted my name through the halls and ran into my parlor. "It's happening, ma'am."

"What's happening?"

"Culver. The crowds came to his in-town residence. They roused him and escorted him back to Westminster. His backers, Lord Lauderdale, Ellenborough, and Siddy."

"You mean Sidmouth?" Stapleton's gaze was on the table. He was probably trying to read the bland niceties my father had penned to his client James Monroe. Even reports of my death hadn't elicited regret. I had defied his wishes to marry, and he'd never forgive me.

Rawlins nodded. "Yes, Mr. Henderson. That one. They rallied. There will be a third reading. If that vote holds, it will be the first bill passed, Lady Worthing."

He was gleeful. My reserved driver radiated with the pleasure of this moment. "All those crazy meetings you made me take you to, ma'am . . . You need to celebrate. I think all of London is rejoicing."

If the town was here at Two Greater Queen Street, we seemed woefully remiss. "Where is everyone gathering, Mr. Rawlins?" I asked. "At one of the elite men's clubs?"

"Yes, because only elite men can celebrate such an accomplishment." Florentina sighed, then must've remembered we were in mixed company. "No offense, Mr. Henderson."

"None taken. But, Rawlins, where is the Duke of Culver gathering the masses? I'm sure he won't waste a minute on his campaign for prime minister."

"You say that like he's not worthy. He's the incarnation of Pitt the Elder and Pitt the Younger to get this done."

Mrs. Smith tsked her tongue as she came in with a tray of her cranberry scones. Though they were delicious, I didn't think I could tolerate anything.

"Funny you mention Pitt," she said. "The gossip Miss Bellows retrieved from the markets is that Mrs. Morton Pitt, no relation, she and her member of Parliament husband are throwing an informal gathering to celebrate at her home on Arlington Street."

"Informal you say, Mrs. Smith?" I stroked Teacup's ear and hoped he wouldn't mind me going out. "Will the Duke of Culver be there?"

"He's the man of the hour. Of course he will."

Florentina had no problem collecting a rich, flaky treat. "I suppose the fashionable who've resisted any movement at all will attend, to pretend they are happy with change or to lament with champagne and music."

"I take it you don't like the duke," Mrs. Smith said. "Maybe this is where age has an advantage, right, Mr. Rawlins?"

"Not sure, ma'am. I have to know where you are leading."

My driver looked to me, and I offered him a treat and then pushed the tray toward Stapleton.

My neighbor blinked, looked at the biscuits, and then glanced at me and Florentina. "I suppose a win is a win, no matter if the leader of the movement should lose."

I pushed off my blanket and let Teacup stand on guard like Santisma. "You all are right. I think I will go to this informal gathering and offer my support."

Rawlins and Mrs. Smith looked pleased, but Florentina and Stapleton gaped.

"What shall I have Miss Bellows lay out for you? Something pink or rose?" Mrs. Smith asked.

"No, I think I will go as I am to see the duke. I think he's expecting dark colors to show the seriousness of the moment. And we should mourn those lost, who won't be able to see this legislation pass."

"Very well, madam. I will get your gloves and bonnet. Are you sure?"

"She looks beautiful as she is," Stapleton said. "She'll make a statement with her presence."

"My party will. Miss Sewell, Mr. Henderson, will you two join me?"

"I'll go get the bounder." Rawlins left with my housekeeper. They looked so pleased. Those two and everyone who'd come before, who'd lived in the tenuous gap between enslavement and freedom, deserved to enjoy the hope this legislation brought.

My cousin shrank back on the sofa. "No, Abbie. We shouldn't go. We should stay and watch the dogs. It's much safer."

Stapleton stepped forward. "I'll accompany you. Let me go get my hat and coat. And I will bring Silvereye to accompany Santisma and Teacup in Miss Sewell's care. The more watch-dogs, the merrier."

As my neighbor left out the door, Florentina's eyes went large. But she'd asked for this by not wanting to come. "Abbie, this isn't wise."

There was nothing wise about confronting a murderer, but if the Duke of Culver knew who had murdered Mrs. Danielson, I needed to see if he could be compelled to confess the name. Someone, even if it was just one person, had to be brought to justice. If a duke was untouchable, some *peerless* killer needed to pay.

Chapter 24

```
Suspects in Anthony Danielson's Murder
         ~~Alexander Hildebrand~~
             Richard Sheridan
              Barbara Banyan
      ~~Lanky Sailor — Lucas Watson~~
              The Mathews
           ~~Unknown Sailor(s)~~
      Martin Simpkins, Duke of Culver
       ~~Joanna Mathews Danielson~~
   Lanky Sailor – Lucas Watson (Added Again)
```

The crowds along Arlington Street were thick. From the window of my carriage, the road looked blocked. It was no surprise when Rawlins pulled to the side and stopped the horses.

He came down from his perch and opened the door. "Ma'am, Mr. Henderson, there's too much to go through. As much as I want to be in this atmosphere, I don't think it wise. Many people are against progress."

Henderson descended and stretched out his arm to me. "I'll protect her, sir."

As good as my training had become, I took my neighbor's arm and stepped out in my jet bombazine gown with black beading that shined in the night.

"Stay close, Mr. Rawlins," I said. "That way we'll know where to find you if we must resort to a quick exit."

He nodded and climbed back atop the carriage. The handle of his blunderbuss showed in his coat pocket. I wished I still kept knives in the yellow bounder, but since I'd become reticent to carry a reticule, I didn't exactly know where to hide a weapon on this outfit.

We walked a little way, carried along by the moonlight and the revelers we passed.

"Do you have a plan, Abigail, or is this some exercise in catharsis? You can't want a scene to confront the duke?"

Maybe. "A young couple is dead. I'm doubting my thoughts on the matter. I must see it, know it in my heart once more that the fate of the abolition movement rests in a murderer's hands."

A noisy group of men sang "When The Stormy Winds Do Blow."

> *You gentlemen of England,*
> *That live at home at ease,*
> *How little do you think upon*
> *The dangers of the seas;*
> *Give ear unto the mariners,*
> *And they will plainly show*
> *All the cares and the fears*
> *When the stormy winds do blow.*

When they ran at us, drunken and swaying, Stapleton pulled me close. I hid my face against his shoulder. I drowned willingly in his bergamot and cedar.

He hummed their tune loudly. We blended into the crowd

and kept moving until we reached paths illuminated by reticulated mushroomlike lamps.

Ushering me into a grove of pines, Stapleton took a breath. "Abigail, I've asked if you have a plan? You can't want us to be here and be bludgeoned by drunks."

"What?"

"My dear, half the people here are in support, but I'm pretty sure the other half isn't. Can't you see our friendly runners scattered about the perimeter? Duncan must be here, expecting trouble."

"I don't have a plan. I have nothing but the desire to see Culver and look at a man who is going to get away with everything, and know that I can live with it."

He released me and pulled his gloved hands to his face. Onyx dyed leather on Stapleton's reddening cheeks was a sight. "You told me the duke didn't kill Joanna. What is he getting away with?"

"He murdered Anthony Danielson. And he must've been told that your friend was killed last night. There is no other reason for him to almost lose the fight today. Who's the link? Which of our suspects is helping him?"

"What if he was sick, then felt better?"

"If you didn't believe me, why are you here?"

A hot sigh came from the dragon. His face deepened a shade. And when I thought he'd explode and argue, like he had when we first met, he whispered, "I've lost enough women in my life. I'll be damned if I lose another."

Hadn't expected that—the honesty, the deep sense of loss. "Stapleton, I'm sorry."

"No you're not. But you coming here alone or even with Rawlins is a death sentence for one or both of you."

"It's not. I can do this. I can get him . . ."

"You are extraordinary, Abigail, but one piecemeal bit of legislation that is full of weak compromises doesn't change centuries of hate and prejudice or the belief that one person should own another."

"Let me see him." I trudged forward.

"You think that you can glance at him and know your suspicions are right? That's the height of naivete and stupidity."

Stapleton raced to my side and held out his arm. When his piercing gaze dared me to be unreasonable, emotional, and too foolish to take it, I did.

"Sir, this is my last try. I have Duncan coming to Drury Lane expecting me to have this solved. When I say I'm beaten, I have to know I did everything. I as much as chased Mrs. Danielson out into the night into the killer's path."

"You didn't. You're not responsible, Abigail."

"I have to do something." My voice choked with unspent tears.

He took off his gloves and clasped my fingers. Then he started us moving.

Crossing the lawn, I saw how spirited music swayed the crowds.

He didn't let us linger. Stapleton had eyed something on the grand terrace, and he headed us in that direction.

The closer we came to the house, the brighter the lights of a massive chandelier in the windows became. After we took the stone steps, our feet landed on velvet carpeting that covered the wide terrace. Seats were arranged all around the edges. Conversations were everywhere, as was dancing. In the corner, by some sculptures, stood my Mr. Vaughn. He seemed stiff and uncomfortable.

The two gentlemen that had helped him with his coffin stunt guarded my godfather.

When his gaze fell upon me and Stapleton, he ventured over to us.

"Lady Worthing," my godfather said, "this is not what I call staying hidden."

"The killer knows who was killed last night. So does Culver. I came to congratulate him on winning."

"Two different people." My godfather's mouth closed. He looked genuinely stunned. "Henderson, although I'm glad you didn't let Lady Worthing travel alone, I suppose there was no dissuading her?"

"None. I believe I'm serving in a similar capacity to your two gentlemen friends."

"The Prince of Wales wanted a firsthand account of the bill's progress while he's at the races."

"Mr. Shaw is at Bibury this week, as well," I said. "Must be prospecting for Carrington and Ewan."

"Really?"

"Yes. The firm sent correspondence to quit my accounts upon hearing of my death. Cold but civil. And I must say efficient."

"Oh, Abigail."

I gripped my godfather's hand. "No. I guess I did choose back then and now. And correctly, Mr. Vaughn. *A Daughter's Love* by the late Anthony Danielson is one accurate and astounding play."

With a dramatic turn, I left the fellows. We were in the light of the chandelier, which was bearing down on my golden-brown face. I had nothing to hide. I'd come for my seat at the party. I was ready to claim it.

With a glass of weak ratafia in my hand, I wandered into Lord Duncan. A tall man, he looked dapper in his formal black and white. "Lady Worthing, I'm surprised to see you."

I offered a quick, respectful curtsy. "Rumors of my death are highly exaggerated, sir."

"You're a supporter of abolition, no doubt. The young Culver is the hero. Lord Lauderdale was bragging earlier about the man's ability to snatch victory from the jaws of defeat."

"Everyone seems impressed with him. Has he arrived?"

"Saw him earlier on the floor. The young man is dragging. Must feel awful the bill almost failed because he wasn't well enough to attend."

My heart constricted. The hypocrisy of feeling sorry for a murderer flooded my stomach with bitter gall. "Excuse me."

The rawness in my throat burned, but I stayed ... only to confront Culver. He'd won. I accepted that. I merely wantonly, recklessly wanted him to know he hadn't pulled the wool over everyone's eyes.

Then I wanted him to tell me who had actually killed Joanna Mathews Danielson.

After a turn around the edges of the open drawing room, which involved counting each of the sconces and crystal-dripping lamps, I walked back out onto the terrace. The crowded lawn had become a raging sea of people. These were everyday faces, the ones seen in the markets or the theater pits. These weren't the diverse crews I'd seen working on the ships along the Thames. Most countenances seemed joyous, but few here were like mine. On the terrace Vaughn and his escorts and I added color. Stapleton was right. One bill didn't change the world.

Without Culver's conviction, would Lord Lauderdale or Lord Ellenborough or the political-interest-shifting Lord Sidmouth have stepped into the lead role?

Duncan came up to me again. "You don't look happy for an alive person. What do you know, Lady Worthing?"

"It's never what I know but what I can prove. I think you taught me that."

He frowned for a moment. "What if I were to listen as a friend? Would you share what you are thinking?"

This was a setup, and once a thing was said, it couldn't be taken back. Duncan was a good man. I didn't hold anything against him. I knew it was a rarity for anyone in authority to want to hear what a woman thought.

But Mama didn't raise a fool.

"I'm sad about Mrs. Danielson. She would've been here tonight. I heard that she was fully accepted by the ton. This was truly her world. The Mathews poured a lot into her education. She might be inside, exhibiting on the pianoforte. The woman was gifted."

When he nodded, I felt him accept this truth. "Her guardians are devastated, Lady Worthing. They'd love to redo the past month. I think they would've protected her and the young man she wed. Hindsight hurts."

He slurped at his punch. Then made an awful face and put the glass down on the stone ledge of the terrace. "I heard the young woman had captured the eye of Culver before his ascension. Funny thing about timing."

It was a funny thing.

Out the corner of my eye, I saw Barbara Banyan coming up onto the terrace with the Duke of Culver at her side. They weren't arguing. They seemed pleasant.

He took her into the house to meet with Mrs. Pitt.

"Lady Worthing, of course you know the actress. You've seen her quite a bit onstage and now backstage," Duncan commented.

Then Culver returned to the terrace. He didn't come close but kept glancing at the magistrate and me.

"I read Miss Banyan grew up in the theater or had a theater background," I said to Duncan.

"Yes. I heard something like that when I questioned her. She's from where Hildebrand was born."

Hmmm. "Acting must be in the air in Surrey."

"Must be," he said. "That is a young woman with ambition."

I nodded and noted the duke straining to listen to this conversation. "She had high hopes for reprising her role in *A Bold Stroke for a Wife*. Without Hildebrand, I wonder if they'll continue the play when the theater reopens tomorrow."

Saying the late actor's name didn't move the duke. Unlike with the actress's name, Culver had no reaction at all.

Duncan tried again to sip his punch. He frowned. "Bitter. We'll have to see, Lady Worthing."

Culver went back inside. I saw him go near Miss Banyan. Unlike at the theater, she didn't seem frightened at all being near the duke.

"Well, well," Duncan said, "it seems as if the love of theater is growing everywhere."

"Why? Because a duke is interested in an actress?"

"No, because Miss Banyan truly does. So much, she's staking her money to promote it. She's become a private investor in Drury Lane. Sheridan says she's determined to keep it going."

Blinking, I tried to remember everything Wilson had said about the actress's finances. I didn't see how she'd be able to pay off Sheridan's debts. "Did she mention starring in its next big play?"

"Yes. How did you guess?"

"It's that theater loving. It gives one the ability to predict what will be performed."

He rubbed his chin. "Never knew that. But no one loves the theater like you."

"No, I'm pretty sure there were some that did."

Duncan went inside to hear Barbara Banyan exhibit. Her pianoforte performance wasn't brilliant, but her voice held power. That play Danielson had written for her, it would catapult her into the same stardom Hildebrand had enjoyed.

I wondered if he could look down or look up and see it happen. Would he be proud, or did antagonism last beyond the grave?

Stapleton and Vaughn passed me several times as I stayed with my ratafia in a corner of the terrace.

Each looked guilty or like overprotective guardians. Each gave up and returned to the drawing room.

When the Duke of Culver came outside to send away the throngs of congratulatory people there to thank him for his tireless efforts, I decided to take my opportunity to extend my condolences for the couple whose fortunes he'd ruined.

Chapter 25

I clapped my hands, timed to the ending of Miss Banyan's song. The Duke of Culver turned on the terrace. The smile he wore faded. "Lady Worthing, you're looking well. I'd heard that you ran into some trouble."

Glass in hand, ready to throw it, I approached him. "You're not the first person to tell me that tonight. I did have a little trouble. While I was rehanging my husband's portrait, the frame split. Old frames are hard to repair. But I'm surprised such trivial gossip makes the rounds."

"Replacing gilding on the finest craftsmanship is difficult."

I stopped breathing, not long enough to faint, but long enough to hear my lungs rattle and my heart pound. "How do you know it's a gilded frame?"

"Isn't it? I know in my father's house . . . my house, chipped-away gilding is the hardest thing to fix. Are you well, Lady Worthing?"

He reached for me, and I nearly jumped out of my skin. "Sorry, Your Grace. I'm shaken. A neighbor was killed yesterday. It's most unsettling. She was a friend of yours. Mrs. Danielson?"

His stare was blank, and then he leaned near, with fire in his face. "That should never have happened. Joanna was a good woman. Please, follow me down the steps. There's a walk along the side of the house. Let's take it."

"You see the crowds on this lawn?" I said. "You don't think they'll provide enough noise to prevent what you have to confess from being overheard?"

A harsh sigh fled his lips; then he drank from his goblet of champagne. "If you want my answer, then walk with me into the garden. Too many ears on the terrace."

Though I knew it was a risk, the number of people fluttering about made me bold. Only a fool would follow him, but only a fool would try to kill me in a crowd.

I nodded and let him lead two paces ahead until we were off the terrace, down a flight of stairs to a grassy knoll. More of the mushroom-shaped lights lit the ground. I let him go a little farther before I stopped.

"Your Grace, this is a good area to talk."

At first, his back was to me, and my gaze landed on his straight brown hair, his fashionable high-necked cravat, which revealed nothing about his frame of mind. He turned, and his expression soured as if I was in the wrong.

"What is it you want to hear, Lady Worthing?"

"The truth, nothing more."

"Madam, you're not owed a thing. You should be grateful to be where you stand and to have the station you possess."

I folded my arms, mostly to keep them from shaking and rattling the beading on my gown. "Are these the 'endearments' you offered Joanna? Did it impress her? No wonder she chose a man who was better with words."

His hand balled. "She loved me. I know it."

"And when she was troubled and went to you, what did you

offer? Love? Or excuses? Daddy wouldn't give you any money to have a Blackamoor bride?"

"You continue to bait me. You will be responsible for my temper."

Those words were so familiar. My father used to blame my mother for his drunkenness, for his pain. So many things that were under his control.

I calmed the fury rising in me.

That was my parents' fight, not mine, and I'd never relive it. "If you loved Joanna as much as you say, why are you letting her killer get away?"

He opened his palm and drew it back, as if to strike me. There were cuts on his hand. From a broken glass? Or from breaking glass at my house?

Keeping my eyes on him, I backed away. "Never mind, Your Grace. You're in no mood to talk. Good evening."

"Wait! Lady Worthing, please."

Close to the terrace steps, I stopped. "Speak from there. I can hear you just fine. But know I'm not looking for any other confession. I know Joanna's killer told you where she was hiding."

"I didn't—"

"But you got the address wrong and you took your frustration out on glass panes and gilded paintings."

"I did no such thing."

"This person told you where Anthony Danielson worked, when he worked, and how to get to him. I'm assuming your own creativity aided you in finding solace with a sharp African spear."

"You're speaking fairy tales."

"But this accomplice still needed Joanna out of the way, so there would be no other claims on Drury Lane. And she knew you'd never kill Joanna."

"No, I would not. I loved—"

"Poor Anthony Danielson, the man who changed his life for Joanna's love, held markers on Sheridan. The debt would go to Mrs. Danielson, the equivalent of twenty thousand pounds or half the interest in Drury Lane."

"Joanna would have been wealthy if she'd lived?"

"Yes. Her claim just needed to be prosecuted by the Court of Chancery. Danielson loved her enough to provide for her."

Culver gulped the rest of his champagne. "You have a gift for speechmaking, Lady Worthing."

"These are mere whispers. No one but you is listening. And I want your help to find the mastermind, the person who set all of these murders in motion. Who enabled your rage? Is this person blackmailing you into financing her investment?"

The duke began to laugh. He smashed the goblet on the stone. Pieces of glass landed by my slippers. A sharp shard from the goblet's stem sat halfway between us. "I'm broke. Barbara Banyan is funding her half of Drury Lane herself. Part IOUs, part an inheritance from a parent she didn't know. That's all her money."

"Then why are you standing up with her, bringing her here on the night of your triumph?"

He rubbed his hands together as if he were cold. "Maybe what you said is half right. Maybe Barbara thinks she can prove I had something to do with Danielson's death. Perhaps I have to be silent because I don't want a scandal. Not now. The old heads came to me. Siddy and Lauderdale came to beg me to show my face in the House of Peers. That gave my side the votes. Abolition will be done because of me. That is my life's work. It's all I have now that Joanna is gone."

I'd be swayed if I were stupid and believed that tortured love was love.

It wasn't.

Love was something calm and fine and lasting. It made you

feel safe and seen. That was what my mama had taught me. That's what every woman should choose.

He'd edged closer. "The question is, What will buy your silence?" The shard from the broken goblet was beside his shoe now. "Or perhaps you need silencing."

"You're not crazed, Culver. You're craven. There's a difference. Would you risk everything in this moment?"

"A slit wrist, a muffled cry until the glass bleeds you out, would be all it takes."

He bent and picked up the sparkling glass shard, sharp as the head of a spear. "Wonder if I could get away with it. I'm a god to the movement. That has to mean more than one life."

"One Blackamoor life that won't be silenced." I hooted for him. "Duke! Well done, Duke! Everyone, let's praise our champion!"

He stopped his advance as others gathered around.

My shouts grew louder as more gathered. "Getting abolition done, Culver is our hero!"

I slapped my palms together hard. More revelers came to this grassy area. Soon the space between me and the man who threatened to kill me filled with supporters shouting his name in unison. "Culver! Culver!"

Lights shined down in this darkened space. I kept my eyes on the vain beast.

The crowd tightened about him like a noose and swung him away from me.

Stapleton ran down the steps. He found me, shaking me.

"Holy hell." He shoved me behind him, then started for Culver.

"No." I clasped his shoulder, jerked him around, and lifted my arm. "I need you to be with me, away from this place. Alive."

He grimaced. The veins along his neck bulged. "Abigail?"

"The duke will stab you." I whispered more about needing Stapleton alive, then lifted my arm again. "Leave with me, sir."

Stapleton complied, his palm falling at my elbow. I led my friend away from this horrible celebration of the evilest man in London.

Chapter 26

Morning light filtered through the slit of my parlor window. I'd barely slept in my tufted yellow chair. Stapleton lay on my sofa, sound asleep, with a musket and an old sword at his side.

The dogs had abandoned Florentina as soon as we came home. We'd made a quick stop at Eleven for the weapons and, apparently, his favorite blue dressing gown, which he'd donned, shirtless, over his breeches. Then my neighbor, now my houseguest, had stood patrol until he couldn't stand anymore.

Mrs. Smith came in with a pot of steaming coffee. "You know we have bedchambers, six, upstairs. You needn't have your guest passed out on the couch."

"He's not hungover. He's on guard."

She looked at him as she eased the tray onto the table. It made a clang.

Stapleton shot up, with his sword drawn.

"Put your weapon away, Commander. You don't need to play soldier. It's morning," I said.

"Right." He drew the weapon down. "Sorry, Mrs. Smith."

Smoothing her white apron over her cinnamon-colored gingham dress, she went to the door with a smile. "It's fine, sir," she said in a voice filled with more charity. "You're protecting Lady Worthing. Given the murder of your friend and the break-in here, I understand and love that you have chosen to do this. Your friend Lord Worthing would be grateful."

Stapleton nodded, tugged at his robe, then sat back down. Blinking his eyes, he focused on me. "Oh, no. Tell me you haven't been awake all night in that chair."

"Fine. I won't tell you."

"Speaking of your reticence . . . Abigail, what part of the plan was for you to take a walk with Culver, the man you suspected of killing Danielson?"

"There was no plan. I told you this last night."

"I know. I was hopeful daylight would change the answer to something reasonable."

"But he did it. He just about admitted that he murdered Danielson and did the vandalism here." I stood and kicked the hem of my wilted gown with my bare feet. "The hate Culver is carrying is incredible. I thought Joanna had chosen Danielson to conveniently wed to make her pregnancy legitimate. She might have chosen him merely to get away from Culver."

"Everyone loves a hero." Stapleton twiddled the short blade in his hand. "But who killed Joanna?"

Florentina, looking sunny and refreshed, entered the parlor. "Oh, I don't want to miss this part." She poured a cup of coffee and sat in the chair opposite me. "Continue. Who killed Mrs. Danielson? Wait, shouldn't we start with, Who killed Mr. Danielson?"

I glanced at Stapleton to see if he wanted to answer, but he seemed more interested in polishing his blade with a handkerchief. So I said, "The Duke of Culver murdered Anthony Danielson."

"But we can't prove it or tell Lord Duncan, as this might

hamper the abolition bills." My neighbor's monotone voice showed none of the frustration he had had last night and none of my fear. Culver would harm me if he felt he needed to. I didn't want to think about how unsafe we were until he could be stopped.

"Well," Florentina said, "who killed Mrs. Danielson? I take it it's not the same answer."

"Why would you say that, Miss Sewell?"

"The way Lady Worthing's pacing, while you're trying to act impartial and unbothered . . . The actions are in conflict."

"That's not new, Florentina," I said.

She laughed. "No, it's not. But tell me if I'm wrong. Did Culver kill Mrs. Danielson?"

I shook my head and forced myself to sit. "It has to be Sheridan or Miss Banyan. Sheridan to get out of paying the vowels. Miss Banyan to remove Danielson's wife as a potential owner of Drury Lane."

"You think a woman is coldhearted enough to cut someone like that?"

"Yes," Stapleton said. His answer was fast and assured. "I know it to be so. Females have the capability to inflict as much pain, knowingly and, in some cases, unknowingly."

He stood, sighed with the creaking floorboards, and headed to the patio door. "I'm going home to refresh myself and shave. I need you two to be alive and here when I get back. Don't leave to go find killers. Here."

Silvereye, Santisma, and my little Teacup rose and went to him.

"Gentlemen, I need you to do your best to guard them. Santisma, no slipping up this time." He waggled his fingers at the dogs, then at Florentina and me. "Best behavior."

"Wait, Mr. Henderson," I said. "Bring the vowels with you."

With a salute, a flintlock musket slung over his shoulder, the sword in a hilt, Stapleton was off.

Florentina popped up and bolted the door. "Must you live in Westminster? This neighborhood will have you constantly fearing intrusion. Abbie, can you seriously stay here?"

Scrambling to my feet, I paced. Then I stood behind my re-upholstered chair and ran my finger along the added nailheads. "This is my home. I won't be run off. That's what Culver wants. Some of my neighbors would probably rejoice, as well."

After moving to my wall of windows, I opened each curtain. The bright sun glittered on the glass. I watched Stapleton, with his strong, straight back, his robe flailing, shield his eyes as he walked across our shared lawn. There was something comforting and humorous and special about witnessing this. "No, Florentina. I won't find a neighbor who cares as much or who'd want to help a woman puzzle out mysteries."

She sipped her coffee. "I wonder if that's all he's going to help you figure out."

Pivoting to Florentina, I rolled my eyes then turned back to the glass. Had to make sure Stapleton made it safely into his study.

Living with this new awareness of fear wasn't sustainable, but I had no intentions of living anywhere else or running away.

After having to circle back to Greater Queen Street because Stapleton had indeed left the vowels, the three of us—my neighbor, Florentina, and I—arrived later than I wanted at Drury Lane.

It was well into the afternoon, and the backstage area seemed oddly quiet. No one rehearsed. The magic of scenery being assembled was missing. The rummaging for props in all the scene stores was absent.

"Is Drury Lane closing?" Florentina's voice sounded scared.

I didn't like how empty the place was. "Didn't Duncan say the theater was reopening tonight?"

Stapleton, who seemed to be moving a little slowly, sat on a bench, one that should have paint for those last-minute scenery touch-ups. "The rumors that Drury Lane would be shuttered are rampant. No one wants to work here if they don't believe they'll be paid."

Florentina nodded, and she and I walked through the cross-over passageway behind the stage. I stopped at the steps where Hildebrand was found. "Who killed him, Abbie?"

Before I could answer, Mr. Sheridan, followed by my neighbor, pounded toward us.

Sheridan's face looked pale. "Are you here to brag? Have you come in to kick a dog while he's down?"

Moving directly in front of him, I crossed my arms, and my black satin reticule slid to my elbow. "I would never kick a dog, or any animal, for that matter."

Stapleton presented the markers. "We're here to see you transfer rightly the assets of Mr. Danielson. You owed him quite a lot of money, and you missed the payment."

"What are you? A bill collector and a physician?"

Sheridan didn't mention that Mrs. Danielson was dead. That would be the first challenge, unless he didn't know.

Before I could point this out, Barbara Banyan and Lucas Watson also came to the crossover space.

"Oh, great," Sheridan said. "You're here. Do you have the investment money? It seems representatives of the late Danielson are here to collect."

"The wrong representatives, Mr. Sheridan." Miss Banyan's eyes were bright. Her curly black hair was perfectly coiffed and accented with a straw bonnet. She looked the picture of wealth and innocence. "Mr. Danielson has no representatives other than me."

She reached into her reticule. "Here's the note Anthony signed giving me possession of his debt markers and its collateral."

Why would Danielson do that? "But what of his wife?" I asked.

"Where is she if one exists? Make her show herself." She handed the paper to Sheridan, and he handed it to me. "It is insurance, to make sure I got what I deserved."

The document looked official. It was an agreement, written in Danielson's curly hand. Something I'd stared at intimately as I read his last play.

Nonetheless, this paper gave Barbara Banyan, also known as Sarah Falls and Lady Barker of Surrey, the sum of twenty thousand dollars or his half of Drury Lane.

Speechless, I stared at the actress.

She took the paper from my hand. "You've defaulted, Mr. Sheridan. Danielson owns half of the theater. It now goes to me."

"Well, I don't know what is true." Sheridan went up the steps, the ones Hildebrand had climbed before dying in the ropes. The theater owner shook his head. "I built this place. I put my blood, sweat, and tears into this, every brick, every seat."

"Come down, Sheridan," Miss Banyan said. "Don't be up there. You're mocking the man we celebrate today."

"You're going to have to wait. I need more time, and Mrs. Danielson's interest in the theater would precede that agreement. I know Danielson got married. She'll just have to show."

Barbara batted her eyes, but she didn't seem flustered. The raven-haired woman looked completely in control. "You know how close Anthony and I were. We had a secret."

I braced for the lies this woman was about to say, knowing she would probably be believed.

"He couldn't tell you, Mr. Sheridan, not before. Anthony and I wed. I was Mrs. Danielson. We didn't want it to affect his position. That is why I've been so tortured."

"Danielson didn't say that, because it wasn't true." Stapleton's tone wasn't so flat. "Joanna Mathews married Anthony Danielson, not you."

"I have proof," Barbara said with a pout. "A marriage license." She waved a document that looked authentic, but I glanced at Watson, remembering he and his slain friend had created forgeries.

Sheridan waved his hands high. "This is going to take time to sort. Barbara, Lady Worthing, nothing will be done today. We go on with my plans of celebrating the legend Alexander Hildebrand."

"No," the actress said. "You will introduce me tonight, during intermission, as the new half owner of Drury Lane. I will stand on that stage, and we'll announce the next play, *A Daughter's Love*, to honor my husband."

Sheridan guffawed. "Let me see that license. I need to see proof that you are Mrs. Danielson. Though you were intimately involved with Mr. Danielson, I don't think he'd marry you or was fool enough to give you his IOUs."

She took more paper from her reticule, an expensive satin one like the one that had belonged to me and had ended up under Hildebrand's body. "Mr. Sheridan, I suspect this is all some sort of trick to deprive a widow and close Drury Lane."

Looking at Watson trying to avoid eye contact made me realize something. "There's a simple way to prove which document is authentic. I have Danielson's play. The last thing he handwrote. Let's see which matches his hand. Mr. Sheridan, you can decide."

The upset theater owner took the markers and the license and then held each next to the pages in Florentina's hands.

"They look the same. The license looks right." Sheridan shook his head. "The courts are going to have to decide. I won't honor —"

"But look at the differences," I interrupted. "It's in the curls.

Notice the way the *Ss* and *Cs* have that extra loop. The true instrument matches the play. Miss Banyan's loops on the contract and the license are backward."

Stapleton's brow furrowed. "How did you know?"

"This is from someone tracing his words. After reading pages and pages of his play, I saw a man who took pride in each letter he crafted. Barbara Banyan has forgeries. The insurance contract is as phony as the marriage license."

Miss Banyan took back the pages and crumpled them. "This is what I get for trusting you, Mr. Watson."

"Well, Cicero says there's no honor among thieves." Watson sort of grinned. "That's what Hildebrand once told me. And it's wrong to be cheating Mrs. Danielson. She's got nothing now. You've got your profession and that inheritance."

"And you have this play." I picked up the play and held it out to the actress. "It's your story. And it celebrates the legend how you want it."

Miss Banyan glared at me, not taking the stack of papers or my bait.

"Tell Mr. Sheridan what it was like to grow up knowing your father was a legend, a king, as in Jasmine's situation in the play," I said. "Hildebrand lost his family. His love ran off. She took his daughter to Surrey and restarted her life. You're from Surrey. Wouldn't she be about your age? Wouldn't she be you?"

Miss Banyan groused. "Can't believe you figured it out."

Sheridan balled his fists. "You are Hildebrand's daughter? Why didn't you tell me?"

"Why would I do that when I didn't tell him until the end? I wanted to be a success. I wanted him to know me as a good actress. We performed only half a play together. Two measly scenes, and then he got drunk."

"He wasn't drunk." Stapleton pointed to where the body had been found. "Alexander Hildebrand was dying. He was in pain from seizures. The man took Dover's pills to ease his sufferings. He may have gotten tangled up in the ropes, but his body didn't have much longer."

Miss Banyan shook her head. "Dying? I saw him struggling and moaning Shakespeare. I whispered my mother's name. He didn't respond. He didn't care. So I waited until I was sure he'd stopped moving and went back to my dressing room."

"You let the man die." My voice sounded strained but the horror of what she'd done struck me. "But you readily accepted an inheritance from Alexander Hildebrand. Yes, a friend of yours told me so last night."

Red in the cheeks, she shook her head. "Lies."

Florentina took the play from me, holding it to her chest like it was a babe. "If Mr. Hildebrand left you an inheritance, you don't think that shows you he cared?"

Tears flooded Miss Banyan's cheeks. "It's all lies. You just want me to feel bad. He had nothing to say to me, his own daughter."

"Strangulation can keep one from being talkative." Stapleton looked at her with disgust but stayed at my side. "What are you capable of? Forging papers. Watching a man struggle and die?"

This act wasn't over. I needed Miss Banyan to confess. "I know what kind of monster she is. One who can lie in wait for a woman to cut her throat."

"You're upsetting me. I need a handkerchief." Miss Banyan wiped her cheeks, then reached into her reticule and withdrew a pistol. From her reticule fell my stolen lorgnette. The glasses smashed on the floor, more proof of Barbara's duplicity.

The actress waved the pistol. "I never liked you, Lady Worthing. You think you're so clever. Duncan should've hauled you away when he found your purse under Hildebrand."

Sheridan, who'd been a statue watching this, stepped forward. "Miss Banyan, why are you holding a gun? What's going on? You tried to commit fraud, and it didn't work. Everyone can go on their way. Nothing to see here."

"Can't quite do that," she said. "Lady Worthing knows about Mrs. Danielson."

"The true Mrs. Danielson, Joanna Mathews Danielson," I said. "Didn't you confess to someone yesterday? At a party on Arlington Street, I heard how devastated your friend was. He's the one who spoke of this to me. Cicero's words about a lack of honor must apply to murderers, too."

Miss Banyan gawked at me, knowing I understood her connection to Culver.

Stapleton stepped forward, and Miss Banyan pointed the pistol at him. "Why kill a woman grieving the loss of her husband?"

"They should never have married. Anthony and I were friendly for months. I poured my soul into him, and he wrote the most amazing play about my father and what my life had been without him. When he threw away everything we could've had, for her, a woman he just met, it made no sense. Then he put her name on the IOUs."

I wanted to clap. Barbara's performance as the femme fatale was perfect, but her crimes were done. "Is that why you betrayed your friend to a man hunting for Mrs. Danielson?"

She started to laugh. "You can't say his name. Too political for MP Sheridan to hear? Fine. The duke was easy to manipulate. My stepfather knew his father, and I knew about the help, the woman the Mathews had brought back from Jamaica. She's the daughter of their deceased son. They raised her to be respectable, but that doesn't change the fact she's common. She didn't deserve Anthony or Culver."

She waved her pistol at Watson and made him move as she backed up.

The woman was going to run, but I needed her to stay and openly admit her guilt. Culver would never testify against Barbara Banyan. I stepped forward. "Did it make you feel powerful to slit the neck of the help?"

"Shut up." Her hand shook as she kept adjusting her aim. "Watson, my friend, help me. I need you to—"

"Miss Banyan, when did you come up with the idea to frame your pal Watson and use his knife for the murder?" I interrupted.

"Barbara," Watson said, "you tried to double-cross me?"

"I said shut up, Lady Worthing."

"Abbie!" With her hands up, my cousin made faces at me. "Perhaps you should listen. She can get one shot off, and at this close range, she'll kill one of us."

Sheridan stepped way back and almost leapt up the stairs again. But I wouldn't be deterred. Joanna deserved better.

"Tell me, Miss Banyan, is life so unfair for a pretty woman like you, one who has talent but never got the right breaks? Pity you couldn't use Papa's name. Imagine if the world had known you were Alexander Hildebrand's daughter. Would've opened so many doors."

"I didn't want to use him. I wanted him to be proud. You wouldn't understand. You don't have to do much but lie on your back to get your title."

"It's more complicated than that," I said, "but if this notion helps soothe your wasted life, so be it."

Watson slid to the side, blocking an exit offstage. "Don't taunt her, Lady Worthing. She doesn't have a sense of humor like Vaughn. And you don't deserve to be killed."

"Noted, Mr. Watson. And I rejoice in the genius of your friend. Anthony Danielson was a true genius. And he took the pathetic story of this ungrateful woman and made it great."

Miss Banyan's fingers curled tighter on the pistol's handle. Her finger stroked the trigger. "I guess we know who I'll shoot."

"Technically, whom you *hope* to shoot." Florentina shook her head. "You backed up more. The navy men joke all the time about the accuracy and rate of misfires of blunderbusses."

Like I had with Culver, I clapped my hands and regained Barbara's attention. Hands snapping together, clapping in applause, I made my voice louder. "That's what you would have heard. The great Miss Barbara Banyan. If Danielson had lived, he'd have finished this play."

Taking the play from Florentina's arms, I made a quick glance at Stapleton, who I knew had his eyes on me. Raising the pages, flicking my wrist, I said, "This play would've made your father see your talent. He would've been proud."

I tossed them at Miss Banyan, and as the foolscap floated in the air like snow, I dove onto Florentina, knocking her out of the line of fire.

Stapleton took out his small sword and threw it at Barbara's hand. It pushed her pistol up as it fired.

Before Stapleton or Watson could get her, the shot cut through a rope holding a curtain winch. The iron block fell and beaned Barbara in the face.

The instant snapping sound as she hit the floor made me cringe. I sat up, stood, and tugged Florentina to her feet, then turned her so she didn't have to see the bones bulging at the base of Barbara Banyan's broken neck.

Watson looked like he'd pass out. Maybe this would scare him to the straight and narrow.

Florentina waved me away. "I'm good, Abbie."

She was fine. Stapleton was, too.

Sheridan ran down and joined us. He looked confused, but he scooped up pieces of foolscap. "Is all what you said true? Hildebrand's Barbara Banyan's father? Danielson didn't finish the play?"

"Yes. All of it. Truth is stranger than fiction," I said as Stapleton checked Miss Banyan for a nonexistent pulse.

Stapleton set down Miss Banyan's wrist, then stood. He didn't look unhappy, not that his face showed any expression, but I felt his gaze, warming me.

Drury Lane's owner scratched his head. "If she killed Mrs. Danielson, let Hildebrand die, who killed Anthony Danielson?"

I glanced down at the fiendish woman's unrepentant blue eyes, ones Stapleton hadn't bothered to close. "I think that's a question for Lord Duncan. The magistrate solves all the hardest crimes."

Sheridan tugged on his coat lapel. "Does Danielson have family? Perhaps I can offer a benefit night."

Stapleton retrieved his sword. "I wouldn't be concerned. Put your efforts into saving the theater. Keeping Drury Lane open will honor the Danielsons. I'll go send Rawlins to alert Duncan. Sheridan, keep people from coming back here. The magistrate will want to do a thorough investigation."

As the two men left the crossover space, Watson came to me. "Anthony became a changed man here. I hope Drury Lane is saved."

"You, a savvy forger, wouldn't make such a mistake unless he wanted to."

"Traveling in a coffin gives one plenty of time to think." He slipped to the rear of the crossover space. "I think I'm going to leave, Lady Worthing. You have enough witnesses."

"Bye, Watson. Do remember to start early on changing your life."

"Just keep your Vaughn from me, and I'll think on it." He took a final glance at the woman who'd tried to pin Joanna Danielson's murder on him, then left.

Florentina had a strange look on her face. "The odds."

"Sometimes luck is all we have."

"But what of Culver? Barbara Banyan would've been the only witness to his crime. There's no proof or confession since she's dead."

"For now, the duke will go free. I'll just have to hope justice catches up to him."

She nodded and let the lofty sentiment hover above us, the unanswered question of whether I'd try to indict the murderous duke fighting for abolition to come to light if there was a living witness.

Honestly, I didn't know.

I'd yet to accept what this omission on my part meant. And I couldn't predict the odds of when the Duke of Culver would try again to get away with my murder.

Epilogue

July 28, 1806, London

The biggest day in the life of Martin Simpkins, the Duke of Culver, happened a week ago. The king has added his royal consent to the Slave Ship Limitation bill, the new name for his compromise bill. It's law. Sauntering at Westminster Hall, passing the big arena where the king held special sessions, Martin sighs.

The memories of the win are fresh. People had cheered for him. Martin had been the talk of the town. The king should have done more to reward the courage it took to pass this legislation. Now it's all over. No more celebration.

He balls his fists and takes a few more steps, looking at the aged roof timbers. The space is too open to contain his echo. It wouldn't dismiss a yell. This is for whispers.

Martin's life is back to hushed words, even gossip.

He has to change this.

Figuring out how to be loved and how best to fix his finances were new goals. His bitter father has locked away all but pocket change for the next three years. According to the man's solicitor, John Carrington, the old duke's will ensures nothing can be freed or liquidated in the ducal fortune and estates until the time has elapsed and Martin has not produced an heir from a woman of questionable heritage.

How can any man write such a vindictive restriction to be enforced against another?

Once tensions die down, Carrington's daughter, a woman who fits such a description, will be visited again. The last time he thought Joanna had been taken there. And although it was the wrong address, it had given him relief to destroy a vacant house.

The cuts to his hand had healed, but it felt good leaving his mark everywhere.

Yes, Lady Worthing should pay. Though she's keeping quiet, it doesn't matter. He gets giddy thinking of seeking retribution.

Sometimes from Saint James's Park he watches her walking with those noisy dogs, looking happy.

She shouldn't be happy.

But as the clever chit hasn't said a word about how Martin dealt with Danielson, he'll let her be for now.

Yet he hasn't forgotten about her, her righteous attitude, her clapping for him. So like Joanna.

She's not the same height as his love, but she shares the same slight build. He wonders what other similarities they possess.

A deep sadness afflicts his chest. He misses Joanna. The love of his life is gone, and now so is the praise.

He walks farther, until he steps away from Westminster. On the frenzied lead up to the bill's passage, men and women would come here. One half protesting. The other side cheering. A rush of pure pleasure came over him when he outtalked and outshouted the naysayers.

Today, like yesterday, he feels the weight of the crowds no longer being here.

A few people gather. They wave at him, and he musters the excitement in his chest over the passage of the Slave Ship Limitation Act.

Lord Sidmouth walks past. Siddy doesn't say anything. Before, when he needed Martin's help to advance legislation, they talked every day. How terrible to be used by Siddy and tossed back into oblivion.

Luckily, there are so many ways the bill was weakened, this couldn't be the last bill on abolition.

Too many amendments have been offered, too many delays about when the act should start for anyone of serious mind to think this fixes the great sin.

No one is happy, but all can claim to have done something.

Martin watches Lord Sidmouth walk away. The man might be heading for drinks at Olive's.

Growing angrier, Martin tugs on his empty pockets. The heiress he's picked out, her father has objected to Martin's request of her hand. The man doesn't want a firebrand for a son-in-law. When did dukes have these problems, people accepting them?

He chides himself.

This was Joanna's sense of humor. She always had a way to soothe his feelings. He came up with too many reasons to delay their secret engagement. Oh, how he enjoyed hunting her, making her forgive him. So many memories of wooing her back when she decided to quit his attentions.

Oh, Lord, he misses her. No woman would ever be like her.

He looks up at the sky. Ready to shake his fists, he calms. Joanna understood and forgave him. If Barbara hadn't killed her, once he found Joanna again, set his eyes and hands upon her, she would submit and be his. That's how it was. It's how it should've always been. He owned her soul. She knew it.

Martin begins walking again. A small crowd stands along the wide pavement.

A thrill courses through him.

Maybe he'll get to say a few words.

Perhaps they'll clap their adulation.

No matter what Lauderdale or Sidmouth or Ellenborough or even Prime Minister Grenville says now, it's Martin who deserves the praise.

He smiles at those who've gathered and wonders what new cause he can champion to keep his name in their mouths?

Just one or two more big wins and old Martin might be up for a position in the cabinet.

"Speech."

An old man shouts this a few times.

Soon eight or ten people are yelling, too. "Culver! Speech!"

Martin waves for them to settle down. When they do, he says, "It's one thing to have this law as a beginning, but we can't stop here. We must keep pushing. We must press. You and I, we are a small cog in the wheel of progress. A wheel doesn't stop, not when there is a job to do."

Claps. A few. It's a start.

"A wheel keeps rolling. I will keep challenging the system on your behalf."

More shouts of his name. More gather. Siddy should've stayed to see this.

"Our brothers and sisters in chains are crying out for us to save them. They hear your prayers for their freedom. And I feel your prayers for me. Never fear, I will win for you."

More accolades are coming; his chest swells with pride.

The cheers get closer. He's again surrounded by praise.

Joanna would've loved this moment. He feels her with him. He keeps on down the steps as people are clapping their hands.

Surprisingly, Lord Lauderdale has joined in. He's clapping, too. He believes. "Once you're done here, join us for dinner.

You have made the difference. Keep it up. Keep holding Parliament to the fire."

The short man walks away, blends into the thick crowd that's pushing to be near Martin.

Something jabs at his rib. Before he pushes it back, a short sharp dagger goes through him.

Crowds disperse.

Martin can't move. He fingers the blood coming from his chest. He sinks to his knees.

In the crowd, he sees Joanna's guardian, Mr. Mathews, walking away.

Before he can scream or accuse the fiend, Mathews mouths Joanna's name and then gets into a carriage with the Blackamoor fixer of the Prince of Wales.

Cold, Martin sinks into the wetness, a sea of red gushing out, stealing his life.

Waiting for my godfather to join Florentina and me at Olive's seemed to take forever. It had been forever since I had felt it would be safe to venture out of Two Greater Queen Street.

"See, Abbie. Isn't this nice? Us. Out. Cheese."

I smiled at her and popped a small piece of creamy goodness into my mouth. "Olive's does have the best cheese."

"Good. I know things haven't been easy. And you've been pretty silent."

"It's hard to explain or even make sense of. I know you and I are leading privileged lives. Yet it feels so small. I hate thinking that one wrong move, being at the wrong place at the wrong time, will make us an example, a wrong example. I don't want to do something to stop abolition or the advancement of equality."

Florentina clasped my hand and kissed it. "You won't. You're helping."

My cousin released me and began taking little bites of a slice of generously buttered bread. Then she wiped crumbs from her mouth. "I hate compromises with the devil, too."

"They chant his name more than those of any of the MPs that pushed this small bill through. I only wish—"

"You only wish you'd been able to get Culver convicted for Mr. Danielson's death without causing this bill to fail. I know, Abbie."

"No. No, you don't. I still dream of how the duke sneered at me. He would've killed me that night if he could. There are three dogs and a neighbor, who I'm sure no longer sleep. They keep guard."

She shook her head. "If you know he's not sleeping, then that means you're not, either. Culver will slip up. Those types of men do. He will get his comeuppance."

Florentina cocked her head a little to the side. Her ringlet of braids peeked from beneath her chocolate bonnet. "Abbie, I never got to ask you about what you and Mr. Henderson were discussing. You and he looked quite intimate standing together at the mantel."

My cheeks warmed. "Probably arguing about something."

"That didn't look like an argument. That looked like the opposite of fussing."

There wasn't much to say other than the truth. "He's becoming a good friend. It's unexpected. I like him. And I respect him. I hope ... all of us ... can continue to become better friends. It's helpful having a physician's perspective on things."

She offered me the "I'll accept this answer for now" look with a small smile and a slight roll of her gray-brown eyes.

The door swung open, and in came Vaughn and my neighbor. They talked in hushed tones. My godfather smiled. Stapleton looked cross, but that was typical. Each had a jet armband for Joanna Mathews Danielson.

It matched the one on my gown. The modiste had dropped

off a new black one, one with onyx lace woven about the waist and long sleeves. She was glad I wasn't dead and that I remained her client.

Stapleton greeted Florentina but took special effort to clasp my raised hand. "Good to see you out and that you're reclaiming Olive's, Lady Worthing."

"I didn't know you'd be out today, Mr. Henderson."

"My sister returns from Paris a day early. I'll retrieve her from the Thames this evening. I know in the upcoming weeks she'll be unable to contain herself from running next door to share all the stories. Of course, she'll be heartbroken about Joanna."

I felt for Stapleton and Mary. Death had visited too often to Eleven Greater Queen Street. "If you need help telling her, I'm more than prepared. The Hendersons are always welcome at Two Greater Queen Street," I said, then pointed to an empty chair. "Please join us. Mr. Vaughn is about to tell us all the new political moves."

"I've none today. It's been quiet since the Slave Ship Limitation bill passed." Vaughn took a seat, too, and summoned our waiter. "Jacob, claret for me and the physician."

The boy nodded, dashed off, and returned with the wine.

Once his glass, as well as Stapleton's, was filled, Vaughn requested that Florentina and I raise our cups of chamomile in a toast. "To progress, no matter how painstaking it may be. Justice and liberty, may they continue to grow and change our world."

Florentina clicked her tea to mine. "That sounds like a prayer, Uncle."

"A blessing," Stapleton added as he waited to tap my cup. "My dear baroness, we need to speak of custody arrangements."

"Custody of what? Don't say the lawn. Not a fence that goes to the end of our yards into Saint James's Park?"

"Dogs, madam. Dogs. Santisma whines if he's not allowed to be walked by you. I'm sure Teacup is bothered."

"No, not at all. He enjoys—"

Lord Sidmouth burst open the doors. "Has anyone seen Lauderdale or Ellenborough?" the reserved man shouted.

Lauderdale stood from his booth. "What the devil is wrong, Siddy?"

"Culver."

"What has the blowhard—"

"Culver was stabbed." Sidmouth waved his arms. "Coming out of Parliament. Right in the gut or chest or both. Blood was everywhere."

Gasps.

Cries of no.

A hushed whisper swept over Olive's.

Vaughn and Stapleton looked at each other, then at me.

I kept my face even, but I wanted to believe the duke had been assassinated. Culver's death would mean justice for Anthony Danielson and freedom for me.

Freedom.

It welled up in my gut. It would express itself in tears, but I didn't want a soul to believe I actually mourned the evil cretin.

Lord Sidmouth looked so shaken as he spoke. "I'd just passed Culver on the pavement. Moments before the attack. Lauderdale, the assailant would've tried to kill me, too. This is revenge for moving too fast."

My heart clenched.

No, it was punishment for the evil that Culver had wrought.

Vaughn grabbed my hand. "Change is not too fast. This won't slow things. The good will keep fighting. The usurpers will fall away."

"Lord Duncan will investigate this," I said. "I wonder if anyone's in custody?"

"I'm sure the magistrate has all well in hand." Stapleton glared at me, as if I'd be compelled to help. Never.

"We can enjoy Olive's in peace. This one mystery, I'm not compelled to solve, Mr. Henderson."

Arguing with each other in fear-stricken voices, Lauderdale and Sidmouth headed out the door. I hoped they'd find Ellenborough safe and sound, likely exercising his ponies.

My anxious stomach calmed when I noted Stapleton's glance. The quiet camaraderie shared with Vaughn eased my spirit. My protectors needed to get along.

We continued sitting as people, mostly peers, ran out into the street.

Soon Olive's settled with patrons merely buzzing and eating.

Florentina patted her mouth with a handkerchief. "In this situation, I believe those who live by the sword often end up with the point turning on them. Culver has gotten what he deserved."

"My, you've become morbid, my dear niece, but you're right. Culver made himself into a spark. Something had to burn."

Slumping against my seat, I sighed. "I hope this legislative win is not a moment like poor Haiti, where progress took one step forward, and then the world took two steps back."

Vaughn nodded. He may have even offered a smile. "I still believe, Lady Worthing, in justice. And things, despite the method of correction, will eventually be made right. If Culver dies, my friends, the Mathews will have some measure of comfort."

If . . . It was wrong to root for death, but Culver deserved it. "The *Morning Post* will tell us everything tomorrow. They always have the latest gossip."

Stapleton lifted his claret as if to toast. "I've no doubt now that they will. Another puzzle solved by my friend, Lady Worthing."

He glanced at me, and I enjoyed knowing that we'd trained each other to be civil and to trust our instincts.

My neighbor cut into the cheese and tore off a piece of the remaining wheat loaf. "I wonder how much longer London will be in chaos. With Nelson's death, then Prime Minister Pitt in January, Britain has been spinning. Isn't six months enough?"

Florentina sat back, stirring milk into her tea. "Well, the world struggles with so many things."

"What are you thinking, Lady Worthing?" Vaughn's fatherly voice reached me. "I truly wish I'd understood better . . . Visions or notions are hard."

"Abbie, you want to save people," Florentina said. "Sometimes you can't. I was wrong in judging Mrs. Danielson. I don't know how she encountered Culver, what lies he told to sway her. But she didn't deserve his mistreatment. She should've been able to love whomever she wanted. And she wasn't owed harm because of her choices."

That was big of my opinionated cousin to say. "When the world allows every woman to have our choices, right or wrong, then I guess true progress will be achieved."

"Speaking of progress . . ." Vaughn pulled a letter from his pocket. "This came today in the morning post."

The lettering, the heavy franking, the tidy script . . . This correspondence was from James.

Hesitating, I opened my palm, and Vaughn placed the letter on it. "I suppose asking for calm during my nuncheon would be too much."

"Well, I wanted to make sure he remembered he had a wife in London awaiting his return." He gaped at Stapleton before winking at me and asking our waiter for more Stilton.

Though I was tempted to open the letter now, I'd wait. Why add more chaos to this day? James, my husband, had taken his sweet time to write me.

Shoving the letter into my reticule, I decided to enjoy my friends for as long as I could. Then alone at Two Greater Queen Street with Teacup, my bartered custody of a greyhound, and a cousin stocked with an ample supply of handkerchiefs, I'd see how James had couched his decision to divorce me.

Author's Note

On July 14, 1806, one of the first abolition bills, the Slave Ship Limitation bill, passed Parliament. It was signed into law (by royal assent) by King George III on July 21, 1806. While this mystery is invented, the bill's difficult passage is not.

I hope you enjoyed this second installment of the Lady Worthing Mysteries. In March of 2022, I went to London for a special tour of Drury Lane. I enjoyed a backstage view of the theater's nooks and crannies, all the places a body could be buried or hung. Our bantering guides shared with us the history and scandals of the theater. It was amazing. The café in the theater makes amazing fare.

The theme of this novel is no good choice goes unpunished. As this mystery unfolds, you are doing life with Abbie, learning more of her backstory, and becoming familiar with some of the struggles this amateur detective faces as a progressive woman in 1806 England. Again, this series is my homage to all the things I love about murder mysteries and crime fiction: it has elements of both a romance and a thriller but is set in the familiar world of Regency England.

As a junkie of the Old Bailey criminal proceedings and a huge fan of *Murder She Wrote*, I intend to bring you crime fiction and mystery solving with a thrilling amateur detective who's trying to define her place in the world. Abigail is bold. She wants her independence in a time when women, particularly women of color, struggle for agency.

The search for racial harmony and acceptance of diversity has always been with us, like the original sin. My approach is to balance the good and the bad of the era while showing a more inclusive side of history, one that matches the facts on the ground. Settle in and enjoy real places, true histories, and actual persons who lived during these times. Every element plays a part in these mysteries. This will be fun. Enjoy my *subtle* homage to *Murder, She Wrote*; *Matlock*; *Remington Steele*; *Dynasty*; and *Dallas*.

I do a lot of research to build these inclusive narratives, and I've included some of my research notes for you. For this mystery, I pulled facts straight from the headlines and stories of London newspapers.

Want to learn more? Visit my website, VanessaRiley.com, to gain more insight. Make sure to join my newsletter, where I share travel stories, history, and a bit of background on my life writing historical fiction. Email me at vanessa@vanessariley.com. I'd love to hear from you or schedule a book club Zoom.

POLITICAL FRAME:

End of Abolition Movement Because of Haiti

When the French colony of Saint-Domingue became free in 1805, under Jean-Jacques Dessalines, all the abolition movements around the world stopped moving forward, curtailing their activities for freedom. The fear of Black rule halted progress. For greater context, read Vanessa Riley's *Sister Mother Warrior*.

Mulattoes and Blackamoors During the Regency Era

The term *mulatto* is a social construct used to describe a person born to one parent who is Caucasian and one who is of African, Spanish, Latin, Indian, or Caribbean descent. Mulattoes during the Regency period often achieved greater social mobility than other racial minorities, particularly if their families had means.

The term *Blackamoors* refers to racial minorities with darker complexions, and these included mulattoes, Africans, and West and East Indians living in England during the eighteenth and nineteenth centuries.

Mulattoes and Blackamoors numbered between ten thousand and twenty thousand in London and throughout England in the time of Jane Austen. Wealthy British with children born to native West Indies women brought them to London for schooling. In her last novel, entitled *Sanditon*, Jane Austen, a leading writer of her times, writes of Miss Lambe, a mulatto from the West Indies, who possesses an immense fortune. Her wealth makes her desirable to the ton.

Mulatto and Blackamoor children were often told to pass to achieve elevated positions within society. Wealthy plantation owners with mixed-race children or wealthy mulattoes, like Dorothea Thomas from the colony of Demerara, often sent their children to England to secure an education and to marry. Read more about a woman who defies accepted notions of agency for Black women in Georgian and Regency times in *Island Queen*.

HISTORICAL PERSONAGES MENTIONED:

Martin Simpkins, the Duke of Culver

The Duke of Culver is an invented character. I made him the contemporary of actual members of Parliament who led the effort to get the Slave Ship Limitation bill passed. The men who championed the act were Lord Lauderdale, Lord Sidmouth, and even Lord Ellenborough.

Mary Edwards

Mary Edwards is considered the first human computer. She calculated positions of the sun, moon, and stars for the nautical almanacs of the British Navy. She was one of the few women paid to do this work, and she received a man's salary.

Elizabeth Inchbald

A famed actress of London, Elizabeth Inchbald was also an author. After the death of her husband, she didn't remarry and was able to live independently due to the financial success of her plays and her novels.

Lord Nelson

Viscount Nelson was an admiral in the British Navy. One of Britain's greatest naval heroes, he led his forces to decisive naval victories against France and Spain in the French Revolutionary Wars and the Napoleonic Wars. The nation mourned his passing at a state funeral in January 1806.

Mrs. Morton Pitt

She was the wife of William Morton Pitt, a member of Parliament from 1780 to 1826. The Pitts had an extravagant house on London's Arlington Street, where they held parties (routs), which often were written up in the papers.

Richard Brinsley Sheridan

Richard Sheridan was a member of Parliament from 1780 to 1812, a playwright, and the owner of Drury Lane. History's judgment of Sheridan is mixed. While he did good things for Drury Lane, he was known to be a heavy gambler and a womanizer. There were rumors of his wretched stalking behavior toward women he pursued. Some of the Duke of Culver's character in the novel absorbed these darker elements of Sheridan's life.

William Wilberforce
Wilberforce was a British politician and a leading activist for abolition. He was a member of Parliament from 1784 to 1812.

William Pitt the Younger
William Pitt the Younger followed in his father's footsteps and entered politics in 1781, serving first in the House of Commons. In 1801 Pitt became Britain's youngest prime minister, and as an eloquent and savvy leader, he did a lot to guide the nation during the French Revolution and the rise of Napoleon. He was good friends with Wilberforce. One of Pitt's regrets was he did not get abolition done before his death in 1806.

Theater Actors and Playwrights
The profession of acting was not highly regarded during the eighteenth century and the early nineteenth century. Unlike today, you didn't want your daughter or son marrying someone from the theater. It would be looked down upon in the upper levels of society. Playwrights, if they were successful, would be advanced, but often they needed patrons to survive financially. During this period, there were a few women who actually became successful playwrights, such as Susanna Centlivre (1669–1723). Also known as Susanna Carroll, she was one of the most successful playwrights of the eighteenth century.

PLACES MENTIONED:

Bibury Races
Bibury Races were held annually in Gloucestershire, near the village Bibury and the banks of the river Coln. The Prince of

Wales often attended the event. Prizes and parties were the typical activities, in addition to watching and betting on the horse races.

Blackfriars Bridge

Blackfriars Bridge, the third bridge to span the river Thames, opened in 1769. It is an Italianate-style bridge, was designed by architect Robert Mylne, and was constructed with nine semielliptical arches of Portland stone.

Drury Lane Theatre

Drury Lane Theatre is one of the royal theaters and dates back to 1663. The original building was destroyed by fire in 1809. The old-scene store is a specific room behind the stage and houses props and old scenery canvases. Several other storage rooms house costumes and scenery items that are being used nightly in current productions. The tunnels that go from Drury Lane to the Thames are now filled in. The tunnels were a part of a network built by kings so that they could travel about the city while sheltering their mistresses from public or wifely view. Sailors used to enter Drury Lane via the tunnels during off times at the docks and would earn extra money working the rigging at the theater, which was similar to their work lifting and lowering sails aboard ships.

Olive's

Olive's was a coffeehouse in London that was more like a restaurant, with history-filled niches around the building.

Saint Bride's Church

Saint Bride's Church is a beautiful church on London's Fleet Street, designed by famed architect Christopher Wren in 1672. The original structure dates back to the 1500s and was destroyed in the Great Fire of London.

Saint Margaret's Church

Founded in the twelfth century, Saint Margaret's Church stands on the grounds of Westminster Abbey and was consecrated in 1523. The church is dedicated to Margaret of Antioch. The east window above the altar contains the oldest stained glass in the church and dates to between 1515 and 1526.

Westminster Abbey

Westminster Abbey was constructed in 1065 under the direction of Edward I (also known as Edward the Confessor). Westminster Abbey has become the church where royal marriages and coronations occur. It is also the burial place for kings and queens, generals, poets, and other famous artists. Westminster Abbey has ten bells and two bell towers.

Westminster Hall

Westminster Hall is the oldest building in the parliamentary area and its architecture encompasses over nine hundred years of handiwork. The edifice's hammer-beam roof, commissioned in 1393, is the largest medieval timber roof in Northern Europe. Westminster Hall is close to the Palace of Westminster, which is the meeting place for the House of Lords and the House of Commons.

Westminster Area of London

Westminster is in the central part of London and extends from the river Thames to Oxford Street and includes Saint James's Park. It is the seat of the British government and Parliament and also contains Buckingham Palace, Westminster Abbey, and Westminster Cathedral.

SIGNIFICANT LITERATURE OR ART MENTIONED:

A Bold Stroke for a Wife

A Bold Stroke for a Wife was written by successful English playwright Susanna Centlivre. A satirical play, it was first performed in 1718. The plot is a metaphor about the British Whig Party, though the play is also critical of the Tories, capitalism, and religious hypocrisy. The play features the characters Anne Lovely and Colonel Fainwell, and Fainwell must gather the consent of Lovely's four guardians before she can wed.

Richard III, Act I, Scene IV

Richard III, a play written by William Shakespeare in about 1592, is about Richard of Gloucester's devious campaign to become the king of England. Richard has his eldest brother, the Duke of Clarence, imprisoned in the Tower of London. In one of the most violent death scenes in a Shakespeare play, Clarence is then stabbed and drowned in a vat of wine in Act I, Scene IV.

The famous lines from this scene uttered by Alexander Hildebrand in the novel conclude with the first murderer's words:

Take that, and that. (Clarence is stabbed.) *If all this will not do,*

I'll drown you in the malmsey butt within.

Acknowledgments

Thank you to my Heavenly Father, everything I possess or accomplish is by Your grace.

To my editor, Wendy McCurdy, thank you for pushing for the best book. Thank you for believing in Lady Worthing.

To my fabulous agent, Sarah Younger, I am grateful that you are my partner.

You are my ride-or-die friend and sister.

To Gerald, Marc, and Chris—Love you bros.

To Denny, Pat, Rhonda, and Felicia. Thank you for helping me elevate my game, the gentle shoves, and every challenge.

The writers of Me and My Sisters, The Divas, and my friends in Black Authors in Residence

To those who inspire my pen: Beverly, Brenda, Farrah, Sarah, Julia, Kristan—thank you.

To those who inspire my soul: Esi, Piper, Vanessa, Kenyatta, Eileen, Rhonda, Angela and Pat—thank you.

And to my rocks: Frank and Ellen –Love you all, so much.